DETAILS & DEADLINES

Book 11 of
THE WARDEN

FELICIA JEDLICKA

I dedicate this book:
To those who feel guilty even after all this time.

To those who were told to get over it even though they still raged inside.

And to those who wanted more, even if they didn't really deserve it.

Details & Deadlines

1

"**D**O YOU WANT THE job or not?" Heaton asked again, quickly losing patience with his former partner.

Jack Macey looked up from his recent catch. At nearly forty-two, his scruffy beard, long brown hair, and thin slit eyes made him look at least sixty. His propensity for no sleeves left his muscular, artfully tattooed biceps exposed. Heaton was sure he had never seen the man clean, but that was at least a testament to his work ethic.

The ten-foot walrus slug lying behind him was not the type of creature Heaton's team usually hunted, but they were quite common in the swamps. Much like the variants of animals across the globe, each region also had its supernatural infestations to deal with.

Heaton would have chosen to hunt in the city over the swamps any day. Vampires may have been blood-sucking parasites, but at least they didn't stink like swamp creatures.

"Let me get this straight." Mace spit some of his tobacco juice, just shy of Heaton's boot tip. Heaton glanced down at the intentional provocation but didn't react. Mace was always about a good show. There was no point in feeding into his need for validation. "You kick me off your team for being too unstable. Now Daniel—the kingpin of excessive force—gets thrown in the slammer again. And you want me back? Is that about right?"

Heaton paused, hoping he wouldn't have to repeat himself a third time. As much tolerance as he had for Daniel's potentially violent tantrums, he had none for Mace's. "Daniel's incarceration is only temporary. We just need a little extra muscle for our hunts."

Mace looked at Nevia on Heaton's left. "Little one not pulling her weight." He snorted and turned away from them both to drag his three-hundred-plus pound, fattened worm further onto dry land. The net encasing it wasn't actually trapping it, but since the creatures never scooted more than a few feet a minute, escape was hardly an issue.

Despite its weight, Mace moved it with ease. His 5-foot-7 stature had never impressed him or Daniel, but they had surmised he could bench press a baby elephant if his adrenaline was high enough. He had been a useful asset in the field. Unfortunately, he was too much of a loner to work cohesively with a team.

Plus, he was an asshole.

"Mace, I'm sweating like I've run a marathon. I've donated enough blood to the mosquito population to warrant a transfusion. And your slug stinks to bloody hell. Do you want the job or not?"

Mace turned back and looked him over. "I want her to ask me." He nodded to Nevia. His raspy words sounded more like a challenge than a request.

"What difference does it make who asks you?" Heaton asked, no longer able to keep the irritation out of his tone.

Mace shrugged, not willing to offer any reason for the request.

Nevia stared Mace down with a venomous glare. Heaton wasn't sure she could smell him over the slug, but whatever she was sensing from him wasn't sitting well with her.

"Shall I say it slowly so you can understand the question better?" she asked him.

"Say it however ya want." Mace crossed his arms, refusing to budge until he got his way. Heaton suspected it was his way of establishing a hierarchy right out of the gates. The strange thing was, it wasn't even about sexism for Mace. He just needed to know he was above someone—anyone. His attitude was the result of too many toilet swirlies and not enough friends growing up.

"We need—"

"Nah, just you," he corrected before she could finish. "You need me." He said with his usual deadpan expression that offered nothing of himself, least of all an inkling of his personality.

Nevia glanced at Heaton, but he didn't insist she continue. If she didn't feel like prostrating herself for the sake of convenience, he wasn't going to make her. As much as he hated Mace, he was his only living former partner. If they couldn't convince him to fill in, they would have to train someone new. It was a toss-up who would be more hazardous to them—his erratic ex-partner or a naïve newbie.

Nevia stepped closer to Mace. He looked her up and down and snorted—obviously unimpressed by her brandished authority. Though her short stature and slender build made her seem diminutive next to everyone, it was her one-quarter werewolf heritage that gave her immunity against intimidation. Any woman who could stand tall in the face of Danato Calibria's wall-rattling lectures would be able to handle Mace's tantrums just fine.

"How about this?" she proposed. "How about you ask to join us?"

Mace shook his head, still refusing without cause or justification. He was a spoiled brat with low self-esteem and a chip on his shoulder called high school. There was no reasoning with this man.

Mace lifted his upper lip, appearing at first to be snarling at Nevia. A fine stream of spit squirted from a gap in his front teeth. The spray landed on Nevia's white linen blouse. She looked down at the tobacco juice staining the cloth.

"God, that's disgusting, Mace!" Heaton griped.

Mace snickered at the shock on Nevia's face, taunting her with yet another level of derision.

Nevia didn't waste any more time with verbal banter and pulled her gun. Aiming her firearm at people was like second nature to her. Anytime she felt... well, any emotion on the bad end of the spectrum, she was liable to start shooting. Usually, Heaton enjoyed watching her wield her weapon, but Mace was not fond of guns. His former partner had never revealed to him or Daniel the cause of his repellent attitude. All Heaton knew was that Mace did not respond well to armed threats. Had Heaton been thinking ahead, he might have asked Nevia to leave her gun behind to prevent any incidents—such as the one unfolding.

Nevia barely got the gun out of its holster before Mace backhanded her and ripped the weapon from her hand. There was room to rationalize PTSD or depression as an excuse for the knee-jerk reaction, but Heaton wouldn't defend any man stupid enough to hit a woman with fem-wolf blood running in her veins.

Nevia stumbled back, holding her face. She peeked at Mace from behind her hand—a wave of almost feral anger overtook her features. Heaton rarely saw the woman's emotion peak beyond haughty or pouty. Even her smiles were subdued. Seeing her raw fury now exposed was almost popcorn-worthy.

He wasn't sure what had pissed her off the most, the assault, the disarmament, or if it was still the defilement of her garment causing her to see red.

Nevia screamed and lunged at Mace. Heaton hadn't expected her to do much damage, and judging by his lack of defense, neither did Mace. However, she surprised them both.

Nevia hooked her arm around Mace's neck, drawing him down to her. She opened her mouth wide and sunk her teeth into his neck like a vampire.

Mace yelped and threw her off to one side. He cussed and groaned, grabbing at his bleeding neck. "Freaking bitch!"

Mace went after her, but Heaton intercepted him. "Fair is fair, Mace. You hit her; she bit you." Heaton frowned as Mace released his neck. Nevia had given him more than a love bite. There was a chunk of flesh missing from Mace's neck—and not a tiny piece.

"If you think I'm gonna help you now..." Mace's rant trailed off into silence as if he had lost focus on what he was saying.

"No, I don't think you are going to help us," Heaton said before he had to listen to more of the man's self-important rhetoric. "I think you are going to stay in this hellhole, dig up slugs for the rest of your miserable existence, and blame your problems on other people. That's what I think." Heaton ripped Nevia's gun out of his hand and turned to leave. "Come on, Jordan."

"Son of a bitch," Mace mumbled behind him.

Heaton looked back to see if Nevia had double-backed for a secondary attack, but she wasn't near Mace. She wasn't anywhere. He looked around the sloppy woods for her, but she was gone.

"Where is she?" Heaton yelled at Mace, but he just kept staring down at his most recent catch. Heaton looked at the walrus slug that was inch by inch trying to escape back to the swampy waters of the Mississippi. Either his eyes were playing tricks on him, or that damn thing was quite a bit fatter than when he had arrived.

Mace's face constricted in disgust even as his eyes remained glazed with shock. "Damn gluttonous thing. I've never seen it eat. I can't believe how fast she went in," he murmured.

Heaton looked between him and the overstuffed pile of pudge. "She..." He pointed at it in disbelief. "Is she in there?"

Mace lifted his gaze to Heaton. "She got too close to the mouth."

"Because you threw her over there! How do we get her out?"

"She went in like a wet fuckin' noodle," Mace said, in awe of the creature. "I didn't even know they could fit two people in there. I s'pose 'cause she's small."

Heaton grabbed him by the shoulders and shook him. "Just get her out of there!"

"I can't." He shrugged off his grip.

"What do you mean, you can't?"

"I mean, there is no way, no how to get her out before..." The bastard seemed almost sympathetic now.

"She's done for. That thing's like pure acid on the inside. It starts dissolving prey the instant it hits the stomach."

Heaton cursed and dug out his pocketknife. It wasn't long, but it was sharp. He leaped to the slug's side and started cutting at its belly—or at least the fattest part of its body. The blade caught on the initial layer of slimy tissue as if he were cutting tree bark instead of skin. He tried to stab the knife in, but it bounced off like he was trying to pop a balloon with his finger.

"You'll never make it through in time," Mace said. "I usually cut these things open with a chainsaw."

Heaton looked back at Mace. "I am not leaving her in there to die, you son of a bitch! Help me!"

"I don't know what to tell you, man. If she doesn't suffocate, the acid—"

"That is Daniel McGrath's wife!" Heaton rasped, pointing at the slug. "He will kill you for this!" He stared hard at Mace, demanding he understand what was at risk if he didn't help. However, even as he said the words, he realized it wasn't Mace who would suffer for this; it was him. Even if Daniel didn't kill him for failing to protect Nevia, it would destroy their friendship.

"I'm sorry." Mace shrugged. "That thing ain't letting anything out until it's a pile of bones and shit."

Heaton frowned and paced the water's edge. He considered shooting the animal, but that still didn't get Nevia out. The chainsaw would work, but Mace clearly hadn't brought it out with him.

He looked down at the slug, trying to fathom how to break the news to his best friend. How would he tell him the only woman he had ever opened his heart to was dead?

No.

He would not watch his friendship fester and die because of an ugly ass slug.

He tossed away his knife and Nevia's gun. He moved around to the rear of the slug—the end without teeth. He kneeled and shifted the tail nub to expose the orifice.

"What are you doing?" Mace asked as if he had just walked in on Heaton doing something inappropriate.

Heaton clasped his hands in prayer and dove at the anus like a human speculum. Mace hollered out a protest as Heaton buried his arms elbow-deep into the creature's rear end.

Working as an underground bounty hunter, Heaton had experienced a good number of disgusting things. It was even gruesome at times, but nothing prepared him for entering the colon of a walrus slug. His final inhalation afforded him a bouquet of rotting flesh and feces. He controlled his gag reflex and pushed on into the darkness...

...down the rabbit hole...

...through the wormhole....

...into the slug's hole.

"Holy shit!"

Even as he heard Mace's last muffled objection, the sphincter muscles tensed against him, trying to push him out. Heaton refused to give up on his forced colonoscopy.

He pushed forward with his feet, maneuvering past the restriction into the great unknown of the digestive tract.

The creature's large intestine wasn't as complex as a human's. Food went into the mouth, and the central stomach dissolved it. After the nutrients were absorbed, the hard bones and residual refuse were slowly pushed out. There were no twists or turns, just in and out.

He traversed, blind and deaf, until he felt a hard object. It wasn't Nevia, just bones. The creature's metabolism couldn't be that fast.

He pushed deeper until his feet were barely free on the outside. His fingers pushed aside a muscle flap, and he felt stinging hot liquid.

The stomach.

He reached through the opening and felt something soft but firm.

A body.

Nevia.

He groped around for what he thought was her arm and found her hand. As if suddenly reviving, Nevia grabbed onto him with the enthusiasm usually reserved for those hanging off the sides of cliffs.

He yanked her forward, guiding her out of the stomach and toward the exit. She moved alongside him, pawing at his clothes as she climbed down his body. He took some liberties as he pushed her, giving her the boost she needed to escape the slippery channel.

When he felt her body slide away, it was time to get himself out. Unfortunately, the slick interior left him with very little purchase. He began to shimmy himself back, but his progress was only inch by inch.

His feet had long since lost grip on the rim of the anus, so he couldn't birth himself as he had intended. It had been a passing thought that the ten-foot span of the creature might be too long to keep a foothold on the outside, but he had ignored it. His only thought was to get Nevia free, and he succeeded.

The creature constricted tightly around him, fervently objecting to its forced enema. What little leverage he had inside the slimy intestinal walls was now gone.

Heaton assessed his lack of air and confinement to be a fatal predicament and released the tension in his muscles. It was an awful and embarrassing way to die, but at least he would go out as a hero. What man could ask for more? Well—other than surviving.

After a moment of coming to terms with his maker, Heaton felt a hand grasp his foot. A second hand grappled around in search of his other foot. Once he was lassoed up properly, he was yanked out with surprising force.

Like a horrific waterslide, Heaton evacuated the slug, getting all manner of vileness in his mouth and up his nose. He felt the final pressure of the anus slap around his head, and the sunlight returned, along with the sound of birds. He coughed, spit, and vomited before he looked up to see his savior.

Mace was standing over him, shaking his head. He looked down at him with a mixture of awe and disappointment. "You know, I never understood why your crazy shit got you branded a badass, but when I colored outside the box, I got written up for being unstable."

Heaton looked at Nevia, who was performing a similar cleansing ceremony. She was red-faced and shaking, but she was alive.

Heaton got to his feet and spat out something he did not want to identify. He stared at Mace a moment, trying to figure out where and when the man's screw had come loose. "Because I'm not trying to be a badass, you prig. I'm trying to save lives."

2

HEATON CARRIED NEVIA INSIDE the hotel room over his shoulder like a sack of potatoes. His phone chirped for the third time—refusing to be ignored. He gently planted Nevia on the floor. Her face constricted in pain, but she didn't cry out as he expected she might. He had been in the slug half as long and his skin felt like it was on fire.

He pulled out his cell phone to answer it. "Start stripping. I'll get the water going," he barked at Nevia as he ran to the bathroom. "Hello," he said into the phone.

"Heaton, where have you been?" Sophie scolded on the other end.

"Where the fuck do you think I've been, Soph? Doing my damn job!" Heaton turned on the water in the white plastic tub. He switched it to the shower spray and slipped off his shirt. "What do you want?"

"Your friend is here—at my office." Sophie's voice was dripping with hidden meaning, but he had no idea what she was talking about.

"Sophie, I am covered in intestinal acid; what do you want?" He held the phone to his chest. "Jordan, get in here now!" he yelled and returned the phone to his ear.

"She's asking about Daniel," Sophie whispered, even though her office wasn't big enough to keep secrets.

"Let me talk to him," a voice in the background said.

"No, this is my—ouch! Bitch," Sophie complained.

Heaton heard a throat clear, and a familiar voice purred over the receiver. "Hey sexy, miss me?"

"Gypsy." Heaton couldn't help but smile at the nuisance woman. "As a matter of fact—" He grunted as he tugged his boots off. "Just the sound of your voice is compelling me to take my pants off."

"Oh, don't tease, honey. My loins can't take it."

"Hang on, Gyps." He pressed the phone to his chest again. "Jordan!"

Nevia stepped into the door frame, holding her arms away from her sides. She was still wearing her bra and underwear. "Damn it," he scolded her and tossed the phone on the sink. He picked up Nevia under the arms and placed her in the shower under the water.

She screeched and tried to get away from it. "No, no, no. I know it hurts, but it will get better." He finished pulling off his underwear and grabbed the phone off the counter. "Okay, I'm back."

"Am I interrupting something?" Gypsy asked.

"Who is that?" Nevia whispered.

Heaton shook his head and hopped into the shower beside her. The water hitting his sensitive skin made him want to jump right back out again, but he fought against the pain. "Yes, actually, I am just about to take the rest of Jordan's clothes off," he said and did just that.

"Heaton," Nevia objected and raised her hands to block him. He batted her hands away, dismissing propriety in lieu of saving her skin.

"You son of a bitch." Gypsy chuckled. "If I find out you lied about being gay..."

"Nope." He grabbed a bottle of gel soap and started washing Nevia's back. She stiffened and shook her head.

"Heaton," she objected again.

"Sorry, sport, I'm standing in the shower next to a naked woman, and no wood for the chipper. So, what takes you to the offices of Walline, Bailey, and whatever?"

Nevia leaned forward, rinsing the soap off her back. She turned around to face him, and he started in on the front, indifferent to the glare she was giving him. "Heaton, stop."

"You can barely move, Jordan. Don't be shy. I'm not getting off on this," he explained, barely present in the room with her, let alone the conversation.

"I am!" she yelled.

His hands stilled, precariously positioned over her breasts. The glare on her face was not simply anger. She was eyeing him... desirously. "But I'm—"

"Doesn't matter," Nevia stated in no uncertain terms.

"I didn't mean to—"

"Then don't treat me so aggressively this close to a full moon," she spat and took a step closer to him. She was only a sliver of a woman, but he was suddenly very aware of her werewolf heritage. "Daniel isn't here to... take care of me." She frowned, thinking of that. "You have to... I need you to..." Nevia's head dipped, and she stepped out of the shower. She grabbed a towel and left the bathroom.

Heaton waited a moment before returning to his phone call. "G-girl, I need to call you back."

"No, wait; just tell me where Daniel is."

"That's classified!" Sophie yelled in the background.

"So are you, sweet cheeks, but my ass is still creasing your leather," Gypsy responded to her. "Heaton, I need his help."

"He isn't available. He's back in prison. We had an incident."

"Damn it."

"How important is it?" Heaton finished soaping himself up to remove any residual acid.

"Important enough that I'm considering taking a trip to the North Pole to break him out."

"I really wouldn't advise that. Cori's liable to fry you at the door this time."

"Yeah, I know. Someday, me and her are gonna have to have a heart-to-heart. Or at least an official brawl so she can get it out of her system. What about you two? You interested in some side work?"

"I don't know. How soon do you need us? We're in America."

"As long as we do it before the full moon, we should be fine, but for reasons which you might already be dealing with, the earlier, the better."

"Alright, we'll need some downtime first. I'll call you when we get back over the pond."

"Deal."

Heaton clicked off the phone and finished showering before he went out to deal with his fem-wolf partner.

He found Nevia on the only bed, wrapped in a towel, watching television. The choice to share the room and save money now seemed unwise. He had never been drawn to Nevia, and he assumed she had considered him in the same asexual way. Had he not been so sure, he would never have treated her so clinically.

"It's not you," she answered before he could broach the subject. "It's me."

"Ouch," Heaton jibed. "I was taking that as a compliment."

She rolled back to face him, wincing from the change of pressure on her tender tissue. "You know how I feel about you, Heaton."

"Like the gay brother you never had."

She smiled. "Yeah, something like that." She frowned. "It's just... since Daniel and I started seeing each other, my lunar cycle has been erratic. I warned him about it, and so far, we've been managing it, but with him gone, I'm scared I might do something stupid."

"Stupid like shagging someone else?" He tightened the towel around his waist and crawled on the bed to settle in beside her.

"It's visceral and chemical and hormonal, Heaton. I can't fight it if I really get drawn to someone."

"Does this lunar moodiness have anything to do with your reaction to Mace?"

"Mace, that hick? Yuck!"

"No, I know, but you bit him." Nevia's face blanked, and her eyes widened slightly. "You bit a chunk out of his neck. And not a small one. You almost hit his jugular."

Nevia's face went pallid, and her eyes darted between his.

"Jordan?" Heaton lost the amusement in his voice. "You do remember biting him, don't you?" When she still didn't speak, he sat up and towered over her tiny supine form. "You need to answer me right now."

"I vaguely remember spitting out a hunk of something before the slug got me."

"Blackout violence?" Heaton watched her bite her lip. "Has this ever happened before?"

"How would I know?" she asked with a hint of amusement.

"Not funny, Jordan." Heaton plopped back down on the mattress and stared at the ceiling. "Partners can't have secrets."

"I know, and I would have mentioned it if I had known I was susceptible. There are a lot of traits that get manipulated when you cross human and werewolf DNA. Some abilities get stronger; others get weaker. Some morph into something undesirable."

"Like feral behavior?" he asked with a good deal more judgment than he intended.

"Yes."

He could hear the annoyance in her voice, but he ignored it. "How dangerous are you?" He rolled over. "Adrenaline spikes included. Should I be worried?"

"No, I'm not strong enough to hurt you. If I get out of hand, knock me out." Heaton reached over and retracted her upper lip. "Heaton, what the hell?" She pulled away.

"Hold still," he scolded her, and she huffed her dispute instead. He lifted her lip and checked for bruising or evidence of deciduous fangs. "When do werewolves start to change?" He pulled his finger away.

She took in a deep breath before answering. "Late teens, early twenties."

Heaton looked her over, not sure how to ask what he needed to. "Can quarter werewolves change?"

Nevia laughed. "Heaton, no, the biologics of a werewolf are fantastical. The human body is barely capable of childbirth, let alone the bone and muscle manipulation that—"

"You did notice the night after next is a full moon."

"Yes, I am acutely aware of the lunar cycle at all times, but despite my violence tonight, my behavior is usually more on par with PMS than any animalistic behavior."

"So, you've never heard of a part werewolf becoming... carnivorous during a full moon."

She frowned, and Heaton's hope dimmed. "My father used to lock my mother in the basement during the full moon." She looked away. "He told me never to let her out. One night, I got brave enough to peek in the basement window from outside."

"And what did you see?"

"She was pacing like a caged animal and frothing at the mouth. I can't say she had truly transformed, but she definitely looked different. To answer your question, no, I have never heard of a mixed werewolf feeding on humans during a full moon."

"Okay." He rolled over, ready to get some sleep and heal his burned skin. He paused in his retreat and turned back to face her. "If that ever changes, I need to know. I'm not going to turn another partner over to Danato." His voice was low with threat, but he knew she would sense the unspoken portion of his meaning.

"I will."

He rolled back over and closed his eyes to sleep.

"We will get him back," she said. "Danato didn't even want to incarcerate him to begin with. If it weren't for the audit, he probably would have just swept it under the rug."

"I know." Heaton exhaled harshly. He was still a little mad at Daniel for turning himself in.

One of the strictest rules of Daniel's probation was he could not harm a human. However, when a transmorph threatened to hurt Nevia, Daniel decided hurting the attacker's human mate was the best way to talk him down.

There was a small chance the couple would have kept the assault secret in order to preserve the transmorph's supposedly civil lifestyle choice, but an amputated limb was not something that could be kept quiet.

The arguments had gone round and round since the incident, but it wasn't until Heaton had convinced himself they should lie about it that Daniel had solidified his resolve to confess. He respected him for the decision, but he couldn't help but feel Daniel was doing it for him, which made Heaton feel like shit.

3

CORI TWISTED HER WEDDING ring as she stared down at the list of duties on her clipboard. Most of the feeling in her left hand had come back, and her mobility was well beyond what the doctor anticipated she would have. However, picking up anything heavier than a pencil was proving to be complicated. The doctor assured her the muscle strength would return, but until then, Danato had placed her on light-duty assignments. The temporary demotion, albeit for her safety and everyone else's, was feeling like a punishment. One that, for once, she didn't deserve.

In addition to that hardship, she had also lost something else since Gypsy cut off her hand and Daniel reattached it. Despite her accelerated healing, the power of her rings had not returned. And that concerned her far more than any physical disablement. Without her rings, she was no longer able to wield the tangible powers they had absorbed from the elementals and other supernatural prisoners.

She was, once again, for lack of a better word, *normal*.

Cori hadn't told anyone about this particular development, although she wasn't sure why. It was the type of error in communication that was likely to bite her in the ass later.

It shouldn't have made any difference to her since the rings were a borrowed source of magic—or, more accurately, a stolen source of magic. The gold used to make them had initially belonged to Ogana—the recently dead wizard who had escaped from the time bubble. It was this incident that ultimately resulted in her amputation—a supposedly necessary step in Gypsy's act of heroism.

Despite the origins of the magic, Cori had gotten used to being able to defend herself without a gun. And if it weren't for her rings, she would have been killed several times over by now. Without them, her daily duties were far more dangerous.

Cori assumed the liability of a secondary handicap might relegate her to even lesser duties than the watch she was being subjected to now. The last thing she wanted was to go back to cleaning cages on the zoological level. She refused to fall any lower in the pecking order than fourth, not after working so hard to gain the respect and trust of her mentors and coworkers.

Even if she wanted to tell Danato about this complication, she wouldn't have. He had enough on his plate without worrying about her safety—more than he already did. The audit had caused his stepmother, a member of the board, to take a closer look at the operations of the prison. She was also supervising the construction work on the top floor—the former quarters of the elementals. The board had apparently found a new tenant, and since financing the prison was always an issue, they bent over backward to remake the space to the renter's specifications.

"Is that a yes, or are you just ignoring me?" Danato asked, slightly perturbed. Since she hadn't been listening to the first half of the morning meeting, she didn't bother to look up to see who had displeased him so early in the day. A pencil landed on her clipboard, startling her back into reality. She looked up and found Danato with his brow raised—waiting for a response from her.

"What?" she asked, looking around at the other faces staring at her.

She wasn't sure what daft expression she had on her face, but it made Danato's mouth curve despite his disapproval. Ethan was also smirking at her, but he hid it behind a contemplative fist. Renee, however, was not the least bit pleased with her befuddled display. Her behavior would no doubt be described in her auditor's report as "lacks focus." Cori didn't bother to look back to see Belus's expression—it was likely the same as Renee's, and what was one more disappointed look from him?

"I asked if there was anything on that list you think you might have trouble with." Danato repeated the question she had missed the first time around. "I can reassign it if necessary."

"Oh, ahh..." Cori glanced over the list, dragging her finger along each task. Aside from the lengthy list, which would inevitably take her three times longer to complete with one hand instead of two, there was nothing physically challenging or dexterously complex about it. "No, I think it all looks fine." She gave him a small, forced smile, as if that might make up for her disinterest in the meeting.

Danato's brow immediately dipped with suspicion, seeing right through her feigned facade. "You seem a little out of it this morning. Is there anything wrong?" Like the flip of a switch, he exuded a genuine warmth and regard. He even extended his hand as if he wanted to touch her, but he was too far away to reach her, so it just landed on a different spot on his desk.

Cori might have told him right then and there about the rings if it weren't for Renee. The woman had turned her scowling face on Danato. Cori wasn't sure what the history was between them, but she got the sense Renee didn't like the familial relationships Danato had developed with her and Ethan. Not surprising since the woman found fault with everything Danato did.

Cori decided this was not the time to bring up her waning superhero powers. It might have been best if she waited for the audit to be over before she told anyone. "I'm just tired. Been a long couple of weeks."

Danato nodded, understanding the pressure Renee had put on everyone since she arrived. Strangely, though, it wasn't the intense scrutiny of the audit that was getting to

Cori. It was the other sudden changes that had transpired since the bubble had popped. With the entire wizard coven dead and the bubble empty, there was little to no risk inside the den. However, due to the entity's desire for electrical power, Danato forbade her or Efrat from entering it. That meant her gardening project was now in someone else's hands.

In addition, Daniel had been taken into custody for a violation of his parole. Levi had become the newest member of their permanent volunteer list and was being trained as a guard. Annette's health had declined exponentially after the battle with Ogana, and rumors were flying that she wouldn't make it through the next month.

Along with all that, a strange camaraderie was growing between Ethan and Efrat that baffled her. Their developing relationship was the polar opposite of what she had expected from her husband and former enemy.

Last but not least, Renee was staying at the house instead of in temporary lodging like other guests. Cori just couldn't keep up with the social changes that were disrupting her normal routine. She wanted everything to go back to the way it was—starting with her rings.

"I understand, sweetheart. If anything changes, my door is always open." Danato smiled at her, and she gave him a nod. "Okay, onto you, Ethan." Danato shuffled through his paper pile for his handwritten list of to-dos.

"Penelope has refused to come out the last three times for her walk."

"Penelope?" Belus asked—no doubt wondering when Danato had started using the pet name Cori had given to the dragon housed within the facility.

Danato shrugged. "If you can't beat 'em, join 'em."

"I don't blame her. It's too damn cold," Ethan said.

"I don't either, but she does need some exercise."

"No problem." Ethan made an air check mark for the task since he didn't have an actual clipboard. He didn't need a clipboard. His duties, unlike Cori's, wouldn't require ten different forms and twenty signatures to accomplish.

Danato continued down his list. "I know Duke has already inventoried the prop room in preparation for the move upstairs, but I would like a second count, just to be safe. I don't want to lose anything in the transition. Especially the small stuff." Ethan gave him a curt nod. "The kitchen staff requisitioned a new stove, and they need it changed out. I thought I would save the men the backache if you don't mind." Danato peeked over the rim of his glasses, almost asking permission to peddle Ethan's muscles for the sake of convenience. Ethan smiled and nodded. "Also, I've got two new guard recruits coming in today. They will need to be briefed and evaluated."

"I want Cori to handle that," Belus interjected.

Danato looked up at Belus. Renee and Ethan added their surprised glances to the mix. When Cori finally looked back, there was nothing to see, except Belus's uncompromising gaze locked on Danato.

"That's an unusual change of delegation." Danato glanced at her, careful not to imply she wasn't capable of the duty. "Would you mind telling me your thought process?"

"I want the new men coming in to see Cori as an authoritative figure. She can answer their questions just as easily as Ethan."

Danato remained quiet, debating the change. He no doubt didn't like it on many levels, the least of which was that it took away from Ethan and Duke's authority. However, since he probably didn't want to get into an argument in front of Renee, he took it in stride. "Any objections, Ethan."

Ethan looked at her. "Not if Cori doesn't."

As generous as it was for everyone to defer to her, she noted that refusal would make her look either weak or defiant. There was no winning. She didn't bother putting on a happy face for the duty; she just extended her hand for the files and subsequent paperwork that came with recruits.

Danato handed them over, once again trying to discern the level of her moodiness. Was it just the standard female drama, or was it something requiring his attention? "I hope that's everything. I don't think this clipboard will hold any more paper," she joked and stood up.

"No, I'm sure that's plenty for today," Danato agreed. "Don't forget your gun, sweetheart." He reminded her as she made it to the door.

She tried to fight the urge to look at Belus, but she couldn't. He was watching her, much as he had been the last two weeks. Waiting for an apology, she supposed, for the argument they had had regarding Gypsy's presence in the prison. An apology she felt she deserved more than he did. Something about her insistence on dragging out the ghosts in his closet for comparison had pissed him off. And since he held onto his grudges very tightly, Cori wasn't likely to get any leniency from him in the near future, regardless of her handicaps.

Belus's taciturn gaze didn't falter when their eyes met, but hers did. She ducked out of the office as quickly as she could, avoiding an unnecessary confrontation. She loaded up her gun, secured her radio, and went off to start her day of mismatch duties.

4

IT DISAPPOINTED DANATO TO see Cori's mood had not improved in the last couple of weeks. He knew she had a lot on her plate, but he had hoped the return of her mobility and nerve sensation would improve her outlook. With so much progress in just two weeks, she was bound to get at least ninety percent of her hand function back.

Of course, there were other reasons for her mood to be so sullen.

"I'm going to check in with my construction team," Renee announced after Ethan had left to start his routine duties, as well as his assigned ones. Her heels clicked as she moved to the door. She stopped there and looked back at him. "You should come up and see it, Danato. It's becoming quite the little laboratory."

"Does it have a table surrounded by big electrical coils so we can make a Frankenstein monster?" he asked.

Renee pinched her lips together in mock thought. "I didn't think to requisition one of those. I'll look into it for you." She winked at him before leaving. He was surprised she was allowing her playful side to show. Actually, he was surprised she still had a playful side. Short of actually being nice, she was at least being tolerable. She had even made an effort to help with the baby, which was enough to make him question her motives. However, so far, the other shoe hadn't dropped.

"Have you slept with her yet?" Belus asked, yanking him from his thought process like a slap to the face.

"Excuse me?" He stared at his second, no doubt wearing the same dumbfounded expression Cori had on earlier. Belus knew his history with Renee and, therefore, should have known she was the last woman on earth he would want to take to bed.

Belus's mouth curved into a smile. He slipped off the file cabinet and took a seat in the chair Ethan had recently vacated. "I asked if you had slept with her yet?"

"Yes, I heard you. I'm still trying to comprehend the level of desire required to have sex with a shark."

"Come on, Danato, shark or not, she's still a woman, staying in your house. It's not like you two haven't done anything before."

"Why..." Danato shuffled the papers on his desk for a moment, but gave up the distraction and leaned back in his chair. "Why would you encourage that? You hate her as much as I do. More, if that's possible."

"True, but I also know how long it's been since you've allowed that particular activity into your nightly routine."

Danato chuckled at Belus's analysis. He wasn't wrong, but he was surprised he was bold enough to bring it up to him. Either Belus wanted new gossip, or they were getting closer to their previous rapport than he thought. "I wasn't aware my sex life was keeping you up at night."

"No, my sex life keeps me up at night." Belus smirked, and Danato laughed. He had walked right into that joke. "I just thought I would let it be known that I wouldn't think less of you for taking an opportunity, albeit a bitchy one."

"I appreciate that. I'm not sure I wouldn't think less of myself. Then again..." Danato shrugged, unsure how to end that sentence. The truth was, Renee always brought up mixed feelings. He would never have a relationship with her, and this trip was the longest she had ever stayed at the prison. He wondered if her loveless marriages were finally making her lonely enough to tolerate the isolation of this place.

He could lower his standards for a night or two. Any concerns he had about betraying Olivia's memory had dimmed with time. He never presumed he would remarry, but that certainly didn't mean he needed to be celibate for the remainder of his life.

"Speaking of girl trouble," Danato spoke to interrupt his subversive thoughts before they made him uncomfortable. "What's going on between you and Cori? There seems to be a lot of tension there."

The humor drained from Belus's face. "I'm sure you got the short and dirty version of it from her."

"I believe her exact words were, 'Ask Belus, he's always right.'"

Belus nodded as if he had expected as much from Cori. "It was an argument. She said things. I said things. It will pass."

"Hmm," Danato added introspectively. He had eventually gotten Cori to give him the short version of the argument. Though he hadn't tried to mediate the dispute, he had determined the problem. Judging by this morning's unpleasant exchange, Belus had not yet reached the same conclusion.

"I know that look, Danato, and I know that smirk. I'm not playing into your hand just to amuse you."

"Oh, was I smirking," he said, genuinely unaware of the facial faux pas. "I barely know my own face."

"This is between Cori and me," Belus cautioned.

"I completely understand. I even told her as much. I haven't said anything to disparage you or defend you in her eyes." Danato leaned forward to speak a little quieter, even though the room was soundproof and didn't require such considerations. "Can I just ask you something, though? Was the guard recruitment duty a punishment?"

Belus stared at Danato. "Of course not," he said with notable annoyance. "Since the incident with Dirk, I think it might be wise to have Cori at the forefront of the disillusionment process. I want the men who come through those doors to see Cori as a figurehead, not just another employee prisoner or vice versa. Not to mention, if she and the other women in this facility are going to be put at risk every time we invite a questionable candidate into our group, she might as well help weed out any undesirables. She'll certainly have better instincts for it than the men."

Danato nodded. "That's a very astute observation. I couldn't agree more."

"Then why are you frowning?"

"Oh, am I? That damn face of mine again." Danato chuckled.

"You think I should have brought it up to you privately before announcing it in the meeting?"

"Well, I think a discussion one way or another should have taken place, but I think the person that should have been included in it was Cori."

"She knows what her obligations are to this place."

"Yes, I'm sure she does." Danato couldn't help but smirk as he said those words. While it was not unusual for Belus to fall back on the rules when he was frustrated, he knew as well as anyone Cori's loyalties were to people, not policies. "Listen, Belus, I know you don't want to hear my side of this, but I hope you'll allow me to reverse our roles here a bit."

Belus leaned back in his chair and nodded, permitting him to speak freely.

Danato rolled a few phrases around in his head before he decided to drop the bulk of his argument right away. "I think you're wrong."

"Wrong to have expectations for my subordinate?"

"Oh, come on, Belus, you're breaking her heart."

"Her heart is not my concern; that's your end of it."

Danato laughed and shook his head. He could only find amusement in the conversation because Belus was the one wearing the furious expression. "That woman, for God knows what reason, has devoted herself to this place. Just short of being its warden, she has applied her knowledge and skill to live up to your demands. Demands, which, by the way, are far higher than she could ever achieve."

"Goals are meant to be set high."

"Goals are meant to be set high, but not personal connections."

"That's not what I'm doing," Belus objected.

"Sure, you are."

"I'm not going to reward insolent behavior."

"Of course not, especially when that insolent behavior involves standing up to one's superior."

"She wasn't standing up. She was lashing out."

"Yes, and had it not been a direct hit to your ego, you might have reasoned with her, but instead, you lashed right back. Now both of you are hurting, and neither one of you wants to admit they've done anything wrong." Belus just stared at him, unwilling to give in but not having a defense beyond the rhetoric of work ethic. "There, I've said my piece. Much like any advice, take what you will of it."

For a moment, they both sat in uncomfortable silence while Danato distributed his papers into different piles on his desk. When Belus still refused to speak, Danato broached another awkward topic.

"Are you sleeping any better?"

Belus took in a deep breath. "Yes, things are starting to get back to normal in that department. How is Annette doing?"

Danato shook his head. Annette was his oldest friend, and despite her past and recent mistakes, he was grateful she had been able to help them fight off the wizards. Unfortunately, she was not the young woman she presented herself to be, and the strain of the magical battle had taken its toll on her elderly body. "She's getting worse, I'm afraid. Between creating the sorceress and defending us from Ogana... It was just too much."

"I'm sorry. I know she's been a good friend to you."

Danato slapped his papers down. "I could have just strangled her for doing that damn ritual, but..." He paused, not wanting to say his thoughts aloud.

"But what?"

Danato twiddled his thumbs a moment before responding. "I just can't help but think if it weren't for that damn ritual, Annette wouldn't have been here in the prison when the wizards escaped. And neither would have Gypsy."

"It was rather fortuitous," Belus admitted.

"It was more than fortuitous. It was..." Danato trailed off. He wasn't sure Belus would view the level of predestination any higher than lucky, but he, for one, found the entire path of events to be fated, right down to Ethan hallucinating the dragon's voice. He just wished it hadn't cost Annette her life.

Danato cleared his throat before continuing to speak. "We haven't had a close call like that in a long time."

"No, we haven't." Belus slipped off his chair and headed to the door. "Makes you want to embrace life," he said as he opened the door. "Eat bad food and fuck worse women." Belus glanced back before shutting the door. Danato scoffed at his incorrigible friend and waved him away so he could work.

5

C ORI TAPPED ON THE door to the critical care unit just down the main hall from the nurse's hub before pushing inside. She gazed at the elderly, comatose woman in the bed. Annette looked nothing like the young, vibrant, thirty-something with taut skin and defined muscles she usually portrayed. Between her stark white hair, draping skin, and a body that looked starved rather than thin, she looked every bit of the eighty years she had lived.

The chirping heart monitor and endless tubes reminded Cori of the hospital rooms she would sit in while her mother slowly died from a virulent form of cancer. Although it seemed like a lifetime ago now, she remembered it vividly. It was an experience she didn't wish on anyone.

Levi, Annette's assistant or protégé—Cori wasn't sure what his official title was—sat in the corner of the room, head hung low as he stared at his folded hands. He looked much like she expected him to—tired, sad, angry, and indifferent to anything beyond the emotional pain he was feeling.

He was just a boy, really—a young man at best. Much as Ethan was when they first met. But like Ethan, Levi was mature beyond his years and just a little broken by the forced growth.

"How is she?" she asked, making him jump. "I'm sorry. I thought you heard me knock."

Levi's wide eyes dimmed as he took her in. He knew who she was and likely her name, but there had never been a formal introduction between them. They, in effect, knew each other as Ethan's friend and Ethan's wife. Beyond that, there wasn't much foundation for a casual conversation.

"I don't know," Levi said. "The nurses keep grimacing when they look at her readings. I don't think she has much time left."

Cori hugged her clipboard tighter. "I'm so sorry, Levi. I know there isn't anything I can say to make it better, but I've been in your situation before, so I hope—"

"You've had to see your lover die, followed by the woman you considered a second mother?" Levi retorted with subdued cynicism.

"Not in that order." Levi narrowed his eyes as if he didn't believe her. "My mother died of breast cancer while I was in college. My aunt not long after that. And the man I was with before Ethan died right here in this prison."

Levi looked surprised by this revelation and a little ashamed. "I'm sorry," he mumbled.

"I'm not trying to compare, Levi. Everyone hurts and heals differently, but I just thought you should know you aren't alone. We're right here when you're ready. I know this isn't where you want to be, and I sympathize with that, too. But this place does get better... eventually."

He nodded, likely taking her words about as seriously as every prescribed sympathy card he had ever read.

"Can I get you anything?" she asked. "Are you hungry?" she added, wondering when his last meal had been.

"No. Thank you." He looked up to convey the full meaning behind his thank you.

She danced at the door, debating if she should leave or reveal the real reason for her visit.

"Do you need something?" he asked when he noticed her pacing debate.

"I know this is a horrible time to ask you a question, but I think you're the only one who will have an answer."

"What is it?" he asked.

Cori moved a little closer to him and lowered her voice to keep the nurses out of her business. "You know about magic, right?"

"Yeah." He shrugged, despite the assurance in his answer.

"I was curious about something. A spell that is cast on someone or something..." Levi nodded, waiting for the question. "The spell caster creates it, but what happens when that person... dies? Does the spell die with them?"

"It depends on the type of spell, but generally, objects can't retain the magic after the creator has passed. Especially if it's dark magic."

"So, for example, Ogana's wand. It would no longer possess magic?" Cori asked.

"No, the dark magic dies with the creator, and the earth magic that inherently exists in all natural objects would become dormant again."

"And there's no way to recharge the dark magic."

"Not without another spell. Why are you asking this?"

"Oh, I just want to take the proper precautions when I dispose of the wizard's wand. I guess it really is just a stick now."

"Yeah, just throw it away. It's useless."

Cori nodded and twisted her wedding ring again. It was officially just a ring and no longer the completion of a spell. Whatever magic had empowered the gold was dead, just like Ogana.

Cori looked at Annette. It didn't take a chart to realize she was on death's door. "Someday, this will all just be a memory, but it won't be what you remember the most. I promise."

Levi did his best to smile at her for the semi-comforting remark, but she knew he was on the verge of tears. She quickly excused herself so he could weep in peace.

She left the infirmary with her clipboard in hand to do her duties.

The duties of a normal person.

6

CORI TAPPED ON THE nine-inch crack in the aquarium. Through the glass, she could see one of her self-appointed sworn enemies. She knew very well how much a bite with his serrated fangs would hurt. Despite the proximity of his glossy black eyes, the vicious look on his bluish face, and the high-pitched sound he was emitting, Cori wasn't concerned for her safety.

The members of the mer population had changed several times since the death of their comrades, but the legend of their demise had been passed down from generation to generation like a lousy bedtime story. Though they weren't capable of dialogue in the humanoid sense, the creatures shrieked intelligibly to each other whenever she was around. This was a warning to all newcomers in the aquatic section that danger was approaching. Unfortunately, instead of hiding from her like they did Danato, they plied themselves to the glass, double-dog daring her to take revenge on more of their kind.

There was no point rationalizing with them, and since ignoring them was about impossible...

"What do you think, Bert?" she asked the merman, staring out of her from tank B. "Ten inches is the standard parameter for glass replacement, but it looks a little too deep to disregard." She tapped the glass again, and he rammed his head into it with surprising speed. When this threat did nothing to startle her, he offered her a water-muffled screech that the resident in tank A across from them mimicked. "I don't know, Ariel," she glanced back at the mermaid, that would sooner take her face off than discuss a crack in the tank. "I think we should consult Danato before we decide to use a filler. We all know what happens when I try to make decisions on my own."

The female screeched again.

"That's right, Ariel," Cori said with a somber sternness, "people get hurt."

"Is this a private conversation," Duke hollered over the water pumps, "or are y'all just takin' a stab at English lessons?"

"Hey, Duke," Cori greeted him with a hint of her boredom threading through her voice. "How's it going?"

"Well, they'd be going a might better if I had five-foot-long arms."

Cori tipped her head, wondering how that would be beneficial to his day. He chuckled at her confusion.

"I got a blockage in the incinerator shaft. It's between floors, and I can't push it down or pull it up. I need to lower someone down to dislodge it, and... well... since you're a might smaller than my boys, I was hoping I could string you up."

Cori looked over her list of unimportant crap. "Hmm." She shook her head. "I'm sorry, Duke. I'm just booked solid with crucial duties."

"Oh." He frowned, "That's alright, I can see if—"

"Duke." Cori laughed. "I'm kidding. This is just busy work, anyway."

"You sure?" he asked, not readily letting go of her joke as her true intentions.

"Yes. Anyway, you are far better company than these guys." The merman screeched. "Well, he is," she insisted.

Duke smirked at her playful banter. "I like to see you enjoying your work, but you are minding yourself around them, aren't you?"

"Yes, Duke," she drawled and tapped her gun. Despite appearances, Cori was ever vigilant of the dangers around her. Even when her rings were fully functional, she had never assumed magic was more lethal than a set of teeth.

Duke gave her a curt nod and led the way out of the section. She followed him through a few more airlocks to a quieter but more humid section. There were a few nondescript reptilian creatures that were never much of a concern to the prison. However, their constantly shedding skin required the incinerator shaft to be cleared as soon as possible.

As Cori approached the propped open chute, she got a whiff of something resembling dead rats and cat litter. "Oh!" She covered her mouth and looked back at Duke.

He gave her a half smile. "I know," he shook his head. "I swear I've been banging on that damn thing for an hour. It won't budge."

She groaned. "Why does everything important have to be dangerous or disgusting?"

"I don't imagine those rings can protect you from stinky."

Cori glanced down at her hands. "Nope, that is beyond their scope. Okay, how do we do this?"

Duke handed her a pair of tin snips and ushered her to the hole in the wall. It wasn't a big opening, but it was big enough that she could depend on getting back out. Duke shifted around her shyly, trying to figure out how to touch her without being indecent. She eventually just flopped herself into the tube, and he caught her ankles and calves to control her drop.

"Oh, gawww!" Cori struggled to control her gag reflex as she pushed through saggy snake skins and nondescript wet debris she really didn't want to identify. "You owe me, Duke."

"Yes, ma'am."

"Okay, I've got it. It's pretty big." Cori could feel the bulbous blockage through the refuse. She couldn't see what it was, but it was big enough she was reluctant to try to shove it down any farther. Lest it just jam up farther down the line. "I'm going to try to pull it up. Hang on tight."

"Will do," Duke called down to her.

Cori put the snips in her mouth and gripped the sides of the object. She expected a lot of resistance, but even with her bum hand, it yanked free on the first pull.

"Okay, reel me in," she mumbled over the tool in her mouth.

Duke pulled her back up. He was once again careful with his hand position as he returned her feet to the floor. "Boy howdy, that..." Duke trailed off as she pulled the load in her arms clear of the shaft. He stared down at the object, slack-jawed. It wasn't until he pulled the gun she understood the emotion lurking behind his disillusionment was fear.

7

"**D**UKE, PUT DOWN THE gun!" Cori yelled, not wanting to be at the aiming end of anyone's firearm.

"Put that down!" he yelled right back at her.

She had never heard Duke raise his voice, especially to her. She dropped the load in her arms and backed away before he shot her because of the damn thing.

"Get yourself over here!" Duke snapped his fingers, and Cori jumped to his side, not willing to argue with him. When she was safely out of his aim, she looked back at the object she had pulled from the chute.

A shiver ran up her back as she looked at the turquoise color visible through the snake skins. She could just barely make out the knobs that did nothing to control the volume or station of the psychic radio.

"Are you alright?" Duke asked, holding the gun on the radio as if it were an actual being.

"How is that thing intact? Danato destroyed it." Cori distinctly remembered the sound of the radio shattering when Danato threw it to the floor. He had gathered up all the parts and taken them to the incinerator himself. There was no way this could be the same radio.

"Yeah, so did Belus. This thing just keeps coming back."

"Wait, why isn't it playing music?" she asked. "I touched it."

"Don't know. Did you have a song in mind?" Cori shook her head. "Well, no need to give it one." Duke holstered his gun and pulled a pair of gloves from one of his many cargo pockets. She wasn't sure they would defend against the psychic connection, but they would prevent him from smelling like garbage, unlike her.

Duke took a step forward to destroy the device again.

Cori grabbed his arm. "Wait." The words were out before she sensed the need for them. As her thought finished, she looked at Duke, who was eyeing her suspiciously. "If it keeps coming back, there is no reason to break it again. Clearly, destruction is useless."

"It works well enough for me." Duke started toward the device again, but this time, she jumped in his path to stop him.

"I want to consult with Danato before we do anything."

"I'm acting on the warden's orders right now." Duke pushed toward the machine again, but she pressed her hands on his chest.

"Duke, we need to sequester this thing in soundproof glass and study it just like the rest of the crap in the prop room."

"That crap should be incinerated right along with this."

"Duke, no!" She gave him a final shove. "That's an order!" She stared at the cowboy, hoping her first attempt at seniority didn't put a halt to their friendship.

"Alright, now listen here, sugar," he reprimanded her with a raised finger. She resisted the urge to smile at finally reaching the status of sugar, especially since it was at the expense of him being mad as hell. "I am more than willing to do as I'm told, but Danato is still the warden and senior on the totem pole. Frankly, he's a bit scarier than you, too. So I'm gonna do what he tells me."

"Duke, please," she petitioned as he stepped by her. "It's just going to come back. We smashed that thing three times now, but low and behold, it's climbing up the garbage chute like the itsy-bitchy spider. We need to try something different."

Duke paused in front of the radio. He looked over his shoulder at her as she did him. "I'll give you five minutes to convince Danato." He nodded to her radio.

"Fifteen. I have to do it in person, or he'll never listen."

Duke's mouth twisted. "Ten and not a minute more. Go," he nodded toward the west wing.

"Thank you!" Cori hollered as she ran as fast as she could through the section.

The elevator was ready and waiting for her when she arrived on the west end. She accepted the offer and arrived safely on the main floor less than a minute later. She popped out of the elevator, coinciding with the usual pink. She ran down the hall toward Danato's office.

With more agility than she usually possessed, she slid into place, deposited her gun, and opened the door at the same time. She jumped inside, prepared to convince Danato of her ideal plan for the radio. Nothing short of death, and what she saw upon arriving, could have deviated her from her purpose.

8

I T WAS YET ANOTHER argument. Renee was an endless stream of opinions and decisions. The fact she had never once consulted Danato before making those decisions was beyond grating. Even from their first introduction, she decided she was attracted to him and, therefore, would seduce him. Never mind that he was a stupid teenager unfamiliar with alcohol or women. Nor was she concerned about the effect it would have on his relationship with his father. All she cared about was getting what she wanted when she wanted it.

The construction was going well, so she was pleased, but that only meant she could focus on other problems. Danato wasn't sure what had set him off. He imagined the slew of passive-aggressive insults she was throwing out were finally getting on his nerves.

Somewhere in the back of his mind, he knew it was because the construction was running ahead of schedule. Renee would be leaving soon, so she had to put her threats into place, lest anyone suspect the audit was a complete sham. She wasn't here to evaluate the finances of the prison. She was just here to be a spy.

Renee was the worst kind of spy. She was a corporate mole. Even though he saw what she was doing, he couldn't do anything to stop it. He just had to sit and wait for the board to figure out their next move. And then he would figure out his.

It was perhaps this underlying thought which caused him to blow. Renee was trying to take away his life's work, and while she was hiding behind a ruse, she had the gall to condescend to him.

If she had been a man, Danato would have put her in the hospital. One or two well-placed punches for the presumption of having control over him. Then, a quick trip upstairs to make it all go away before she left.

But of course, she wasn't a man. And since he was vehemently opposed to hitting women, there was only one thing he could do to release so much anger without actually hurting her.

Danato stood and shoved his desk as he reached for Renee. She was wisely backpedaling away from him, but he caught her arm and dragged her back. He glared down at her, and she stared back at him, fearful of his intent.

He caught her mouth up in a forceful, unromantic kiss. She whimpered against his mouth and gripped his biceps, steadying her failing knees. Without slowing his insistence, he lifted her onto his desk and bunched up her ugly floral skirt around her thighs. He pushed against her, demanding her submission. To his surprise, she started pawing at his pants, more than willing to accept his aggressive offering.

He had thought nothing of the interaction other than satisfying that need Belus had mentioned earlier, as well as regaining some of his control of the situation. There wasn't an ounce of shame in his heart for caving to such brutish standards of domination.

That was until he heard the tiny voice at the door.

"I..."

Danato broke from Renee and looked at Cori's gaping expression. She looked down the instant his eyes hit her. The floor was the only safe place to look since he and Renee were putting their impromptu sex scene on display.

"Cori," Danato helped Renee pull her dress down as she slipped off the desk. She discreetly zipped his pants while still blocking Cori's view.

"Did you need something?" He moved around the backside of his desk to intercept her. He kept his movements slow and controlled. He didn't want to appear embarrassed or panicked by the interruption. That would only make them more uncomfortable in the long run.

"I forgot my clipboard," Cori mumbled as she searched her hands for the missing accessory. She looked positively dazed.

"That's alright, sweetheart." He placed his hands on her shoulders and gently ushered her to the door, giving her permission to escape the awkward moment that had her frozen in place. He couldn't imagine what she thought of him. She only knew Renee as his stepmother. Although that designation probably sounded like the plot of a bad porno to her, Danato had no intention of explaining the details of their relationship to Cori. There were still some things in his life that needed to remain private. And his love life was one of them. "Why don't you go grab it and let me know what you need?"

"The crack in the tank is nine inches," she said, as if she were just remembering what she had meant to tell him.

"Then fill it." He pushed her out the door.

"It's almost an inch deep, though," she said.

"Use your best judgment, Cori." He gingerly shut the door behind her, trying not to make it seem like he was kicking her out of the office. Especially since he had only made a point that morning of telling her his door was always open. Apparently, that excluded times when he was making out with women he hated.

Cori turned back to look at him through the glass, but he ignored her and turned his attention to Renee. She looked a little amused by the entire situation. Leave it to her to find her sense of humor when it was at his expense.

9

Cori stared at Danato through the window as he walked away from the door. She couldn't comprehend what had just happened. He had all but shooed her out of the room—the room where she had caught him making out with his stepmother.

Aside from the weirdness of the pseudo-familial relationship and the fact that Renee was a complete bitch, there was something else.

Danato...with a woman.

Cori shuffled down the hall, trying to wrap her mind around that thought. She had never thought of Danato as a man—in that sense. She had thought of him as a father figure for so long that it was almost defiling to her mind to think of him as a sexual being with... needs.

Still, why was that so bothersome to her? Why did she feel betrayed?

Was this jealousy?

Was she just a spoiled child who didn't want to share her daddy's attention with anyone else?

Cori shook herself from the thought process before it required her to sign up for therapy sessions. Naturally, she forgot her gun in the bin, so she turned back to grab it. Once she returned to her previous path, she remembered her true purpose in seeking Danato.

She ran back to the office and burst in with slightly more zeal than she had earlier. The door slammed on the back wall, and Danato looked up from his conversation with Renee. This time, they were in the chairs in front of the desk instead of on top of the desk. They were also keeping their hands to themselves.

"Cori." Danato sounded annoyed by her second interruption.

"The radio is back," she said before he had a chance to run her off again.

"What?!" He jumped up. "Did you destroy it?"

"Not yet."

"Why the hell not?"

"Because I want to talk to you about not destroying it," she interjected civilly before his anger could reach a full boil.

"Where is it?" he seethed.

"Second floor," she disclosed immediately, "reptile section." She jumped out of the way as he charged out of the office.

"Is that the radio I think it is?" Renee asked behind her.

"Yes."

"Oh, honey, you are definitely poking the bear with this stunt."

"Yeah, I know." Cori gathered her gun and ran down the hall after Danato. She missed the days when he relied on a cane to get around. His long, pain-free strides made it impossible for her to keep up with him. "The radio isn't playing any music," she hollered after him. "There's no connection."

"All the better to stop it before it starts." He swung around the steps to head to the elevators. As part of her continued bad timing, Belus was coming out of the elevator as he arrived. "Hold the door!" Danato yelled, and Belus put his hand out to stop the carriage from leaving again.

Danato jumped in, with Belus right next to him. The doors started to close immediately, indicating that Danato was pressing the door close button. She barely caught a glimpse of his angry face before it disappeared behind the doors. Hopefully, her face projected that same depth of anger.

The second elevator *ponked* and opened promptly. At least someone was on her side. She jumped in, and the doors shut right away. The lift's speed nearly made her motion sick, but she arrived on the second floor in record time. She even had time to wait for Danato's carriage to arrive.

10

D ANATO SAW THE ANGER on Cori's face as the
doors to the elevator closed. He was in no mood
to negotiate about the radio. That damned thing cost him
his wife. He would not entertain any notion beyond its
destruction.

"What's going on?" Belus asked beside him.

"Cori found the radio again. I'm on my way to take
care of it."

"You've got to be kidding. Do we count that by
real-time or bubble time?"

"Hopefully, bubble time."

"Either way, that blasted thing is returning faster than
we thought. Why didn't Cori destroy it when she found
it?"

"A question I will be happy to ask after it's in pieces."

The doors to the elevator opened, and Danato found
Cori waiting outside. He might have assumed she had run
up the stairs to beat him, but judging by her un-winded
state and the smug look on her face, her elevator had
arrived before his. He didn't like the connotations of the
entity siding with her—especially on this matter. In truth,

he didn't want any connection between Cori and the entity, but that was beyond his control now.

"I know your concerns, Danato," Cori began as he brushed past her to get to the reptilian section. She kept pace with him, nearly running to match his long strides.

"You know nothing of my concerns," he yelled. "That thing killed my wife!"

"That thing almost killed me!" she yelled right back, surprising him with her ferocity. "Don't treat me like an imbecile. I know what she is capable of."

"Then why didn't you destroy it!" He stopped to open the airlock and pinned her with his gaze.

"Because it's not working." She sounded the words out carefully, in case he had forgotten how English worked. "It keeps coming back."

"Of course, it keeps coming back. It's evil!" He slipped through the airlock, forcing her to wait for him to get through before she could enter.

By the time she made it through, he was nearly at the next section. She sprinted to catch up with him. "So, we trust the elevators, the house, and your office, but not the radio?"

"The radio isn't a radio. It's a conduit into the mind. You know this."

"Yes, I know what you know. Which, if you haven't noticed, is jack shit."

Danato whipped around to face her, and she nearly collided with him. "You are skirting dangerously close to getting a consequence for this behavior," he threatened in a tone that promised pain and punishment if she did not appease him.

He could see her debate. It had been a while since he had to scold her for her actions. He had hoped she had grown beyond this level of obstinacy, but he was starting to think her obedience had only been building up pressure for rebellious moments like this.

"You don't really know anything about this creature. It's been pushing into this universe for a century, and you don't know any more about it than what Roland Latham figured out in a lightning storm."

Danato was disappointed she was pushing so hard to save the radio. "Did you touch it?"

"Oh, geez. It didn't affect me. Duke was there. You can ask him."

"I will, right after I destroy it." Danato pushed through the section again and ignored Cori's muffled objections. He made his way to the reptilian section, where he found Duke poised with his weapon, which was trained on the turquoise atrocity.

"Hey, warden, I take it Cori talked to you."

"Yes, she spoke to me. Why didn't you destroy it the minute you saw it, like I had ordered?"

"I gave her ten minutes to consult with you, sir. She's got one left."

"No, she doesn't." Danato barreled toward the radio. Duke seemed reluctant to deny Cori the remaining minute, but he certainly wouldn't stand in his way.

"Danato, stop!"

"Let it go, Cori," Belus reprimanded her as he entered the section.

"This is the very definition of insanity," she insisted.

Danato looked at her, more than a little disappointed by her behavior. He shook his head and picked up the radio. He raised it high over his head to make sure it turned to shrapnel on impact.

"Danato?" A soft, faint, feminine voice spoke, but this time it wasn't Cori. The voice was coming from the radio.

Olivia's voice.

11

CORI GASPED AT THE sound of a voice coming from the radio. Not a song. Not an evil being. A woman. Cori couldn't have known who it was since she had never met her, but she knew from the tormented expression on Danato's face that it was his wife.

His deceased wife.

"Is that you?" The sweet, trembling voice froze Danato. His eyes widened and brimmed with tears just at hearing her voice. "I need you, bear."

Danato's eyes instantly turned cold, and his biceps tensed.

"No!" Cori yelled as he slammed the radio to the floor. She shielded herself as fragments of the radio's shattered plastic shell ricocheted off the floor toward her. Danato finished the job with his foot, breaking the metal components back down to their original parts.

Once it was all done, he stared down at the dispersed remnants of the device, blinking away his tears. The emotions building up inside him were hidden by a veil of anger, as usual.

Danato moved to Duke. "Clean this up."

"Yes, sir," Duke said with a curt nod.

"And the next time you see this radio. You will destroy it immediately! Have I made myself clear?"

"Yes, sir." Duke swallowed hard.

"It wasn't his fault," Cori defended. "I ordered him—"

"Your orders do not supersede mine!" Danato stepped up to her, and she nearly backed away, as close as he got to her. She wanted to look him in the eyes, but she still couldn't muster the courage to do that—not at such close proximity to his anger. "You will never undermine me again. Do you understand?"

"Yes, sir," she said respectfully.

He moved away from her, heading back to his office, or perhaps a quiet corner, to bury his emotions. She should have left it be. She should have kept the remainder of her dignity intact—or, at the very least, her head.

"And you will never close those elevator doors on me again," she said firmly, but there was enough of a waiver in her voice to make her sound like a child in a room full of adults.

Danato halted, his shoulders rising with a breath even as his head bowed down. His anger was nearly palpable, as if the room itself was warming with its rise. He turned back, cornering her in the vacuous space with only his eyes. He was well past the stage of threats. His fuse was gone, and he was about to blow.

"Excuse me?" he asked so quietly she feared her eardrums would shatter when he finally spoke up again.

She looked at Belus, but he was backing away from the impending battle, no doubt out of respect for Danato, but also because she hadn't left even a sliver of room for her defense.

Danato moved to her with three quick steps, drawing her attention back to him. "Look at me!" His voice boomed. "What did you say?" He towered over her, and for the first time, she really thought he might hit her or, quite possibly, throw her in a cell.

She panted, nearly in tears, but she felt compelled to stand up for herself. If she was struggling for his respect now, what would happen when he found out her rings were useless? Downgraded to janitor—that's what.

"I brought the radio to your attention. I wanted to discuss the options with you while we were still safe from it. Not only did you not listen, but you closed those doors in my face. You completely disregarded my opinion." Her tears were pouring down her face, but she continued to speak. "From now on, when I wish to discuss a matter. I would appreciate your attention for at least a few minutes."

"We will not discuss that radio again, Cori!" Danato lowered his volume to a human level, but he stepped even closer, dominating her and forcing her to strain her neck to maintain eye contact. But maintain it, she did—although the constant tears were not conveying the courage she was aiming for.

"We didn't discuss it this time; you just brushed me off like an insect." Cori could sense her well-crafted argument turning bitter, but she couldn't let it go.

"Then stop being a pest!" he yelled in her face, forcing her to lose what was left of her composure. She took in a stuttered breath and turned her gaze downward. He stomped away, not bothering to clean up his mess—the shattered radio on the floor or her heart..

12

"I CAN GET THAT, Duke," Cori offered after Duke began to sweep up the radio bits.

"Nah, I got it," he smiled at her. He was sympathetic to her plight, but it didn't change the fact that she was mortified to have been reprimanded in front of him.

"Sorry for getting you in trouble."

Duke shrugged. "Don't you worry. I've been at the shit end of that man's temper before. I'll survive. Always do." He gave her a wink before returning to his work.

She picked up her clipboard and looked over the duties she had left before her recruits arrived. There wasn't enough time to get them all done. She would be home later than usual, which wasn't all that unusual. Busy work always takes longer than one anticipated.

She headed back toward the aquatic section to fix her cracked glass, but Belus stepped out of the corner he had been taking cover in and blocked her path. "Cori, can we speak?"

She sighed. "Please, no."

"Please, yes," he insisted.

"My self-respect is already a puddle of goo on the floor," she motioned to the white tile beneath her. "Do you really think you can berate me any further into submission?"

"Actually, I thought you had some good points." He glanced over the figurative goo. "You're timing, on the other hand, is absolute shit." He looked her over carefully before turning to leave. "Come with me."

She didn't bother arguing with him. She followed him through the airlocks to the infirmary. As they stepped through the doors together, a round of quick betting broke out as the three nurses at the desk debated which of them was injured. They settled down when they realized neither she nor Belus was wounded.

"Ladies," Belus nodded to the three young women. There was some whispering between the two of them, and then one giggled. "Would one of you be so kind as to fetch the archive files on the 1953 murders?"

The pleasant and playful smiles melted away, and one of the nurses bounded off to the file closet. Cori followed Belus into the dimly lit meeting room, just ahead of them. He sat down at the long table usually reserved for medical staff meetings or the occasional show-and-tell when a new species arrived at the prison. Along the chalkboard at the back of the room were three carts. All of them held various projectors—overhead, slide, and film. Cori was still begging Danato to let her order subtitled movies so she could have some form of visual entertainment, but so far, he hadn't caved to her request. Anything new tended to make him nervous.

Cori sat down catty-corner to Belus and patiently waited for her homework assignment to arrive. She peered out the open door at the women at the nurse's hub. They were reading magazines and debating which of the latest mainstream actors was hotter. She didn't even recognize the names they were bandying about. She used to keep up with celebrity gossip, but with such a minuscule budget to play with, she tended to buy more important things than magazines, like deodorant that didn't come out of a can and chocolate.

"I should have gone into nursing," she mumbled.

Belus glanced back at the door, but didn't agree or disagree with her potential career change.

The beck-and-call nurse arrived a moment later with the files he had requested. She gave Belus a warm smile as she handed them to him. He thanked her with a meaningful wink and watched her leave—no doubt getting a good look at her shapely buttocks.

Cori couldn't help being irritated by the flirtatious display and met Belus's returning gaze with a glare.

"Does every woman in this facility have a crush on you?" she asked snidely, turning her attention to the chipper young women now snickering about something the returning nurse had said to them. None of them had a care in the world about the hardships permanent residents had to deal with. Cori knew the minute a life-or-death situation came through their doors. They would jump into action and justify their presence, but until then, they just seemed like freeloaders.

In truth, she was envious of them. They got to spend the majority of their days trying to fill the empty time so they didn't get bored.

Oh, how she missed boredom—and television, and movies, and music, et cetera, et cetera, et cetera.

"I have a reputation," Belus said. "One that has taken me years to cultivate. Some women are curious if I can live up to it. It provides a little amusement to an otherwise dull day." Belus narrowed his eyes at her. "Does that bother you?"

Cori continued to glower at the nurses as she tried to formulate the words to describe what it was that bothered her about Belus's frequent dalliances with the female staff. It wasn't quite the same emotion she felt when she saw Danato kissing Renee. "You're nicer to them than me."

"I have different intentions with them." She heard the smile in his voice even before she looked at him. "I wouldn't call it nice."

"You're rubbing off on Danato. I just walked in on him and Renee making out—and then some."

"Really." Belus sputtered a laugh. "That's interesting."

"That's weird. She's like his—"

"Hardly, but that's none of your business. What Danato does in his—"

"Office?" Cori blurted out.

Belus did his best to hide his smile, but he was completely unsuccessful. "I do recall interrupting you and Ethan on the roof once, so let's just give everyone a little leeway for their hormones, shall we? Me included." He continued to smile, but the sturdiness of his gaze told her this was his way of reminding her that his personal life was personal. Nothing new there.

"What are we doing here?" Cori rubbed her face. "It's been a shit day, and I still have recruits to deal with," she noted acridly.

"You seem a little on edge since you got back to work."

"You think?" she snapped, proving his point.

"Cori, you need to stop. I'm not your enemy. Neither is Danato."

"You could have fooled me."

"You know, he was defending you earlier this morning. Now I feel like I have to defend him to you."

"What was he defending?"

"Your outburst prior to the wizard's escape."

"Is that what that was? I thought it was an observation."

"I'm not going to do this. I'm not going to be baited into another argument. You've been off ever since that day, and as much as I want to make nice and get past this, I can't help but think your attitude stems from something more than my harsh words." He raised his brow. "Any thoughts on what that might be?"

Cori pulled her hands into her lap and fiddled with her rings, twisting them, begging them to work. They wouldn't, though. They were unplugged. No more power. And admitting it would only make it real. "I'm just tired."

"You were just tired this morning. Would you care to add to that explanation?"

"Sick and tired." She added less than constructively. "Don't look at me like that," Cori objected when Belus's only response to her sarcasm was a hard stare.

"How am I looking at you?"

"Like you can't believe you got stuck with me."

"Oh, my, that is a burdensome look. Are you sure you aren't projecting a little of that into my facial expression? Because I'm pretty sure I'm just trying to get you to quit being a pain in the ass."

"From pest to pain in the ass in less than an hour, is that an upward move or a sideways move?"

Belus chuckled, but it wasn't a mirthful sound. "We should have had this meeting over drinks."

"I don't need a drink."

"I do," he complained. "I'm trying to help you, and you're redirecting my every effort to attack me. I know I hurt your feelings, Cori, and I truly am sorry, but I hardly think I deserve the animosity that's peeling off you right now."

Cori quieted for a moment. She was being too defensive. Her anger was meant for Danato and the nurses outside, and for a slew of other problems that didn't have any faces. She couldn't use Belus as a scapegoat for all of them. "You're right, I'm sorry. I'm sorry about what I said two weeks ago, too."

Belus nodded. "You had some valid points then, too, but much like today, you had horrible timing." He leaned back in his chair. "I had just come out of a year in the bubble with little to no reprieve from the dream feeders. You attacked my vulnerable state with the very thing that had made me vulnerable."

"I just wanted you to see my side of things."

"Yes, kid, I know that. Just like you wanted Danato to see your side of things today, but listen…"

Cori slumped down, ready to receive her reprimand from Belus.

"Don't dismiss this, Cori. I really am trying to offer you helpful advice."

"I'm listening." She nodded for him to continue.

"I like that you're taking the initiative to stand up for what you want. I think it's a side of you that has been missing for a while now, but you really need to think your arguments through. I agree that destroying the radio is pointless. It will just come back."

"That was my whole point."

"No, that's my point. If you would have destroyed it and then gone to Danato to discuss some potential options for when it returned, you might have found him more receptive to your ideas."

"It's just... he never listens. It takes so much to get him to hear me sometimes."

"I know the feeling. He never used to listen to me either, but trust me, diplomacy is your answer, not dictatorship. He loves you, so his knee-jerk reaction is to rescue you. Let him rescue you, and then speak to him when he's calm. You may find that the more you listen to him, the more he'll listen to you."

"I get that, but..." Cori fiddled with her rings again. She wasn't sure how to explain how she felt. She wasn't even sure Belus would sympathize. "I feel so useless right now."

Belus frowned and shook his head. "Just give it some time. You'll be back to normal soon."

"And if I'm not?" She locked eyes with him.

His brow dipped slightly. "Why wouldn't you be? Has the doctor said otherwise?"

Cori stared at him, debating if she wanted to answer that question, or even if she wanted her question answered. "Does it ever bother you to be normal?"

Belus perked his brow and shook his head. "I'm not sure normal is ever how I would describe myself."

"No, I mean human. Just human. No superpowers."

"What is this about?"

"I think I just need to know that I'm not going to be stuck on clipboard duty forever."

"Of course not. You don't really have to be on clipboard duty now, but since you aren't working the gardens, Danato wanted to give you something to do."

Cori let out the breath she had been holding. "Good."

"Is that what has been distracting you lately?" Belus asked, seemingly unconvinced.

"That and the usual worries." Cori shifted to look at the files the nurse brought in. "What's all this?" she asked, happy to change the subject.

"Have a look." Belus pushed the files over to her.

She flipped open the top manila folder, unprepared for what it contained. "Oh, God!" Cori closed the folder before the melee of blood and evisceration in the photo could fully register. "What is this?" She stared at Belus—slightly annoyed he hadn't warned her about the pictures before she endangered the contents of her stomach.

"That is why Danato doesn't want to listen to any negotiations regarding the radio."

Cori frowned and shook her head as Belus reached over and started opening all the files. She covered her mouth as he put eight horrific photos out on display.

If it weren't for the vicious nature of the dissections, she might have assumed she was looking at autopsy photos or medical cadavers. The bodies were skinned down to the bone, guts splayed and rearranged. In one photo, the victim's eyes had been pried from their sockets. In another, the skull had been cracked open, and the brains removed.

Cori gagged, no longer able to keep her breakfast secured. She ran to the trashcan by the door and made her deposit. She noticed the nurses outside staring at her. Thin, flat smiles were perched on each of their faces as if they were restraining the grimaces they wanted to give her. They were probably intending to be sympathetic since they likely knew what she had just seen, but she didn't like the idea of entertaining them with her reaction.

Cori stood up and slammed the door shut, so she didn't have to see them. Belus glanced at her to see what had inspired her rudeness. He looked like he wanted to say more, but he let it go. He started to collect the files, but she stopped his hands. She didn't want to look at the images anymore, but she wanted to understand what she was looking at. She pulled one of the files toward her and flipped the page to read the report that documented the event.

"How did the radio cause this?" She frowned at a paragraph mentioning the removal of the testicles.

"The entity possessed one of our men, and he did this."

"One man, did all this?"

"Yes."

"This is like Silence of the Lambs shit. Sadistic, but purposeful."

Belus nodded. "She wanted to know more about the humans she couldn't replicate, so she cut them open... while they were still alive."

Cori gaped at him. "Like a child pulling wings off a fly."

"Very much so. When she didn't get the answers she wanted, she dissected her own vessel."

"What?" Cori shook her head. "She—she dissected herself."

"We assume she was becoming frustrated that her projects kept dying on her before she could truly understand them, so she found a mirror and started cutting." Belus pulled a file forward to show her the photo of a man with a long incision across his belly. "Naturally, she was unable to tolerate the pain, so she stopped. We later executed the vessel and did an autopsy on him. We found three sets of testicles in his stomach."

Cori stood up and walked away from the table. Her laughter, albeit completely inappropriate, was the only thing that kept her from permanently checking into the padded room down the hall. "I made the Silence of Lambs reference too soon." She paced behind Belus. "Why would she do that?"

"Now, I think perhaps it was a misinterpretation of the sex organs. Back in those days, there weren't any women here, save a few pictures and the occasional visitor. I think she thought she could multiply the men simply by ingesting their seed. The distinction between stomach and uterus is difficult to identify from an exterior perspective."

"Why have you never shown me this?" Cori asked.

"I didn't feel it was necessary until today."

"You wanted to prove to me that Danato was right about destroying the radio?"

"No, I showed you this because if you have any chance of making a case for keeping the radio intact, you need to know all the gory details of its history."

Cori glanced at the files. "You don't think she would actually pull something like this again, do you?"

"Do you?" Belus asked as he gathered the files.

"No."

"Why not?" Belus glanced back at her, waiting for a legitimate reason for her belief.

"This is old hat for her—like those model T's—been there, done that. She doesn't want to be a factory. She wants to explore and discover new things. Besides, she knows that's not how it works anymore."

"Right. Now she knows she needs a woman." Belus leaned against the table. "She knows she needs you."

"Me?"

"Yes. You are the only human being she is certain will be capable of reproduction."

Cori instinctively touched her rings. She hadn't considered all the ways her rings had protected her up to that point. She had only been thinking about the physical threats.

"Have you noticed the house responding to your emotional state?" Belus asked.

Cori nodded. "The elevators come right away now, just like they do for Danato."

"She's imprinted on you."

"What does that mean?"

"It means she is anticipating your needs and protecting you."

"That's a good thing, though, right?"

Belus took a breath. "Cori, I'm not sure there will ever be anything good about this entity. We have seen evidence she is learning, but she doesn't always understand the nuances of human emotion. You've seen what she can do when she's disappointed in us."

"Am I in danger again?"

"The imprinting seems to be similar to Danato's rather than mine. Either way, she hasn't tried to harm either of us. She just remembers us. However, I would strongly advise that you don't touch the radio when it returns."

"I did touch the radio, but nothing happened. When Danato touched it—that voice came through. I know that was Olivia." Belus looked away. "This isn't the first time she's come through, is it?"

"It isn't Olivia. It is just the entity."

"Are you sure?"

"Am I sure that Olivia is dead?" Belus barked at her.

Cori grimaced and sat back in her chair. "I didn't mean it like that."

"I know." He shook his head. "Look, kid, I really don't want to have a repeat of our last argument, so let's just establish something right here and now. Olivia isn't gone because of a skewed timeline, or a genie wish, or even because the entity took over her mind. She is gone because I put a bullet in her face."

Cori stared at him, unable to refute that statement.

"And she wasn't a monster when I did it. She was my best friend, pleading for her life and begging me to stop. And when I was inside of the bubble, I relived that moment every fucking night for nearly a year." Belus's face crumpled. "And you had to throw it in my face to defend your actions rather than just do as you were told." Belus pulled back the files and stacked them again. "I meant what I said. I'm sorry I hurt your feelings, but what you said to me did not leave me unscathed."

With still nothing to add, Cori stared at the table while Belus gathered the files before heading out. He paused at the door and looked back at her. "Are we good, Cori?"

Cori thought about that statement. They weren't good. She was a constant reminder of the woman he had loved and killed. There was never going to be anything good about that.

"Yeah, we're good."

13

C ORI STARED AT THE three faces before her at the docks. Two new ones and one familiar one. Trevor, the fast-talking eager guard, was already raising his hand to ask a question. "Trevor, what are you doing here?"

"Oh, yeah, I'm here for a recap. Duke says I make special sound smart, so he said I should redo my entries."

"This is just an intro to the prison. We aren't going to go over anything you don't know."

"I know, but I got some questions, and he said questions are for beginners, so here I am." He shrugged and smiled, revealing a missing tooth in the back of his smile.

Cori smirked at his enthusiasm. The truth was, she was happy to have a familiar face in the group, especially since the two new recruits looked a little sketchy.

The one to Trevor's left was black and bald. His expression was permanently set to murder mode. She knew it was probably just a defensive technique to keep people away from him in prison, but it was unnerving as hell.

The one to Trevor's right was Latino. He also looked a little familiar. She looked at her clipboard. "Paul?"

"Pow-ul," he corrected her with a thick Brazilian accent.

"Have you been here before?"

"No, ma'am, first day," he responded.

Cori checked her chart and saw nothing to indicate he had been trained before, as Trevor's paperwork suggested. She presumed it was just her memory playing tricks on her.

"And Cain?" she asked, looking at the black man again.

"Yeah, like Cain and Able. From the bible," he added as if the connotation of murder wasn't strong enough. "You mind telling us what the hell we're doing here with you?"

"Short answer: you signed a paper. Long answer: I didn't get to sign a paper. So, listen up and follow me," Cori grumbled as she made a note in her log about the time.

"That ain't no damn answer, woman! What the fuck are we doing here?"

"Hey, man, chill, she's just doing her job," Trevor defended her.

"Bitch is just a paper pusher. Anyone can see that. I want to talk to the man in charge."

"No, you don't," she and Trevor said simultaneously.

"Look, you guys are about to be introduced to a whole new view of life," she continued. "I would strongly advise shutting up so you can keep up with everything I'm about to throw at you."

"Bitch, I ain't takin' orders from you; or anyone else in this place."

Cori shrugged. "Then don't. Get back on the bus, go back to your 4x8 cell, and rot until your term is over. You signed up for this because you wanted something different to pass the time. Well, you got it, but nothing will change if you don't. There are a lot of people to give you orders in this prison. Orders that are intended to save lives, including yours."

"I didn't say I wanted anyone to get hurt. I just want some answers."

"Good. Step one is to shut the hell up so I can give you those answers." Cori paused to see if he was going to mouth off again, but he didn't. He just rolled his eyes. "This prison is designed to harbor special prisoners."

Trevor smiled and muffled his laughter behind his hand.

"What is so funny?" Paul asked.

Trevor smiled at her. "Can we show 'em, Penelope?"

Cori chuckled. "Well, that would jump-start their acceptance."

14

"**D**ON'T SHOCK HER!" CORI scolded Efrat again as she paced the sidelines in front of the slack-jawed recruits. Ethan found a great deal of amusement in watching the new guys see the dragon for the first time. He was almost disappointed Belus wanted her to do that part of the roster today.

"Efrat, stop!" Cori yelled. Efrat turned from his battle and threw up his hands as if reminding her he couldn't help shocking the animal even if he tried. Because of the distraction, he narrowly missed getting his hand nipped by Penelope. She seemed to be reacting to Efrat's electrical sting like a dog. If Efrat wasn't careful, she might try to eat his hands just to be rid of them like a pokey sticker or a stinging bee.

Ethan turned his attention to Cori, finding further amusement in her motherly agitation. He was surprised at how protective she was of the dragon. If she knew the mammoth creature was such a condescending gripe, she might not have had so much sympathy for her pain.

Penelope shifted to look at him. He wasn't sure the reptilian face was capable of a glare, but he sensed it was her attempt. "Relax, Cori, he's not hurting her. Keep going, Efrat," he called over to the elemental, since he had relinquished his attack strategy at Cori's beckon. Or perhaps he was only taking a breather.

"How do you know?" she asked.

"Because Efrat is still alive," he said. Cori frowned, dissatisfied with his arbitrary conclusion. "Sweetness, her skin is like four inches thick. That's why I'm having Efrat train with her. He needs a sparring partner that he can't hurt, and she needs the exercise."

Penelope wailed and whipped her tail around, knocking Efrat back. He landed between Ethan and Cori on the sidelines. He lay there a moment, groaning as he held his hands up, keeping them clear of his body. "Would you focus so I don't get killed!" he rasped over his deflated lungs.

"No problem." Ethan grabbed him, pulling him up by his wrist. He still got a slight shock from the proximity, but he didn't let his pain show. Ethan, much like Cori, was starting to grasp the level of guilt Efrat was feeling from his condition. Maintaining physical contact with him was going to be vital to developing a relationship with him. Though Ethan couldn't shake his hand, that didn't mean he couldn't find other ways to interact.

Ethan looked Efrat over for signs of blood or cuts in his clothing. "You, okay?"

"Yeah, just tired," Efrat said.

"Good." Ethan slapped his back. "Now, just remember." He pointed toward the tail-twitching dragon. "She needs at least twenty more minutes of this, so pace yourself."

Efrat turned a wide-eyed stare at him. Ethan resisted laughing at him. "Twenty minutes!" Efrat cursed. "I hate you."

"I know you do, buddy." Ethan squeezed his shoulder and gave him a good shake. "Now, you take that hatred, put it in the pit of your stomach, and go exercise my dragon." Ethan shoved him back into the arena and chuckled as Efrat rolled under a paw swipe from Penelope.

"Ethan," Cori said quietly beside him. He looked over at her sad, slightly disappointed face. "Are you sure you aren't just doing this to get back at him?"

"No, this is a guy thing, Cori. Despite the motivation for it, this actually has very little to do with you."

"A guy thing?" She waggled her head. "Really, you're pulling that card. I think I know punishment when I see it."

"Duck!" Ethan yelled, saving Efrat from Penelope's tail. "Look, sweetness." He glanced between her and Efrat so he didn't lose track of his responsibilities on either end. "If I really wanted to punish Efrat for making a pass at you, I would just throw you to the floor and make out with you right here in front of him." Cori's mouth gaped, and she looked down at the floor in anticipation of the aforementioned act. "But of course, that would be cruel, since he does have legitimate feelings for you."

Ethan shifted away, seeing that Efrat was in trouble again. "Don't let her corral you! She's trying to corner you in the hangar!" When he looked back, Cori was staring out at Efrat. She looked annoyed and sympathetic—her usual twist of emotions when dealing with the man. Despite Efrat's feelings for her, Ethan was certain she was still loyal to him, and that was all that mattered.

"Trust me, Cori," he said, drawing her attention again. "I know what I'm doing. This is going to help him more than hurt him. Besides, you've been carrying all the guilt for Efrat's unlawful incarceration. It's time you let me help you."

She looked at him with visible relief at this epiphany. Her eyes fluttered over his, and her breathing quickened. He smiled at her, quickly recognizing her inappropriately timed desire to express her love, gratitude, and overall appreciation for him. He hadn't seen it in a while, so he was happy to know she still felt it. Unfortunately, without doing exactly what he said he shouldn't, they couldn't act on any part of it. And he didn't have time for a broom closet tryst.

Ethan glanced over to Efrat, who had resorted to running from the beast. "Listen, I've got to help this nitwit before she eats him, but I would very much like to see you later if you can fit me into your schedule." Cori glanced at the clipboard in her hand as if she might literally need to pencil him in.

"Yeah," she said breathlessly. "I'll see what I can do." She didn't move.

Ethan glanced at Efrat again and smiled back at her. Her lust-inspired, dumbstruck expression was priceless. It was as alluring to him as any temptress. "You really need to leave, sweetness, or you're going to create an awkward situation for me."

She smiled at first, but then his meaning dawned on her, and she blushed. "Oh, sorry." She backed away, nearly tripping, which made him want her that much more. "I have to finish my tour, anyway." Cori barked an order at her recruits, and they filed out, only releasing their gaze on the dragon when they were out of the gym.

Ethan watched Cori slip out the door with a shy smile on her face. For a moment, he imagined every scenario in which he might receive his reward for helping Efrat. When he finally came out of his fantasy, he realized he had neglected his student for a little too long. He found Efrat pinned under Penelope's massive toe pads. His arms splayed like a flattened bug as he tried to find an angle to give the dragon a proper zap. "Oh, damn it, Efrat! How is that exercising her?"

15

"THE GROUNDS ARE FAIRLY extensive," Cori hollered over the wind as the three men trailed behind her, huddled into themselves as tightly as they could get. She didn't relish the cold weather either, but she decided to start with the exterior tour, since she didn't have the luxury of stopping for a cold shower. "That over there is the greenhouse." She pointed to her second favorite place in the world—outside of Ethan's arms, of course. She didn't spend as much time there as she used to, but she still stopped in to tend to the more persnickety plants that didn't grow well in the bubble.

"The next two buildings are mostly storage," Cori continued to point out the other outbuildings she rarely, if ever, went into. "The one over here in the back corner is the garage." She pointed to the largest building in the far corner. "And up ahead of us are the stables."

Cori picked up her pace and jogged to the stable entrance. She pulled back the large sliding door and ushered the men inside for a reprieve from the wind. She slid the door shut behind them and pulled out a packet of tissues, which she offered around like gum.

Cain yanked one from the pack and blew his nose hard. "Is it ever warm here?"

"Warm?" Cori shook her head and wiped her nose with a tissue. "No, but it is less cold. The summers are actually nice. Jacket weather."

"I hate the cold." Cain's face pinched in disgust.

Cori ignored his pouting and guided them past several stalls. "We always have a few horses on hand for emergencies. The main road is usually pretty reliable for the trucks, but if we have to go off the beaten path in the winter months, the horses are a better option.

"We keep several cows and goats around as well. So don't be surprised if you are assigned to feed them or change out the hay." She pointed out a deep stall that held two cows and another with four sheep.

"Is that where we get our milk?" Trevor asked.

"No, they aren't for milk." Cori frowned. "They're for blood. We bring in live animals for most of the vampiric inmates and divide the meat among the carnivores, but once in a while, we get a sick one or one that has died during transport. These guys are the understudies."

"Can't you just give the creatures a bag of blood?" Paul asked.

"Some we can, but in most cases, the creatures don't recognize it as food unless it is coming straight from the tap."

"You really have vampires?" Cain asked quietly.

"Yeah, quite a few. We'll head there next, but first, I need to check something off my roster." Cori handed her clipboard off to Trevor and grabbed a rope from the wall. She unlatched the gate to the sheep stall and chased down a small one. She looped the rope around his neck as a makeshift leash and dragged him out of the pen. Trevor shut the gate behind her.

She slid open the rear door of the stable and motioned for everyone to exit.

"Can't we just wait in here where it isn't subzero?" Cain asked.

"It will be plenty warm where we're going."

Cori booted her sheep along, urging him forward across the span of the back acreage toward Rodan's cage. She heard Trevor laugh behind her and clap. "Oh, yeah, this guy's awesome," he whispered to the others.

"Rodan!" Cori banged on the bars. The mound of rock inside the cage snapped and creaked as he slowly came to life. "There you go, big guy; rise and shine."

"What do you want?" His vibrating voice was barely translatable today. The wind was cooling him to near immobility.

"I brought you an extra treat," she said, but he didn't warm to her offer. "For your help with the digging."

"They are not virgins," he retorted.

"I don't even want to know how you know that, but they aren't the sacrifice. I brought you lamb chops."

"I want a virgin," he objected.

"I am not bringing you a virgin sacrifice; stop asking! Do you want the sheep or not?"

"Yes," he agreed.

Cori lifted the small cage door used for feeding the big lug and pushed the baying fluff ball through it. She walked away, unwilling to watch the mammoth rock man devour the animal alive. It was bad enough that she could hear the bones crunching. Judging by the horrified looks on her trainees, it was the right choice not to watch.

She trudged back through the snow, taking the opposite way around so she could point out Belus's house and the staff quarters. Trevor ran up beside her and handed the clipboard back to her. "That was freakin' awesome. Gross, but genuinely cool."

She smiled at his enthusiasm. She imagined she could show him just about anything in the prison, and he would find it "awesome."

"Hey, what's that?" He pointed to a spot well away from everything else.

"What?" She couldn't quite see what he was referring to, but then she saw it—a patch of grass, clear of snow and green as a spring day. She furrowed her brow at the phenomenon. It was easily ten degrees below freezing, and it had been for a while. Nothing should be growing, let alone something bright green.

"What's that about?" Trevor asked.

"Just a reaction to fertilizer, I think. I wouldn't worry about it," she dismissed the question, but even as his curiosity waned, hers piqued, especially since she knew what was buried under that lush patch of grass.

16

CORI STOOD OUTSIDE OF the cell, staring at herself inside the cell. Her inner self glared harshly back at her. "And these are the transmorphs," Cori said, hiding the shiver she felt every time she walked past them. Much like the merfolk, the transmorphs had grown to hate her. She had helped Danato find a way through their camouflage, and she was also one of the few humans who had survived being imbibed by them. "They can change their body composition to match any being they see."

"They can also mimic voices to perfect pitch." The transmorph Cori continued to speak for her. "The way you walk." She walked along her bars, displaying what Cori assumed was her particular gait. "And even your mannerisms." She stopped in front of Cori and smirked at her—very proud of her impersonation.

The men looked back and forth between them, trying to decide if this was an expansive ventriloquist act. It wasn't, of course. This was just one of the many downfalls of having a being intimately connected to her mind. She resented the fact that there were so many beings that had raided her mind and could torment her with it.

Cori crossed her arms, and the transmorph mirrored her less than a second behind her. They rolled their eyes at the same time. "Do you want to do this speech?" she asked it. "Frankly, my voice is getting tired, anyway."

"Sure." The Cori transmorph smiled and turned her attention to the recruits. "If you are so unfortunate as to wind up in the clutches of one of these... things." The transmorph glared at Cori as if she were the parasite. "You will most certainly die inside of it."

The men looked between them, unsure if they should take this as a threat or fact. Cori nodded, agreeing with her facsimile.

"If, by some miracle, you survive, you still won't be free of them." The transmorph looked down at her hands. "I am forever connected to them now. My hopes and dreams are entrenched in their shared memories. This allows them to taunt me, torment me, and manipulate me. In a way..." The transmorph pressed her hands together. "I am a part of them now."

Cori swallowed hard, not wanting to show any discomfort in front of the recruits. The creature held her gaze as she stepped closer to the bars. "Can you feel it, Cori?" it whispered. "Can you feel me... inside you?"

Cori could feel it. An unmistakable tug in the back of her mind. The same tug she felt when Leona stared her down. However, the mental block gifted to her by Cleos was still blockading everyone's attempts to control her.

"Holy shit," Trevor exclaimed. "You really were inside of one of these things. I thought the guys were just yankin' my chain. What was that like?"

"I don't remember it."

"I do." The transmorph smiled. "I remember it very well. Especially the part where I got to fuck your husband." The transmorph bit her lip seductively. The men behind her offered a subdued groan, apparently amused by the prelude to a "catfight."

She glared back at the men, reminding them that this was a prison and not a bar. "I'm sure you do remember that. Do you also remember the part where Daniel McGrath ripped two of your friends to shreds in pursuit of me?"

The transmorph Cori smiled even more. "Oh yes, Cori, I remember that very well. Every second of their agony is scarred in my memory. But don't you worry about that; I won't hold you accountable for his crimes against my kind?"

"That's very generous of you. I won't hold you accountable for being a predacious, parasitic prick that feeds on the livelihood of others. Oh, wait..." Cori kicked the bars—against the rules, of course—but she couldn't help but add to her performance. "Yes, I will hold you accountable for that."

The transmorph lost her smile, but only for a moment. "We'll see," she murmured. "I look forward to the days to come. Perhaps I'll have a chance to be on the giving end the next time I'm outside of these bars. It will please me to be inside of you one way or another." The men snickered, pleased by any suggestion of girl-on-girl action—even if it did trespass into the territory of katoptronopholia.

Cori cleared her throat and moved further away from the bars. She hated getting caught up in the drama of prisoners. She didn't have the quiet reserve that Ethan had when it came to these situations. When she turned her attention back to the men, she found Trevor unabashedly smirking at her.

"While walking these halls, it is important to rely on your logic over your eyesight," she continued to lecture. "As you can see, it's easy to get caught up in unnecessary interactions. It's a good rule of thumb not to interact with any prisoners, no matter which floor you are on."

"I don't get it. How did you get inside that thing?" Cain asked.

Cori instinctively wanted to defend her foolish actions that resulted in her capture, but she realized Cain's question was more about the specifics of the creature and not her specific screw-up. "In addition to molding new faces and bodies, the ones on this end can actually envelop a person. So don't get too close—ever," Cori explained.

"Okay, okay," Trevor waved his hands. "I don't get it. Why don't they just like get really skinny and slide through the bars and escape?"

Cori frowned. "No, it's not like they are a bowl full of jelly, plus they can't just activate that transition at will.

There has to be something to wrap around like a snake unhinging his jaw to swallow prey. It involves pressure points and reflex reactions. They have a very complex autonomic response to specific stimuli."

Trevor wrinkled his nose, still trying to understand.

"It's like a hug." Cori handed her clipboard off to Paul and moved behind Trevor. She wrapped her arms around him from behind. "I can wrap my appendages around you, arms and legs, but my body stays behind you." Cori released him and stepped to the side to see if he was getting it yet.

He pursed his lips and nodded. "So, it's like this." Trevor moved behind her and wrapped his arms around her to give her the same backward hug she had just given him. Only he made it a point to wrap his arms tightly around her waist and chest, encapsulating her but not technically touching her breasts. The other two men snickered.

Cori knew he was playing up any opportunity he could to touch her, and since she had initiated the contact, he probably thought it was an opening for flirtation. Men always misinterpreted physical contact as more than it was.

If she had her rings, she might have just shocked him. If she had any confidence in her self-defense skills outside of near-death encounters, she might have elbowed him or flipped him over her back, but it had been a while since she had to defend herself in that way, and embarrassing herself would only reduce her credibility.

When all else failed, there was always her mouth. "Yes, Trevor, it is very similar to this. An unwelcome invasion from a creature that has no comprehension of boundaries or moralities." There was another snigger from the others, and Trevor let go. His face was sullen from her chastising, but she resisted the urge to do or say anything to comfort him. It wasn't until that moment that she realized she had just handled this situation precisely as Belus would have. Years and years of the sharp tongue and cold stone facade that had tormented her and broken her heart suddenly made perfect sense to her. She resisted the urge to smile at her epiphany and continued her lesson.

"I don't get it," Cain said, clearly perturbed by anything he didn't understand. "If that thing was on your back, you'd look like a hunchback with two heads. How's it supposed to hide like that?"

Cori knew from experience that this part of the prison tour was difficult to understand. Without seeing it for yourself, it was almost impossible to believe. "Transmorphs are composed of very little hard bone structure. They have a more expansive reach. When the transformation is activated, their flexible tissues surround the hostage like a second skin. That part of the transition is fast—fast enough that you can be unrecognizable in seconds. The organs, including the brain, flatten out, molding to the body like an extra layer of clothes. The firmer, less mobile structures, like the spine and ribs, spread and adhere to the host as closely as possible. The skull, which is paper thin, will spread apart at the fissures before fastening over the head and face. The positioning is usually so exact that palpation or even X-rays reveal no substantial changes from the original body being encased. To further disguise its presence, the creature will expel nearly all of its water composition and dehydrate the victim so there isn't any evidence of weight gain when the transition is complete."

"So how do you know when someone is inside?" Cain asked.

"You don't," Cori answered flatly. "Once you are inside of one of these creatures, you are indistinguishable. You will eventually die after your body gives out, but until then, you are a puppet for them to play with. Fortunately, transmorphs usually tire easily of their toys."

"So, there could be someone in there right now?" Paul asked.

Cori debated whether to bring up Nevia or Daniel, since that was a whole other can of hard-to-swallow worms. Instead, she opted to be evasive. It is better that these men assume there is no way of escaping a transmorph. "Because of the mineral composition in their pliable bone structures, empty transmorphs look no different from a regular human body on scans and x-rays. Given enough time, they can even shift that mineral content to mimic dental restorations and artificial joints with staggering accuracy."

The men seemed to gape at that surprising nugget of information.

She didn't even bother to mention the aspects of the transmorphs that were truly frightening to her. Since she had been tasted by several of them, they could now not only impersonate her, but they could effectively become her in every identifiable way. Not just externally, but also internally—hormones and blood type.

"How do you get someone out after they are inside?" Paul asked.

"You don't."

"But you were in one of these things for weeks," Trevor objected.

"There was a very specific set of circumstances leading to my successful extraction. Circumstances that will probably never be repeated." Cori unconsciously twisted one of her rings as she thought back to her incident with the transmorph. Reading the books and files was still not enough to make her respect the danger involved in housing transmorphs. Perhaps she could change that for these men. She could tell them the gory details and save them from a fate she narrowly avoided.

"The entity doesn't just cover you. It gets inside your body. Layers of fluid tissue enter your orifices—lining your lungs, intestinal tract, and, in my case—the vaginal canal." Once again, the men smirked a little—as if any mention of female anatomy would make them titter like ten-year-old boys. Rather than show any sign of embarrassment, she circled them as she explained the reason for the invasion.

"Through the internal liners, they begin to sap oxygen and nutrients from your body—putting you and the transmorph in a parasitic, symbiotic relationship. It will decide how much food you get. It will decide how much oxygen you breathe. It can even decide what you hear and what you see. After several weeks, the creature will have grown internal blood vessels that will splice with your own. By that point, extraction is fatal for both the host and the transmorph. On the rare occasion that someone is removed before that deadline, they still have long-term damage to heal from—physical and psychological."

"But you came out unscathed," Trevor pointed out as if trying to plant seeds of hope into her warnings.

"The creatures inside these cells have an intimate knowledge of me–my mind and my body. Because of that, they are a constant threat to me. If just one of them escaped their confinements, it would be difficult for me to prove that I was the human and she was the transmorph. So, yes, I did get out of the clutches of a transmorph, but I will never truly be out of danger. Not now, not ever. So, going back to my first statement. Don't interact with the prisoners."

The men glanced around at the other transmorphs on the floor. Some of them had taken on their physical likenesses, bringing their discomfort to the max. Cori shouldn't have been pleased, but she was. That was precisely the reaction she wanted from them. She needed them to be afraid.

Satisfied with her show and tell for this floor, she headed to the section break.

"You're righter than you know, kid." She turned her attention to the last cell, where a transmorph was impersonating Belus. No one was ever off limits on this floor, including ghosts from her past, but she was surprised to see one of them mimicking her mentor. She caught his gaze and noticed the dark circles under his eyes. He looked just like he did after the bubble went down. Apparently, this one was trying to appeal to her compassion. Little did he know she was not feeling very sympathetic to either of her superiors right now.

"Moving on," she announced loudly and pushed on to the next section.

17

"WHAT THE HELL ARE we doing here?" Nevia asked as she took Heaton's hand and slipped out of his vintage leather seats—an expensive accessory to his brand-new Porsche, but well worth it.

"I told you, a favor for Gypsy." He kissed her hand, distracting her from the three-story cottage mansion in front of them. "You look fabulous, by the way." He nodded to her loose-fitted navy blue dress that hid the firearm strapped to her thigh. She had put on a little extra makeup and even spiked her hair for the evening out.

"As much as I like dressing up and as much as I'm enjoying seeing you in that suit." Nevia stepped forward, running her fingers along his slim black tie. At the very end of it, she yanked it down, bringing his face down to her level. "I don't like surprises. What's the catch?"

He sighed and disconnected her hand from his fine clothing. "The catch is, this is a party in celebration of Leona's triumphant rise to head bitch of the werewolves."

"Werewolves?" Nevia frowned and grabbed his lapels in place of the tie he had just smoothed out. "You brought me to a party full of werewolves the evening before the full moon!"

"Jordan, this suit is Armani." He pulled back on the jacket. "Listen, it will be fine. We just need to escort her, keep her from saying something that would unravel a year's worth of work, and diffuse any arguments that might result in her killing someone."

"I'm not worried about Gypsy. Heaton—" Nevia glanced at the valet as he interrupted them.

"Nice wheels," the young man complimented as Heaton handed over the keys.

Heaton watched his youthful body bound around to the driver's side. "Nice ass," he murmured. He caught a potential smile as the young man ducked into the car.

"I don't think you're taking this seriously," Nevia continued. "Forget Gypsy. I need you to keep me from doing something stupid. I need you to keep me from breaking your friend's heart."

Heaton frowned. "You would really do that?"

"I'm sorry, Heaton, this isn't an issue of moral judgment. This is heat. I wish there was something I could do to make you understand how little control I have over it. If you can't control me, then you shouldn't have brought me here." Nevia turned around and started hoofing it down the driveway.

"You've got to be joking," Heaton called after her. As he debated chasing after her, a motorcycle pulled around the circle drive and stopped right in front. The long, exposed legs of the rider were sheathed in black stockings and mid-calf, high-heeled boots. When the helmet came off, a bevy of dark brown waves fell onto Gypsy's shoulders. She glanced over at him and nodded her hello as she extricated herself from the bike and pushed down her bunched-up black dress. "A motorcycle?"

"As opposed to that douche-mobile you pulled up in."

"Well, some of us prefer to spend our money on non-lethal accessories."

"I think we can agree that I don't need accessories to be lethal." Heaton smiled at her, but refused to boost her ego any further. "What's up with the bloodhound?" Gypsy nodded to Nevia's extended exit.

"She's in heat, and apparently, I'm the tosser who brought her to a party with horny werewolves."

"Is there any other kind?" she mumbled.

"I guess it's just you and me tonight."

Gypsy let out an exasperated sigh. "No, offense to you, butch, but if I can't have Daniel, she would have been my second choice."

Heaton chuckled at her, but when she didn't laugh, he frowned at her. "So, what the hell am I doing here?"

Gypsy smiled and moved closer to him. "Eye candy." Gypsy tugged on his tie. "Sweet, sweet—"

"Yeah, yeah." Heaton batted her hand away from his tie and smoothed it out again. "I'll get her back." He stalked away, ignoring Gypsy's laughter. He jogged down the long drive and caught up with Nevia before she could reach the street.

"I can't." Nevia shook her head as he arrived.

"You won't." Heaton came in front of her and cut her off. She bumped into him before she could stop. "I won't let you cheat, no matter how much your hormones say otherwise." He helped her situate her stance on her fashionable peg legs.

"I don't want you to feel like you have to babysit me. That wasn't my intent."

"Well, I have some free time now that I don't have to babysit Daniel."

"I just don't want you to—"

"Lose respect for you? See you as a werewolf instead of a woman? Judge you for the person you are one week out of every month?" Heaton smirked at her.

"I don't want you to resent me like you do, Daniel."

Heaton's mouth dropped. He stared at Nevia, trying to find the words to counter her accusation. "You best button that up." He thrust his finger in her face. "I love Daniel like a brother."

"But if you didn't, you could retire with a nondisclosure clause tattooed on your brain and be done with all of this."

"You're wrong, Jordan."

"I'm not saying—"

"You're wrong!" Heaton pushed up on her and pressed his hands against her cheeks, tipping her face to look at him. "Sometimes we think things that we don't actually mean. Besides, just because we want something doesn't mean that it's what's best for us. You hear me, Jordan?"

"Yes," she hissed.

"Stay out of my head, or scent, or whatever," he conditioned gently. She nodded, staring up at him. He didn't notice her hand creeping forward until she had a firm grip on his crotch. "Holy shit!" he jumped back, alleviating himself from the contact. Nevia looked away, chagrined. "Damn girl, stay out of my pants too."

"I'm sorry. You just aren't getting the domination connection here."

"Perhaps I can help." A low voice spoke from the depths of the darkness beside them. Between the bushes on the side of the drive, a figure moved, stepping from his upwind position into the moonlight. Callin Caldwell's usual sloppy waves were combed back and tamed with gel. He, like Heaton, had donned an expensive suit for the evening. Between the glimmer in his eye and the natural upturn of his relaxed lips, he looked smug. "I can keep Nevia true to her husband," the werewolf volunteered.

18

"SO LET ME GET this straight," Heaton said as he pushed Nevia back again. The tiny woman was like an escape artist–a horny little escape artist. Her target had thankfully shifted away from Heaton, leaving him to hope that their friendship might survive the night. However, Callin's stiff upper-class facade, with just a hint of danger lurking in his eyes, was making her gravitate uncontrollably toward him. Not that he could blame her. The dude was hot. "You, a werewolf—aka domination nation—want to play chastity belt to my little bitch here."

"Hey!" Nevia slapped his face for the insult.

"Ouch, that's the correct terminology."

"For a dog!" she yelled and raised her hand to slap him again.

Callin intercepted the attack and pulled her back. He lassoed an arm around her, cupping her to his side. Rather than complain about the manhandling, she leaned her head back against his chest and took in a deep whiff of his scent. Callin ignored her, keeping eye contact with Heaton.

"Look, Callin, I get that you can control her, but I gotta be honest with you. I don't see you controlling yourself."

"I consider Daniel my friend. If he were a werewolf, he would have no desire to keep his lover to himself."

"Wife," Nevia corrected, but he ignored her.

"Since he is human, he desires monogamy. I can respect his wishes."

"Yeah, again, I feel that you would want to do that, but I'm not sure if you are capable of it this close to your change."

"With respect to you, Heaton, but you have no idea what I am capable of."

"No, man, I do." Heaton reached forward and pulled Nevia from his grasp, which he allowed. She tried to tear away, but he kept a tight, probably painful, grip on her hand. "That's why I can't leave my partner in your care."

Callin eyed him carefully, seemingly insulted he wouldn't trust him.

"He means it," Nevia whispered to him. He looked at her. "He..." she glanced at Callin. "He knows what Daniel can do to him."

"That hasn't stopped him before."

"Only because there was a threat to Gypsy. He won't go against a stronger male unless there is a threat against him or one he cares about."

"Is that true?" Heaton asked him.

Callin gave Nevia a slight smirk that was as much threat as amusement. "I give you my word. No one will trespass on Nevia's marriage vows this evening, including me."

"Alright, man, I'll trust you, but don't underestimate me in this scenario. I may be next to useless against a fem-wolf, but I'm not afraid to take on a male werewolf."

"I'm sure you aren't." Callin's eyes glinted with delight.

Heaton resisted the flirtation since he knew it wouldn't go anywhere. He looked at Nevia at his side. He was still pinching her hand, but she didn't seem to mind the pain. He had never really assumed much about her pain tolerance, but he presumed being bulletproof made a good foundation for it. "Jordan, we are here to do a job. Don't flake out on me. Clamp your damn legs shut and act like a professional. Got it?"

He could see a flare of anger in her eyes, but rather than yell at him for scolding her, she dove at him, planting her lips on his. He pulled her off and pushed her toward Callin. "Oh, hell, just take her."

Callin chuckled and forcefully dragged her away.

19

"WHERE THE HELL HAVE you been?" Gypsy sniped at Heaton over the German techno music inside the mansion. There was a mash of people in the central area, dancing and gyrating to the heavy beat. If this party went the way he suspected it would, the dance floor would turn into an orgy by midnight.

"Had to find a babysitter for Jordan." He nodded back to where Callin was entering the foyer with Nevia on his arm.

Gypsy's face blanked for a moment, offering nothing to the scene but observation. Heaton might have assumed she was jealous, but unlike everyone else, he had accepted her living heart donor status and moved on to more important matters.

"You really think he's going to keep his hands off her?" she asked.

"He gave me his word."

Gypsy's face came back to life with a pleasant smile. She chuckled and turned to observe the dancing couples in the expansive hall before them. "I love promises. It's the best way to convince someone of something that they would otherwise have no reason to believe."

Heaton glanced back at Callin as he brought Nevia up beside them. Heaton shifted over, allowing any onlookers the impression that Gypsy was his date. To add to the effect, she looped her arm in his. "Hello, Callin."

"Grace." Callin looked over her tight black dress. His eyes settled on her cleavage. "You are aware that this is a strictly social occasion?" he asked with disdain.

"That's why I'm only armed from tit to tit. You are aware that Daniel McGrath will turn you to dust if you so much as kiss that little girl."

Callin pinned her with a hard stare. "Unlike you, I can resist my baser instincts. That's the advantage of having an emotional response. It allows for control."

Gypsy's smile grew. She managed to stifle her sputtering laughter, but it still came out as a giggle. "You should hear that from my side." She motioned to her head. "It's really funny—since it's a load of bullshit."

What little amusement Callin had for the conversation disappeared, and anger gripped the muscles of his jaw.

"That's enough chit-chat, wouldn't you say, G." Heaton pushed her forward, interrupting her imminent death. "Weren't you going to meet with Leona and discuss the next step?"

"Yes, back to work it is." Gypsy bowed her head slightly.

"We'll join you," Callin added, tugging Nevia to come with him.

"Oh, good. I was hoping to see how many egos we could fit into one small room." Gypsy stalked off, leading the way through the melee of the dance floor to a room at the back of the mansion.

Heaton paused in the double doors to observe the fem-wolves lining the path to Leona. The beige uniformity was unsettling even with—or perhaps because of—the adornment of beautiful smiling faces. He would have preferred keeping himself out of the werewolf community entirely, but that was becoming increasingly more difficult as time went on.

Callin cleared his throat behind him, and Heaton stepped into the lion's den with false bravery. He reached Gypsy just as she made it to the head of the suck-up line. As the couple before her bowed and retreated from Leona's presence, the women came eye-to-eye with each other.

Heaton felt the shift as much as saw it. Leona's civil, political smile slipped, and she took a deep breath. Gypsy puffed her chest, either unconsciously or to show off whatever weapon she had hidden there. He once again caught sight of something in Gypsy's eye that might have been fear, but it wasn't as simple as that. Attentiveness to danger was all it could be for her.

"Hello, Grace." Leona didn't smile, but she did nod politely.

"Hello, Leona." Gypsy nodded in return. "My employer has sent me to congratulate you on your ascension to the high seat in the council."

"That was kind of him. He didn't feel the need to attend."

"He sends his deepest apologies. A matter of great concern is putting pressure on his time management, but he wanted me to relay that his alliance with you is by no means secondary in his priorities."

"I should hope not." Leona looked at Heaton. "I'm afraid I don't remember your name, sir."

"Heaton Reid. I'm Nevia Jordan's partner." Leona's eyes narrowed as she tried to remember that name as well. "Formerly Ethan Pierce's partner."

"Oh." Leona's eyes widened, and her jaw locked. "I see. Yes, I remember. The trial, right? Are you working with Grace now?"

"I'm just a rental for the night." Heaton smiled.

"Mmm." Leona smiled back. "Are your services available to anyone?"

"He's gay," Gypsy muttered.

"Oh." Leona's interest faded right along with her smile. "Nice to see you again."

Heaton glanced at Gypsy to see if that was the end of the interaction, but whether or not it was, Callin was already pushing his way between them for his meet and greet.

"Leona, my love." His voice purred at her. "How are you?"

"Good, thank you. Are you—" Leona stopped as he pulled Nevia forward, keeping her on a tight leash. Despite the debasement of it, she seemed far more content to latch onto his bicep than to be free of it. Leona stared at the woman, her eyes tracing her features with a fine-tooth comb. "I wasn't aware that you had taken another human mate."

"She is part werewolf," Callin said, only correcting a portion of the assumption.

"She's a quarter werewolf, and that's hardly the point," Leona said. "Do you really think flaunting your new girlfriend is appropriate at a party honoring your matriarch?"

"I wasn't aware that you were planning to have me over tonight. Or ever again, for that matter."

"You are more than welcome to join me anytime you want."

"Provided I'm willing to pick which half of you I get and in what order."

"I should have been born a werewolf," Gypsy grumbled under her breath.

Leona stood slowly from her chaise lounge and closed the distance to Callin. "I'm sorry if you are uncomfortable with my choices, but I at least keep my playthings where they belong."

"I am not his plaything," Nevia ground out.

Leona looked down at her. "Don't talk. The grownups are speaking," she said dryly.

Heaton knew Nevia wouldn't be happy about the condescension, much as she hadn't appreciated it from Mace. However, he hadn't expected she would pull her gun. Before anyone could stop her, Nevia raised the weapon and shot Leona in the face.

20

H EATON DOVE AT THE gun as soon as it popped up from beneath her skirt. Nevia was a deadly aim at sniper range. He had no hope she could miss a target at point-blank range.

Since Callin was unfamiliar with her resume—and likely underestimated her as most people did, he didn't know what was happening until the shot fired and Leona's head was flying back. "Leona!" he cried and leaped to aid her.

"Frickin' A!" Gypsy jumped to attention and yanked a small pistol from her cleavage. "What the hell did she just do?" She wheeled around, aiming her weapon at the approaching fem-wolves, who were only beginning to figure out what had just happened.

Screams engulfed the room, drowning out the techno-rock. Humans scatted while the werewolves clustered around the door, searching for the problem and hoping to be the solution.

"Callin! Help me!" Heaton barked as he struggled to keep control of Nevia's weapon. She was small, but she was utilizing every dirty-handed fighting technique she could, including biting and ball-bashing. He shifted away from two knee kicks, but he knew he wouldn't be as lucky a third time.

"Leona!" Callin was on his knees, cradling the fem-wolf. The worry in his voice didn't sound promising.

"Oh, fuck it!" Heaton yelled and punched Nevia in the face. The cold cock was harsh, and he knew Daniel would get his revenge for it later, but he needed to get a grip on the situation. Nevia dropped to the ground, but Heaton kept her gun. He aimed it back at the angry, snarling faces surrounding them.

"Goddammit!" Gypsy screamed, shifting back from the encroaching wolf pack, male and female alike. "You two were supposed to keep me from getting myself killed. Now you got us all killed!"

Heaton took a step back from the mob as well. He knew that someday, this job would get him killed. He had always assumed that it would be Daniel's fault. He never suspected Nevia would be responsible. He also never suspected his final memories in life would be of his limbs being ripped from his body.

"Enough!" Leona's voice sounded behind them.

He looked back and saw her standing, hands raised to inform her followers she was alive. Aside from the drop of blood on her forehead, she was unharmed.

"She shot you," one of the fem-wolves pointed out.

"Yes." Leona looked down at Nevia. "And she shall be punished."

"It's not her fault." Heaton stepped in the path of Leona's gaze. "She's going through some kind of hormonal changes." Leona perked a brow at him. "Look, I don't pretend to understand it, but it's like having PMS and going into heat at the same time. I guess."

Leona frowned and looked at Callin. "Is this true?"

"Her pheromones are erratic. I didn't smell anything too alarming, though."

"Very well." Leona peeked around Heaton and waved to her minions. Two fem-wolves approached. "Take her upstairs."

"Whoa!" Heaton wheeled around, pointing his gun at one woman and blocking the other with the pressure of his hand. "My partner is not leaving my side."

"Then follow her," Leona suggested sardonically.

"No one is going anywhere." Gypsy stepped closer, joining Heaton's stand.

"Are you sure that your boss would approve of you defying my orders?"

"I'd be happy to have him weigh in on it." Gypsy smiled. "Shall I call him?"

Leona frowned and stepped breast to breast with Gypsy. "No need. You would be dead by the time he arrived, anyway."

"Ladies." Callin joined the mix of the argument. "Perhaps this is one of those times where simply explaining your motives would solve the situation."

Gypsy tipped her head at Leona. "I am motivated by the importance of having my friends stay alive."

"I have no intention of killing anyone, Grace. I'm not my sister." Leona shifted her attention back to Heaton. "Your partner is going through a hormonal change, only familiar to partial werewolves."

"Like menopause?" he asked.

"She is going feral, and if you do not let us take care of her, she will kill you."

"I can handle her temper tantrums."

Leona looked at Callin before moving in front of Heaton. "You are a competent man. I can see that. I appreciate that you wish to protect your friend. At another time in my life, I might have enjoyed leaving you to your ignorance, but I am endeavoring to use my knowledge for the betterment of the werewolf community, as well as revitalizing the waning connection we have with the enlightened human population.

"So, allow me to share my knowledge with you, Heaton. If you remain with Nevia through the next full moon, she will go feral, kill you in your sleep, and eat you." Heaton's mouth went instantly dry, and he felt faint. "Unless you relish the idea of your partner waking up next to your dead body with pieces of your liver caught in her teeth and no memory of the vile crime, then feel free to take her away."

Heaton stared down at Nevia. He couldn't believe she was capable of all that. Then again, she did have a habit of surprising him. "What will you do to her?"

"I will nurse her."

21

"Yeah, I gotta be honest; I was picturing something else when you said you were going to nurse her, Leo," Gypsy commented as she entered the guest bedroom behind Heaton. The plush interior décor was gold with accents of orange that didn't seem to match—as if someone's grandmother had suddenly gotten rich but wouldn't throw away her old furnishings even after she got the new ones.

"That is disgusting, Grace—and don't call me Leo," the fem-wolf retorted as she rolled up the sleeve of her blouse. With little more preparation than a swipe of an alcohol pad, she poked a thick needle into her arm, tapping a vein. The dark red blood fed into a connected IV line leading to a machine on one of the bedside tables. Leona taped down her line and sat on the edge of the bed where Nevia had been lying. She picked up her limp arm and began probing for a healthy vein. When she found one she liked, she swiped the skin with alcohol and pulled over a second IV line from the machine.

"How will you get that through her skin?" Heaton asked.

"It's a diamond tip; it will go through," Leona insisted, but as she started to penetrate the skin, the needle caught. With a slight readjustment and a forceful push, the needle finally went in.

"So, this is just happening?" Gypsy asked. "No blood tests first. An STD panel, perhaps?"

Leona glared at her before motioning one of her minions over to the other side of the bed. She did the same on Nevia's other arm, forcefully tapping a vein there as well. They deposited the blood from that arm into a blood bag.

"What exactly is this accomplishing?" Heaton asked, coming to the foot of the bed to monitor his friend. The machine on the bedside table whirred quietly, transfusing Leona's blood into Nevia.

"The human body was never meant to have the hormones of a werewolf. During the lunar phase, our species is flooded with a dozen different growth hormones that allow our bodies to restructure, expand, and heal at astounding rates. Despite the drain on our energies, this is normal for us." Leona touched Nevia's face in an unexpectedly maternal way. "Your poor friend is going through what we lovingly call werewolf puberty. It's late for her, but it usually is in hybrids. The problem is that her female cycle is coinciding with her lunar cycle. This is producing the erratic behavior that on the surface appears to be anger and arousal."

"What do you mean appears to be?" Heaton asked.

Leona grimaced at him and shrugged slightly. "We are carnivorous by nature."

Heaton shook his head, hoping he misunderstood her. "You're saying she wasn't getting turned on; she was getting hungry?"

"It's complicated," Leona said. "She's never felt the desire to hunt before. She wouldn't have understood it."

"What's the matter, Heaton?" Gypsy hooked her arm around his neck. Fortunately, he was too tall for her to belittle him with a noogie. "Haven't you ever licked whipped cream off a lover?"

Heaton blinked at Gypsy. The amusement on her face was disturbing, even to him. "Sure, but the biting always stops before I hit blood." He shrugged her off. "How long will this take? Don't you all need to be sequestered soon?"

"I have a containment facility on site," Leona dismissed his concerns with a wave of her hand. "I'm almost done, but she won't wake for several hours. You're welcome to stay the night if it's more convenient."

Heaton grimaced at that thought. He wasn't sure staying in a home with an onsite containment facility for werewolves sounded any more appealing than spending the night in Danato's prison.

"So, just to be clear." Gypsy leaned on the footboard of the bed. "You keep a fully equipped blood transfusion machine in one of your guest bedrooms."

Leona looked at Gypsy with measured disdain. "And it's saving your friend's life. Do you have a problem with that?"

Gypsy smirked at her. "I don't have a problem with much. I was just curious what you do with this device in your spare time, that it's required to be a permanent fixture in your home."

"It's none of your concern, Grace." Leona stopped the machine and disconnected her IV. She pressed a cotton ball to her wound while her minion finished disconnecting Nevia. "If it was, I'm sure your boss would have already told you about it." Leona moved around to the end of the bed, and Gypsy turned to face her. "Oh, when you do see him again, tell him that everything is ready at my end, and I will be happy to accept his invitation. He'll understand."

Gypsy grimaced. It was an odd sight to Heaton since she usually wore a smirk, even when the situation was intolerably uncomfortable. Something about Leona's knowledge had pissed her off. Or perhaps it was Gypsy's lack of knowledge that was irritating her.

"As I said, Heaton, you are welcome to stay if it is more convenient. My staff is almost all human; they can attend to you and Nevia. And here..." Leona raised her hand behind her head and waited. When nothing magically appeared in her palm, she snapped her fingers. The sound alerted her assistant phlebotomist, and she jumped forward, pulling a card from her side pocket to hand to her boss. Much as Gypsy had observed, the women seemed prepared for just this occasion. He couldn't imagine that too many hormonal half-breeds stumbled into Leona's lobby, but then again, what else was the council of the moon for, if not to help werewolves?

Leona clamped the card between two fingers and twisted her hand in a flourish to hand it to him. "The blood is only temporary. You should seek out my doctor as soon as she is mobile."

Heaton took the card and slid it into his breast pocket. "Is that really necessary? I mean, you're describing it as puberty. Won't it just pass?"

"I am describing it as werewolf puberty, which is an entirely different situation when confined to a human body. You may do what you like, but in the interests of mutual respect and maintaining a cordial relationship with Danato's people, I strongly advise that you call that number."

Leona offered a handshake, and Heaton gently squeezed her hand. "Thank you," he said, almost bowled over by her courtesy. This wasn't the same woman that Ethan described from his experiences. Perhaps she was growing into her role as a leader. Or maybe she was just a better actress than he realized.

"As much as I hate to be a bad hostess, I'll be much worse if I don't get sequestered soon." She winked at Heaton and moved to the door. She paused and looked back. "Are you coming, Callin?"

Heaton looked back to where she was looking. Callin was standing in the corner of the room, innocuously observing them. Heaton hadn't even realized the werewolf had followed them into the room.

"No, thank you. I'm going to head out." He checked his watch. "I'm already late."

"You best hurry. Danato does not appreciate tardiness in his werewolf clientele," Leona chided. She glanced at Gypsy and slipped out the door with her assistant in tow.

Callin stepped from his corner position and approached Gypsy. He eyed her carefully, and she did likewise. Heaton expected an argument to break out or a make-out session, but neither of them said anything. Callin raised his hand to touch her face but lowered it again before he actually made contact. He whisked out of the room as if he were finally giving credence to Leona's warning.

"Well, this was the worst party ever," Gypsy grumbled. "Only one shot fired, and it wasn't mine. Plus, I have no chance of getting laid." She looked him over and shook her head. "What a waste." She looked at Nevia. "You staying here or taking her home?"

"I don't know. I'm not sure I want to hang out two stories above a werewolf den this close to a full moon. On the other hand, I'm not sure I want to take her with me." Heaton moved to the bed and looked at his partner. He couldn't believe that one night earlier, he had thought nothing of sleeping next to her. Now, he was almost afraid to be alone with her. "It was bad enough when I thought she was considering cheating on Daniel. That was just a morality issue. Now that I know she wanted to eat me... That's just too damn weird."

Gypsy stepped up to the bed next to him and crossed her arms. "You want me to come with you? I'd be happy to take over the uncomfortable, unwanted advances if that makes you feel better."

Heaton tried to be annoyed by her endlessly ill-timed humor, but along with her usual thin smirk, he could see a tinge of sympathy in her eyes. He knew Gypsy wasn't anybody's favorite person, but there was something about her lighthearted determination that appealed to him. "Too bad you already have a top-secret employer. We could use a third for a while."

"I can moonlight for a couple of nights." She nodded to Nevia. "You carry her; I'll get the valet to fetch your douche-mobile."

22

Heaton tossed his keys on Daniel's coffee table and headed into the bedroom to drop Nevia off. He heard Gypsy scoff from the living room. "Why do hunters have such shit apartments? You would think with all the money you guys make, you could at least afford a house."

Heaton laid Nevia on the bed, positioning her head gently on the pillow. He clicked off the light and shut the door on the way out. "I don't recall your flat being that spectacular."

"My money goes into my weapons. You wouldn't believe what spider silk costs."

"Mine goes to my cars."

"And Daniel's, where does his go?"

"His mother."

"Mmm." Gypsy nodded, deeming that to be an acceptable use for his surplus income. She moved around the room, observing the details.

"Not to mention it's in our contracts that we can't draw attention to ourselves, which includes flaunting our wealth."

"And your blow-job mobile accomplishes that?" Gypsy leaned against the tacky wooden divider between the kitchen and living room.

Heaton ignored her quip and settled into the couch. "So, what's the deal with Leona and your boss? What's going down that your employer isn't telling you about?"

Gypsy's expression of subdued amusement shifted into a less than subdued pre-murder stare. "I'm not quite sure, but I'm going to damn well find out."

"I never understood why you guys were getting involved in a werewolf coup, anyway. Who in their right mind gets into bed with the mob when they aren't even the same species? Or is your boss part werewolf?"

Gypsy chuckled and opened her mouth to speak, but she seemed to struggle with the words. "I'm afraid I can't say much about it."

Heaton tipped his head to examine her. "You really can't, can you? What can you say?"

Gypsy smiled. "I can say that his plots go as deep as his pockets."

Heaton frowned and leaned forward, bracing his elbows on his knees. "Are his intentions good?"

Gypsy thought about that. "They aren't bad. His intentions are to restore the old system of hunting."

"The old system?" Heaton shook his head. "You mean he wants werewolves to go back to being hunters? That's ridiculous. The reason they stopped allowing that was because they were too unstable. I mean, props to your boy toy for his control, but every werewolf I ever met was an egotistical prick on a good day."

Gypsy shrugged and nodded in agreement. "And that's just the males."

"Why would he try to go backward?"

"Pr... preser... vation," Gypsy struggled to say.

"Preservation of the werewolves?" Heaton asked, and Gypsy shook her head. "Preservation of what?"

Gypsy panted and tried to speak, but she finally shook her head. "I'm sorry, I have restrictions. I can't fight them."

"Are you okay?" Heaton moved to her, legitimately concerned about the sweat forming on her brow.

"Yeah, it's just his insurance policy to keep things on the down low."

"Insurance policy? Is he hurting you?" He squeezed her arm.

Gypsy smiled at him. "Aren't you sweet. No, he doesn't hurt me. He fiddles with my brain a bit. But hell, who hasn't had that done? Don't worry; we're getting close to completion. You'll know everything soon enough, and all my mental blocks will crumble away. I'm going out for a cigarette. Wanna join me?" She tugged a soft pack from her bra.

"No, go ahead." Heaton dropped his hand and headed back into the bedroom to check on Nevia. He opened the door and peeked inside, but the bed was empty. He pushed in and scanned the room. The room was empty, and the window was open. "Shit!"

23

H EATON JOGGED DOWN THE road with Gypsy right beside him. He thought her dress would slow them down, but she switched to boots before they left so she was able to keep a steady pace with him. Moreover, she didn't complain about the cardio like Daniel always did.

"Are you sure she went this way?" Gypsy asked.

"She ditched her heels a few blocks back." Heaton scanned the side roads as they passed them. "Bloody hell! She can't run that fast. How far could she get?"

"Far enough to find a late supper," Gypsy joked morosely.

"Damn it, somebody should have told us this was a possibility with part werewolves." Heaton huffed. "What good are all those damn books if they're missing half the information?"

"In the council's defense, this is a really embarrassing aspect of the hybridization. No wonder they look so poorly on half-breeds. Mutt doesn't quite cover it."

"Shut up—do you hear that?" Heaton stopped in his tracks. Gypsy did the same and bowed her head to listen for movement.

He heard the sound of feet scratching the concrete, followed by a feminine yelp. He popped his head up just as Gypsy did. They both took off down a tight back alley.

Three houses in, they found an open gate leading into a small backyard. Heaton jumped through the door and found Nevia straddling a red-headed woman's back, pinning her arms behind her.

"Nevia, stop!" Heaton shouted.

Nevia looked up at him, a visceral anger in her eyes. Gypsy pulled her gun and aimed it at her. He pressed Gypsy's arms down, but she only lowered the gun enough to prevent an accident.

"Listen to me," Heaton spoke softly. "You have to stop."

"Help!" the woman beneath her shrieked. "She's fucking crazy."

"Yeah, workin' on that, sweetheart. Just shut up." Heaton moved forward with his hands raised in surrender. "Come on, Jordan, I need you to calm down."

"What are you doing?" she asked, narrowing her eyes on him. "Help me tie her up."

"No, I think we should talk about this," Heaton insisted.

"Talk about what?" Nevia looked at Gypsy. "Why are you pointing that at me? Point it at her."

Heaton looked back and saw that Gypsy had raised her gun again. "Gypsy?" He raised his hand, urging her to stay calm.

"I'm good," Gypsy assured him. "It's just my security blanket."

He turned his attention back to Nevia, knowing he wouldn't make any leeway with Gypsy. "I know you are going through some whacked-out hormonal stuff, but I don't think you understand what you're doing."

"That doesn't have anything to do with this."

"Are you sure? Are you feeling the desire to bite anyone?"

Nevia scoffed. "Not yet. Would you please help me take this bitch transmorph into custody!"

"Transmorph?" Heaton looked down at the woman beneath her. "Oh."

24

"I AM NOT A transmorph! I am human!" the woman screamed at them from the living room. Although securely tied, Heaton maintained his line of sight on her while speaking with Nevia and Gypsy in the kitchen.

"Are you sure about this, Jordan?" he asked for possibly the third time.

"Why do you keep asking me that? That is a transmorph, and it is encasing a human."

"How did you—"

"Help!" the woman screamed.

Heaton rushed into the living room and shoved his finger in her face. "Look, I am still working on this! If you are a transmorph, then just deal with the fact that you are being arrested. If you are a human, then deal with the fact that you are being kidnapped. Either way, if you don't shut up, I am going to have to punch you in the face to knock you out!"

The woman gulped at the threat, her golden-brown eyes glistening with tears. She ducked her head down. Soft whimpers were the only noises she made after that.

Heaton returned to the kitchen where Gypsy had taken her perch on the counter instead of joining Nevia at the table. He wasn't sure if it was an issue of fear or if she simply didn't want to get blocked in by the table. He took a cue from her book and stayed standing for the conversation. "How did you find her?"

"How do you think? I smelled her."

"No, I mean... You were passed out."

Nevia rolled her eyes. "And then I wasn't. I smelled her. I peeked out the window, saw her strolling by, and decided that since our job is to recover humans, that I should maybe go catch her."

"Why didn't you come get me?"

Nevia froze and grimaced. "I didn't even know you were here. Besides, I was a little dazed when I first woke up. I just woke up and jumped out of the window. I didn't really think much beyond that. The exertion cleared my head, though. I feel fine now."

Heaton frowned and scratched his head. He wasn't sure that sounded good. If she had jumped out the window initially by feral instincts, and her head cleared on the way. She might be assuming the woman was a transmorph because of crossed signals.

"Why are you questioning me so much?" Nevia stood up, and he took a step back. "And why are you afraid of me?"

"I'm not afraid, just concerned."

"About what?" She frowned. "Did I act inappropriately tonight? Did we..." Her voice trailed off as she glanced at Gypsy.

"You're kidding, right?" Gypsy raised her brow. "You shot the fucking werewolf queen!"

"What? Leona?" Nevia's eye darted between them. "When did I do that?"

Gypsy laughed. "Oh, damn, you need to call that doctor."

"Doctor? What the hell is going on here, Heaton? Why is she here? I am your partner!" Nevia pushed into his space. He could see the anger in her eyes and the pursed pout on her lips. She was feeling like a third wheel on her own team. Since he didn't like that feeling either, he needed to fix it.

"Let's talk. Gypsy, you mind watching our guest." He nodded toward the living room.

"Not at all." She jumped off the counter and paused behind Nevia to tap her ear. A little signal to remind him she would be listening if he needed help. A comfort, except he was pretty sure she had no qualms about shooting his partner if she so much as nipped at him.

"Did I kill her?" Nevia asked after Gypsy had left.

"No, you missed the eye."

"I missed?" Nevia asked, appalled by any suggestion of inadequacy in the firearm department.

"Let's just assume for the sake of argument that you never intended to kill her." Heaton hoped more than believed that Nevia had that much control during her blackouts. "Let's sit down." Heaton ushered Nevia to take a seat at the table.

"I don't like how you're treating me." She plopped back in the chair. He took the one catty-corner to her. For a moment, they just looked at each other. She was broadcasting her ire while he was no doubt revealing his unwelcome commiseration.

Before he spoke, he unbuttoned his white dress shirt, tugging it open. With his chest exposed, he invited her to take a whiff. She grimaced at him, but leaned over and took a long drag of his scent. She paused as if her mind was computing the data and then sat back in her chair again. The hardness in her eyes was gone. Her lips pinched into a thin line, almost disappearing entirely.

"What do you smell? What am I feeling?" Heaton wasn't just asking for proof; he actually wanted to know. His mind roiled with doubts and concerns, but he couldn't define his emotional state.

"You're worried about me." She reached her hand out on the table. He didn't hesitate to lean forward and take her fingers in his. As her slender fingers gripped onto him, he realized he needed this contact. He needed to know she was still human. "You feel a lot of pressure to protect me now that Daniel's gone, don't you?" Nevia continued.

"You're my partner."

"It's more than that, though. You're scared that if anything happens to me, he'll blame you."

Heaton took in a breath, digesting the verbalization of his feelings from someone else's mouth. Confronting Nevia's nose wasn't always fun, but it was definitely enlightening.

"Look, Jordan." He drew his hand back. "I didn't do this, so we could discuss my loyalties. I did it because—"

"He won't, you know?" Heaton froze and stared at her. "Daniel doesn't see the world the same as you and me. He believes that he's a monster—he always has and probably always will."

Heaton frowned at that. He knew Daniel was hard on himself—and with regard to how dangerous he was, his discontentment was appropriate. But... a monster?

"Daniel will never judge anyone as harshly as himself. Certainly not a friend. If anything were to happen to me under your watch—Daniel would ultimately blame himself for not being here to help you."

Heaton blinked at Nevia, wondering if she had intended to make him feel better or worse with that insight. He took in a breath and shook his head. "Never mind about my insecurities. I wanted you to understand that my motives are honest. I need you to believe that I have your best jnterests at the forefront of my mind."

"I didn't need to smell you to know that."

Heaton's lip perked up a little at seeing the stony resolve on her face. It reminded him of why he didn't mind having a female partner. It was the same reason Daniel had fallen in love with her. She didn't require the constant coddling that some women did.

Nevia shifted back in her chair and crossed her arms. "Now, why don't we skip the bullshit, and you can tell me what's eating at you."

25

CORI STARED AT HER pile of paperwork on the clipboard. All her tasks were complete—except one. She thumped her pen on the empty box that should have already had a time stamp. Callin had not checked in for his full moon containment.

The werewolf was new to their program, but he knew as well as anyone he couldn't come in late. Being late meant he would arrive in a predacious state. The closer to the change he was, the more volatile he would be.

Cori checked with the doc manager, hoping that Callin had simply sneaked in and not announced himself, but no one at the docs had seen him come through. She checked the schedule and found that there was another shipment coming in early tomorrow. Callin could be on that one. If he wasn't, he would violate his parole. The last thing Cori wanted was for another of Ethan's friends to end up behind bars. However, she wasn't the one to make that call.

On her way out, Cori dropped by Danato's office to update him, but he wasn't there. Since it was barely six o'clock, she was surprised to find the office vacant and dark. If Danato wasn't around, Belus would usually toil away on paperwork. She dropped the clipboard on the desk and headed home to report to Danato there.

After a bracing walk through the cold wind, Cori reached her front door—sounds of activity filtered through the wood. Bright light streamed out of the kitchen and living room windows, lighting the porch better than the dim bulb hanging beside the door.

"Shit." Cori rested her head against the door to the house, suddenly remembering why Danato and Belus hadn't stayed late tonight.

The beautiful ting of a live piano accompanied the cheerful voices of the prison's least tone-deaf staff. They were singing Christmas carols, just as she had wanted them to.

A house full of drunk, sugar-high guests was what she had petitioned for. She didn't want the Christmas season to go unnoticed as it had so many years before. She wanted a slice of the real world. Unfortunately, that's precisely what she had gotten.

Her miserable day had left her exhausted and hoping for a quiet evening, but instead, she was going to be surrounded by noise and forced to converse with people she only nodded to on a daily basis.

Then again, this could be for the best. She could bury her woes in spiked eggnog and cookies. Everyone would be too drunk to notice her sullen mood. As soon as she made the rounds, she could discreetly disappear into her room and pass out.

Cori reached for the knob and pushed on the door, but it wouldn't budge. She pushed again, but the door was jammed shut. She realized this wasn't a physical impediment and stopped fighting it. She rested her hands on either side of the door and massaged the wood frame with her thumb.

"I know you think you're giving me what I want," Cori spoke to the house, "but the truth is, sometimes humans have to do things that they are uncomfortable with. Sometimes, what we want and what we need are two different things." Cori waited, but nothing happened. "Alright, you don't understand. How about this? Inside that house is my husband, my baby boy, and a buffet of wonderful food that I really want to stuff myself with."

The door shifted open slightly. Cori laughed. "That's a good girl." She patted the jamb and pushed the door open.

26

DANATO SAW THE DOOR open, and he immediately checked to see who else was invading his normally peaceful home. He knew Ethan was trying to be fair to his poker friends, but he wasn't sure he needed to invite every guard that had ever crossed the threshold of the house. As if that wasn't enough, he had invited Efrat and Daniel.

He understood the reasoning behind that as well, but he couldn't help but monitor Efrat's electrical hands near the fine leather on his furniture. And as far as Daniel was concerned, he was already taking heat from Renee for that minor breach of security. He politely explained that Daniel was not a prisoner so much as a grounded child, but she didn't understand. Never mind the fact that any imprisonment for Daniel was technically voluntary.

He was relieved to see Cori walk through the door, but he quickly recalled their argument that afternoon and realized this celebration wouldn't be as cheerful as it should have been. He wanted to rush over and hug her, but he was still angry about her behavior. Much like Belus, he felt he was owed an apology. Unfortunately, he owed her one, too.

Cori glanced over, noting his location in the rear corner opposite the Christmas tree. Before she could maneuver through the crowd to get to him, Daniel plowed into her, giving her an all-encompassing hug. She smiled at his enthusiasm as he dipped her back for a mistletoe kiss. Danato saw Ethan come behind him and grip his shoulder. He wanted to monitor the interaction to make sure neither of them got carried away, but Efrat's sudden arrival obstructed his eavesdropping view.

"Efrat?" Danato frowned at him.

"It must really shake you to the bone to see me standing in your house." Efrat was smirking smugly, a slight change from his acerbic frowns. Judging by the dimness in his eyes and the slight drag in his words, he was pretty drunk.

"What?" Danato asked.

"You." Efrat poked his chest, offering a slight static snap against the festive sweater he had donned for the evening. Danato glanced down at the contact, but didn't react beyond that. "Me. Here." Efrat gestured around the room with his half-full beer. "That's gotta be a slap in your egotistical face, doesn't it?"

Danato narrowed his eyes, examining the man's casual bravado disdainfully.

Duke noticed their interaction and abandoned his conversation with Chuck to run over and fetch Efrat. "Sorry, sir. Come on, partner." Duke tugged on Efrat's arm, but he yanked himself free.

"No, no, no. Danato and I are just having a conversation. Right?" Efrat chucked him on the shoulder. The snap of electricity that accompanied it was slightly more than static, but nothing Danato couldn't handle. Duke grimaced and pulled Efrat's arm back.

Danato gave the elemental a thin smile. "That's right, Duke. Efrat was just coming over to prove he has the balls to talk to me face to face... when he's drunk." He perked his brow at the wobbling man before him.

"You think you're so fucking tough," Efrat snarled.

Duke shifted closer to whisper to him. "Knock it off. This is a party."

"Yeah, it's a party." Efrat broke into a slight dance, jiving to the cafeteria ladies' rendition of jingle bells like it was a dance mix.

Danato glanced over to Belus, who was chatting with half the nursing staff by the Christmas tree. He was monitoring their interaction with interest. No doubt wondering if he should mediate. Luckily, Duke was serving just fine in that capacity.

"Say your piece, Efrat, and move on," Danato said.

"My piece?"

"Yeah, you obviously stepped in my face for a reason. Let's hear it so I can say my part, and we can both move on with our lives."

Efrat looked at Duke and smiled. "Don't you just love this guy? I mean, come on." He laughed. "There's just no room for apologies or remorse."

"For what?" Danato asked.

"For what you did to me," Efrat said.

"I didn't do anything to you. I signed paperwork for a military contract."

"See what I mean." Efrat pointed at Danato. "Not an ounce of compassion."

"Is that what this is about? You want an apology?"

"It's about what I'm owed."

Danato pushed into his space and grabbed his hands before he could defend himself. He forcefully pressed them behind his back and together to reabsorb the energy. Strangely enough, a trick he had taught them himself via his attack on Cori. Efrat grimaced under the pressure and bent his head away from Danato's looming face. The room stilled a moment as everyone noted the socially stunted mingling.

"Okay then, Efrat, here's your apology. I'm sorry you were stupid enough to sign up for a military-sponsored Dr. Moreau experiment. I'm sorry that in the six years of your confinement, you thought it would be better to electrocute me rather than talk to me." Danato lowered his voice a little further. "What I'm most sorry for, though, Efrat. Is that you thought it would be a good idea to challenge my authority in my house, full of my men. The next time you take issue with me in this manner, I will put you back in a cell... for good. Understand?" Danato smiled warmly to disguise his threat from the onlookers. "And to answer your initial question, no. You don't shake me to the bone. You irritate me. You're like a child demanding something they've never bothered to ask for to begin with. You may not like me, Efrat, but don't ever assume that I owe you anything."

Efrat glared back at him but said nothing.

"Quite right, sir," Duke insisted. "I'll make sure he stays out of your way from now on."

"Thank you, Duke." Danato released Efrat. "You boys have a good time."

Duke nearly dragged Efrat away. Danato smiled after them, shaking his head. He noticed a movement to his side and turned to see Cori approaching him. She might as well have been coming up to a wild animal as carefully as she moved. Despite the elephant in the room, her presence made his lips turn up a little. "Hi," he said to break the ice.

"Hi," she said back.

"I was wondering when you would get here. Seemed a shame for you to miss your own party."

"Yeah. I kind of forgot about it until I got home." Cori glanced around the busy room and then back at him. Her eyes drifted down to his navy blue sweater with a line of white reindeer across his chest. One of the reindeer had a tiny red jingle bell in place of his stitched nose. "Nice sweater." Her mouth tipped up a little.

He reached up and flicked the nose to make it ring. "I got it in honor of you. I thought you might appreciate the fashion choice."

"I do." Cori shifted her gaze to the floor, but she didn't make an excuse to leave. Her hands rubbed against her pants, and she fiddled with the pockets on her cargo pants.

"Is there something you want to tell me?" he asked, careful not to use any ill tone in his voice.

Cori turned back to him and nodded her head somberly.

He frowned at the serious expression on her face. This wasn't an apology conversation. This was a bad news conversation. He didn't even want to guess what words would fall out of her mouth. What deception would be unveiled? What action had she taken without his permission? What twisted truths would she admit to? "What is it?"

"Callin Caldwell wasn't on the last truck."

Danato took in a relieved breath, but then realized why she was so chagrined to admit this to him. He looked over at Ethan, who was laughing at the drunken animation of Daniel's story. He assumed she hadn't shared this information with Ethan.

"Are you going to release them?" Cori asked.

It was protocol to send the collectors out for absentee werewolves, but Danato was always reluctant to do so until he absolutely had to.

He checked the clock on the wall of the kitchen and did a quick calculation. "There's a truck in the morning, isn't there?" She nodded. "If he isn't on that one, we'll send them."

"Okay," Cori nodded and abruptly moved away. He reached out for her, but she was already gone, and he didn't want to make a scene by chasing her down.

He wasn't sure what he intended to say to her. Maybe he wanted to beg her for forgiveness or maybe demand an apology. Either way, it would have to wait. He didn't want to disrupt the party any more than he already had.

"Is she normally so sullen?" Renee approached him, fresh from the restroom. She had loaded herself up with another batch of lipstick despite the fact that it would end up on her wine glass along with the previous applications.

"No, she's not happy about what happened this afternoon."

"Are you referring to the radio or our long overdue kiss?"

"The radio," Danato ground out.

"Speaking of that kiss." Renee jingled his reindeer bell. "What do you say we try it again? But this time, let's try it closer to a bed."

Danato grabbed her hand and pulled it away. "Do you know why I kissed you this afternoon?"

"Because deep down inside, you know we belong together."

Danato couldn't even muster the feigned amusement required to chuckle at her stupidity. "We don't belong together, Renee. I don't doubt that you're lonely, but the only reason you're here is to spy for that collective of wallet-stuffers."

"You don't know what you are talking about." She ripped her hand from his grip.

"Once again, you underestimate me. So, let me make this easy for all of you. This prison is mine, and no one, not your white-collar business associates or your military minions, will take it away from me."

"You should be careful about the threats you make, Danato." Renee's face turned back to its familiar coldness. "You don't want me on your bad side."

"Do you still want to know why I kissed you this afternoon?" Danato pushed into her space. She took a breath but didn't answer. "Because I don't hit women. Now get out of my face before I have to kiss you again."

Renee's face melted, and her eyes watered. She attempted to glare at him, but her narrowed eyes only served to release her tears. She turned on her heels and headed upstairs to disappear into the guest bedroom.

He looked around the room to see if there was anyone else he could verbally beat down yet tonight. He caught Belus's eye. His second nodded at him and raised his glass. He wouldn't have begrudged Danato if he had sneaked off with Renee for a tryst, but he was just as entertained by seeing the woman put in her place.

27

ORI MANEUVERED THROUGH A few tall bodies in black to find a seat. One particular body hooked her neck and pulled her over to mingle. "Hey, Kitten!" Efrat's beer-heavy breath yelled in her ear over the music. His hand lobbed in her face, safely away from her body.

"Easy, Sparky," Duke looked at her to see if she was amused or pissed. She rolled her eyes but gave him a smile to let him know she was okay. She nodded at Chuck, who looked surprisingly coiffed for the evening's affair. A night out was a night out.

"I fought a dragon today," Efrat slurred in her ear.

"I know, you did... pretty good."

"Hey, that was my first time. We aren't all dragon slayers like you and Ethan." Cori chuckled at that description. "I still can't quite believe you took that bitch on and won."

"I didn't fight Penelope. I just trained with her." Cori turned a little to look at him, but the proximity to his baby blues made for an awkward interaction.

"She fought a male dragon," Duke explained.

Efrat looked over at him. "What's that like?"

"They're quicker," Duke answered.

"And meaner," Chuck added.

"And they breathe fire," she couldn't help but add, since she thought it deemed emphasis—at least as she remembered it.

"No way," Efrat smirked and tugged on her neck. "You did not."

"Yes, she did." Duke insisted. "It was spectacular."

She looked at Duke. "I don't remember you being there."

"Oh, yes ma'am. That was the fight of the century for our lot. I had a front-row seat at the window. Worth every penny of overtime it took to earn it, too." Duke winked at her. With such a low immunity to his charms, Cori blushed and looked away.

"Well, we should bring him back and have a rematch. Sell some tickets," Efrat suggested. "What do you think, kitten?" His hand shifted to her shoulder, and she jumped at the electrical shock he was unwittingly exuding.

She flinched and fled from his grasp before he could do any damage. She bumped into a hard chest as she moved away. She looked up and saw Ethan. Confusion and threat marred his face as he looked between her and Efrat. "What's going on?" he asked.

"What'd you do, man?" Daniel stepped up behind them, asking the same question.

Cori looked back at Efrat, and she found his face filled with the same confusion. His eyes flitted over her, looking for an explanation for her impulsive rejection, but she didn't have one. She didn't want to get into a long explanation, especially since she realized Efrat was going to be the one most affected by her powerless rings.

"Nothing," Efrat answered. "We were just talking."

"Cori." Ethan drew her attention back to him. "What's wrong?"

"I'm just... um... jumpy. Sorry everybody, PSOD: Prison Shit Overload Disorder." Cori chuckled and stepped away. "I think I need a drink."

Cori moved away, but Ethan caught up to her and pulled her into a kiss. After he released her, he leaned into her ear. "Are you really okay?"

"I just had a tough day."

He leaned back and looked her over. "I heard about the radio," he said apologetically, as if he didn't want to admit that her antics were already hitting the rumor mill. Of course, with a prison full of mostly men, it wasn't gossiping so much as reporting. "Are you sure you're okay?"

"No," she frowned. "I really want all these people to go home so I can take you upstairs and make love to you."

Ethan smiled and shook his head. "This was all your idea."

"I know. How stupid was that?" Cori clasped her hands behind his neck, and they swayed back and forth to the O' Holy night, which was being played by their pianist for the night.

She tucked into him, and he slow danced with her for three more songs, which made the entire party worthwhile.

28

"I WASN'T ACCUSING YOU," Daniel defended against Efrat's accusation. "I was asking you."

"You asked me what I did?" Efrat grumbled.

"Yeah, I asked," Daniel clarified. "If I really thought you had hurt her, you'd be missing some skin."

"Nice to know where I stand on your list of friends. What do you have two categories? Ones you'll peel and ones you'll peel for."

"Alright, boys," Duke interjected, but neither one of them broke their stare. "No need to make it worse. The girl just got her hand cut off. Who knows what might set her off?"

"Whatever, I just don't like getting my head bit off before I've done anything wrong?"

"Oh, don't play the victim here, Efrat. We all know your history with Cori." Daniel pointed out.

Efrat smirked at him. "Yeah, but hey, I never successfully took her hands off. That burden goes to Gypsy now. Maybe you two can form a club. You can be the president, though, since your victim is permanently handicapped."

Daniel strained to hold in his temper. He wanted to smash Efrat's pretty boy face in, and he probably would have if Chuck hadn't spoken up.

"It's Christmas." Chuck's blanket statement didn't tell either of them anything they didn't already know, but they broke their deadlock gaze to look at him. "This is the first time I've seen a Christmas tree in six years and the first time I've heard carols in ten. I don't get to visit my family or wake up at home on Christmas morning. I don't even get to unwrap my own damned gifts because they've been searched ten times before they make it to me." Chuck looked between all of them, including Duke.

"I was fortunate enough to be invited here to share in something that still means something to Cori and Ethan. I got no right to be telling any of you what to do. I'm not a tough guy. I don't have any superpowers, but I do have common sense. And my common sense says that if any of you break out in a fight, then this won't ever happen again. Not for any of us."

Chuck shrugged and, having said his piece, meandered off.

"Well, I hope you two are happy?" Duke admonished them. "You made Chuck use his big-boy voice."

Daniel smirked at the joke and glanced at Efrat. His anger seemed to diffuse as well. "I tell you what. This Cinderella only has until midnight. Who wants to get me drunk and try to ride my pumpkin?"

Efrat smirked at the joke. "I'm not touching your pumpkin."

29

C ORI FLOPPED ONTO THE couch next to Belus. She was a few beers in and feeling pretty good, but she was losing steam. She had never entertained for a full house. Even just directing everyone to the food and keeping their beverages away from the living room was a full-time job.

"Where's your date?" Belus asked.

"I got ditched for guy time."

"Where are they?" he asked, looking over the couch for the guys.

"I can't say."

"Why not?" Belus frowned.

"They don't want Danato to find them," she whispered conspiratorially.

"Why?" He narrowed his eyes at her. "What are they doing?"

"If I tell you, you can't tattle."

"It depends on what they're doing."

"Pinky swear?" Cori lifted her hooked pinky finger. Belus eyed the offering with amusement, but eventually caved and looped his finger in hers for the legally binding contract of the pinky swear.

"Now spill," Belus mildly demanded.

Cori giggled. "They're skeet shooting."

"Did they think Danato would miss the sound of gunshots?"

She giggled again. "No, they're using Efrat as the gun."

Belus seemed to find some humor in that, but he was still trying to remain passive. "And what are they shooting at?" Cori bit back her lips, refusing to answer despite having revealed most of the secret already. "Cori?" Belus said with just a hint of warning.

"We may have accidentally gotten an extra box of plates that we didn't report." Cori laughed at Belus's head shake. "You pinky swore," she reminded him.

"That's why I'm going to pretend I didn't hear that."

"What about you, playboy? Where's your date or dates?"

Belus smiled and shook his head. "No takers tonight."

"Mmm, not curious enough."

Belus's chest shook with a quiet laugh. "No, not curious enough."

"Oh, well, their loss," Cori said through a yawn.

"I saw you speaking with Danato when you first arrived." Belus changed the subject. "Anything important."

She frowned. "Callin hasn't checked in yet."

"Strange, he doesn't seem the type to miss a curfew."

"I'll check on the morning bus. I hope he's just late." Cori knew as well as anyone that the cause of a missing werewolf could be premature shifting. It was the first sign of a werewolf's final terminal change. Callin wasn't yet geriatric, but age was meaningless for a creature that regularly pushed his body to extreme limits.

"What was the deal with that incident behind the couch here?" Belus asked. "I missed most of it, but it seemed like the boys got pretty tense for a moment."

Cori's eyes flickered to Belus and then her lap. "The usual. Efrat was getting a little too friendly." She could feel Belus staring at her as if he was evaluating her honesty. Rather than wait for him to dissect the truth from her, she opted for a quick exit. "I suppose." Cori pulled herself off the couch, rubbing her tired eyes. "That morning shipment is going to come way too early for me as it is. Do you need anything before I go up?"

"No, I can find my way back to the eggnog. You go ahead. Sleep well."

"Goodnight, Belus. Merry Christmas."

"Merry Christmas, kid."

Cori made a discreet exit upstairs, but instead of heading to her room, she tapped on the door to the guest room. Renee opened it and looked her over—as if the reason for the interruption might be a delivery.

"Do you have a minute?" Cori asked.

Renee's brow dipped, but she opened the door wide enough for her to slip inside. The prison auditor should have been the last person Cori would seek out for conversation, but there were a few questions lurking in the back of her mind, and she needed to ask them before she lost the opportunity to receive impartial answers.

Cori looked around the sparse guest room. The furnishing looked older than it usually did. She wasn't sure how the house knew everyone's styles, but it always gave a little insight into a guest's character.

If she had to guess, only from the room, she would know that Renee had simple but expensive taste. She was the type of person who would spend thousands of dollars on a tiny framed painting rather than hundreds on art that would actually fill her wall.

"If this is about this afternoon, don't worry about it. Danato and I have decided not to pursue a relationship."

Cori nodded. "That's fine," she said, slightly disinterested, but then remembered how weird that moment was. "When did you two... I mean..." Cori looked at Renee and realized that Belus was right. Some things just weren't any of her business. "Sorry, I just wasn't expecting that."

"Neither was I, but men do surprise us once in a while, don't they?" She folded her hands in front of her. "Was there something else?"

"Yes, I've actually been meaning to talk to you for a while now. I have some questions."

"Why ask me? I thought Rutherford was your teacher?"

"I don't know?" Cori shrugged. "Maybe because you won't sugarcoat it. Or maybe because I want an outsider's perspective."

Renee sat on the bed and crossed her arms. "All right, let's hear your questions."

Cori rested against the wall to alleviate her wobbling stance. "How many other time bubbles are there?"

Renee smirked and nodded as if she had been waiting for her to ask this question. "The only existing time bubble is right here. That we know of, anyway."

"When you arrived, Maddox said that there had been another breach and that it pulled out of our world. What happened to that one?"

Renee's amusement died back. "We didn't manage it correctly, so the entity pulled out. It imploded."

"What do you mean, imploded?"

"I mean that when it left, it took a gaping chunk of earth with it. It's now a reputed borehole, about seven and a half miles deep. The geologists love it. Nothing like a big hole in the ground to get them excited."

"I thought the entity couldn't go beyond the earth barrier."

"Can't or won't." Renee shrugged. "Ramifications of pissing off a dimensional creature, I suppose. The truth is, we know so little about these things; it's scary to consider the risk we are taking just being near it. If it weren't for the steady feed that this one gets here, this prison might be hopping all over Europe like the wandering village."

"The village?" Cori frowned. "You mean the one that Danato took us from? That's an entity."

"Oh, yes. She pops in and out at will, with little more warning than the changing weather."

"The village is her creation?"

"Yes, she takes it with her wherever she goes. Right along with all the residents."

"You said there was only one time bubble."

"Yes, because the village isn't a schism in time. It's just a spatial displacement, but it has a fluid barrier so that anyone can pass in and out."

Cori knitted her brow and stared at the floor. "Why are they even here? What's the point?"

"No one knows. And we may never know, Cori."

"Surely, in the course of your tenure, someone has given you a theory that made some sense to you."

Renee sighed and thought about that. "It's been so long since any of us have questioned the reasons behind what we see every day. We no longer care what the answers are. But if I could dare to give you a bit of advice."

Cori shrugged.

"Danato and Belus are alive for very good reasons. They are suspicious of everything they see and hear. You, my dear, seem to be on the curious side of things. And I'm sure I don't have to remind you of what happens to curious creatures."

"And yet, when all of you were running for your lives, I was standing my ground, saving everyone."

"At what cost?" Renee cleared her throat. "Don't get me wrong, Cori. I'm ever in your debt for saving... my investments, but the very definition of a hero demands that you place yourself in harm's way to save others. I've read your files front to back and back again. How long do you suppose that your luck can last? Who is to say that the next risk you take isn't your last?"

"I understand what you're saying. And I appreciate it, as far as I appreciate anyone watching my back. But it is a little hard to take from you. I mean, after all, I'm only here because of your demented business endeavors."

"Are you?" Renee tipped her head to one side.

"I may have chosen to serve here in the end, but that doesn't negate your involvement in my captivity in the first place. The board is just as culpable for everything that goes on here as any of us." Cori pushed away from the wall and opened Renee's door.

"You know Cori..."

Cori reluctantly paused in the doorway and turned back to allow Renee her final vindictive word, whatever it might be. Perhaps an insult to her intelligence or just a personal attack on her general character.

"I sometimes think about that wandering village and all the people who live in it. It must be absolutely frustrating to live there. Electricity is virtually impossible to maintain. Water pipes are useless there. Let's not even get into the outhouse situation. And the earthquakes must wreak havoc on one's nerves."

"What's your point?"

"My point is that people still live there–impoverished and isolated. Unsure of what the future holds or the dangers that could be lurking within the very ground that they walk upon, and yet they still choose to live there."

"Maybe they're happy there."

"They would have to be very happy though, wouldn't they? I mean, no one would endure such a difficult existence if they weren't happy to do it."

"Am I missing something, Renee?"

Renee smiled warmly at her. "Nothing that you would understand in your current predicament. Forget I said anything. Merry Christmas, Cori."

"Merry Christmas," Cori grumbled and shut the door on her way out. She hated Renee to the very core. Something about her screamed deceit, yet Cori couldn't think of one time she had lied to her.

30

"READY?" ETHAN STOOD BEHIND Efrat, holding his outstretched arm like a cocked rifle. Despite being treated like a piece of machinery, Efrat seemed to be enjoying the inventive distraction.

"Ready," Daniel signaled.

"Go!" Ethan yelled, and Daniel threw the white plate like a Frisbee up into the night sky. The plate was just glossy enough to reflect the light from the snow, giving Ethan a clear target. "Fire!" Ethan yelled again when he felt his aim was good.

Efrat released an electric pulse that came out like a shot from a gun. He gave it just enough power to shatter the plate.

A collective, "Ohh!" sounded as everyone celebrated his hit. Ethan gave Efrat a pat on the back for his part.

"My turn." Daniel shifted behind Efrat while Duke took Ethan's spot on the clay pigeons. "Now, how do I cock this thing again?" Daniel reached around Efrat, pretending to go for his crotch.

"Oh, back off, perv," Efrat bucked him away, and everyone laughed.

"Sorry, I have to get those jokes in while I can. They aren't as funny when your bud is actually gay." Daniel moved back into position. "Okay, okay, I'm ready now." He grabbed Efrat's arm and yelled, "Pull!"

Duke spun the plate into the air. It was an improvement from his first throw, which ended up whipping into the side of the prison. After a high arc, the plate crashed to the ground without a shot being fired.

"You have to tell me when to fire," Efrat said to Daniel.

Efrat looked back to see what the holdup was, but Daniel wasn't paying attention to the game anymore. He was staring out at the night sky.

"What are you looking at?" Efrat followed his gaze to the sky.

Daniel pushed past him slowly and walked forward. Ethan could see the confusion on Efrat's face, and he jogged forward to see what was wrong with his friend. "What is it?"

Daniel didn't answer except to buck his chin forward in the direction he was staring. Ethan looked out at the night sky. The clouds were masking most of the stars, so there wasn't much to look at, but Daniel had excellent night vision. If there was something to see, he would see it. "What do you see, Daniel?"

"It can't be," Daniel mumbled.

"What?" Ethan asked again.

"They've never traveled this far."

Ethan looked at Efrat and Duke, hoping they could make sense of what Daniel was trying to say.

"Well, I'll be damned," Duke murmured as he moved forward, squinting at the sky. "Is that what I think it is?"

Ethan looked at Efrat, but he shook his head. He couldn't see anything either.

Daniel finally looked away from the sky to Ethan. "They actually followed her here."

"Anyone want to share with the rest of us?" Efrat asked.

"Right there, boss." Duke pointed up at the sky, where the moonlight was peeking out through a cluster of separating clouds. Ethan came in tight behind them, trying to catch a glimpse of where Duke was looking.

Ethan frowned and peered into the sky. He could see the movement now and though it initially looked like three birds, flapping and gliding, they couldn't be mistaken for any animal in the realm of ornithology.

"What the hell is that?" Efrat's eyes widened in disbelief.

"Dragons." Just as the word escaped Ethan's mouth, a deep caw resonated through the sky, like the cry of a hawk with a sore throat. "Those are the three dragons Annette cared for and used in her magic."

"The ones from China?" Efrat asked, flabbergasted. "But that's like..."

"Really far away," Ethan said. "Except for Penelope, none of them have been outside of a hundred-mile radius of the caves in decades."

"Why are they coming here? Why now?" Efrat asked.

"Annette," Daniel answered. Ethan turned to look at him. "Well, she's dying. Maybe they've come to pay their respects?"

Ethan nodded, but he wasn't sure that was it. The dragons didn't seem to have much respect for Annette. It was unlikely they traveled thousands of miles to pay tribute to her deathbed.

Ethan heard a screech and a bang that echoed between the outbuildings. He whirled around, searching for the cause. The bang sounded again, and everyone joined in the search. Something big was hitting against something metal.

"Penelope!" Ethan ran to the east side of the building. The others followed behind him, and they shoved through the exterior door that accessed the hangar. Inside, the usually calm and contented dragon was rearing, pacing, and ramming her head into her dragon-sized doggy door.

"Penelope! Stop!" Ethan raised his hands to her.

Release me. She insisted in his mind.

"Do you want me to get a tranq gun?" Duke offered when she hit the door again.

"No," Ethan grimaced. "Penelope—"

RELEASE ME!

The resounding impact of multiple minds shouting inside of his brain doubled him over. He groaned and grabbed his head, trying to keep his skull from exploding. It was more than enough torment to get his compliance.

"Alright!" Ethan shouted back at the dragon. He shifted to open the exterior door and noticed that everyone was looking at him with concern. His outburst no doubt seemed unprompted from their perspective. "We can't afford a new door." He attempted to explain and pulled the lever to raise the exterior hangar door.

Penelope moaned or mooed—whatever the creature's happy noise was. She continued the groans until the doors were open, and she could walk out on her own.

Ethan expected her to fly off, leaving him to explain her loss to Danato. However, he was afforded the freedom of that embarrassment. Penelope just sat down on her haunches like a cat and pointed her snout toward the sky. She wasn't more than ten feet out the door.

"That's it?" He raised his hands at her back and stalked toward her. "You couldn't have done that from ten feet to the west!" The dragon did not respond in his mind, but he did have to jump to avoid her swatting tail.

"What is this?" Efrat asked. "What is she doing?"

"I think we're all in the same boat of WTF right now, Sparky." Duke patted his back as he passed him up. He stepped outside and pointed north. "One just landed outside the perimeter."

Ethan stepped outside and spotted heavy flapping wings disappear behind the east side of the wall. Another one flew over, blasting them with a gust of air. Ethan already suspected where she was headed. "They're setting up the corners," he said.

"What's that, boss?" Duke asked.

"North, south, east, west."

"How do you know that?" Daniel asked, coming up behind him.

Ethan shook his head. "I don't know. Some earth magic bullshit."

"So, they're just sitting there paying homage?" Daniel asked.

Ethan shrugged. He looked north to where Duke had spotted the other dragon. He noticed a green patch of grass among the piles of snow. "Or they're standing guard."

31

"FORGIVE MY PESSIMISTIC ATTITUDE, but I don't like change." Danato pressed the button on the coffee machine. His troublesome house guests had long since vacated, but there was no sleep in sight since three new arrivals were trespassing on his prison property. Not to mention the six men standing in his kitchen, circumventing his REM sleep with more questions than answers. "Especially when that change involves several tons of dragons."

"The dragons are not dangerous," Levi explained to him from his seat at the island. Belus had wisely brought him in on the conversation. The boy hadn't left Annette's side since the doctors had declared her prognosis for recovery as "unlikely," but Belus convinced him that this was a consult that required Annette's expertise, therefore, his expertise. Despite the recent stresses in his life, he graciously provided his objective knowledge. "They're presence, no matter how unusual or unexpected, should be viewed as a good omen."

"What about the grass over Addy's grave?" Ethan asked from the stool next to him. "Is that a good or bad thing?"

Levi turned to Ethan and shrugged. "When a witch or wizard dies, their magical energies dissipate almost instantly. Their power over the surrounding world becomes obsolete. However, in Addy's case, she wasn't just summoning and directing the power through spells; she was a vessel."

"That's the part I don't get," Daniel asked from his seat on the counter in the far corner. Danato ignored the indiscretion for the sake of moving the discussion along. He also didn't mention he was past his agreed-upon midnight curfew. "You make it sound like she sucked up all the earth magic. If that were the case, wouldn't the Earth die?"

"Vessel might be a bad description. Magically inclined beings summon the energies of natural magic. They funnel it, magnetize it, and direct it toward its intended target with the power of spells. Once the spell is locked in place, it will remain until they undo it or a stronger witch overpowers it."

"Or they die?" Belus clarified from his spot in front of the stove.

Levi nodded. "Right? However, witches and wizards can't actually hold earth power; they only manipulate it. They are basically traffic cops directing busy traffic to the proper channels. That's how standard magic is performed, regardless of skill level. Even Ogana worked his magic this way, but with the help of his coven, he could direct traffic that was much heavier and faster. It wasn't until he opened himself to too much power that the spellcasting backfired."

"Like what happened to Addy?" Daniel asked.

"Addy is... was different. Her expansion was successful. She became a highway for magic. It was just too much for her. The earth is a far greater power than any one man could wield. In many ways, our planet is its own entity, taking from—"

"Hang on, partner," Duke shifted away from the fridge where he and Efrat were leaning. "Now you're saying that Mother Earth is really a being."

"Well, no, I mean, not in the strictest sense of consciousness, but it does produce its own field of magical energy. All living things do, whether by extension of the earth—like a rock, or by their own devices—like humans and animals."

Duke frowned. "By their own devices?"

"Dark magic."

"You mean voodoo?" Duke asked warily.

"Yes, but what you are thinking of is death magic—which is a separate genre. My point is Addy didn't take the earth's power away from it. She wasn't just going to be a traffic cop, either. Rather, she had... melded with the earth. Binding herself to it would have allowed her to use it as free-flowing magic. She would have simply thought something to make it happen."

"Also known as a sorceress," Danato couldn't help but point out. Levi paused and stared at him.

"So, getting back to the grass," Ethan interrupted the tense moment. "If spells die with their creator, why is Addy's grave covered with green grass in the dead of winter?"

"Because she's the spell."

"Oh, for the love of God," Daniel complained. "What the feck does that mean?"

Danato gave up on ever sleeping again and pulled a coffee cup from his cupboard. He dumped the first trickles of brew into it. "Levi, while I appreciate your thoroughness, I just need to know why the hell I have three more dragons than I'm supposed to. Are they here for Annette? Are they here for Addy? And in either case, are they here to save her?" Danato clenched his jaw before taking a sip of his bitterly strong coffee.

Levi looked him over before answering. "Annette is beyond saving. I sincerely doubt that we would have different results with these dragons' saliva. Besides, trying to cure wounds caused by magic, with magic, is a bit like trying to cauterize burns."

Danato swallowed hard, trying to hide his disenchantment. He had hoped the dragons were a sign that his friend could be saved, but obviously, he was the last one holding out hope for that option. His ignorant bliss was finally on its last leg. "So, they're here for the girl."

"They aren't here for her. She's dead." Levi's veil of indifference faltered for a moment, revealing the anger and pain that Danato would eventually have to deal with. Danato had already predicted that their future would hold as much bitterness and projected blame as his and Efrat's.

"Then they are here for what follows her death," Ethan said. Everyone looked at him for an answer.

"What do you mean?" Levi asked.

Ethan took in a breath and scratched his head. "If it's melded to her, then maybe some of the magic that has been coursing through her is still here. Well, it's obviously still here; the damn grass is growing, and the dragons are drawn to her like a beacon. If witches are traffic cops, then she's a road. And if she's a road for magic, what happens when the road closes?" Ethan stared into space as he considered the metaphorical situation. "What if it's all building up until it…"

"Until it what?" Danato asked.

"I don't know, explodes?" Ethan shrugged. "Could it do that?" He looked at Levi for the answer.

"Yes, I think that's possible." Levi sucked in a breath as the realization dawned on him as well. "That's genius, Ethan."

"Share with the rest of the class, lads," Daniel said.

"What Ethan is suggesting is that—I mean, if we go back to the traffic metaphor. Addy would have been like an interstate road. She was a pathway for the magic. It coursed through her, and if she had awoken with that power, she would have been able to shift it and rearrange it at will. Create new exits and on-ramps. Effectively directing the traffic much as the traffic cop would have, albeit with a much greater degree of control."

"She would have been a full-fledged sorceress," Danato summed up, urging the young man to get to the point, since he was already familiar with the basics.

"Yes," Levi nodded. "That was the risk, but killing her hasn't necessarily stopped the flow of magic. Just her ability to direct it. Just because there is an accident on the interstate doesn't mean the cars stop coming. The traffic never ends."

"So, killing her was like causing a fifty-car pile-up during rush hour?" Daniel asked.

"Killing her was like placing a giant brick wall across six lanes of traffic and then walking away." Levi glanced at Danato, but he refused to show any remorse for killing a potential sorceress.

After everyone had a moment to imagine that scenario, Efrat cleared his throat. "What happens when a bunch of earth power gets jammed up, and the road crew meant to fix it doesn't show up for work?"

Levi glanced at Ethan before speaking. "This is, of course, just a guess, but based on my understanding of magic and the principles of basic physics, as it occasionally applies to those forces. I think the reason the dragons are here is that we might have inadvertently created the magical equivalent of a Mount Vesuvius."

"Wait, wait, wait." Danato waved his hand and put down his coffee. "I thought you just meant she was retaining the magic she possessed at the time of her death. But you're saying that new power is actively being poured into her?"

"Yes, that's what I'm saying."

"Even though she's dead?" Belus clarified, disbelief written all over his face.

"Yes," Levi stated, irritation bleeding into his voice.

Danato shook his head. "Why would it do that? How could it do that? Especially after what you said about the spells dying out with their creators."

"Oh, jaysus!" Daniel threw his hands up. "I finally get it!"

"Glad somebody does," Duke mumbled.

"Don't you get it, guys? Addy is the spell," Daniel said, but no one claimed any new understanding in the conversation. "If Addy is the spell, then who cast the spell?"

All eyes shifted to look at Ethan and Levi.

"If Annette was the one who cast the spell," Danato surmised. "Perhaps this will end when she passes."

"Unfortunately, it's not that simple," Levi said. "Since it took all three of us to complete the ritual, we are all the spell casters. The only way to make the magic dissipate is to kill all three of us." Levi looked at Danato. "Should I fetch your gun?" he asked without a hint of sarcasm.

The air in the room instantly cooled, and everyone froze in their positions. Danato stared back at the boy with a level of anger he had not felt for another human being in a long time. The sting of the insult was enough to ignite his temper but to do it in his own house, in front of so many others. He had sympathy for Levi's loss, and he bore the guilt of Addy's death as much as he sanely could, but he still needed this young man to mind him as a superior, or this arrangement would never work.

Danato debated his next statement carefully as his silence penetrated the room a little longer. When he had finally made up his mind to allow the boy a stay of execution, as it were, another voice surprisingly spoke on his behalf.

"You watch your mouth, boy," Daniel reprimanded. Everyone looked at him in surprise, including Danato. "You got no right to be riding high on your horse after the shite you just laid at our feet. There is one reason and one reason alone that we are in this situation, and it's got nothing to do with bullets. It's got to do with magic. Your magic."

Levi might have been ready for Danato's condescension, but Daniel had caught him off guard and put the boy in his place. Levi's face tinged pink, and his eyes drifted to the floor. His first and perhaps last attempt to criticize Danato was lost without a single remark from the accused.

"Gentlemen, I think we should call it a night," Belus jumped in before the moment could fester into further discomfort. "Everyone, back to your bunks and beds."

Everyone filed out the front door without more than a few words among them. He wanted to give Daniel an appreciative nod, but the disgruntled look on Daniel's face told him he was still ruminating on the final words of the night.

32

ETHAN WALKED DANIEL BACK to his cell. He didn't assume that Daniel wouldn't return as he was supposed to, but he wanted to do everything by the book, so he didn't put Daniel's future parole in jeopardy.

He was surprised that his friend wasn't joking about the impending doom that had just foreshadowed their existence. He wasn't usually the type to let a serious mood take root. Certainly not one as serious as a magical apocalypse.

When they reached his cell, Daniel stepped inside and shut the door for himself. Ethan locked it per protocol, even though it was pointless. There wasn't a prison in all the world that could hold Daniel McGrath. This was his second stint inside the walls of Danato's prison, but just like the first time, the only thing truly containing him was his guilt.

"Goodnight," Ethan nodded to him. Daniel reached through the bars and grabbed his wrist. Ethan frowned at his friend's austere expression.

"Why did you do it?" Daniel asked.

Ethan almost asked what he meant, but there was no point in pretending. There was only one topic on everyone's minds right now, and Daniel wasn't likely to be fooled by his placation.

He moved closer to the cell, and Daniel let him go. Ethan braced his hands on the bars and thought about his answer. An answer that would satisfy his friend.

"Because she would have died otherwise."

Ethan had hoped that it would satisfy him, but he seemed more irritated by it. "You aren't ready for this job."

"Excuse me?"

"You have no idea what it takes to save people."

"I think I know what it takes."

"No." Daniel shook his head. "You're strong enough. You're brave enough. But you don't have a killer's instinct."

Ethan narrowed his eyes at him. "I thought we were talking about saving people, not killing them."

"And how do you think that happens? Do you think I save lives with diplomacy?"

"I understand your perspective, but what I do is completely different."

"No, it isn't, Ethan. You risked everything. The whole fecking world for one girl."

"I had my—"

"Cori would have considered the risks."

"What does she have to do with this?"

"Cori would have let her die."

Ethan frowned and stared at him. "Don't be ridiculous. Cori is compassionate and humane."

Daniel chuckled, his eyes sparkling behind his darkened lens. "You can't even see how much she's changed, can you?"

Ethan's fingers pinched into a tight fist, but he resisted punching a dent into the bars. "Please don't belittle my knowledge of my wife."

"You didn't see her when that bitch was threatening to wipe us out. She's compassionate, alright, until someone she loves is threatened. Then she's just passionate."

Ethan didn't disagree with the statement, but he didn't like that Daniel thought he wasn't just as protective of his loved ones. "What's your point, Daniel?"

"My point is, we are sitting on a potential fecking magical rupture, and I want to know, once and for all, why you didn't have the balls to let her die."

Ethan gritted his teeth and backed away from the bars. "I think the question you should be asking is what transpired in China to give me the balls to defy Danato and endure baseless accusations from my best friend." Ethan turned to walk away, but stopped. He turned back and tipped his head to look at Daniel. "You know, I never once asked you why you did what you did to end up behind these bars. I just assumed you felt it was necessary, and I trusted your judgment. I would have appreciated the same from you." Ethan headed out before Daniel could offer a response. Whether he would have been apologetic was

irrelevant. He had already let him know where he stood in
his eyes.

33

DANATO WATCHED CORI YAWN as she made her way to the office door the next morning. She dropped her gun in the plastic bin and came inside to sit beside Ethan with her precariously full cup of coffee and a Danish from the cafeteria. He knew she must have been tired if she was succumbing to coffee for her motivation. He and Belus were already entrenched in a conversation about magic and the physical ramifications of a breach. There was still speculation about whether a rupture would actually harm them. Not that it was likely to be a good thing, but was it actually—as Levi had insinuated—explosive?

"Morning," Cori mumbled over another yawn.

"Morning, sweetheart. Has Ethan filled you in yet?"

"Not yet." Ethan shook his head.

"Filled me in on what?" she asked.

"Our meeting last night," Ethan answered.

Cori perked a brow. "You had a meeting? Last night? While I was sleeping?"

"You were already in bed. I didn't want to wake you." Ethan said.

Cori looked at Danato for an answer. "The three dragons from China have arrived and parked themselves around Addy's grave. After some discussion last night, we have determined that we might be dealing with a potential magical breach. Which we aren't familiar with, so we are debating what the physical and magical ramifications might be so we can get prepared."

"Dragons? A magical breach? Magical ramifications?" Cori repeated and turned to Ethan. "You didn't think I should be woken for this conversation."

"You said you had a tough day. I didn't want to interrupt your sleep," Ethan defended. Cori stared at him, frozen in a state of disbelief.

"At any rate, we are filling you in now?" Danato glanced at Belus, hoping to get his help in dispelling the marital argument about to erupt before them. He honestly had not even considered waking Cori up for the meeting the previous night, but only because he hadn't really thought of it as a meeting, more like an impromptu conversation.

"Danato and I were just discussing the potential impact of a sudden increase in magical energy," Belus jumped in on cue, making some leeway at drawing her attention from Ethan. "We were thinking that a surge of that magnitude might strengthen existing spells and wards. My first thought was about your rings. I'm not sure that we want them amped up any more than they already are. What do you think?"

Cori blinked at him and looked down at her rings. She frowned and stood up. "How would I know? Ethan's the expert on magic. I just plant vegetables. Excuse me, my clipboard is calling." Cori yanked the clipboard off his desk and stuck it under her arm before heading out the door.

"Cori," Ethan objected, but she just grabbed her gun from the bin and headed down the hall. "Damn it." Ethan stood up to go after her, but Renee came in, blocking his exit.

"I have good news, gentlemen," she said cheerfully. "The construction is officially complete."

"Good," Danato said. "When does our tenant arrive?"

"Soon, actually. He's rather anxious to get here, but as I understand it, he prefers not to travel this close to a full moon."

Danato's brow knitted with concern. "Please tell me you didn't rent out the top floor to a werewolf."

"Of course not." Renee's face paused in thought. "No, no, I don't think I would have done that. At any rate, he'll be here after the full moon, so he'll be in no condition to quarrel if he is. As for me, I will be catching a ride out with the construction crew. Good luck with everything."

"Goodbye, Renee." Danato noticed she was fiddling with the doorknob. If she had expected him to be courteous enough to walk her to the dock, she was going to miss her ride.

"Goodbye, Danato," she whispered and nodded to Ethan and Belus before leaving again.

"Where were we?" Danato voiced loudly to get them back on track. "Oh, yes, Cori is now unhappy with all three of us at the same time. That might be a record for her."

"I honestly didn't think she would mind getting sleep instead of bantering hypotheses," Ethan defended.

"She's just got a lot on her mind right now with all the changes." Belus dipped his brow in thought.

"What is it?" Danato asked, seeing the consternation on his face.

"Nothing."

Danato knew it wasn't likely to be nothing. He tapped his pencil on the desk, waiting to see if his friend would give in.

"What is it?" Ethan glanced between him and Belus, trying to determine what the problem was.

"Belus?" Danato asked again.

Belus glanced between them, realizing the spotlight was on him. "Oh, I was just trying to remember if I had seen Cori use her rings since the accident."

Danato looked at Ethan, but he shook his head. "I assumed the injury was encumbering her abilities."

"So did I, but last night, Levi explained that a spell is locked into place until another spell dismantles it or the creator dies. Ogana is dead."

"But I created the spell with our marriage vows," Ethan said.

"Yes, but you didn't initiate the magic. You added the directive, but Ogana put the power into the rings."

"Cori obviously knows her rings aren't working by now. She didn't tell any of us." Danato frowned and leaned back in his chair. Why was he surprised? Why did Cori's lies ever surprise him?

"She probably didn't say anything because she assumes the power will come back," Ethan defended.

Belus nodded. "I'm sure he's right."

"Of course, because Cori would never lie to me about her rings. She would never keep a secret that would ultimately put her life in danger. And the lives of my men." Danato felt his skin prickle as his body bloomed with heat. He shifted to stand, but Ethan stood.

"Let me handle this."

"Ethan—"

"I know." Ethan raised his palms to calm him. "A hundred times over, I know. But... If she didn't tell any of us..." Ethan glanced at Belus. "Then she is probably feeling pretty vulnerable. Maybe a superior is not what she needs right now."

Danato shook his head. "Are you sure you want to put yourself in that position? It's not as easy as I make it look, you know?"

"I know. I'll start with an apology for leaving her out of the loop. I'm sure the irony won't be lost on her." Ethan grimaced and left.

When he was gone, Danato took his seat again and stared down at his desk. He wanted to smash it in half like he usually did. He wanted to punch his fist through the wall. He wanted to, but the truth was, he wasn't half as mad as disappointed.

"I guess this explains her behavior as of late," Belus said. Danato nodded in agreement. "How mad are you?"

The pencil Danato forgot he was holding broke in two. He frowned at it and tossed it aside. "Mad enough that I'm glad Ethan is handling it. Aren't you?"

Belus took in a breath and looked around the room. "I think I've long since given up trying to expect the complete and absolute truth from her. I think she needs secrets. I think there will always be a part of her that doesn't trust the men in her life."

Belus was right. There were a lot of reasons that Cori kept her secrets. Deeply embedded rationales that stemmed from abandonment, traumas, and any number of lies she had been fed from the day she was born. But that didn't change the fact that she lived in the most dangerous place on earth. Surrounded by creatures that would take advantage of any weakness in the ranks.

"Danato—"

"I don't want to talk about it right now. We've each taken our turn to defend her this week. I'm not in the mood to bicker about it."

"I was actually going to bring up a different tender topic."

"What's that?"

"What are we going to do about Adrianna?" Belus asked.

34

"C UTTING IT A LITTLE close, aren't you, Callin?" Cori stared at the werewolf as he exited the back of the semi-trailer. The dock manager gave him a weary look before giving him a wide berth to unload his supplies.

Callin's head slowly turned to look at her. It reminded her of the creepy slow motion of a possessed toy. Unfortunately, Callin wasn't doll-sized, and the only thing possessing him was a predatory monster. "I'm late, yes," he said tersely.

"You should have been sequestered at midnight last night," she conditioned quietly. "Danato is not happy."

"I can hardly change the time," he stated, eyes locked on her.

Cori gulped and moved away from him to the platform stairs. She should have called someone else in to transfer him, but she didn't want to relinquish any more of her duties. She was already heading in the direction of a demotion, with or without her rings. She didn't want to reach useless any sooner than she had to.

"Let's get you..." She looked back to usher him along, but he was already right behind her. His folded hands and stiff-as-a-board posture belied the intensity in his gaze. He was a strong-willed werewolf and would do everything he could to maintain his dignity until the very last hour, but she could tell he was struggling. "...locked up."

She guided Callin away from the docks and to the elevators. The doors opened right away, and Cori debated if a shorter time in an enclosed space was better than a longer time in the stairwell. Either way, she had no defense other than her gun, and she already knew she wasn't a good enough shot against a werewolf.

Without instruction, Callin brushed past her and stepped to the back of the elevator. He looked out at her, somehow daring her to enter with him. Cori held her hand on the door, preventing it from closing. "Do I need to call Ethan to do this?"

Callin's jaw clenched. "I'm fine. Do your duty?"

Cori frowned and moved into the carriage. She pressed the button for the part-time level and leaned against the wall to watch him. She moved her hand to rest on her pistol—just in case.

"Don't," he scolded. "It will provoke me."

Cori sighed and moved her hand away from the gun. So much for self-defense.

As soon as the elevator arrived, she vaulted out of the enclosed space and moved toward his designated cell for the remainder of the day. She glanced back to make sure he was following. His long, intentional strides easily matched her insistent pace.

As she reached his human confinement, she was relieved to see Efrat through the glass door in the next section. He was on duty to monitor the inmates. Since he was a walking-talking cattle prod, it was an ideal duty for him. The fact that he enjoyed it a little too much was thus far being filed under stress relief.

Cori pulled out her key ring to open the lock. A sudden vibration in the bars and a growl startled her, and she dropped the keys. "Here, puss puss puss," a werewolf down the line called to her, pressing his face to the bars of his door. "Big bad wolf wants what's in that basket." He chuckled, biting his already bleeding lip.

A low rumble sounded beside her. She glanced at Callin and saw he was more than ready to defend her. Unfortunately, anything edging him into violence was going to test the control of his civility.

Cori grabbed the keys from the floor and slipped them into the lock. Naturally, the antiquated lock and key system required just the right jiggle and twist to pop it open. She had done it a hundred times, but not necessarily with a werewolf less than 24 hours from his transition breathing down her neck.

Callin pressed against her back and reached around for her hand. "Allow me." His previous irritation was now replaced by a smarmy tone. With a flick of his wrist, the latch popped, and she slid the door open. He slammed it shut again and pushed her against the door.

"Shit," she whispered and glanced to where Efrat was producing blue orbs of potent electricity. "Callin," she said calmly. "It's time to go into the cell."

"You smell delightful," he pressed his face into her neck, taking a long whiff of her.

"Yeah, showers are a wonderful invention."

"Ethan is a lucky man," he purred into her ear. "He is very fond of you. Unfortunately, he doesn't approve of sharing." He leaned in to nuzzle her ear. Her heart was thumping so hard she was certain he could hear it. His lips parted and nipped her earlobe. Then she felt his teeth.

"Ouch!" Cori pushed him back and flipped around to face him. She touched her ear and confirmed what she felt. Blood. He had actually bitten her.

Her instincts told her to pull her gun, but even the movement to reach toward it made Callin's eyes alight with something even worse than what was already there. Instead, she shoved the cell door open. It clanged loudly, and Callin's eyes flickered to it. "Inside!" she yelled the words, hoping they would seep into his still human consciousness. "It's time, Callin!"

He stared at her, seemingly barely understanding the words, or at least not wanting to comprehend them. Cori bolstered her bravado and deepened her voice to an unmistakable authority. "Get in the cell now!" she yelled.

Callin's eyes glowed with contempt, but something must have registered because his eyes drifted from her, and he moved into the cage without further insistence. To add to his impressive display of control, he slid the door shut.

Cori rushed to the door and twisted the key in the lock without difficulty. She moved to leave, but he grabbed her hand. She immediately tried to rip it away, but that was useless, as she knew it would be. She had a better chance of getting out of handcuffs.

"Cori," Callin said softly, drawing her gaze back to his face. "I'm so sorry." His other hand brushed back her hair around her ear, revealing whatever damage that had caused it to bleed. "I have never in my life wounded a woman—not without the precedence of pleasure, at least."

Cori nodded and pulled her head away from his hand. "I understand. You shouldn't have come in late."

"I am far more controlled than other werewolves."

"Yes, but that's a quality to exhibit, not test." Cori moved away again, but his fingers were still latched around her wrist. "Callin, you have to let me go." Cori shook her wrist, displaying the werewolf's hand hanging from it.

Callin smiled, entranced by the connection. "I can barely feel my hand." He looked up at her, holding his smile. "Did you know that a werewolf's nerve endings start to pinch off before the transformation?"

"No, I didn't," Cori admitted. "I don't prefer to research werewolf transformations."

"Why is that?" he drawled. "Is that because of Vince?" Cori frowned at his knowledge. She forgot she had mentioned her former lover to him. "It must have been difficult losing him."

"It was a long time ago."

"Do you miss it?"

"Miss him? Of course, but that's in the past."

"No, I mean, do you miss fucking a werewolf?"

Cori cleared her throat and shook her head. "No, I'm pleased with Ethan."

"Mmm, I suppose he's fairly comparable in that department, but still..." Callin trailed off as he rubbed the soft skin on the underbelly of her wrist.

"Callin, you need to let go of me. I have to get back to work." She reasoned with him.

"The nerve endings have to be stunted to minimize the pain, but of course, you know that it's a minor consolation for what is to follow." Callin pulled her forward, bringing her face as close to the bars as her now bruised cheekbones would allow. "Water is the key. Without the water, the process stays in a constant state of preparation. The stress would kill me if I didn't get enough."

"Callin, let go of me; you're hurting me." Cori finally grabbed her gun, but she was too close to her target. Callin grabbed the muzzle of the weapon and tossed it away. "Efrat!" Cori shouted, resorting to the tried-and-true defense of damsel in distress screams.

"I don't know when the desire for blood comes into play," Callin continued to babble.

"Efrat!" she screamed louder. Finally, Efrat's face perked up, and he looked around for the faint sound that had alerted him. He caught sight of her through the door and sprinted toward her.

"I suppose between the animal's hunger for meat and the man's desire for water, the craving becomes blood." Callin raised her wrist to his mouth and licked it before opening his jaw to bite down. Cori screamed in preparation for the pain that would not be numbed by pinched nerve endings.

"Oh, no, you don't!" Efrat arrived just in time, reaching through the bars to pump a hefty bolt of energy into Callin. Unfortunately, Cori was still connected to him. She shrieked, feeling the full rebound of the surge as it propelled her back, freeing her from Callin's clutches. She hit the floor and inspected her wrist, which ached with a pain that felt remarkably like a ghostly hand was still holding her captive.

"What the hell, Cori?" Efrat moved toward her. "Why didn't you just..." His sentence trailed off as he observed her condition. "What's wrong? Did he hurt you? Shit, you're bleeding." He moved toward her to assess her bleeding ear.

"No!" She backpedaled, not wanting another shock. "Don't touch me."

Efrat looked at her with a pained expression that broke her heart. He shrugged and shook his head. "What the hell is wrong with you? I thought we were good. Why are you treating me like a fucking leper?" His eyes searched her for some explanation. She knew the truth wouldn't make him any happier than her dismissal, but she hated letting him believe she was indifferent to his struggle. "Whatever." He gave up and turned to leave.

"Wait," she murmured. He stopped and looked back at her. "You can't touch me anymore, Efrat."

"I know you want to do right by Ethan, but I didn't think you would go this far. This is just cruel."

"No, Efrat, you don't understand." She groaned and forced herself to stand up. "I can touch you, but you can't touch me." She frowned at his confused face. She lifted her hands to him, displaying her rings. "It's gone. The power put into the gold died with Ogana." His face donned understanding. "If you touch me, you'll hurt me. Just like you do everyone else."

Efrat stared at her hands a moment, taking in her words. She expected an angry, blasphemous retort, but he just turned around and left the section.

She followed him and found him sprawled on the floor, leaning against the wall opposite his pacing lycanthrope detainees. The vacant stare on his face wasn't the usual bitter tantrum. He looked empty, as if the last of his hopes for the future were gone.

"Say something." Cori crouched next to him. "You know I had no control of this, right?" she asked, trying to absolve herself of her burden of guilt.

He didn't move.

"I don't want this any more than you do," she mumbled and sat down cross-legged next to him. "I was just getting the hang of everything. I was actually starting to feel confident, maybe even a little cocky." He said nothing. "I know what you're thinking." She chuckled. "This stupid woman is bitching about losing the power that I wish I could lose," she said in a mock male voice.

He wouldn't even look at her.

Cori rubbed her face and scooted back against the wall partition with him. She looked out at the men eyeing her from their cages. She presumed they could smell her bleeding ear. "I suppose that's it then. I can almost hear your heart hardening up. I mean, don't get me wrong, I know whatever this was, it wasn't exactly a healthy friendship. It had more to do with the rings than any actual connection between us, but still... kind of stings." She looked over and saw Efrat staring at her, glaring at her through glistening eyes.

"The only thing that has ever been between us is one ring, and you know it," he croaked over his emotions. "Don't you dare pretend to be indifferent to this just to make it easier on you," he hissed.

Cori looked down at her rings. She had nothing to say to that. At least nothing that hadn't already been said a dozen times.

"Why did Danato let you escort Callin if you didn't have your ring power anymore?" Efrat asked, under control of his tone again.

Cori didn't look up at him.

"Son of a bitch," he whispered. "You haven't told him yet? Cori, you need to tell him."

"I was just waiting until after the audit," she rationalized.

"Why do you do that?" he asked. "You put so much faith in him, and yet when it really counts—when you really need his help, you just drop him like a bad penny. You drop everyone."

The accusation rang true in her ears. It was her greatest downfall. One she had been trying in vain to overcome. "I don't know." She shrugged and looked at him. "I never really thought about it. I just assumed that I suck at my job." She laughed, but ironically, Efrat didn't seem to appreciate her efforts to lighten the mood.

"I think you're afraid he won't be there for you."

"He overreacts."

"He overreacts because you never tell him anything until it's too late for him to fix it."

"And what if it's something he can't fix?"

"Then at least tell him it's broken."

"You don't understand, Efrat. The minute he knows that I am just regular boring Cori again..."

"What's wrong with regular boring Cori?"

"You wouldn't understand."

"Try me."

"Danato is the strong one. Ethan is the brave one. Belus is the smart one." Cori shook her head. "What the hell am I? These rings were my only chance to fit in here."

Efrat looked her over, mouth parted, still searching for the right words to comfort her. "What a load of bullshit?"

Cori scoffed and stood up. "I should have known better than to confide in you." She felt a static shock on her butt and then a tug that yanked her back to the floor. She frowned at Efrat. "Ouch. Remind me to stop wearing jeans around you."

"I wasn't done talking." Efrat looked out at the werewolves across from them. "I don't recall everything about last night, but I do recall Duke saying something about you fighting a male dragon. Do I remember that correctly?"

"Yes." Cori sighed.

"And if I'm not mistaken, that took place before you married Ethan. Before the rings were bound to you."

"Yes."

"Okay, and what about the day we met?"

"Technically, the rings were protecting me during my time jumps."

Efrat laughed and shook his head. "Oh, no, kitten, I mean the very first time." He shifted to face her. "Say what you want about me now, but back then, I was a pretty dedicated asshole, and I know I was scary," Efrat smirked at her and raised his finger. "There I was, waiting for my impending doom and revenge, one way or another, and some sassy girl came sauntering into that gym like she owned the joint. You should have been pissing in your panties, but you were smack-talking. Then, before I knew it, you and your little band of merry men were overthrowing my entire operation."

Cori couldn't help but smile at that memory. It was one of her better moments, but it was certainly not without pain or guilt.

"You are a smart-ass. You are strong-willed. And you have braved every horrific thing I have ever done to you and still managed to find the good in me." Efrat paused to look her over. "You have the strongest heart of anyone I've ever met." Efrat reached forward but paused, remembering he couldn't touch her anymore. He shifted his hand and caressed the side of her cheek with his forearm. "And I'm grateful for that heart. Since it's probably the only reason I'm still alive."

Cori smiled and touched his arm.

"You don't need magic rings to be a part of this place, Cori." Efrat shifted his arm away from her and lowered his head to stare at her from beneath his brow. "But you do need to tell Danato that they aren't working anymore."

"You told him about your rings?" Ethan's voice made them both jump. As Efrat shifted from her view, Cori saw Ethan standing in the section with them. As usual, he had arrived without a single sound. The expression on his face was no less scathing than what she expected from Danato.

35

"ADRIANNA?" DANATO STARED ACROSS the desk at Belus, who was gritting his teeth. "What did you have in mind?"

"I'm not sure what you got out of last night's little meeting, but I'm under the impression that a magical breach anywhere near this prison would not be beneficial to our detainees. Especially the bubble."

"I shot the girl, Belus. I buried her—at your request, I might add. What more do you suggest I do?"

Belus shifted uncomfortably in his seat. "I think there are other measures we could take."

"You're not seriously suggesting that we kill three people, are you?"

Belus paused a moment, but shook his head. "No, but I think Levi may have been wrong about the spell being cast by all three of them. He and Ethan certainly played a part in the ceremony, but it was Annette who initiated the spell and summoned the energy for it. If Cori's rings have gone dormant after Ogana's death, it is reasonable to assume that Adrianna might go dormant if Annette were to pass."

"So, you are only asking me to kill one person?"

"I'm not asking you to do anything. I feel it's an option we should consider, but only because the situation seems to warrant a more proactive move. I don't mean to be morbid, Danato, but it would hardly be murder. She is already at death's door."

"And there she will stay until he sees fit to let her in."

"Danato—"

"It won't help."

"How can you be sure?"

"Magic has never been my strong suit, but I don't think it will help to kill Annette."

"Why not?"

Danato picked up a new pencil and tapped it on the desk rhythmically. Belus glanced at the anxious tick, but waited for him to answer. "Because I don't think that Annette was the sole creator of the magic that fueled Adrianna's creation."

"And what makes you think that?"

"Annette has been trying for years to reach the strength required for that ceremony. I doubt that after so many failed attempts, she managed to do it on her own."

"What are you suggesting?"

"I don't think Ethan was a benign part of the sorceress ceremony like Levi was. I think he may have some innate power in him."

Belus stared at him, losing the last of his argument for terminating Annette. Had he been having this conversation with any other man, they might have laughed in his face, but Belus simply took in the information with little more reaction than a slight gape of his mouth. "Innate power?" Belus clarified. There was doubt in his voice, like he was still searching for a polite way to tell Danato he was off his rocker. "Something that even Annette couldn't detect?"

Danato nodded. He knew what he was suggesting was ludicrous, but it was the only explanation he could think of.

"You think Ethan is a mage?" Belus asked.

Danato racked his brain for the correct definition. Witch, mage, enchantress, they were all powerful and potentially dangerous. It was just a matter of personality and goals. However, a mage was much rarer than the rest. A mage didn't require the same ceremonial stimulus as Annette to create magic. They also didn't need a ritual to connect them to power like Adrianna. A mage was inherently connected to the earth, a birthright carried down from one or both of their parents. Since Ethan lost his parents at a young age, it was possible he possessed magic and just didn't know it.

"You believe Ethan harbors a powerful natural magic that can be called upon without the use of spells or fetishes, and he simply never uses it?" Belus's tone sounded more like mockery now.

Danato shrugged. "I suppose it's just a theory."

Belus narrowed his eyes at him. "You aren't one to casually drop a theory—certainly not without evidence. Unless you've witnessed him performing magic." Belus looked at the door as if he suspected someone might be listening in. "Is this why you sent him to Annette? Did he discover his ability?"

"No. In fact, if, by some slight possibility, Ethan is a mage, then I don't think he knows he is."

"How could you know and not him? Did Annette know?" Belus shifted anxiously in his seat. Danato wasn't used to seeing his friend feel discomforted by a subject, but he suspected he wasn't the only one who felt inadequate in his knowledge of spellcasting. Something that both of them would soon have to remedy. "What haven't you told me, Danato?" Belus's eyes narrowed slightly. He was probably more than a little put off by the thought of a secret between them. After so many years together, there were no more secrets. Not even the really private ones.

"I wasn't sure it was worth mentioning. I wasn't even sure it actually happened. It was during our time in the bubble, so I wasn't exactly the very definition of clearheaded," Danato said, trying to defend his lack of open communication.

Belus nodded. "Go on."

"I took Ethan to donate his blood to one of our inmates. She got a little carried away. I had trouble getting her off. When I finally did, Ethan was completely zonked. His pulse was thready, and he was practically unconscious.

I knew I needed to get him some food as soon as possible, so I just flopped him over my shoulder and headed toward the elevators. He was babbling on about something I couldn't understand, so I ignored it. But then I started to feel something shift in the air. It was like a fog, but I don't actually remember seeing a fog." Danato shook his head, still not believing what he was about to say. "From one step to the next, I went from the seducers level to the cafeteria."

Belus blinked at him for a moment. "You teleported?"

Danato paused, debating whether he wanted his statement to go down on record. "Yes."

Belus stood and paced in front of the water cooler. "You should have told me this?"

"At first, I thought it was caused by the entity—something about being inside of the bubble—time and space bending. I thought she was assisting me to get his blood sugar up. As I said, I even questioned my sanity. Ethan wasn't the only one low on blood. I knew what had happened, but the farther away the experience was, the more I denied it."

"Perhaps it was the entity, just as you said—helping you."

"I've considered every angle. Ethan might have cast a spell that activated the bubble. Some spell he came across years ago, fed by the entity's power of spatial disruption. A coincidence, like the rings, but..." Danato stared off into the blank space ahead of him.

"But what, Danato?"

"When it happened—when the air started to shift... You know how it feels, standing next to Annette when she is casting a spell?"

"Like a hurricane in a bottle?" Belus frowned.

Danato nodded. "I felt that same thing... coming from Ethan."

Belus moved to the office door and stared out the window. There was nothing more than a blank white wall to look at, but that was likely what he needed at the moment. "Annette worked very hard to reach her skill level." He commented, though it was nothing Danato didn't know. "If I recall correctly, Annette has never been capable of teleportation, and she is considered the third most powerful witch in the world." Danato clenched his teeth. He knew Belus would have nothing new to offer for his consideration, but he waited for his friend to gather his thoughts, connecting the dots he had already been working on the past few months. "If what you're saying is true. Ethan's power—which he hasn't trained a day in his life—has surpassed Annette's."

"Yes."

"That means it is entirely possible that Ethan wasn't just participatory in the spell that created Addy, but the key ingredient?"

"Yes." Danato leaned his head back and stared at the ceiling. He knew where this conversation was going.

"Is there any chance that Ethan knows about his powers and just hasn't told us?"

"I sincerely doubt it. If Annette couldn't sense the power on him, then it must be a translucent connection."

"Maybe he's remained hidden because he's so powerful."

"What are you talking about?"

"I'm talking about a mage that has been right under our noses for years, in the presence of magical entities, left and right, going unnoticed by anyone—including Ogana. That is not possible," Belus said, casting away his theory even before Danato could.

"You think Ethan knows and is actively cloaking his power?"

"I think there is more going on here than we think." Belus chuckled and turned around. "What if Ethan actually did communicate with the dragons, and he wasn't just high?"

"Why would he admit that to us if he were trying to keep his power a secret?"

"Everything that has led us to this moment is because Ethan admitted to hearing the dragons. A sorceress was created, brought back here, killed, and buried in our yard—a decision I regret participating in now. A magical seed planted in the most magically infused place this side of the hemisphere."

Danato sighed and rubbed his face. He had not thought about it in such a criminal way. He had not considered that every play, from the moment Ethan mentioned he had heard the dragons, was leading to this pinnacle ending. "No." Danato shook his head. "I refuse to believe that Ethan is manipulating us."

"Refusing to believe it doesn't disprove it."

"Ethan has never lied to me."

"He's lying to us right now. Danato, we have dragons outside howling at the four corners of the earth. The equivalent of massive talismans surrounding the most potent altar on earth, and we might have a secret mage in our midst. Something is going on, and we have to figure out what it is before this magical bullshit literally blows up in our faces."

"You can't possibly believe that Ethan is behind all of this."

Belus moved to his desk and leaned over the edge. "Look, I'm out of my area of expertise here. I'm mostly just spinning my wheels, but you have to admit, it is interesting that on the verge of a major magical shift, the most powerful witch we know is lying on her deathbed, completely incapacitated and unable to defend us against it."

Danato leaned back in his chair, and his eyes pinned to Belus as he held back the bellowing argument that nearly passed his lips. "Ethan didn't release the wizards intentionally."

"Whether he did or not, this chain of events has reached critical mass, and we have to do something to stop it."

Danato nodded in agreement. "If Ethan is as powerful as we suspect, then he could help us with that."

Belus scrunched up his face and shook his head. "How do you find comfort in the fact that the only person we have to defend us against this seed of magic is the one who created it to begin with?"

"I'm still running under the assumption that Ethan doesn't know what he is. Until I have proof, I will assume that what is happening is... a very awful series of events."

Belus paced the length of the room before returning to Danato. "You need to question Ethan about what he's hiding."

"I've already—"

"No, I mean, really question him." Belus swallowed hard and braced his hands on the desk. "If he won't give you the answers you want... take them."

36

ORI STARED BLANKLY AT Ethan, unable to formulate the words to defend herself. She could only imagine how betrayed he felt—her receiving console from Efrat instead of him. It was like Cleos all over again.

"Great," Efrat mumbled and stood up. "Look, Ethan, I just found out about the ring situation and I told her she should report it to Danato ASAP."

Ethan continued to stare at Cori past Efrat. "Yes, I heard. You seem to have more sense than my wife."

Efrat groaned and backed away. "I think I should give you two some privacy."

"Not at all." Ethan grabbed Efrat by the shirt to keep him from leaving. "You seem to be Cori's new confidant. Congratulations, you've even one-upped Belus."

Cori scoffed and stood up. "I had to tell him. I'm not immune to his electricity now."

Ethan looked at Efrat to confirm this. Efrat smirked at him. "A dream come true, right?" Ethan knew the man probably wasn't taking her lack of resistance as anything more than another hit to his streak of bad luck. He was just hiding his disappointment under humor, as usual.

"That doesn't change the fact that you didn't tell me the rings weren't working?" Ethan dropped his grip on Efrat.

"Because I knew you would be worried and overprotective."

"In his defense, he was that way when the rings were working," Efrat pointed out.

"Shut up, Efrat," Cori scolded him.

"And what if we scheduled you for a duty you weren't equipped to deal with, and you got hurt or worse?"

Efrat coughed into his hand. "Like werewolf duty," he mumbled into his fist.

"Shut up, Efrat," Cori seethed.

Ethan turned to look at him, then back at her. He shifted his gaze to her ear, where she was bleeding. "What happened?"

"It was nothing," Cori insisted.

"It wasn't nothing," Efrat snapped.

"One of you, answer me!" Ethan yelled, making the feral men behind him rattle against their cage doors.

"Callin got a little handsy when I was putting him in his cage," Cori tried to downplay what had probably been the stupidest mistake of her life, second only to getting too close to a transmorph.

Ethan looked toward the section where Callin's designated containment was. "When did he come in?"

"About a half hour ago," Cori admitted.

Ethan huffed out a stuttered laugh, but it wasn't out of humor so much as extreme shock. "And you took him to his cell? By yourself?"

"It was on my duty roster yesterday. I was just finishing my list."

"And what happened?" Ethan asked. Cori stared blankly at him, not wanting to explain the details. "Efrat?"

Efrat looked at her before answering—not so much asking permission as giving her an opportunity to fess up. "She called out, and when I got there, he had hold of her through the bars. He bit her ear and was going back for more."

"Son of a bitch," Ethan whispered.

"It's not his fault. He can't control himself right now," Cori defended his friend.

"I know that, Cori, but you bloody well can! You should have followed the standard protocol."

"Yes, sir." Cori mock saluted him.

Ethan's face darkened, and he lunged forward, closing the distance between them. Cori shrank back, surprised by the sudden movement.

Efrat jumped forward with him and shoved his shoulder in front of his. It was hardly an obstacle, but the look on Efrat's face was what kept him still. The elemental obviously didn't want to make waves and would undoubtedly prefer to leave his post than go head-to-head with his superior. However, just like Ethan and Danato,

Efrat felt obligated to protect Cori. He was just as enslaved by his hero call as the rest of them.

Ethan stared at Cori for a moment, heart racing, panting through his clenched teeth. Cori stared back at him, eyes dancing over his face, questioning what her next move would be, entirely contingent upon his. He even sensed a little fear in her. That wasn't what he wanted, but he wasn't sure he had a choice. "I always wondered what this would feel like."

Cori's brow dipped slightly, and she glanced at Efrat, possibly unsure of who he was talking to. "What what would feel like?" she whispered, playing along.

"The moment I gave you an order, and you disrespected me in front of my men instead of taking it seriously."

"It's all good, Ethan; I'm barely one of the men. I'm like a stray dog that you guys keep feeding."

"Efrat?" Ethan turned to look at him. The contented smile on Ethan's face must have thrown him because he looked worried, especially since they were nose-to-nose. "Do you take inmates to their cells by yourself?"

Efrat glanced back at Cori as if answering would betray her. "No. I can't open the doors very well, though."

"To your knowledge, does Duke take inmates to their cells alone?"

Efrat swallowed. "No, sir."

Ethan nodded. "That's interesting. It seems to me that everyone in this facility is following the rules except you, Cori."

"Callin said…" Cori trailed off, as if realizing that her only defense was useless. "I thought I could handle it. I thought he could handle himself."

"And you were wrong." Cori rolled her eyes and nodded. "Because werewolves are not something that anyone in this facility can handle. I have gone head-to-head with that man in a full-on brawl. Do you know what happened?"

Cori nodded. "He wore you down."

"I lost, Cori. I lost the minute the fight started. There are only two people in this facility I would trust alone with Callin this close to a full moon: Daniel McGrath and Efrat." Efrat looked up in surprise, unaware of his status. "But do you know what?" Ethan paused. "I still send him with a second!" Ethan poked his finger into Efrat's chest, making him wince at the pressure. "Because we have protocols!"

Cori nodded and walked away, hiding whatever emotions she was feeling besides abject hatred for her husband. Ethan sighed and shifted to look at Efrat. "Thank you for helping her."

"Yeah, well, she's no use to me anymore, but I guess we could keep her around to look at."

Ethan nodded rather than laugh at his joke. "I know you'll always do right by Cori, Efrat. Even if it doesn't get you what you want."

Efrat smirked and shook his head. "I'm used to not getting what I want."

Ethan shook his head. "No one gets used to that." He gripped Efrat's shoulder, giving it a squeeze and a shake. "Hang in there. I see good things in your future. Maybe this twat with the lab upstairs can figure out a way to cap that energy."

"I'll keep my fingers crossed." Efrat raised his sparkling blue crossed fingers.

Ethan laughed and left him to his babysitting duty. By the time he reached the elevator, Cori was already inside, and the doors were closing. He picked up his pace and leaped through the closing doors just in time.

Cori gave him a tepid look before continuing to stare in front of her. He cracked his neck and adjusted his t-shirt. He took up a position beside her, staring forward just as she was. When she didn't speak, he looked over at her. He even dipped his head down to see her pouting face.

"Do you want to talk about this?" Ethan asked.

"That depends; who am I talking to? My husband or my boss?"

Ethan leaned forward and pushed the stop button on the elevator. After a slight jolt, the carriage stopped. Ethan turned to face her. "We knew this would be difficult. Working together. Living together. We've done as much as we can to separate our lives, but at some point, we are going to be the ones running this facility. Just you and me."

"Just you, by the sound of it."

"If you are acting as a guard, then you are under my supervision. And yes, that means I expect you to listen to me. I've been in command of these men longer than I have been with you, Cori. If you think that I am going to compromise safety just because you might make me sleep on the couch tonight, you're wrong."

Cori glanced up at him and took a slow breath. "I wasn't compromising their safety."

"If you start a fire, then you endanger yourself and the firefighter who has to come put it out. What if it hadn't been Efrat nearby? If you aren't equipped to handle the duties of this prison, then you will endanger whoever you work with. I know you don't want to hear this, Cori, because you think that I am being overprotective, but the truth is that without your rings, you are not going to be able to do certain things."

"Then what do I do? The time bubble is off-limits. Prisoner transport is going to be limited. Maintenance and janitorial work?"

Ethan shifted in front of her and cupped her face in his hands. "We'll figure it out, Cori." He gave her a gentle kiss. "I'm not going to let you become insignificant, if that is what you're worried about." He pulled out the stop button, and the elevator continued to descend.

"It's not you that I'm worried about."

"Don't worry about Danato. As long as I have any say in this prison, he isn't going to demote you to a janitor." The doors to the elevator opened on the main floor. Danato and Belus were waiting just outside. "Speak of the devil."

Ethan moved to exit the carriage, but Danato raised a hand and pushed inside with him. "Cori, get out. I need to speak with Ethan."

"What's going on?" Cori asked as she maneuvered to let Danato into the small space.

"Are your ears broken?" He turned a harsh look on her, so she scurried out to stand next to Belus.

"Are you planning on telling *me* what's going on?" Ethan asked him, almost amused by Danato's seriousness.

"Yes, as a matter of fact, from now on, everyone is going to tell everyone the truth. Starting with rings." Danato pushed the button for the seducer's level, then turned a hard stare on him. "And ending with what really happened in China."

37

A S THE DOORS TO the elevator closed, Cori caught a glimpse of the worried look on Ethan's face. She wasn't sure what was going on, but it was clear Danato was done taking evasive answers from Ethan.

"Come on, kid. Let's go have a drink."

"Son of a bitch," Cori grumbled and followed Belus out of the prison.

When she made it home, she left the door open but didn't invite Belus inside. She turned around and crossed her arms. Belus patiently watched her and waited for permission to come in.

"If you're not going to let me in, at least bring me a bottle of whiskey."

"Every time we come here to have drinks, something horrible is happening. Something that requires alcohol to deal with."

"In that case, you should know the routine." Belus stared at her a little longer. "Brandy will do. Or scotch if he has any left." Cori still didn't move or give verbal consent. "Are you enjoying this, Cori? Are you enjoying the power you have over me? Or do you really want me to leave without explaining what's going on?"

Cori sighed. "Come in." She waved him in and headed into the living room. She took her usual position on the couch while he closed the door and joined her.

Belus moved directly to the hidden bar, sliding open the wood panel on the wall to reveal two shelves of fancy and expensive liquor. He pulled out two glasses and set them on the coffee table before returning to contemplate his choice.

"You do realize it's not even 9 o'clock in the morning, and I think I'm still hungover from last night."

"You are going to want a drink for this, trust me." He chuckled and pulled out a tall green bottle. He turned back to her and smiled. "If you've ever had any doubts about that man's love for you, you have your proof right here." He displayed the bottle to her.

"What is it?"

"It's Chartreuse. It's pretty strong, but sweet. I requested it on your behalf a while back. I wasn't sure he would get it. He doesn't allow much in his budget for his liquors anymore." Belus pulled the cork out of the bottle and smelled the liquor inside. His smile broadened, and he poured a little into each glass. He added a little tonic water to each before handing one to her.

She took a tentative sip of it and immediately tasted honey in the background. After several more sips, it was difficult to tell if what she was tasting was spice or fruit.

"If you don't like it, lie to me. You don't want to know how much he spent on this."

"I do like it. I like it a lot, actually." Cori leaned back on the couch and sipped the aromatic beverage. Belus did the same, easing himself back into Danato's chair and enjoying the simplicity of the moment. At another time, she might've been begging Belus for the answers to her questions, but she knew he would eventually tell her. He always told her the truth, even when the truth was only to tell her he wouldn't tell her the truth. "I take it you already knew about my rings?"

"In the discussion last night with Levi, he mentioned that when the source of magic dies, his spells die with him."

"Yeah, he told me the same thing yesterday morning. Are you mad?"

Belus perked his brow and pursed his lips in thought. "No, I don't suppose mad is the word for how I feel."

"I would've told you, eventually."

"I know."

"I just didn't want to bring it up around Renee."

Belus leaned forward in the overstuffed chair. "Cori, I didn't bring you here to lecture you about the rings or to dole out a punishment for your behavior."

"Why did you bring me here?"

"I'm not really sure how to say this, so I'm just going to say it. Danato and I have reason to believe that

Ethan might be responsible for the magical breach that is threatening us."

"Well, yeah, I guess. I mean, he helped create the sorceress."

"No, Cori. The problem has become more complicated than that. Danato suspects he has innate magical abilities, and he has been hiding them from us in order to achieve this breach."

Cori laughed. She hadn't really heard anything so ridiculous in all of her life. Ethan was the one constant in her life. He was the epitome of the hero and the good guy. For them to doubt his loyalties was outrageous. "Is this about the thing with Ogana? He was obviously being controlled by him."

"For now, we believe that was a separate incident, although possibly necessary to eliminate Annette as a threat."

"Ethan adores Annette—like a weird grandmother. He wouldn't want to hurt her."

"Cori, do you remember reading about witches and sorcerers?"

"I'm going to be honest with you. If it came out of one of those red books, I not only don't remember it, but I probably blocked it out."

Belus opened his mouth to speak, but his lips drew back in a cockeyed smirk. He huffed out a breath that might've been an attempt to laugh before he composed himself again. "What we suspect is that Ethan is a mage."

"And which one is a mage again?"

"A mage is a person who has a natural gift for magic. You see, Annette always qualified as a witch because she uses rituals and spells, and sometimes even dragon blood, to summon her magical power. She is very gifted and very powerful, but it took her years to learn her craft.

"A sorcerer, as you already know, is a being that has been imbued with earth power. The power filters through them and is always with them."

"And the mage?"

"A mage is arguably between the two. This person could access the power of the earth with little more than a thought. They would not require the extensive training that a witch undertakes, and they would not require any physical objects to focus their purpose."

"You said that a mage is between the two. You mean in terms of strength or danger?"

"To be perfectly honest, I've never heard of the existence of a mage. Up to this point, I would've considered a mage to be a myth, or at least something extremely rare. Since we don't know much about mages beyond how they draw their magic, I can't really speak to their level of abilities. I will say this, though. Ogana tried to make himself a sorcerer with a full coven and failed. Annette tried to do something similar with her protégé and nearly lobotomized her. However, when Ethan got involved, they were at least able to complete the ceremony. Not to mention that long before any of this, he was able to create a rather complex spell on your rings just because they contained magical energy already. That's without any training whatsoever."

Cori smiled at Belus—an expression that belied her discomfort. "Where is this coming from? You can't just jump to conclusions based on a couple of incidents. You can't just suddenly decide he's bad."

"I haven't decided anything, and neither has Danato. I'm just telling you that we have suspicions."

Cori shifted forward and set her glass on the coffee table. "Okay, if he is a mage and if he intended to make a sorceress... Why? What would be the point? You will never convince me that he is trying to hurt anyone. He's... the good one." She sputtered out a laugh, but like her smile, it was covering a deep emotion.

"Yes, he is? And yet, he has refused to explain why he performed that ceremony."

"To save a girl!" Cori jumped up. "That's what he does! He's a good man!"

Belus raised his hand to calm her. She was near tears, but she resisted the urge to cave to them.

"All I'm telling you is that Ethan might be a mage. If he is, that would make him a very powerful person. In our experience, power brings problems. Since Ethan has been very evasive about his motives, Danato and I have decided he needs to be interrogated. To make sure he is not a danger to us, himself, or the prison."

"But this is Ethan. He loves us. I have a child with him. How can you even suspect his motives?"

"There are other possibilities. Danato suspects that Ethan may not even know that he's a mage."

"How could he not know?"

"Again, we don't know much about mages, but that might be because the people who are either don't know they are, or they hide it extremely well."

Cori sat back down, trying to remember any time when Ethan had done something miraculous. However, through her rose-colored glasses, Ethan was already superhuman. Maybe that was the point. Maybe his heroics were more than just manly acts. For some reason, that made Cori sad—as if there was another reason to feel unequal to the world she lived in.

"Another theory is that someone may have discovered his gift and started using him against us. Manipulating him with their magic. Much as Ogana did to him."

"You mean Annette? She's basically a vegetable. She couldn't maintain that."

Belus stared into the fire that had spontaneously lit for them on their entry and bit his lip. "If he is being used, it would have to be someone extremely powerful. Or something." He looked back at her.

Cori stared at him and then at the fire. "You mean the entity?"

"I have no proof of anything, Cori, but I didn't want to have this discussion with you after I did. I'm trying to prepare you for the worst-case scenario."

"The entity is always the worst-case scenario. We don't understand it, we don't trust it, and we are deathly afraid of it, and yet here we are sitting in the home she created, warming ourselves by her hearth."

"Because the alternative is just as dangerous." Belus groaned and shifted out of his seat. He placed his glass on the coffee table and crossed his arms. "This isn't the way that I like to do things, Cori. I prefer to at least have some idea of what the hell is going on before I bring you into the loop. I like to be prepared for your questions, but the truth is I can't wait for the answers. I need to know before anything else happens where you stand."

"Excuse me?" Cori felt a shiver run through her body.

"Whatever is happening here now involves four dragons, a dead sorceress, and likely Ethan."

"How did we go from a possibility to a likelihood?"

"Whether Ethan is being controlled or not, if he has done this intentionally, that would mean his loyalties could have shifted in an unforeseen direction."

Cori shook her head. "You and Danato are just being paranoid."

"Cori, listen to me. I know when push comes to shove that I can trust you with my life."

"Belus." Cori chuckled. "You're kind of freaking me out."

"I also know that when push comes to shove, you don't trust anyone but yourself."

Cori frowned and looked down at her glass. She didn't want that to be true, but what evidence did she have to disprove it?

"If something should happen with Ethan, I need to know where you stand."

Cori took a quick breath—almost a gasp. "That's not fair, Belus."

"I know it isn't, kid, but I need to ask."

Cori glanced in the direction of the prison, suddenly wondering what sort of interrogation Ethan was experiencing. It doubtfully involved drinks. "Where did Danato take Ethan?"

"I know you don't want to choose between your husband and your friends—"

"Where's Ethan?" Cori shifted forward.

"I need to know, Cori!"

"Know what?" she yelled back at him.

"Are you going to trust us and support us, or are you going to abandon us!"

Cori stared at Belus, her head shaking slightly. She didn't like any suggestion of abandonment. She would never interpret her actions as leaving anyone behind. Regrouping, doubling back, but not abandonment. "You said you needed proof. What happens if Ethan is a mage? What does it mean if he is one?"

"I don't know."

"Don't lie to me!"

"I'm not lying! I told you. I don't particularly appreciate discussing these things without more information, but if Ethan is a liability, we may have to take negative actions. Actions you may not approve of."

"Like you did for Addy?" Belus didn't answer. "Goddamn it, Belus! Are you talking about killing my husband!" Rather than wait for an answer, she jumped up and went to the door. Belus followed her.

"Cori, you have to leave this be."

She grabbed her coat off the hook.

"Do not go out that door?"

"And what if I do!" Cori glared at him as she slipped her coat on.

"Then I call ahead and have two guards drag you back here in shackles." Cori raised her hand to throw out a fireball, but there was no fire to conjure from the dead rings. Despite his knowledge of this, Belus took a step back. "You don't have any power anymore, Cori. It's just you and me. Do you want to keep fighting, or do you want to talk about this?"

"There is nothing to talk about. If something is happening to Ethan, then we will fix it. Without resorting to guns."

"You know that Danato and I always exhaust our resources before resorting to that. I'm just giving you a heads-up on the possibilities."

"You aren't telling me about the possibilities. You're warning me about them. And I'm warning you that no one is killing Ethan."

Belus stared at her for a moment. "I doubt it will come to that."

"It won't come to that."

"Cori—"

"I don't care, Belus," Cori reaffirmed. The lights in the house began to flicker, but she ignored it. "Mage, magician, or mathematician, Ethan is not our enemy. There will be no more discussions about eliminating threats."

Belus looked at the lights as if he were seeing this behavior from the house for the first time. His expression was angry but also concerned. As unhappy as everyone was about her connection to the entity, she was starting to appreciate that someone had her back.

"I think you should go." Cori motioned to the door, and it opened on its own. Belus stared at it a moment, then grabbed his coat. He slipped it on, but before leaving, he turned back to her.

"I know it's an impossible decision. For a long time, Danato refused to entertain the idea of killing his spouse to protect the world from the entity." Belus nodded to the surrounding room. "But eventually, he came to realize that it was his only option. I don't think Ethan is compromised enough to warrant a death sentence, but I hope when the time comes... When you have to make a decision equally as

difficult, you have the strength to do it before it's too late."
Belus stepped outside, closing the door behind him.

33

38

"ARE YOU GOING TO tell me what we are doing up here?" Ethan asked Danato as they walked through the seducer's level.

"I need to get answers."

"Have you considered asking me for them?"

"I've tried that already. You either won't answer or can't answer, and in either case, I need to know which it is."

Ethan nodded. "I see." It didn't surprise him that Danato was tiring of his enigmatic responses to his queries regarding China. He wanted to tell him more, and without actually revealing the dragons, he had said as much as he could. The problem was, even he didn't know if he wouldn't or couldn't tell Danato the truth. The words just didn't come out, even when he tried. "What exactly happened between the time I left your office and when I came back?"

"Belus and I were discussing the magical breach."

"And you decided I have the answers, but just won't reveal them."

"In summary, yes." Danato's jaw tensed.

"I wish I did, but I really don't. The truth is, I am almost as in the dark as you are."

"See." Danato stopped and turned to him. "It's the almost part that has me questioning your motives."

"I've told you as much as I can."

"Ethan, answer me once and for all. Who has been making requests of you? Who are you keeping hidden from me?"

Ethan once again searched for the words to answer him. To let it all be out in the open, but he couldn't even part his lips. The best he could do was smile, which didn't make him seem any less guilty in his refusal to speak.

Danato scoffed and pushed into the airlock, conjoining with the next section. Ethan hung back for his turn in the transitional space and caught up with him on the other side. He kept pace beside Danato, preventing himself from being led. "Where are we going?"

"Mezula."

"Ah, man," Ethan grumbled. "Isn't there anyone gentler than her?"

"She is the strongest psychic we have in the prison."

"And the most sadistic. You might as well stick me in a chair under a hot light and have Efrat poke me."

"It may come to that."

"Really, Danato?" Ethan stopped in his tracks to confront him. Danato stopped to face him. "I get that this is the Danato show. I get that you're mad and frustrated, and this is how you react when things don't go your way."

Danato's jaw tensed, and he looked away. "Look at me!" Ethan yelled at him, drawing his feral eyes back to him. "I'm right here, Danato." Ethan pressed his hand to his chest. "I'm not running away, and I'm not going to cower away from you. Talk to me."

Danato's gaze softened, and his tense muscles relaxed. "There's something going on with you, and I need to find out what it is before this magical breach occurs."

"What do you mean, going on with me?"

"I need to know if you are being controlled."

"I'm not being controlled."

"Then why can't you tell me the truth?"

Ethan shrugged. "Why can't you take me at my word?"

"Because everything you've done has led us into this situation."

"You make it sound like I'm causing the breach."

"I think you are." Danato marched on.

Ethan frowned. He couldn't imagine how Danato had come to that conclusion. Ethan jogged again to catch up with him. "You want to explain that logic to me?"

"I need to know if you possess any power."

"Power?"

"Magic," Danato clarified.

"You want to know if I have any magic? You mean other than a knack for spell casting at weddings?"

"It's not just that." Danato stopped outside Mezula's cell. She was naturally standing at her bars, waiting for them, arms looped through the metal like she was leaning out a window. "I need to know if Ethan is a mage."

"You think I'm a mage?" Ethan asked, waiting for the punchline to this awful joke.

Mezula perked her brow and looked back at Ethan. "Ooh, this just got interesting."

"And I need to know if anyone is controlling him."

"Oh, no, now it is interesting." Mezula winked at Ethan, but turned her attention to Danato.

Ethan scoffed. "You do realize she has read me multiple times during our year in the bubble?"

"She was cleaning the house, not exploring. She could have missed something." Danato looked at Mezula for confirmation, and she nodded.

Mezula wiggled her fingers at Ethan. "I'd be happy to take a deeper look." She returned her hand to Danato and dragged a finger down his cheek. "My dear warden, you look heavy with stress. I do wish you would let me unburden you."

"Enough, Mezula. Do your job?"

She sighed and extended her hand to Ethan. "Come, boy, it's time to share your deepest, darkest thoughts with Mama."

Despite the odd request, Ethan stepped forward and took her hand without hesitation. He didn't want Danato to think he was doing anything to prevent the truth from coming out. He wanted the truth to come out. He had no wish to keep secrets. Not from him. Not from Cori.

Just as Mezula closed her eyes to begin, Danato reached through the bars and grabbed her neck. Her eyes flapped open, and she stared at him with wide eyes. "Skip the theatrics, or you'll go a month without clean sheets. Understand?"

Mezula pursed her lips and harrumphed. "Fine," she said, narrowing her eyes and shaking his hand away from her neck. She closed her eyes again, but instead of the electrical shock that usually accompanied her reads, Ethan felt nothing.

After a moment, she released him and examined him. "There is something blocking me."

"Blocking you?" Danato asked. "Can you get past it?"

"I can't, but whatever it is, it isn't a foreign presence. Just a hypnotic suggestion of sorts."

"Is it controlling him?"

"Not in the least, save perhaps preventing him from admitting what you want him to."

"Is he a mage?"

"Magic is difficult to detect in the mind, especially when it is naturally occurring. Even those with a skill for it would have difficulty sensing a mage."

"How much do you know about mages? Have you ever encountered one?"

Mezula tipped her head up to the ceiling as if recounting every person she had ever met. "I recall many witches and more than a few enchantresses, but I can't think of any mages. But then that is what a mage would want."

"What do you mean?" Danato asked.

"Mages are reputed to be excellent at concealment. I imagine I could have met a hundred in my life prior to being incarcerated and never known it. I'm not sure if Ethan is a mage, but he definitely fits the profile. That is assuming you've actually seen him perform magic. That is the most important qualifier."

"I have performed two spells in my life. One by accident and one with the assistance of a witch." Ethan explained.

Mezula looked at Danato and then back at him. "I think you'll find that Danato can think of a third time."

"What?" Ethan shifted, trying to see the expression on Danato's face.

"Dear, sweet Ethan. I really hope that you are a mage. Because short of that, nothing is likely to prevent that bomb outside from exploding."

"First, you think I caused the breach; now you think I can fix it." Ethan looked at Danato. "Well, which is it? Am I the good guy or the bad guy?"

Danato stared at him, eyes locked on him, but he wasn't mad. The roiling emotions in his gaze were contemplative and worrisome. "When has life here ever been as simple as that?" Danato waited a moment more before turning his eyes to the floor. "Go home, Ethan.

Until further notice, your duties in this prison are suspended."

"What?" Ethan scoffed. "You can't just—"

"I can, and I did."

Ethan smiled and nodded as he backed away from Danato. He let out a small chuckle and looked at Mezula. "Did you see this coming?" he asked her.

"Oh, honey, no one saw this coming," Mezula answered in a soft, sympathetic whisper.

39

IT WASN'T TRUE THAT no one saw this coming. There was at least one resident of the prison who had seen his future. One who had prepared him for it. Except the betrayal he had been warned about was from the wrong person.

"Is it true?" Ethan yelled up at the statuesque beast before him. Penelope had taken up her position with the rest of the dragons, who were now inside the courtyard of the compound. He wasn't sure how Belus would feel about having the ass end of a dragon in view from his kitchen window, but it wasn't like he could ask them to move. The dragons quietly sang to the four corners of the earth in low hums that, in unison, sounded like a didgeridoo. He looked at the other three female dragons, each standing stock still, with their necks stretched high. In the center of them, the snow had receded, revealing more of the patch of green grass that had apparently grown in size since their arrival.

Ethan moved to the green growth and kneeled to touch it. He expected to feel something when he touched it, but it was just grass. "What's happening here?" he asked.

The vessel must be protected.

Ethan turned back to Penelope, but she hadn't moved. Her mind was present, but the rest of her body was in perpetual ceremony.

"The vessel is dead."

The vessel will hold the power until the threat has passed.

"What threat?"

We will guard the vessel until it is time.

Ethan sighed. She was talking in circles again, telling him just enough to pique his curiosity but not enough to satisfy it. "Danato thinks I'm a mage. Is he right?"

Penelope's head dipped down slowly, and she looked at him with her big golden eyes. *Why do you think we chose you?* Ethan flushed and took a step back. He hadn't expected her to confirm the suspicion. *We are the guardians of the earth. You are her shepherd.*

"Why didn't you tell me this before? Why didn't I know?"

The magic is not your true nature. Until you accept it, the forces within you will remain buried and hidden.

"Did Annette know I was a mage?"

Mages are undetectable—even to themselves.

"What did you intend for me to do with this power?"

We seek a resolution.

"To what?"

To the imbalance.

"You want me to stop the breach?"

The breach is necessary.

"The breach could destroy us."

The breach will save you.

Ethan looked back at the grass, somewhat hopefully. "Is she still alive?"

The vessel is not living but does have life.

Ethan sighed, disappointed that the dragon was back to nonsensical explanations. He assumed that the beast was speaking in the grander sense—that all things have life. He was tempted to dig up the earth and see for himself what was transpiring beneath the green grass, but he suspected that was why the dragons had arrived. They would prevent anyone from disturbing the incubation of the magical pressure.

"Why won't you allow me to tell Danato that I'm speaking to you?"

We have not forbidden your speech.

"Then why do I have a block in my brain?"

It was not placed by us. We do not meddle with the mind.

"Except to eavesdrop," Ethan mumbled. "If you didn't place it, then who did?"

You.

"Why would I place a block in my own mind?"

That is a question to ask yourself.

Ethan considered that question on his walk home. He was certain he hadn't placed any kind of block, but considering he was a mage and didn't even know it, then perhaps he had. But why? Was he determined to keep everyone else from knowing what his motives were?

Or was he simply avoiding the truth about himself? Was that possible? Could he have lied to everyone around him because he wanted to lie to himself?

Or was he doing it to protect himself—to avoid the same fate as wizards and sorcerers?

Ethan stepped through the door to his home, walking in on an argument between Cori and Danato. They both turned to look at him, faces constricted and red. The lights flickered, and the chandelier over the table swung back and forth. The room was intolerably hot on one side from the blazing fire in the hearth, while the kitchen seemed to emanate cold like someone had left all the windows open.

Ethan didn't have to ask what this fight was about. It was about him. Who he was. The man Danato suspected him to be.

He hated that Danato's suspicion had pitted him against Cori. This secret was dividing them. And it wasn't worth it. No secret was worth this.

He took in a deep breath and focused on the very act of speaking. Thinking the words and opening his mouth to release them. "I've just spoken with Penelope." The moment the words were out, Ethan felt something shift inside of his mind—as if the mental block was literally opening a door for him. "She's confirmed your suspicions. I am a mage."

40

"**A**RE YOU KIDDING ME?**"** Sophie rasped from behind her desk. The oversized mahogany furnishing took up three-quarters of the room, leaving Heaton, Gypsy, Nevia, and the transmorph just enough room to squeeze through the front door to talk to his human resources director. AKA the woman who tells him where to go and when. "She can't stay here."

"You have a temporary holding facility on sight, don't you?" Heaton asked.

"Yes, but..." Sophie glanced at the woman in Gypsy's grasp. She looked downtrodden, as if she had finally accepted her fate. Of course, that meant nothing, since she was probably a transmorph. Everything out of their faces was a lie—including their faces. "No one has used it in years."

"Does it lock?" Nevia asked.

"Yes." Sophie shifted back in her seat, returning to her usual perfect posture. "I don't have a problem with the facility. I have a problem with babysitting."

"It's only a few hours away. We will be back tonight to collect her and be on the next truck out."

"Why can't you just take the transmorph to... you know where and then go to your doctor's appointment?"

"It's urgent," Heaton said.

"Then split up," Sophie squawked.

Heaton took a cleansing breath and leaned forward. "She's my partner. My other partner is in... you know where. If we split up, then we are just two people going to potentially dangerous places by ourselves."

"We could always just take her with us," Gypsy suggested. "Stuff her in the trunk." Heaton threw her a glare. "What, she's a transmorph, she'll fit."

"Why is she here? Again!" Sophie objected. "This is supposed to be a top-secret operation."

Gypsy chuckled. "Sweetheart, I probably know more about this top-secret operation than you do."

"Oh, really?" Sophie tipped her head in disbelief.

"She was the one who suggested we use the holding facility," Heaton admitted. "I had actually forgotten about it." Sophie stared at him. "Like you said, we haven't used it in years."

Sophie's annoyance faded, and she reached back to her file cabinet. She opened a drawer and leafed through the file folders until she found the one she wanted. She dragged out a manila envelope and opened it up. She pulled out a skeleton key with a rubber grip and a pink form to go with it. She set it on the desk in front of Heaton.

"We're kind of in a hurry, Sophie. Can we skip the paperwork?"

"You already know the answer to that. Maybe your girls could go ahead and get her secured for you." Sophie handed the key off to Nevia. "Here you go, Jordan. I'm sure Miss Gypsum can show you the way."

Gypsy gave her a broad smile. "As a matter of fact, I can." She shoved the transmorph forward, guiding her out the door. Nevia followed after her, leaving Heaton to his paperwork.

When they were both gone, Sophie smacked her hand over the pink sheet and ripped it away from him. "Don't fill that out. It's a requisition for toilet paper."

Heaton frowned. "You put the toilet paper requisitions with your cell keys?"

"Not the point, Heaton." Sophie shoved the paper back in her envelope and tossed it to the side of her desk. "Listen, does it not bother you at all that this woman is just suddenly in our lives, in our business?"

"She's actually been quite helpful."

"But why?" Sophie whispered. "Why is this rogue military group suddenly interested in werewolves and our prison?"

"I've been asking those questions since I met her, but she can't answer any of them."

"That's my point. Neither can any of the higher-ups. I've been investigating this little divergence in our otherwise extremely zipped-mouth group, and no one seems to know anything about her or her group."

Heaton cleared his throat and glanced back at the door. "Are you saying... What are you saying?"

Sophie frowned and looked around the office. "I thought that I would be done with this position in six months, like the rest of the up-and-comers. Something changed, though. They stopped bringing in new people. Nevia was the last hunter to be recruited. I've been trying to fill over a dozen empty positions around here. The American constituencies have lost nearly fifty men in the last year, but the board refuses to hire anyone new."

"So, are we talking budget cuts?"

Sophie smiled and shook her head. "You know, it's just silly. I'm sure it's nothing. I'm just inventing gossip."

Heaton reached back and shut the door to her office. "I've known you long enough to know that you don't gossip. You're a pretty no-nonsense woman." Heaton braced his hands to lean over the desk. "If you have something to say or a concern I should know about, say it."

Sophie's smile dimmed, and she looked down at her desk. "The money is still there. It's just shifting in a different direction. At first, it was just because Danato lost his upstairs tenant, but now they have one, and the money hasn't shifted back."

"I don't understand. The prison is still getting supplies, right?"

"Oh, yeah, they aren't in danger of starving or anything... yet. This is all about next year's budget. They send out a report every few months updating anticipated expenses. I'm supposed to go over everything with a fine-tooth comb to make sure I'm not being allotted a penny more than can be accounted for. It lists everything in detail, including Danato's budget."

"And how much are they anticipating the prison will need next year?"

"Twenty percent of what they usually do."

"You mean twenty percent less?"

"No, I mean only twenty percent of what they normally require."

"That's got to be a glitch. Twenty percent would barely keep the lights on, let alone maintain the food and supplies."

"Actually..." Sophie shifted uneasily in her chair. "Twenty percent is almost exactly what it takes to feed the chrono-tear. If that's all they are allocating for next year, it pretty much means that they are not anticipating any expenses related to the prison or its personnel." Sophie cupped her hands together on her desk and stared at him. Heaton stared back at her, his mind spinning a thousand different scenarios. "You're a good guy, Heaton. I just want you to be on the lookout—for the sake of job security. You know, get your resume in order." She was downplaying her concerns, but Heaton could see the worry on her face, and it had nothing to do with the condition of his resume.

Heaton nodded and shifted off the desk. "I'm sure they're just waiting to put the numbers in until after the audit." He rapped his knuckles on her desk. Sophie nodded and gave him a thin smile. Neither of them agreed with that explanation, but they were happy to delude themselves with it for the time being. "But you will warn me if I need to... beef up my resume?"

Sophie lost her smile and nodded. "Yes, of course."

Heaton left her office and headed down the hall. He didn't even want to think about the prison's state of unrest, especially while Daniel was still a prisoner there. Then again, if there was going to be a shutdown, perhaps Daniel would be the best man to have on site.

41

GYPSY HELPED DIRECT THE transmorph down the hall to the holding facility. As laughable as the little cage tucked inside one of the office rooms was, it did have an intricate system of bare wires running across the surface. Whatever it lacked in strength, it made up for in pain.

As Nevia unlocked the cell door, the woman began to struggle as if she was only just figuring out what they intended to do with her. "No, you can't do this," she whimpered. "I haven't done anything wrong. I haven't done anything wrong!"

"You are encasing a human," Nevia responded flatly as if she had had this conversation with many other transmorphs and didn't have enough energy to do the cop routine it demanded.

"No, you don't understand. It's not like that." The woman flailed, nearly throwing Gypsy out of her grasp. As it was, her skin was feeling slick from sweat or whatever else the damn thing might secrete.

"Oh, please don't tell me that this is a symbiotic relationship." Nevia shook her head. "I just can't take any more bullshit from you. I can smell you a mile away."

"Okay, I'll admit that I am a transmorph, but I am not encasing."

"Then prove it." Nevia crossed her arms and leaned on the cage entrance. "Do the butterfly thing?"

"I can't do that."

"You got hold of her, Gypsy?" Nevia asked, and she nodded. She stepped forward, and the transmorph stiffened. She turned around and backed into the woman. "There you go. Your retractiles must be going nuts. Go ahead, spread your wings."

Gypsy heard the girl scoff. "I can't."

"Because you already have a human inhabitant. There's no more room."

"No, because I'm not capable of that movement. I can't even change my face that much."

Nevia turned back to the woman. "What kind of transmorph can't change her face?"

"The kind made of bone." The woman braced against Gypsy, lifted her legs, and kicked Nevia back into the cage. Before Gypsy could even think about retaliation, the woman's arms, slick as snakes, ripped from her grasp.

The transmorph shut the door to the cell, and the latch clicked into place. Nevia moved back to unlock it again, but the excess of wires, suddenly now activated by the cell's occupant, was impeding her progress.

The transmorph whipped around to face Gypsy. Her eyes were bright, almost yellow, with anticipation of the fight. Gypsy wondered if she shouldn't have been more prepared to fight transmorphs. Werewolves were one thing; their bodies were hard and muscular. All she had to do was duck and brace for impact. Transmorphs, on the other hand, were soft and malleable; even if she could get in a good punch, what damage could she possibly do?

To her surprise, the woman didn't attack. She only darted back and forth, trying to get around her to the exit. "Please! You have to let me go! They'll kill me. Don't let them take me to the doth seola."

"The what?" Gypsy was at a loss for the definition. The transmorph saw her distraction and leaped toward the door. Gypsy gave it her all with one powerful punch. The woman's head snapped back. The sound of her nose cracking reverberated through the hollow room.

The redhead yelped and stumbled back, cradling her bloody nose. She was instantly back to crying. Gypsy followed her as she backpedaled, prepared to hit her again, but when the woman reached the wall, she just hunkered down and bawled.

Gypsy reached out her hand, and Nevia maneuvered the key through the wires for her. She unlocked the cage and let the very perturbed Nevia out. "See," she said. "You can never trust transmorphs."

Gypsy would have to agree, but she was still surprised by the ache in her knuckles. Transmorphs were reputed to have more cartilage than bone. And although the woman's nose shattered like cartilage, the face that backed it up seemed as hard as a human skull. At least judging by the throbbing in her hand.

42

G YPSY AND HEATON SAT inside a small waiting area with stale coffee and magazines older than the invention of paper. She had gone back and forth on the coffee, debating the need for caffeine over the torture of her taste buds. She opted for the caffeine and sank back down in her chair to face Heaton.

She could see his muscles tense as he nibbled on the inside of his cheek. He didn't like waiting, certainly not when his partner was on the other side of the door going through God knows what. She admired his devotion to his friend, but she couldn't quite understand how the three of them could function in the field with such close relationships. How did any of them keep their heads on straight during a crisis? Of course, that was probably why Daniel was in jail.

"You never told me what Daniel did to get himself locked up again."

Heaton looked up at her, surprised by the question, or insulted; she wasn't sure which. He looked down and shook his head. "He hurt someone. A human."

"Got in the way of the death eyes?"

"Sort of." Heaton effectively shrugged away the conversation and picked up a magazine to read.

Gypsy smiled at the subtle "fuck off." He should have just said it. Subtlety was not her strong suit. Even when she recognized it, she rarely abided by it. If someone wanted something from her, they just had to ask. Whether it be "fuck off" or "fuck me," simplicity was the key to getting her to comply.

She glanced back at the receptionist behind the glass pass-through window. Even if she were paying attention to them, the earbuds blasting rock music into her ears would have prevented her from eavesdropping.

"That transmorph, she said something to me."

"I can only imagine." Heaton rolled his eyes. "Don't believe anything they say."

"I get that, but she said something I didn't understand. I think it was in reference to Daniel."

Heaton chuckled. "Daniel has a reputation. Her kind is not fond of him."

"She called him a doth seola. What does that mean?"

Heaton's eyes landed on her and didn't move. She could see him debating the next sentence carefully. His following words could very well end up being that "fuck off" he had been too polite to say earlier. She kept her face blank so he couldn't determine her question to be nosy. It was merely a casual inquiry that would save her a trip to the dictionary later.

"It means dead soul," he said and immediately went back to flipping through his magazine. "It comes from a time when they still believed the eyes were the window to the soul. All that bullshit."

She waited for his page-turning to lessen before she spoke again. "Dead soul. That sounds like a name for a supervillain in a comic book."

"Daniel is not a villain," Heaton defended. "He's a good man."

"Daniel is definitely unique. And seeing him in action is singular, but I think you know as well as I do that good and bad have more to do with circumstance than morality."

Heaton stared back at her. He was about to skip the "fuck off" and go straight to punching her in the face. She settled back against her chair. "You're right, though. He is a good man. If only because he knows he isn't."

Heaton's gaze burned into her. "And what about you? What side of that line do you fall on? Are you a good person, or just playing at being one?"

Gypsy smiled, unable to resist seeing his anger as flirtation. It really was such a waste that he preferred men. They had too many flare-ups in their interactions to be alleviated by handshakes alone. One or two hard turns through the sheets would have gotten them back on track in an instant.

She opened her mouth to answer, but the swinging door near the reception window popped open, and an older man came out. "Are you with Nevia?" He removed the green mask from his mouth, which blended perfectly with the light green scrubs he was wearing.

"Yeah." Heaton jumped up. "Is she okay?"

"Yes, we are still going to run a few more tests on her, but we are ready to offer the answers she is seeking. She said it would be easier if you joined us for the diagnosis." His accent was a little more Swedish, she thought, than English, but she had long since given up trying to dissect the crossover dialects. As long as she could understand the words, she couldn't care less what inflection was put on them.

"She's okay, though, right?"

"Yes, this kind of thing is my specialty. You were wise to bring her here."

"What exactly is your specialty?" Heaton asked.

"Please." The man motioned for them to come through the door.

Heaton passed through the double door. Gypsy gave up on her coffee altogether and went with him. She wasn't sure Nevia had included her in the invitation, but she was bored as hell and had no intention of staying put.

"I am Dr. Reine, by the way." The man took up the lead again, guiding them down the narrow wood-paneled hallway. "I will be taking care of Nevia from here on out. If you should ever have a problem with her, you are to call me. Is that understood?"

"What sort of problems would we have?" Gypsy took the liberty of asking after they passed an exam room with stirrups familiar to a gynecologist's office.

"Violence, aberrant sexual aggression, much the same as, I imagine, brought you here today."

Gypsy did a double take on another exam room they passed. The table was twice the size of a regular exam table, and the stainless-steel surface was marred with deep scratches. "What the hell do you do here?" she asked, not willing to let the observation go unanswered for.

Dr. Reine glanced back at her and sighed. "Werewolves need doctors, too. In some cases, surgeons. As you know, they are difficult patients to work with. Please have a seat in my office." He motioned to a room on his right. Yet another wood-paneled paradise. "I'll be with you shortly." He stepped through the door that capped the hallway. She only caught a glimpse of the white, sterile floor and transparent plastic curtains before the door shut again. The door read "Personnel Only" and had several translations.

"This place seems like a back alley abortion clinic," Heaton mumbled and moved into the tiny office to take a seat.

Gypsy stepped inside and shut the door behind her. She looked down at the chair and wondered if she could stand to sit another minute, let alone repeat the last hour and a half. "Maybe it is," she said haphazardly.

"What do you mean?" Heaton looked up at her, suddenly very interested in her interpretation.

She sighed and shrugged. "I don't think it's hinky or anything, but it would explain the problem."

"What would explain the problem?"

She sighed, wishing for once she had kept her mouth shut. "Didn't it occur to you that the reason she's having such a sudden hormonal imbalance is that she might be pregnant?"

"Pregnant?"

"Come on, Heaton. Don't play dumb just because you have a penis. There are only three things that make a woman's hormones freak out: menstruation, pregnancy, and menopause."

"Shit." He lowered his head into his hands. "If she's pregnant. I can't have her working with me."

"Well, maybe that won't be a problem after we're done here."

Heaton raised his head and blinked at her. "You don't think she would... She can't do that. Daniel would be devastated." Heaton stood up as if he were about to rush into the personnel-only zone and rip the speculum right out of her.

"Whoa, easy!" Gypsy held up her hands and blocked the door. "We're just guessing here. And even if we weren't, this is her decision."

"She's not in any position to make that decision right now."

"If that's the case, she's in the only position to make that decision." Gypsy pushed on his chest. "Her life might depend on it."

Heaton frowned. "This day is beginning to suck."

"Beginning?" Gypsy asked just as the door popped open, bumping into her shoulder. She shuffled out of the way so Dr. Reine and Nevia could get into the room.

Dr. Reine took the swivel chair behind the desk. Gypsy motioned for her to take the seat next to Heaton when she didn't readily sit down. She looked a little embarrassed, so Gypsy leaned in behind her. "Do you want me to go?"

Nevia turned back enough to acknowledge she had heard her. There was a slight pause, but she shook her head. Gypsy wasn't sure if she preferred to have her company or if she just wanted a female in the room to balance things out.

"So, before we get started..." Dr. Reine clasped his hands together. "I assume we all understand that this is a private facility. The things that go on here are not to be mentioned in mixed company."

"We're all trustworthy," Heaton summed up.

"Good, then I think we should talk about two different options for Nevia's care. The first option is that we treat her lunar cycle much as we do a full-blood werewolf. She would simply need to be detained for approximately three days. One day in advance to the full moon, and at least four hours after the sunrise following."

Heaton glanced at Nevia, but neither of them seemed to like that idea. "What's the other option?" he asked.

"The other option is a hormonal replacement program that is only in its infancy. I have used it on many fem-wolves, partial-breeds such as Nevia, and pure-bloods. We have been getting amazing results. Unfortunately, at this stage, it would require a biweekly visit to our facility. I'm guessing that in your line of work, it would be even more inconvenient than caging. And, of course, there's the cost. As you might imagine, we are underfunded for our services, so we unfortunately have to put the lion's portion of our bills on our clients."

Heaton sighed and leaned back in his chair. "How long will we have to do this?"

Dr. Reine exchanged a worried look with Nevia. "Every case has varying degrees of severity—"

"How long?" Heaton asked again.

"For the remainder of her life." Heaton slumped upon hearing that news. Nevia didn't seem as surprised.

"The werewolf endocrine system is very complicated. We are making great strides in understanding the lunar impact, but as of now, we are still trying to fight magical influences with internal medicine. You can guess how well that works."

"Is she..." Heaton glanced at Nevia, giving her an apologetic look before asking his question. "Is she safe to be around? I mean, will she ever turn?"

Dr. Reine cleared his throat and scanned a paper in his chart with figures and numbers on it. "Her issues appear to be fully hormonal at present. I see no evidence of hair growth, muscular hydration, bone decalcification, or nerve retardation. She has an abnormally thick muscular structure, even for a werewolf, and her tissue has an internal matrix that... Well, bulletproof to sum it up in layman's terms." Dr. Reine smiled at Nevia, his eyes creasing with delight at her anatomical beauty. "Anyway," the doctor said, returning his diminishing smile to Heaton. "She technically has the ability to change—to some degree, but so far, her structure shows no sign of a transformation. My guess is she will never change."

Heaton breathed a sigh of relief and fell back into his chair. Despite the good news, Nevia did not relax. Her breathing hastened slightly, and she gripped the arms of her chair even more tightly.

"And?" Gypsy probed further, since Heaton's state of mind was too deep into his own worries to be objective. Dr. Reine once again drew his smiling eyes from Nevia. "What caused this sudden change in temperament?"

Dr. Reine shifted uncomfortably in his chair. "A hormonal shift such as this could be caused by—"

"Is she pregnant?"

Nevia took in a deep breath and looked back at Gypsy. She didn't seem angry, but she was obviously appalled by her question. Either she was overstepping her bounds, or Nevia hadn't thought to ask this question herself.

The doctor stared at Gypsy, his eyes skirting over her, trying to interpret her character based on her outward appearance. When he couldn't find her translation written on her clothes, he gave up.

He closed his chart file and turned his attention to his patient. "I was not certain if you wished to discuss the remainder of your diagnosis?"

"Remainder?" Heaton shifted up straight again. "What haven't you told us?" Heaton looked at Nevia. "Are you pregnant?"

Gypsy could have punched the man right then and there for the glimmer of hope and excitement on his face when he asked that question. He was a fool not to see what was coming next. If not for her extensive studies on werewolf anatomy and maturation, she would have been just as blindsided as him.

"It's okay," Nevia whispered. "I don't like secrets."

"Are you sure?" Dr. Reine asked.

"Please, just tell them so I don't have to."

Heaton leaned forward as the doctor spoke.

"We have determined that Nevia *was* pregnant. Just a couple of months along, but it was likely miscarried recently. Due to the fragile nature of her hormonal fluctuations, I have advised her to suspend her efforts to get pregnant. I believe that all of her pregnancies will result in miscarriages, even with hormonal therapy. Her physiology, unfortunately, is not compatible with motherhood."

Heaton rubbed his face before looking at Nevia. "That's alright. It's not like she doesn't have options. Her werewolf side may not want to be a mother, but that doesn't mean her human side agrees. What about a surrogate? Could another woman carry her eggs?"

Nevia gave Heaton a somber expression that in a more emotional woman might have resulted in a flood of tears.

"The issue here is not Nevia's fertility. I'm certain that it would be possible for her to provide offspring through other methods. However, she would have very little time left to raise it."

"What are you talking about?" Heaton stared at the doctor.

"As you know, werewolves have a diminished lifespan."

"She's not a werewolf. She's human!" Heaton stood as if he might attack the doctor. Gypsy moved forward and placed a heavy hand on his shoulder. He tried to shrug her off, but she kept it firmly in place.

"No, sir, she is not." Dr. Reine pushed back his chair and stood, calmly meeting Heaton's level. "I understand your perception. You are thinking of her heritage as a combination of two races. You understand that a single drop of black in white forever makes gray. However, that is not the case here. Werewolf physiology is always dominant. It may be subdued in one way, but it is almost always exacerbated in another. We frequently refer to persons such as Nevia as partial-breeds or, in her mother's case, a half-breed. This is extremely inaccurate, though, because werewolf DNA does not thin when added to human DNA. The transmutation process is generally quelled, but that does not mean she is human. You see, Mr. Reid, Nevia, and those like her are not a mixture, resulting in gray. They are just painted white. On the inside, they are still pure black. Nevia is a full-blooded werewolf, whether she changes during the full moon or not."

"Heaton," Nevia whispered, and he looked down at her. "I'm dying."

Heaton's shoulder sank in Gypsy's grip, and she let her hand slide away. For a long moment, he just stood there, staring at her—though he wasn't really seeing her. His mind was flipping through the conversation, looking for an emergency exit, and all the while closing up the access to his heart. He would try, as all men do, to fix the problem instead of preparing for the pain that it would cause.

"I don't understand," he finally admitted. "You said that you had a treatment."

"I do," Dr. Reine confirmed, "but it is not a cure." He sat back down in his chair and motioned for Heaton to sit. After he had, the doctor continued his explanation. "The flood of hormones that Nevia is being subjected to on a monthly basis is designed to inflate her body. During these transformations, the majority of the brain is shut down, and the werewolf functions only with his or her hindbrain. This is the reason for their animalistic behavior. There is no memory in this part of the brain, so all they know is instinct and survival until the transformation wears off. It's also why they retain no memory of their change.

"The blackouts and abrupt anger that Nevia has experienced are an indication that her hormones are affecting the connection between her brain stem and her frontal cortex. This blocking effect is only temporary, but the damage being created is permanent. The hormone therapies that I am suggesting will reduce the impact of her monthly lunar cycle and eliminate her female cycle entirely. However, as I said, this is not a cure. It will prolong her life, but the degradation will continue to—"

"How long does she have?" Gypsy asked.

Dr. Reine stared at her. He opened his mouth to say something, but stopped. Gypsy sensed that his efforts to stay optimistic were wearing thin. He took a deep breath. "With intensive therapy and stress management, I could foresee Nevia living well into her twenty-eighth year."

Gypsy could hear the strained hope in Dr. Reine's voice, and she knew that twenty-eight was already a stretch. Heaton leaped from his chair and walked out of the room. Doors slammed in his wake, all the way to the front entrance of the building.

Nevia's eyes shifted to the floor, and Gypsy could see her body shake. Once again, she would have anticipated the theatrical tears of a woman in despair, but Gypsy knew better than to fetch tissues for her. Those eyes would sooner bleed than cry.

However, that didn't mean the woman wasn't in anguish. While Heaton was dealing with his own grief, she was confronting the mortality of her existence by way of the complete obliteration of her human identity.

Gypsy moved to Heaton's seat and pulled it away from the desk. She sat down, propped her feet up on the doctor's day calendar, and crossed her arms.

"So, our little pet werewolf is going feral." Gypsy's dismissive tone and belligerent attitude drew Nevia's hardest gaze. She ignored her rearing anger and spoke only to the doctor. "I'm told that feral wolves have to be put down." Dr. Reine looked between the two women, no doubt appalled by everything Gypsy was offering to this situation. "Unfortunately, Jordan is a very valuable member of the prison's hunting staff. Losing her would set back transmorph detection to the sticks and stones stage of this war. We can't lose her, and we certainly can't have her leashed to a goddamn transfusion machine every fucking month. Talk to me about our options."

Gypsy glanced at Nevia and noticed that her anger had subsided. She lifted her nose slightly, breathing in Gypsy's scent. Even after all this time, she was trying to figure her out. Searching for the core of her motivations. Much like Callin, she wanted to dig deep, past the darkness and into the center of her aberrant personality. Unfortunately, there wasn't a scent profile for her convoluted version of morality.

Dr. Reine nodded and opened his file again. "I can provide Nevia with a hormone blocker. Rather than draining the existing hormones, it will block them. It will provide the same reduction of damage and slow her disconnection."

"Great! Set us up with a batch." Gypsy jumped up to leave.

"However!" Dr. Reine said firmly and also jumped to his feet.

"Always a fucking catch," Gypsy mumbled before turning her attention back to the doctor.

"The stressors that frequently lead werewolves to an early grave will be especially concerning for her. She must limit her stress or the hormone blockers will be useless."

"What do you mean limit her stress?" Gypsy frowned. "She's a bounty hunter, for Christ's sake."

Dr. Reine's mouth twisted as if he was reluctant to speak. His anger seemed to be rearing up. Gypsy could tell he wasn't used to speaking his mind, so it was taking him a moment to get the words out. "If Nevia goes feral, she will not die as other werewolves do in a final exhaustive transformation." Dr. Reine paused, letting that nugget of truth set into Gypsy's cold brain. "But she will kill. There is no stopping that. I will report my findings to the council as I must, in good conscience, do. However, you were correct in your earlier statement. All feral wolves must be put down." Dr. Reine turned the last of his sympathy to Nevia. "It is the law and for good reason." Nevia nodded, understanding the burdens of her heritage. "I will get the medication." Dr. Reine left the office in search of the band-aid Nevia's condition required.

Gypsy dropped back down in the chair and stared at the wood-paneled walls. She wanted to storm out like Heaton had. She wanted to pound the walls and demand that the world be changed by man's will alone.

She wasn't kidding that Nevia's loss would set back the war with the transmorphs. Her boss would not like this. Not one bit.

43

"**N**EED ANY HELP WITH her?" Gypsy offered when she saw Heaton struggle to get a grip on the transmorph after taking her out of the cage.

"Nope." Heaton switched one hand to grip the woman's hair. She yelped as he yanked her head back hard. Gypsy smiled at his disregard for the usual male gallantry. As far as she was concerned, it was just a turn-on.

What a waste.

"We are going to take her straight to the prison, anyway. I'm pretty sure Danato would have a fit if we showed up with you again. Especially when he finds out that your block didn't take."

"Well, what can I say? I have a good memory."

"You should stop while you're still ahead," the transmorph said to Heaton.

"Yeah, whatever," Heaton pushed her toward the hall.

The woman struggled against Heaton, turning to face Gypsy as she passed her. "I see what you're doing, but you won't succeed."

"What is she talking about?" Gypsy asked.

"The downfall of interactions with transmorphs," Nevia said. "She's just trying to get into your head."

"Relinquish this fight, and I will take pity on your friends," the transmorph fumed.

"Sweetheart, you are barking up the wrong tree. I am not helping you?"

"I wasn't talking to you, Grace." The redhead snarled at her. "I would never ask for your help. I see what you are. You're a demon. You swallowed the world's pain in one bite with nary a tear."

Gypsy barked out a laugh. "Excuse me, I swallowed what?"

"You belong in hell with the doth seola."

"Don't listen to her," Heaton finally yanked her away, forcing another yelp from her after they were out the door.

Gypsy headed that way as well, but stopped as she neared Nevia. "What's the deal with the transmorphs and Daniel, anyway? What is a doth seola?"

Nevia frowned. "He doesn't like that name."

"I'm sure not; it makes him sound like a Star Wars character, but what exactly is a dead soul to the transmorphs?"

Nevia took a breath and let it out slowly. "A devil."

Gypsy smiled. "They believe Daniel is Satan?"

"No, not the Devil, a devil. Transmorphs believe that Satan sent demons up from hell to kill them. They also believe that God gave them the ability to change their faces to hide from them."

"Oh goody, the transmorphs are religious zealots."

"That's not even the half of it. Some of them actually believe that they are a crossbreed between humans and angels, which is why they were blessed with the ability to change their faces. To disguise their true hybrid angelic form from Satan's minions."

"Oh, make it stop. Don't tell me; when they kill their victims, they believe it's petitioned by God."

"To be fair, not all of them kill, but I imagine the ones that do would tell you they do it because they enjoy it. They just can't resist."

"Eating a doughnut or screwing your therapist is something you just can't resist. Sucking another being up inside of you and mummifying them while you mind rape them is not something anyone should have trouble resisting." Nevia looked at her, analyzing her features. "What?"

"Nothing, you just seem a little more animated on this topic than usual."

"I take issue with religious freedoms. I'm still pissed off about the reformation." Nevia gave her a weak smile. She wondered if the woman's face would break if her smile ever pushed into her cheeks. "I suppose she got to me a little with that psychic crap."

"Don't worry about it. She probably calls everyone she doesn't like a demon."

"No, that's not what bothered me." Gypsy clenched her jaw.

"What then?"

"I think that bitch just left a message for my boss, using me as the answering machine." Gypsy glared out the door the transmorph had just been dragged through. "Which means they know what he knows."

"What do you mean?"

Gypsy looked at Nevia and, for a moment, allowed herself to take in her sharp facial features. It was hard to imagine the wolf inside of her. Gypsy would sooner peg her to be a vampire than a lycanthrope.

While Heaton was still lingering in the throes of denial about Nevia's diagnosis, Gypsy was settling into her bed of acceptance. Death had never been something she feared. She faced it daily, on occasion shaking hands with a reaper only to arrive back in the world of the living. It was just routine now. But for others, death was not a welcome sight.

Gypsy understood what the doctor meant by reducing Nevia's stress. Every werewolf she knew, save perhaps Callin, would throw themselves into the path of conflict at the drop of a hat. It was an adrenaline rush laced with testosterone. That was what drove their bodies to an early death—not just the burden of the change itself, but the mental fatigue of being inundated by mind-altering hormones. While testosterone can increase the cognition of a human, it has the opposite effect in a werewolf. To say they get stupider would be an understatement.

In the end, all wolves go feral. The mind, much like the body, can no longer bounce back. They fall victim to a final change that morphs their body past the point of even the most absurd levels of water retention. And then... they burst.

Gypsy could already see the future. The choice she might be faced with. She usually relished the idea of killing a bad wolf, but this was not the face she pictured in her fantasies. Nevia was not the blood she craved.

"What does your boss know?" the fem-wolf asked.

Gypsy tapped her head. "I couldn't say even if I wanted to."

Nevia stared at her, no doubt sensing the lie, but she didn't call her out on it. "Until we meet again."

Gypsy looked down at Nevia's extended hand. She pressed her palm to hers, admiring the soft skin as she squeezed her a little too tight. "Take care of yourself."

An odd crooked smile threatened to crease the woman's perfect stone face. There was even a slight glisten in her eyes. Could it be she possessed tear ducts after all? "Goodbye, Grace."

Gypsy's face twitched as Nevia slipped her hand from hers. "Goodbye, Nevia." The words felt strained and far more meaningful than any two indifferent people should require in an exchange as simple as a farewell, but it was not entirely surprising. Nevia had skipped the other stages of grief as well and crawled straight into that bed of acceptance with Gypsy. Huddled together, they were ready for the inevitable, even if no one else was.

44

ADMITTING HE WAS A mage was one thing, but acknowledging he was speaking to the dragons was something else entirely. After a quick recap of his experiences with the dragons, minus a few details involving the prediction about Cori, Danato called Belus in to get his opinion on this revelation. By the time dinner rolled around, not only was everything out in the open, but all the animosity of the day had transformed into hunger.

Most of it, anyway.

"So, what happens now?" Ethan asked, scooping the mashed potatoes he had made into a smaller serving bowl that was more appropriate for passing around the table. He glanced back at Danato, who was making quick work of his deconstructed chicken pot pie on the stovetop. "I mean, I'm assuming that I've convinced you that I have no motives to destroy the prison or take over the human race."

Danato looked over at him and nodded. Ethan noticed Cori had stopped her salad preparation next to him to stare at Belus, who had taken up a stool to watch the meal preparation. Ethan looked at him for the same answer. Belus shrugged at him. "Never had a doubt in my mind."

Cori scoffed and dropped a pair of tongs into her bowl before taking it to the table. Belus watched her go with a look that Ethan rarely saw on the man. Amusement.

"What do you want to happen now?" Danato asked him.

"Well, if I'm a mage, I might have the ability to stop this breach... Should I practice or something?"

"I'm actually not sure." Danato shut the heat off his skillet and similarly dumped his chicken mixture into a suitable serving dish. "This is the type of question I usually ask Annette," Danato said solemnly before taking it to the table. Ethan followed him, putting his potatoes next to the other dishes. He took a seat across from Cori while Belus took a seat at the far end, opposite Danato's usual spot.

"Is Renee joining us?" Cori asked when Danato returned to the table with a basket of rolls.

"No, she's gone," he said.

"Am I the only one extremely happy about that?" she asked.

"No," Belus and Danato said in unison.

Ethan opted for a scoop of mashed potatoes over the rolls and poured a heaping serving of the gravy with veggies and chicken over it. As prescribed in Danato's original recipe, he crushed a fistful of potato chips over the top of that.

"When does our new renter arrive?" Cori asked, loading her plate with the same combination.

"After the full moon, apparently." Danato loaded his plate and perked a brow to offer Belus some of the main dish.

"Just the salad," Belus said, and Cori shoved the bowl down to him, making it crash into his plate. Ethan could sense the tension that had only been getting worse since Belus arrived. Danato, apparently dismayed by this behavior, put a hand over Cori's. Ethan was certain it was intended to remind her of her manners at the dinner table, but she ripped her hand out from under his and put it under the table where he couldn't touch it. Danato watched her for a long time, considering his next move. To his surprise, Cori held his gaze, not caving to her fear as she usually did. He could only imagine the conversations that had taken place outside of his earshot. If Danato was willing to kill a sorceress, what had he considered doing to a mage?

"It's okay, Cori." Her eyes latched onto him, prepared to be angry with him, too, but she seemed to release some of the anger when she saw the endearing look on his face. "They're just doing their jobs." Cori bit her lip, restraining whatever accusation was about to fly out of her mouth. "Listen to me, sweetness," he said softly, and she focused on him. "If I were doing anything to hurt you or our son, I would want them to stop me." Cori shook her head. "I know it seems like an impossibility that I would ever hurt you, but this place is full of impossible scenarios. Things that neither one of us can predict. It's their job to..." Ethan looked at Danato. He was holding his tongue, allowing Ethan to say his piece. "It's their job to assume the worst."

Cori looked away and dug into her food. Bite by bite, she shoveled her food in, ignoring proper etiquette until her mouth was too full even to swallow. She pressed her face into her hands and shook with quiet sobs. Ethan pushed back his chair and moved to her. He kneeled beside her and urged her to come out of hiding. When she finally did, she melted over his shoulder and wept.

Ethan rose, bringing Cori upright with him. He looked at Danato. "I think we just need some time to regroup." Danato nodded, and Ethan took Cori upstairs.

45

ETHAN AND CORI STEPPED out of the elevator onto the top floor. There was no longer a wall separating them from the entrance. It looked more like the infirmary level, with tiny windows lining the walls and dropped fluorescent lighting. The white vinyl tiles, as usual, were polished to a high sheen. According to the blueprints, the floor was partitioned into four main sections. Each had designated areas with nonspecific titles like quarantined, unclassified, and analysis. The new tenant wasn't just collecting the prop room gizmos; he was going to dissect them.

"What is all this stuff?" Ethan asked. He moved forward to examine the rows and rows of empty glass enclosures. "This looks more like a museum than a lab."

Cori followed behind him, peering into the various enclosures. "I always thought someone should organize the crap in the prop room. Apparently, someone else had the same idea."

"Organize is one thing, but this place is intended to study them like ancient artifacts." Ethan moved over to a giant fume hood in the center of the section. He couldn't imagine anything in the prop room that would require a fume hood, but then again, why be caught without one?

"Why is this door locked?" Cori tugged on the door that theoretically should have led to the next section.

"Danato said the tenant requested private access to the interior sections. We'll still be able to access the level from the east and west elevators, but only as far as the first sections."

"Great," Cori mumbled. "More secret government shit." She looked around the room, but soon noticed that Ethan was staring at her. "What?"

"Oh, nothing, I guess."

"You guess?" She crumpled her brow. "What gives?"

He paused, thinking about what he really wanted to know. "Are you happy, Cori?" Ethan and Cori had indeed regrouped after dealing with the accusations against him, but most of their morale had been achieved in bed. They hadn't really discussed the situation.

"Happy? I'm not that concerned about the lockout."

"No, I mean, happy in your life. You, me, us, the baby."

Her mouth dropped open, and she froze for a moment. "Yes, of course. Why are you asking me that?"

Ethan smiled, not wanting to worry her. He didn't want to admit that this recent incident was just another reason for him to question his role at the prison. Yet again, Danato had disregarded him as an equal and relegated him back to the status of an underling. While Danato certainly had reason for concern, his lack of trust was proof he had no intention of sharing the duties of his wardenship with anyone.

"I just wanted to make sure that our argument the other day hadn't soured our working relationship," he said, temporarily bypassing the real issue.

Cori's eyes flickered over his, momentarily confused, and then she frowned. "It was more of an ass-ripping than an argument, wasn't it?"

Ethan smirked and nodded. "True, but you wear very naughty."

Cori snorted, unable to maintain her annoyance when he made the situation seem more sexual than serious.

He moved close to her and leaned in to whisper in her ear. "Your ass doesn't seem to be too damaged, though." He wrapped his arm around her, squeezing her buttocks firmly as he pulled her against him.

She gasped at the abrupt contact, making him wish they were still in bed. Her eyes glittered with delight. "I suppose I can forgive you, but you—"

Ethan couldn't resist just one more domineering move and muffled the conditions of her pardon. The truth was, he didn't give a damn about her rings or his magical status. As long as they had each other at the end of the day, they could figure out the rest.

Cori relaxed in his grip, allowing him to handle her as he wished. He loved it when she did that. Her surrender wasn't just a signal of her love, but of her trust. He had no idea, until recently, how important that was to him.

"Come on, you two," Duke interrupted as he popped out of the stairwell. "If you think I'm dragging all this crap off the elevator by myself, you have got another thing coming."

The service elevator buzzed, and the doors slid open. Efrat stepped out of the oversized compartment with a pair of boxes hanging from each arm by a special rubber cargo netting that Duke had devised for him. He noted everyone's attention on him as he exited the lift. "What?"

"I thought you were still on duty with the werewolves?" Ethan asked.

"I reassigned him," Duke said. "The men have been complaining about the smell of burned fur when he helps with clean up."

"No skin off my back." Efrat dropped his boxes to the floor. "I hate cleaning up after a full moon. Nobody warned me that the damn things shed a freaking haystack on the way back down."

Ethan shrugged. "Furs got to go somewhere. They're harry enough as humans as it is." He nodded to the cargo netting still hanging from his forearms. "How are the nets working for you?"

Efrat shrugged. "They cut in a bit, but I haven't melted them yet."

Ethan moved forward, removed one of the straps, and pulled up Efrat's sleeve. "We'll have to add a wider strap to balance the pressure." Ethan looked at Duke, and he nodded.

"Where do you want all this crap, anyway?" Efrat asked.

"Just bring it in. Cori will stack it for you." He glanced back at Cori to confirm this, and she nodded. "Duke, why don't you and I get the big man?" Ethan headed to the service lift, and Duke followed.

"Sure thing. We've got him on wheels now, so it shouldn't be too much trouble." Duke motioned to the casters under the giant pontificating statue.

"Got your gloves?" Ethan asked, pulling out his own from his back pocket.

"Don't leave home without 'em." Duke whipped out an identical pair of black gloves and slipped them on.

"Okay, here we go. I don't have to remind you to keep your hands on the base."

"No, sir, I got my lesson on this baby early on."

Ethan situated himself behind the huge square plinth with Duke. On the count of three, they started pushing the heavy marble out of the elevator. Despite his supernatural strength and Duke's own natural brawn, they had to use every ounce of their body weight and leg muscles to get the stony artifact to move.

"Where do you want it, boss?" Duke rasped beside him.

"Let's put it on that wall, under the windows," he grunted back. "Let's hope our tenant doesn't want to move it again."

"If he does, he can bust his groin to do it," Duke grumbled through his exertion.

Ethan could feel the momentum they had achieved diminish as if someone were pushing the beastly statue in the opposite direction. "I think it's getting heavier."

"It doesn't like to be moved," Duke said. "Just keep pushing and don't give up until we're there, or it won't budge again."

"I'd give you boys a hand," Efrat said from behind them, humor bleeding into his words. "But Danato was very specific about not introducing elemental magic to the artifacts."

"Yeah, yeah," Ethan said. "I remember."

"Looks like those dragon steroids are starting to fail you." Ethan could hear the smile on his face before he saw it. "Your face looks a little red."

"Shut up!" Ethan yelled back at him.

Efrat chuckled. "Now, Ethan, you just take that hatred, put it in the pit of your stomach, and shove that stony bastard as hard as you can."

Once they were in position, Duke gave the okay, and they both slumped to the floor, panting. "Bugger me," Ethan huffed. "Forget the dragon; I'm gonna train on this thing from now on."

Duke let out a breathy laugh. "I wouldn't advise that. This thing is more dangerous than you know." He sat up and rolled his shoulders out. "Did I ever tell you about my run-in with this thing?"

Ethan smiled even before Duke began. He always had the best stories about his past. There was not one mundane thing he couldn't make hilarious. "No, I think I got the rundown about lamps and masks, but that was about it. Probably should have given Cori that lecture, too."

Duke nodded and looked to where Cori was piling the boxes into Efrat's cargo net by the elevator. He was playing the part of the mule better than Ethan thought he would. "Yeah, I should have, but she was pretty skittish back then. Not sure she would have listened to me." Ethan noted a peculiar sadness in his eyes. An emotion he had never seen on Duke before, certainly never in regard to Cori. He knew there was no reason for it, but he felt his territorial instincts flare.

"You were talking about the statue," Ethan said, drawing his attention back.

"Oh, right." Duke turned back to him, instantly back to himself. "Well, you know I have a hankering for pocket-sized valuables. It's what got me here to begin with. I've been in and out of the prop room more times than I can count, gathering little trinkets that I thought might be of value someday. I'm not entirely sure how I thought I was going to sell them. It's not like the local pawnshop was a few blocks away.

"There was a guy working here at the time by the name of Riley. He was a lot like you. A good guy with a talent for managing a bunch of reckless convicts. In fact, I think if things had gone differently, Danato might've put him in charge of this place."

"You mean as warden?"

"Yeah."

Ethan frowned. "I can't believe Danato never mentioned him. Scratch that, it's not that surprising. What happened to the guy?" Duke nodded up at the statue. "Seriously? That's him up there?"

Duke nodded as he looked up at the man, frozen in perfect contemplation. "He caught me sneaking about, doing my usual pilfering. He tried to lecture me about safety and rules. I was a bit of a prick back then—I thought I knew everything. I mouthed off some bullshit. Hell, I don't even remember what it was. Didn't make a lick of sense, I'm sure of that. Riley came at me and grabbed my shoulder. He wasn't on the juice yet, so naturally, being the cocky son of a bitch that I was, I gave him a good shove." Duke's expression turned hard, with no sign of the humor that usually brightened his eyes. This story wouldn't have a happy ending. "I've been in and out of prisons all my life. Stolen my fair share of diamonds and hearts, but I never felt as sorry for anything in my life as I did when I saw that man's hand nick that marble and turn to stone."

Ethan frowned at his friend, searching for the words to ease his guilt. The statue wasn't technically a death sentence, but it may as well be. Spending the rest of one's life as a block of stone was worse than death, in Ethan's opinion. "Mistakes happen. Especially here. Unfortunately, sometimes people get hurt."

"Yeah, that's true. I've been telling myself that for years." Duke hoisted himself off the floor and offered his hand to Ethan. "Do you know what I figured out?"

"What's that?" Ethan took his hand and let the man hoist him up with his not-so-unadulterated strength. He certainly wasn't as strong as Ethan, but with the help of an occasional "protein" shake, Ethan ensured Duke would be more than capable of handling his fellow co-workers without contest.

"I'm not the man that I was then," Duke said.

"No, you're not." Ethan cuffed his shoulder before releasing his hand. He may not have known Duke when he first arrived, but the man he knew had made leaps and bounds, becoming not only his best friend, but he had become a commanding presence in the prison. There were only a few people that Ethan truly trusted with his life, and Duke was one of them.

"No, I'm a better man than I ever was." Duke looked up at the statue as if he were talking directly to the man inside. "And I'm not going to stand by and let someone else take the punishment that was meant for me."

"What are you talking about?" Ethan tensed. "What punishment?"

Duke looked at him, the sadness returning to his eyes. "I made a mistake, Ethan, and another man is paying for it. I'm afraid I can't let that go unanswered for any longer."

Duke nodded over to Cori. "Tell her I'm sorry things didn't work out. We're all better off this way."

"What?" Ethan looked at Cori, a panic settling into his toes. What hadn't worked? Why was Duke looking at his wife in such a forlorn way?

Ethan turned back to accuse Duke of something that, in a million years, he never thought he would have to do. However, all thoughts of marital misconduct went to the wayside when he saw Duke's ungloved hand extending toward the statue above them.

"No!" Ethan yelled, and dove forward to save his friend from his wretched scruples. He tackled him to the floor. "What the hell were you thinking?" He leaned back to reveal his glaring eyes to his friend.

Ethan blinked down at the strange man beneath him. His longish black wavy hair was not the blond it should've been. The green eyes that were supposed to be blue rolled back in his head, and he passed out.

As he tried to figure out where he had gone wrong, Ethan looked back up at the statue. New features were carved into the stone. Subtle, occasionally errant curls topped chiseled cheekbones, and a dimpled chin. A subdued yet friendly smile adorned the statue's face.

Duke.

He was crouched on the base, bent over in permanent thought. The pure white marble magnified and memorialized his beauty. He looked like a Greek god, but he was far from it. He was a perpetual prisoner inside the stone.

Stuck... forever... drawn in by a burden of guilt and his obligations to his duty.

Ethan stood and stared at his best friend. It was too much. He couldn't just leave him there. He couldn't walk away. He wouldn't let his friend stay locked up inside that stone for years on end, slowly dying. He wouldn't let him stay there for one more second. Ethan reached up to pull his friend back off that plinth.

46

CORI LAUGHED AND MOTIONED to Ethan and Duke, who were lying on the floor panting after shoving their statue into place. Efrat looked back and smirked. "They certainly are determined; you gotta give them that."

Cori nodded and loaded her boxes into the netting for Efrat to carry. He kneeled to help her, but a small snap of electricity forced him to retreat his hands. "Sorry." He shook his head. "I keep forgetting."

Cori gave him a thin smile. "I know. We'll get used to it, eventually."

"Yeah, I guess." Efrat frowned. It was his usual frown. The one that reminded her he was never truly going to find happiness in his life. It was frustrating for her. She had spent far too much energy trying to help Efrat, and none of it seemed to improve his demeanor. At some point, she was just going to have to accept that Efrat was the Ejor of the prison. "What?"

Cori blinked at Efrat, realizing she was staring at him instead of helping him. "Nothing. Are you worried about this magical explosion everybody has been talking about?"

Efrat's brow dipped. "Doesn't have much to do with me?"

"Efrat. Anything supernatural nearby is bound to affect you."

He looked down at his hands. "I hope not. I have no intention of powering the western hemisphere."

"You think you could get stronger?" Cori frowned at him. "You already have a lightning storm's worth of power. Surely your body couldn't take anymore."

Efrat scoffed and shook his head at her. A small smile played across his lips, but the lingering amusement disappeared as he spoke. "This body was never meant to have this level of power to begin with. If I get more, I don't think I'll survive it."

Cori stared at him, fighting the imagery of Efrat's heart exploding from the stress of his proximity to his own hands. It bothered her, maybe even a little more than it should have. She reached across to him and touched his forearm above his scar line. She opened her mouth to speak, but Ethan's outcry drew her attention.

"No!" Ethan leaped forward and tackled Duke.

Even watching the event, Cori couldn't quite understand how the dark-haired man had arrived beneath Ethan in place of Duke. She looked up at the statue, which featured a different face—a familiar face. "Oh, no," Cori whispered and looked at Efrat.

Efrat stared at the statue with the same wide-eyed shock. "Did that son of a bitch just do what I think he did?"

Cori pressed her hands to her mouth and shook her head. "No, no, no." She couldn't begin to understand what had just happened, but she was certain Duke was gone.

Ethan stood and stared up at Duke's marble figure. She already knew what he was thinking. The blind leap of heroism that his mind was demanding. "Ethan, no!"

Ethan was not thinking clearly. He was stupidly going to sacrifice himself for Duke. As much as she loved Duke, she wasn't willing to lose her husband for him. Ethan wasn't thinking about her or their child. He was only thinking about rescuing his friend. Admirable, albeit stupid and shortsighted.

Cori ran to stop him, but her legs got tangled up in the cargo netting she was loading for Efrat. She dropped to the floor, and the mirage of the genie came into view, reminding her with three fingers that this was her third and final minor inconvenience. But, of course, it wasn't minor; it was life-altering.

The distance between her and Ethan might as well have been a mile now. His hand rose to touch the statue, but apart from a terrified scream, she couldn't do anything to stop him.

Ethan's hand was less than an inch from the stone when a burst of electric blue convulsed his body. He spasmed and fell safely against the base of the statue. Cori scrambled to her feet and ran to him.

She slid to a stop and dropped to her knees. She pulled Ethan into her arms and pressed his head against her chest. He was wavering in and out of consciousness. Tears spilled down her cheeks, and it was all she could do to stop herself from punching him for his stupidity. Instead, she cussed him out between ill-placed kisses.

Efrat approached, and she noticed the slightest disappointment on his face. As if he knew that no matter how many times he played the hero, he wouldn't get the girl.

She gulped away her hiccuping tears and grabbed his leg, pinching his calf as she thanked him. He glanced down at the contact and gave her a nod. He reached to touch her head—to offer some human contact, but he drew back his hand before touching her. He looked up at the statue. A new, discontented frown took over his expression. He looked at the stranger lying on the floor in place of Duke. "Who the hell is that?"

Cori looked at him as well. She didn't recognize the unconscious man. He would no doubt be happy to have been rescued from his stone confinement, but she was certain that Efrat was thinking the same thing she was. It wasn't a fair trade.

47

D ANATO STEPPED FROM THE elevator into the first section of his newly designed top floor. It was formerly the home of an elitist military group he was thankful to be rid of. The smell of cinder and sweat was gone, replaced by drywall and fresh paint. As clean as the rest of the prison was, this new portion of the facility was immaculate. He had already suspected that his new tenant would have prospects of doing chemistry in here. Still, looking at the maze of plastic cubicles and sterile stainless-steel tables, he wondered if anatomy would be on the list of activities as well. He wasn't sure how he felt about that. Perhaps he had traded in one sadistic asshole for another.

As he looked around the room, he saw all the sullen faces he expected to see. Cori was on the floor, holding Ethan. Her hands twisted in his shirt as if she had no intention of letting him go. He could tell she had been crying.

Ethan, on the other hand, looked hollow. Only a few stray tears defied his indifference and revealed how hard his heartstrings had been tugged.

Efrat turned as he came toward them, a certain accusation rising in the ire behind his eyes. He already knew how this argument would begin. He also knew how it would end. It was the same conversation he had with Duke so many years ago.

Danato had hoped and prayed the Texan would recover from his guilt and leave the statue be. And as far as he knew, that was the case. Duke had accepted his role in the accident and learned from it. Ever since that day, he had been an obedient member of his staff. One of his best, in fact.

But now this?

Perhaps it was Danato's fault for allowing him to get so close to it again. And yet, it had always been there. What changed? What prompted him to cave to his guilt? Or was he rising from it?

Danato looked up at the hard, white stone of the pontificating man. The majestic Greek god interpretation of him was seamlessly sculpted. Every muscle accentuated for the perfect physique. Smooth calcite glorified the skin. His face and hair, perpetually frozen in the image of his last thought. Was it relief or pride? Danato wasn't sure what expression the statue was trying to capture, but he knew it wasn't fear. Whatever motivated Duke to choose this path, it also gave him the strength to endure it.

"Where is he?" Danato asked.

"Right here, warden." A voice sounded behind him. It was a low rasp, as if the vocal cords didn't quite know how to work anymore.

Danato froze, trying to remember his name. He had blocked it out—pretended the man hadn't existed. It was easier that way.

In truth, he hadn't known the man long, which was a shame since he was designated to take over the position of warden after him.

Danato turned around to look at his face—a face he hadn't seen in years—at least not in the flesh.

His chiseled cheeks looked a little hollower than when he had gone into the statue. His black hair had grown some during his containment and now fell into his eyes. The staunch five o'clock shadow marked the beginning, middle, and end of his day. Though the statue allowed him to age, the skin around his eyes only had slight creases. He would have been over forty by now. Nearly a decade of his life was gone, and he could never get it back.

"Hello, Riley."

Riley's eyes skirted over him as if he were calculating the years that had passed on Danato's face. A few more wrinkles and a few more gray hairs. Maybe a lot more. Time he had missed. The people who might already be long gone from his life. "How long?" Riley croaked through his disused vocal cords.

"Nine years," Danato said without hesitation. There was no point in trying to conjure a different definition of time. No matter how he phrased it, Riley knew what the consequences of his lengthy captivity meant. He was officially dead on paper, and there was no coming back from that. The life he once knew was lost to him. He couldn't re-enter society in any form or fashion without raising suspicion about the prison. He was free from the statue, but the stone walls of the prison were still containing him.

Riley swallowed hard and forced a stuttered breath into his lungs. He roared through gritted teeth and threw himself at Danato.

The first glancing blow to his cheek surprised Danato. It had been a long time since anyone had dared to punch him. He took the impact with civil determination and hoped his tantrum might be done, but Riley took a second swing that wasn't as easy for his ego to dismiss. Riley threw his fist a third time, but he didn't let it land. Danato caught Riley's hands and yanked them down to his sides.

"That's enough," he said in warning, but Riley still thrashed against his grip.

"How could you leave me in there! How could you do this to me!"

"We need to get him down to the infirmary," Danato announced, but Ethan just stared at Riley. "Ethan!" Danato shouted, but Ethan only blinked at him, unmoving.

"Where is Tessa?" Riley asked.

Danato shook his head. He didn't want to get into all of this. He hated giving bad news, but he hated it more when there was so much of it to give at once. Why didn't people just let him dole it out one bite at a time?

"Where is she!" Riley screamed in his face and pressed his chest against his.

"Gone!" Danato yelled back at him. Riley's eyes volleyed over his, searching for the lie, waiting for an explanation that would soften the blow. "She left, Riley."

"What?" Riley fell away from him. His attempt at intimidation melted into devastation. "She said she would stay."

"She had a chance to live her life. I couldn't let that be taken away from her because of a promise that was too unreasonable to keep. When her term was over, I made her go."

"You made her leave? You made her forget!"

"Of course I made her forget," Danato seethed. He knew he was needling the man's pain, but his selfishness needed to be reigned back in. He needed logic to penetrate his grief. "She was a flesh and blood woman. I wasn't going to allow her to pine over a goddamn statue the rest of her life."

"Where is she? I'll find her."

"Riley..." Danato sighed and shook his head. "She doesn't remember you."

"I'll make her remember. We can start over."

"She already started over, Riley." Danato crossed his arms. "She's happily married now, with two kids."

Riley tipped his head back and stared at the ceiling. A tear trickled down his temple. "This can't be. I just went in there. I was arguing with…" Riley looked back at the statue. He took in the features in the stone and pointed at it. "That son of a bitch put me in there."

"That son of a bitch just brought you out, too," Ethan snapped.

Riley barely acknowledged Ethan's statement. "You left me in that thing for nine years while that asshole roamed around this prison."

"If there was a way to release you—"

"There was a way!" Riley screamed and motioned to the statue, as if this conclusion should have been obvious the moment he went in.

"It was an accident. Duke never intended to put you into the statue."

"Fine, then you put back in whoever the hell came out of it."

Danato shook his head and took a breath. "They were already dead. The statue only receives living people."

"Then you should've found someone to put in," Riley said coldly. "Someone old. Someone bad. Someone with a death wish. I don't care who, but you should have found some way to get me out!"

Danato wasn't surprised by his anger, but he was surprised that Riley would sacrifice someone so easily. "I couldn't do that."

Riley narrowed his eyes. "You chose that slackjawed hick over me?"

Ethan heaved himself off the floor and got in the man's face. "Call my friend a name one more time."

"Ethan," Danato said, but he didn't stop him. There were too many emotions to keep bottled up at the moment, and he knew it.

Riley looked him over carefully. "Who the hell are you?"

"I'm the warden of this prison."

"Ethan is my successor," Danato corrected, since he wasn't retired just yet.

Riley perched a smug smile on his face and laughed at Ethan. Despite the delight he seemed to take at his expense, tears filled his eyes. "You're the new me? I thought I was the last." Riley looked at him.

"You were. Ethan was brought in from the outside."

"Last of what?" Ethan turned his attention to Danato.

"Last of the bloodline." Riley gave Danato a smug glance before puffing his chest. "I'm Riley Latham. I'm the youngest living heir to Roland Latham, the prison's founder. And I own this prison."

48

TENSION FILLED THE ELEVATOR as everyone, except Efrat, rode down to the infirmary to get Riley checked out. Years of living as a statue were bound to have ramifications on his body.

The shock of Duke's entrapment had only just set in when this stranger revealed more startling news. While she was focusing on not openly bawling over the loss of her friend, Ethan looked like he was ready to start swinging his fists.

She knew exactly what he was feeling. It was the same betrayal she always felt when Danato didn't tell her something important about his past. Ethan usually took everything in stride, but with his friend trapped and this newcomer staking claim to the prison, his patience was razor thin.

"And who's this?" Riley looked at her.

"My wife." Ethan shifted a little closer.

"Easy champ. I wasn't going to hump her leg. You got a name?" he asked her.

"Cori," she answered."

"You a nurse?"

"No." Cori lifted her chin. "I'm second-in-command to the warden. I'm Belus's successor."

Riley snorted and laughed. Instead of impressing Riley, she had apparently amused him. "Since when does a pity position for a handicap require a successor?"

Cori reached her hand out to throw a blast of fire right into Riley's face, but nothing came out. Riley looked at her outstretched hand with a cocked eyebrow. "Is that supposed to scare me?"

Cori put her hand back down, embarrassed and more than a little infuriated by her lack of threat. She was going to have to get used to pulling her gun instead.

"Riley, I know you've been through a lot," Danato said as the elevator doors opened. "But it would be in your best interest to keep your thoughts to yourself." Danato left the elevator. Ethan motioned for Riley to go first, but he motioned right back.

"Please, ladies first."

Ethan grabbed Cori's hand and pulled her forward out of the elevator. She wanted to claw Riley's eyes out on the way by, but she didn't get the chance.

"Must be nice," Riley mumbled after them. He stepped out of the elevator just as the doors slammed shut, clamping his foot in a vice-like grip. Riley yelled and dropped to the floor. "What the hell! Ahhh! It's crushing my ankle."

Danato and Ethan ran back to aid him, but even with both of them tugging on the doors, they wouldn't budge. The power behind them had nothing to do with machinery. This was the entity. The same entity that had tried to kill her on several occasions in response to Danato's conflicting emotions.

All at once, Cori realized Riley was caught because of her. Not intentionally, but the entity was fighting on her behalf, hurting him in retaliation for his unkind words toward Belus.

Since dealing with the expanded time bubble, Cori had received more positive attention from it—swift elevator rides and warm, welcoming home fires. However, it had also been reading her emotions like a book and responding to her anger like a protective force.

For a moment, she considered how much power was placed in her hands. Her rings may have been useless, but she was not defenseless. She shook away the egotistical thoughts following this revelation. "Let him go!" she yelled at no one in particular.

At first, nothing happened. Elevators did not have ears, nor did the entity, but if she could express herself with the emotions she was feeling, that would be enough to make her command understood. Clearly, she was not going to be friends with Riley, but she recognized the pain on his face. Regardless of her previous desire to hurt him, she did not want to hobble him. "Let him go," she said softly, allowing her pity to be conveyed in the request.

The elevator doors released Riley's ankle and opened with a happy yet sadistic little *ponk*. Ethan and Danato pulled him free and set him down to check his foot. Riley yelped in pain when they tried to touch it.

"I think it's broken," Danato said.

Ethan and Danato exchanged a worrisome look before turning to look at her. Their concerns regarding her connection to the entity were nothing new. However, this time, she noticed their expressions were a good deal more fearful.

49

"I DIDN'T MEAN TO do it," Cori defended after Riley had been wheeled away to surgery.

"I know you didn't." Danato squeezed her shoulder before leaning over the counter to speak with the nurse stationed in the hub. According to her nametag, she was "Vera," but she could have been anyone since the nurses liked to switch their tags to see if anyone paid attention. It was sad, but he had stopped paying attention to names a long time ago. He, like most of the staff, used to partake in a bit of fraternizing with the nursing department, but he was much too old for most of the women trickling through the prison these days. "Vera, would you mind fetching me some headache medicine?"

"Not at all, warden," she said cheerfully and headed down the hallway toward the pharmacy stock room. He looked back at Ethan. "That will take her at least ten minutes, so get it out."

"Get what out?" Ethan asked, though the look of contempt he was aiming at him didn't change.

"Whatever it was that stopped you from obeying my orders earlier."

Ethan's lip twitched upward, bearing little resemblance to the humored smile he was trying to convey. "I didn't want to get in the way of a family argument."

"You're mad. I get that."

"I'm not mad, Danato. I'm worried. I'm worried that the same thing is going to happen to Duke as what happened to Riley. I mean, hell, if you didn't fight to get your own blood out of that rock, how hard will you try for an ex-con?"

"There were extenuating circumstances with Riley. I made a decision. Maybe it wasn't the right one, but it was for the best."

"And Duke?"

Danato waved his hands toward Ethan and Cori. "You are the next generation of wardens. What is your decision? Do we put Riley back in? Do we choose someone new? Do we rotate? Shall we add six months of statue duty to every recruit? What is your best solution?"

"This isn't a joke," Ethan said.

"No, it isn't. It's your job. I don't recall making either of you happy with my latest decisions; perhaps it's time you start making some for a change." Danato walked away. "Let me know if you need help dragging your victim to the statue."

"Convenient that you finally give up the reins when there is an impossible choice to be made," Ethan called after him.

Danato froze. The heat of his anger burned through him, warming his ears and making his hands tremble. He turned back to Ethan and found him squared off and ready for this battle. Cori, meanwhile, was wide-eyed behind him. Even she was surprised by this outburst. "What was that?"

"You heard me."

Danato moved slowly back to him, but Ethan didn't flinch. Not an inch. "Is that what you think I'm doing? Giving up the reins?"

"Let's just stop this," Cori petitioned. "We're all stressed. We all love Duke, and we want to save him."

"You're right, Cori, but this isn't about Duke anymore. This is about the way I wield my authority. So, Ethan, please enlighten me on my vacillating decision-making."

"Tell me that Duke is coming out of that statue."

Danato shook his head. "I don't know that he is."

"I won't let him stay in there."

"Then don't. I've already decided the fate of one man in that statue. If you want me to make this decision, then I will, but you may not like the one I make, and I don't want to listen to your sarcastic pre-pubescent backtalk for the next twenty years because of it."

"I am trying to save my friend!"

"I am trying to run a prison, which, believe it or not, is more important than Duke."

"It's thinking like that that got Riley stuck in there in the first place."

"Actually, it was an attitude like this that got Riley stuck in there in the first place."

"Duke doesn't deserve to be punished for a mistake he made years ago."

"I'm not talking about Duke. I'm talking about Riley." Danato glanced behind them, making sure that no one else would be privy to this dirty little secret. "You want to know the real reason I didn't get Riley out of that statue? Because he was a mouthy, egotistical brat, who thought he could run this prison without my help." Danato leaned in close. "I was glad that piece of shit got stuck in there, and I barely made an effort to look for a way to get him out. I'm not going to find a way to get Duke out of that statue either, because it will look bad to the board. So, one of you will have to do it. That's why I'm handing you the reins. Not because I can't do it, but because I don't want the Board to know what measures I will take to relieve myself of a nuisance usurper." Danato walked away again, but this time, there were no snide comments in his wake.

50

HEATON STEPPED OFF THE truck with the transmorph that called herself Eve. She was handcuffed and gagged, but she was still struggling against every move he made. He nearly had to knock her out just to get her into the truck to begin with. Her slurred cusses were getting on his nerves, especially since they were getting more personal, which was no surprise since transmorphs only needed proximity to get a psychic read on people. They did their best work through encasement, but they had gotten plenty close on the ride over.

Nevia trailed out behind him, still rubbing the sleep from her eyes. She had insisted on being sedated for the journey, just in case. It was probably for the best, but it only reminded him that they needed a third in their group. Until Danato released Daniel, there was no one to assist with the heavy lifting portion of this job.

"What are you doing here?" Heaton asked when he saw Efrat leaning against a crate, waiting for them instead of Ethan or Duke. His bent elbows made his crackling hands look like a perpetual threat, but his expression wasn't sinister. If anything, he looked contemplative.

Efrat looked up from his inward thoughts and stared at the woman in Heaton's grip. "Seducer?" he asked.

"Transmorph," Nevia answered as she stepped down off the platform. She stopped in front of Efrat, tipping her chin to sniff the air around him. "What's wrong?"

Efrat turned his attention to Nevia, his eyes skirting her petite frame before landing back on her face. "Transmorph level it is."

"First, a quick stop at the part-time level," Heaton said.

Efrat stood, but Nevia barred his exit with an outstretched arm. Efrat looked down at it before glancing at Heaton. He wasn't sure if Nevia could ever be a threat to an elemental, especially such a mercurial one, but he wouldn't put anything past her again.

"Tell me."

Efrat shook his head. "Just because you can smell it, little girl, doesn't mean it is any of your business."

"Jordan—" Heaton attempted to interject.

"No," Nevia snapped. "Someone has gotten hurt, and I want to know who it is."

Heaton grimaced and shoved Eve to the edge of the platform. "We got a lot of friends here, mate. If you got bad news, spit it out."

Efrat scoffed and shook his head. "Duke put himself inside of the Medusa statue."

"Bloody hell," Heaton murmured.

"I don't know what that means." Nevia looked between them.

"It means Duke is gone and we can't do shit about it," Efrat said.

"Fuck that. I'll put this bitch in there before I let him stay in."

"Don't you dare!" Eve snarled.

"Shut your trap." Heaton shoved the girl down the steps and led the way out of the docks.

"She's got a passenger, I take it?" Efrat asked from behind him.

"No!" Eve screeched.

"Yes." Both he and Nevia answered.

Before Heaton could stop her, the girl squirmed from his hands and flung herself at Efrat. His reaction was naturally to avoid electrocuting her, so he spread his arms. She landed against his chest, sobbing and wailing. "Please! Please! Don't let them kill me. I'm not what they say I am. I'm human. Please, help me!"

Efrat stared at the woman crumpled against his chest. He lowered his arms slightly to embrace her as best he could and leaned his head down to speak into her ear. "There, there, now. What's your name, girl?"

"Eve," she whimpered.

"Eve, look at me." The transmorph looked up at him with glistening eyes and hair matted to her wet cheeks. "Let me tell you a story."

Heaton almost pulled the woman off him and broke up the cozy moment, but he saw Nevia just behind Efrat shaking her head. Instead, he took a step back, allowing room for error if necessary.

"Once upon a time, in a land far, far, away called America, there was a group of young men and women who stupidly signed up to be the pet project for a madman. These men and women were meant to be supernatural warriors who could fight any manner of creature. To find their vulnerabilities and defeat them. And whether it be fire to kill vampiric vermin, ice to penetrate the hardest armor of the stone men, or water to drown the biggest beasts too strong to fight—we all had our lethal specialties."

Eve shifted away from him, but Efrat clasped his hands behind her, blocking the retreat. "Don't you want to know what my specialty was?"

Eve shook her head.

"It was my job to dispose of conniving, theatrical parasites such as yourself."

Eve tried to shift away, but Efrat pulled her in tight. "If I had it my way, every last one of you leeches would be dead, so don't come to me looking for sympathy." Efrat released the woman, and she fell back, more than eager to get back into Heaton's restraining grip.

It surprised Heaton to hear that Efrat's butchers may have actually had a purpose for him. However, it made sense. The Americas were rampant with vampires and transmorphs. The military would be wise to seek alternative combat tactics—although perhaps not via transplanted hands.

51

HEATON SAW THE EXPRESSION on Daniel's face as he left the confines of his small cell. He should have been elated to see his wife. He should have been well-humored in the presence of his friend, but all he could focus on was the prisoner he had in his custody. Even as he hugged Nevia, his eyes drifted over to Eve—already sensing she was someone he was meant to hunt.

Daniel McGrath was a good man at heart. He didn't want to be the destroyer of life. He didn't want to be the man that an entire race feared. Causing fear inevitably created power, but what no one ever considered was that the power could scare those who wielded it. Daniel lived with that fear every day of his life. Who would he hurt next? Who would he have to kill in the name of heroism? How many more lives would end at the hands of his wicked eyes?

Daniel did his best to pretend he was happy to see them. He smiled and joked about bad room service, but he wasn't fooling Heaton, and he certainly wasn't fooling Nevia.

Since she didn't want to bring up the revelations the last few days had brought, Nevia was also doing her part to pretend that their reunion was joyous and untainted. Her small smile wasn't nearly enough to hide the burdens of an uncertain future. Heaton knew Daniel would find no fault in Nevia's hybrid burdens, but she was young and probably still had dreams of a traditional married life with children and pets. She hadn't been a hunter long enough to realize that a life like that was just a fantasy.

"And what have you brought me there?" Daniel finally asked, nodding to Eve.

Eve's earlier fits were all but a memory. She was holding deathly still now. Her eyes gravitated to Daniel's, and they held each other in a stalemate gaze.

"A transmorph," Nevia said. "She has a victim."

"I have no victim," Eve said, surprisingly calmly. "I am the first of my kind. A hybrid between man and transmorph."

The excuses transmorphs gave to gain their freedom did not impress Heaton, but this excuse gave him pause. At least it was original.

Daniel snorted. "What a load a shite."

"I am the future of both our species." Eve turned to look at Heaton. "I know you don't believe me, but you must find a way to prove it. Poke me, prod me." She looked at Efrat next, who was patiently waiting by the entrance of Daniel's cell, though there was even less sympathy there. His predatory gaze was even more sinister than Daniel's.

For the first time since they had deemed the man a "good guy," Heaton wondered if that was a mistake. "Take my blood. Take my bones," Eve offered.

"That human blood and bone is just skin deep, lass. You're gonna have to find a new argument because we've heard it all before." Daniel stepped forward, and Eve shifted back, pressing into Heaton. "Do you know what I've never heard one of your kind say? I've never heard them apologize for ripping someone's life apart. I've never heard them cry over the pain they've caused."

"Have you?" Eve asked.

Daniel paused a moment before nodding. "Aye, but my days of crying are over. That went right out the window, along with teddy bears and prayers."

"There must be something you can do." Eve turned to Heaton again. "Something..." Eve frowned and looked at Efrat. "How did the military find transmorphs?"

Efrat scoffed. "You don't want to know."

"My life is on the line; of course, I want to know!"

Efrat shifted uncomfortably. "We would knock a bit off and fry it up. If it smelled like chicken, we let 'em fly. If it smelled like rubber boots..." Efrat shrugged.

"How did you distinguish between empty transmorphs and those with hosts?" Nevia asked.

Efrat shook his head. "Up until I heard about Daniel, I didn't know that it mattered."

"That won't prove anything," Nevia said. "If you fry her flesh, it will smell like both human and transmorph.

No different from what I am telling you. She has a human inside of her."

"I'm not denying what you smell," Eve insisted. "I am simply denying the reason for it. I am half human."

"That's ridiculous," Daniel said. "You can't be a human hybrid. The DNA isn't compatible."

"Transmorphs have a history of aberrant evolutionary leaps. Our entire lineage is based on one mutation after another. My ancestors used to be nothing more than glorified chameleons. Now we thrive alongside humans, as equals."

"Don't you dare call yourself equal to humanity!" Daniel threw a finger at her. "I've seen what your kind can do."

"And I've seen what humans can do! We are no worse than the worst of humans. Don't allow your prejudice to decide my fate." Eve looked around at all of them, accusing them of the same bias. "The only thing I am guilty of is being different. And that is hardly worth a death sentence."

"We can't prove it," Heaton mumbled.

She looked at him, disappointed. "You can't disprove it either." Eve looked at each of them again. "If you raise your weapons against me, I will die for sure. By the time you know the truth, you will have caused yet another rift in our tenuous relations. I know you can't trust me. I know you must assume I am lying, because that is what we are known for. I won't defend the deception that is built into our very makeup. I won't defend the many of my kind abuse their God-given privilege for money and sex and power. I won't even pretend that I am not guilty of some deceit, even in this limited form. I can't ask for trust. I can't ask for freedom. But what I can ask for is time."

"Give me enough time to prove my innocence or for you to confirm my guilt." Eve's eyes landed on Daniel. Heaton could see him wavering. "Please, stay my execution for a few days or hours if you can't offer me more."

Daniel looked at Heaton for an answer. Heaton honestly didn't have one. He knew Nevia wouldn't be happy about them distrusting her evaluation of the woman, but at the very least, they needed to consult with Danato before proceeding one way or another. Knowing Danato, he would most likely approve the removal if for no other reason than to confirm or deny the existence of hybrid transmorphs.

"Nevia and I will get her locked up," Heaton said. "Efrat, why don't you go let Danato know we have some questions for him."

Efrat shook his head with irritated disapproval, but he headed out to do as he was told, anyway.

"I'll just put myself away." Daniel motioned to his cell. "Maybe after all this work stuff, you and I can have a proper hello." Daniel winked at Nevia, and she finally gave him an honest smile. "You too." Daniel threw him a wink as well, along with a click of his tongue. Heaton chuckled at his theatrics. He liked that Daniel was getting more comfortable making jokes about their relationship. It meant he had finally come to terms with his best friend being gay, or at the very least, he was hiding his discomfort better. Daniel certainly wasn't a bigot, but the secret had thrown off their dynamic for longer than either of them would admit.

"Thank you," Eve whispered beside him.

Heaton looked at her and frowned at the relief on her face. "I hope you aren't expecting this stay of execution to last long. The warden isn't exactly a fan of transmorphs. I doubt a hybrid will make it any higher on his list."

Eve's eyes flickered over Heaton's, and a small smile tipped the edge of her lips. "I have faith that everything will turn out okay. Unlike your friend, I haven't given up on teddy bears... or prayers."

52

"I T'S PRETTY QUIET AROUND here?" Nevia commented while she, Heaton, and Eve waited for the elevator to arrive.

Heaton checked his watch and calculated the time difference. "Nearly lunchtime. They're probably passing out blood packs to the vampiric prisoners upstairs. Never pays to make them wait."

Nevia glanced at Eve between them, giving her a subtle sniff before crossing her arms. It was a subtle change to the average on-looker, but Heaton knew she was just positioning her hand closer to the Glock tucked under her arm.

Heaton shifted back to look at her behind Eve's head. Nevia caught the movement and turned her worried expression on him. He dipped his brow, demanding an explanation, but she seemed reluctant to speak within earshot of Eve.

Heaton grabbed Eve's shoulders and commanded her to kneel.

"What? Why?" She looked between them frantically.

"Because I need to have a word with my partner, and I don't want you wandering off."

Nevia drew her gun and pointed it at Eve. "Do as he said." Heaton didn't bother reminding her that bullets did little to transmorphs, but if she really was a hybrid, perhaps that immunity had been eliminated from her resume.

"Is that really—"

Heaton pushed his foot into the back of her knee, forcing it to buckle. He assisted her fall and leaned onto her, pressing her shoulders down hard. "Stay."

He moved far enough away to give them privacy for their whispers. Nevia backed away with him, keeping her eyes on Eve as she did. The transmorph watched them for a moment before rolling her eyes and staring ahead to the elevator doors.

"What is it?" he whispered.

"Something's wrong," Nevia whispered back. "She's relieved."

"She just narrowly escaped death. Why wouldn't she be relieved?"

"No, she isn't out of danger yet. She should still be nervous, but she's not."

"You think she has something planned?"

"I don't sense guile. Just contentment... and pride."

"Let's get her upstairs. We can call Danato and let him know what's going on. The sooner he gives the go-ahead, the sooner we can get back to our normal, weird lives."

Nevia nodded just as the lift arrived. Heaton jogged back over to Eve before she could attempt an extremely slow escape via the elevator. The doors opened, and Heaton pushed her inside. He leaned against the back wall, holding her against him. Nevia stepped in, holstered her gun, and pushed the button for the fourth floor.

As the doors closed, Heaton felt Eve press back against him a little harder. Her foot rose fast, kicking Nevia in the back. The lightweight woman flew between the closing doors with ease and landed on the floor outside. She pulled her gun and turned to fire. However, it was too dangerous for her to shoot with him in the path of a through-and-through bullet—not to mention the potential for a ricochet in the small enclosure. Heaton glimpsed Nevia's infuriated face before the doors closed completely.

"Prat!" Heaton shoved Eve aside and pushed the door open button so he could catch Nevia before she had to jog up a flight of stairs. Unfortunately, he could already feel the lift moving. "Why did you—"

Eve raised her elbows and pulled her hands clean out of her cuffs with little more effort than removing bracelets. It wasn't uncommon for transmorphs to do this, but usually not while they contained a human. Apparently, her victim had tiny hands. She dropped the handcuffs on the floor and eyed him with lethal intent.

"So, you were lying about being a hybrid," Heaton said.

"No."

"You know, even if you manage to get past me—which you won't—you'll never get away. We've got your scent now. The collectors will be on you like stink."

Eve rolled her head, making her neck crack loudly—or perhaps it was her victim's neck that was cracking. "We'll see."

Heaton rolled his shoulders and positioned himself across from her. "You really want to do this?" he asked. Eve smiled and nodded. "It's your funeral."

"I doubt it."

Heaton lunged forward and buried his shoulder into the woman's belly. He had no intention of holding any punches, not that he usually did. He expected her to bellow and cough, but she just grabbed him and threw him back against the wall with surprising strength.

Once he regained his footing, another look passed between them—that of a mere mortal meeting a dark horse for the first time. Heaton's concerns were there and gone. He had always been a mere mortal. There was no sense in letting it bother him now.

Heaton threw his fist into her jaw. A spray of blood ejected from her mouth, temporarily appeasing his ego.

She responded with a powerful uppercut. His chin erupted in pain. He hit the wall, and a dizzy sensation like shock nearly overwhelmed him.

He pushed himself to fight on and kicked the woman in the stomach, sending her into the wall on her side. She recovered, and they met again in the middle.

Their arms locked in a tight, defensive embrace. Heaton pushed her, slamming her back into the wall. Then she pushed back, slamming him into his side. They twisted, entwining themselves in a standing wrestling match as they bounced around the small space.

Heaton finally gained enough leverage to lift her and flip her over his back. She hit the elevator floor with a loud bang. Heaton didn't give her a moment's rest before punching her. Once, twice, and a third time for good measure. His fists bloodied themselves on her face.

He stood upright and panted over her. He had hoped the violence would be enough to wound her, but she wasn't showing any signs of bruising, and he was quite certain the blood on her face was from his knuckles.

The lift announced its arrival with an unmelodious *ponk*, and the doors opened. Heaton had anticipated seeing Nevia there waiting for him, but she wasn't. He noticed the sign designation on the wall ahead of him: Level 5. Seducers. He was on the wrong floor.

Fucking elevator buttons.

A kick pushed Heaton forward. He stumbled forward and whipped around to face his attacker. Eve's fist hit him first in the cheek and then in the throat. He sputtered, barely breathing through the pain. An uppercut arrived before he could recover.

His world finally stopped spinning and just fell.

It was only a moment of unconsciousness, but that was all it took. He heard a grunt and felt the world rise again. He opened his eyes and looked at Eve below him. She was holding him up high. She was so strong. Stronger than she looked. It was the first and easiest rule to break regarding transmorphs. Never trust anything you see.

"Why did you let us take you?" Heaton croaked over the pressure in his throat. "You could have escaped anytime you wanted?"

Eve looked up at him. The unassuming curve in her lips wasn't maniacal or vicious, but it was no less intimidating. "How else was I going to get in?" she answered. She dipped her arms and pushed him back up, launching him into the air.

Heaton hadn't recognized the stairs until that moment. He dropped past one railing and landed on the next set of steps. His back roared in agony, and the ache in his head sent a second shock wave through his body. If he could have moved, he would have turned his head to vomit. As it was, his foggy vision was signaling another blackout. Which he was grateful for, since the pain was too much for any man to bear.

53

"D ANIEL!" NEVIA PRACTICALLY SLAMMED into his cell door. She was panting and slightly sweaty. He wasn't sure what was the matter, but he was certain if his wife had taken to using her lesser skill of running, then something was wrong.

He jumped to the door. "What's the matter? Don't tell me she got away."

Nevia nodded. "She kicked me out of the elevator. I tried to follow them, but I couldn't get up the stairs fast enough."

"What do you mean, fast enough?" He frowned.

Nevia shook her head. "It's Heaton. She... She threw him down the stairwell. I think his back is broken. You have to help him."

Daniel huffed out a breath that was part worry and part exhaustion. He hated leaving Heaton on the job by himself. The fool was too brave for his own good. He also didn't like the idea of patching a broken spine. What if he couldn't get it put together, right? What if he ended up paralyzed because of his amateur surgery?

Since no one had bothered to lock him back up, Daniel pushed the door aside and stepped out. "Show me," he demanded.

Nevia led the way to the stairwell, and they jogged up to the next flight of stairs. She stopped and turned around, looking at the floor number on the wall below them. "He was here. Someone must have taken him."

Daniel could see red smears on the steps. Heaton had indeed been here.

"Unless she..." Nevia trailed off and ran back to the door where they had just passed. She pulled it open and sniffed the air before running through it.

"Feck!" Daniel followed her inside, even though he knew they were getting into dangerous territory. If the transmorph was free, she could now be anyone. If she released the rest of the transmorphs, they would be in a load of trouble.

He followed Nevia into the next section, but she was already halfway to the next one. "Oy! Wait up!" He jogged after her, fearing that any distance between them would put his heroism out of reach.

When he arrived in the next section, he found Nevia an entire section ahead of him. "Nevia!" he yelled and outright sprinted after her.

He caught up to her in the following section. She had stopped running and was standing stock still, staring at the floor, facing away from him. He noticed the transmorphs residing in the surrounding cells were none too happy to see him. One spit at him, and another hissed like a snake. He frowned at that one, trying to figure out what emotion he intended to reflect.

"Nevia!" Daniel grabbed her arm and turned her to face him. "Don't ever..." He looked at the tears pouring from her eyes. "What's going on?"

"I shouldn't have dropped my guard. I should have put a bullet in her brain when I realized something was wrong."

"Now, now, you can't solve everything with a bullet." Daniel pulled her close. "We'll find Heaton and get him patched up. Okay?" He drew her back and looked at her.

"Okay." She gave him a small smile. "I love you," she whispered.

He smiled and brushed his thumb across her damp cheek. He was certain he would never tire of hearing her say that. "I love you too." He leaned in and gave her a sweet, albeit wet, kiss.

A sharp, stinging pain in his stomach forced him to draw his lips away from hers. For a moment, he only stared at her, not entirely understanding what had just happened.

He looked down and saw the knife in his belly with her hand on it. There was no time to think. There was only a blink between the blood pooling beneath him and his instincts activating. Nevia's face disintegrated before him. Her mind crashed into his just as the ash of her body crumbled into a pile on the floor.

Daniel stared down at the gray heap—a thousand thoughts crowded in all at once, but none as deafening as his only sane thread.

It wasn't her.

It wasn't her.

It wasn't her.

It couldn't be her because if it was, he couldn't endure it. He was barely able to live with the guilt of a murder, let alone uxoricide.

The second searing pain came as almost a relief. This time, he recognized the pain right away. The pain of a knife penetrating his back between the ribs—making his breath escape.

He tried to turn to face this unknown attacker, but a weight wrapped around his neck. It pulled his head back and forced his eyes upward, pointing the sights and muzzle of his weapon toward the ceiling.

The third stab was just a repeat of the second withdrawn and re-inserted. The pain was worse now. His lungs begged for air but despised every breath he took to get it.

Then came the fourth.

And the fifth.

His senses should have dulled, but he was now acutely aware of the woman hanging on his neck stabbing him.

Again.

And again.

And again.

54

HEATON'S TRIP TO THE infirmary was a blur of guards' faces. They had locked arms and carried him on a human stretcher down two flights of stairs. It was painful as hell, but he was glad to feel the pain. At least he was alive. At least he wasn't paralyzed.

He tried to be brave, but he could feel tears streaming down his face, and the wails that echoed through the stairwell were surely his own. He hated to lose face in front of other men. He would have to keep the fact that a girl beat him up a secret as long as possible. However, the minute he got to the infirmary and five eager nurses and the doctor jumped to his side, he lost all will to maintain his dignity and turned into a toddler.

They poked and prodded at him, determining the location of his spinal injury. All the while, he groused about the pain and cold hands. Had he a tickle in his throat—he would have announced it at that moment—anything to distract himself from his pain and his failure.

He hated that a transmorph of all creatures had gotten the better of him. Tricked him and beaten him bloody, senseless, and useless.

Sometimes, he considered trying to weasel some of the dragon shake from Ethan to give himself an advantage. He never felt inadequate with Daniel around, but when it was him and Nevia, he felt like the burden of manliness was put on him. And yet, for some reason, that burden had not translated to the nursing staff.

"Ouch! Blasted woman! Can you make that hurt anymore?" he yelled at the nurse, placing his IV.

"Yes, I can! Would you like me too?" The woman labeled Vera snarled right back at him.

"Mr. Reid," the doctor interjected. "Thankfully, you haven't broken anything. We had to manipulate a couple of discs back into place. You should remain immobile for at least a few hours. And no vigorous activity for at least a week."

"You know what my job is."

"That's why I'm telling you this. Most people understand the concept of rest. You might also have a concussion, so we'll need to keep you here to monitor you."

"You don't understand there is a—" Heaton immediately cut off his words. There was no point causing alarm. Hopefully, Nevia had caught up with Eve and detained her. That is, assuming she wasn't lying in another stairwell.

Though the prison staff needed to be alerted as soon as possible, he didn't want to get everyone in a panic. He wasn't even sure if Eve could take on new forms. The fact that she hadn't already was a good sign, but if her ultimate goal was to get to the prison, she may have hidden those skills, much as she hid her strength. To appear as less of a threat than she actually was. But why come to the prison? Surely, she wasn't stupid enough to try a prison break. "I need to speak to the warden right away."

"Which one," the doctor grumbled.

"Excuse me?"

"I'll get the message to him, but he's in the middle of a rather difficult problem. I wouldn't expect an immediate response." The doctor headed out, leaving Heaton to the torture of Vera as she desperately tried to find a vein on him.

She glanced up at him, and he smiled at her. "Vera, let's forget about what I just said. Let's talk about pain meds."

Heaton heard quiet laughter coming from one of the beds across the way. He hadn't even noticed the man with his casted foot propped up on a pillow. "You should know better than to piss off the nursing staff, Heaton."

Heaton tried to shift to sit up, but the pain forced him back down.

"Don't you understand the concept of rest?" Vera asked before taping off her IV and connecting it to a saline drip.

"Who is that?" Heaton whispered to her.

She shrugged and injected a flood of pain medicine that made him want to kiss her.

"Don't you recognize me? My face hasn't changed as much as yours." The man rose from his bed and hobbled over on his crutches.

Heaton blinked at him, still willing his memory to find the name that matched the face—a face that, by rights, he had only seen a few times in his early years of service but nevertheless dreaded. "Riley?"

"There you go." Riley sat down on the bed next to his. He propped his crutches on the two beds and lifted his foot into the elevated position. "Long time no see."

"Why are you...? Shit. Duke."

"Yeah."

Heaton suddenly remembered the sad look on Efrat's face. As sullen as he was, he could only imagine how Ethan was feeling. He was no doubt demanding to save Duke. However, Danato wasn't likely to allow an unwilling sacrifice just because Ethan had lost a friend. Fortunately for everyone, Heaton had arrived with the perfect person to put into that statue. It was probably against the rules, but what Danato didn't know, the board didn't have to know.

"Did you know him?" Riley asked.

Heaton nodded. "He was a good guy, as far as I knew."

"Funny, everyone is saying that, but he was a prick when I knew him."

"Well, everyone's a prick when you're an arse."

"Nice." Riley scoffed. "You should probably be nicer to me."

"Why is that?"

"Because I'm back, and I intend to start where I left off."

"Where you left off? You mean you intend to be warden?"

"Yeah. That is what I trained for. That is my birthright."

Heaton wanted to laugh and even started to, but he wondered if it wasn't true. Did Riley's blood ties overrule Ethan's claim to the wardenship? If so, what would happen to Ethan? What would happen to Cori? Nothing in this prison made sense, but there were definitive rules and guidelines. Until Ethan and Cori arrived, the prison had been handed down from generation to generation, like bad luck and male-patterned baldness.

"Is that what Danato says?"

"It doesn't matter what Danato says. I'm next in line. The only one left in the line. The board will back me in a second. Hell, I'm related to half the board, anyway. They'll side with family over some outsider."

Heaton shook his head slowly, thinking about the budget Sophie had shown him. He still wasn't sure what it meant for everyone employed by the prison, but he was certain adding a new name to the roster wouldn't be on the top of their to-do list. "The board has changed over the years. From what I hear, there are a lot of new, young faces. Who's to say they will have the same family values?"

"There are rules, Heaton. Whether you or anyone else likes it, I will be your boss soon. The sooner, the better, if you ask me. This place has gone to hell in a handbasket. Did you know they have an elemental on staff now?"

"You have no idea. A word of advice. Before you start spouting your authority on high, you might want to research your new staff."

"Thanks, I'll take that under advisement."

"Hey, if you really want to get back in Danato's good graces, do me a favor. Find that big lovable mug and let him know that I have to see him right away."

"I have a broken ankle."

"And I have a broken back, Riley. Get me the warden, now."

55

"WHAT DOES THAT EVEN mean? 'I own this prison.'" Cori used a mocking voice to impersonate Riley. Belus poured her another cup of coffee and placed a batch of fresh-baked cookies on the coffee table in front of her. Despite the sour nature of the conversation, she couldn't help but revel in the delight of Belus giving her sweets to eat. It was the one perk of visiting his home. It was a strange little habit he had, but as she understood, it was a valuable seduction tactic for his lady callers.

Given their recent disagreement, Cori wasn't even sure he would let her through the door, let alone offer her hospitality. However, he seemed prepared for her visit. The cookies were already in the oven, and the coffee was brewing.

Belus didn't answer her question. He just returned the carafe to the kitchen and sat in the chair catty-corner to the couch to observe her.

After a moment to dwell on the chocolaty goodness in her mouth, she went right back to ranting. "He talks like an over-privileged adolescent teenager. How old is he?"

Belus shrugged. "He was in his late twenties when he went in, I think. I'm not sure what the age delay is for the statue."

"Can he do this? Can he pop out and stake claim to the prison?"

"Well, it was originally intended to be his responsibility."

"But... We're here now. Ethan and I. We..."

Belus held her gaze a moment before looking away. "No one's going to kick you out, Cori. This is your home. Danato wouldn't part with you without a fight." He looked at her, his eyes narrowed, practically rolling as he spoke. "And neither would I."

Cori chuckled at his reluctant admission of attachment. "Belus." She groaned and threw herself back on the couch. "I hate myself for asking this." She bit her lip before speaking. "Can't we just put him back in?"

"Do you think that's the right thing to do?"

"No!" Cori put down her cup and scooted down the couch closer to his chair. "Of course, it isn't the right thing to do, but neither is leaving Duke in the statue. I hate to be this person, but couldn't we just put him back in and get Duke out?"

"We could, and truth be told, I don't think anyone would object once it's done."

"See!" Cori raised her hands in a eureka moment.

"Except Duke." Cori's excitement fell along with her hands. "He sacrificed himself for a reason... guilt.

Despite our grief, Duke won't just change his mind, especially since his mind will be in the exact same state of determination when he is taken out of the statue. He'll go right back in until we all accept his choice. I think you know the man well enough to know that's true."

Cori did know that. Duke was an honorable man, but at the moment, she hated him for it. She put her face in her hands and grumbled a few cuss words. "Why did he have to do this now? Ethan has enough to deal with." Cori looked at Belus, debating whether or not she wanted to poke the elephant in the room. "Danato really hurt him when he killed Addy."

Belus nodded. "I know."

"He... I think he's losing confidence in Danato's choices."

"What about you?"

"What do you mean?"

"I mean, are you losing confidence in Danato's choices? How do you feel about Danato killing that young woman?"

"I think it sucks," Cori summed up.

"But?" Belus offered.

Cori dithered a bit, searching for the right words. "But... after seeing what the wizards could do... I can't even imagine what a full sorceress could do."

"I'm glad you understand."

"That doesn't mean I think Ethan is dangerous," Cori quickly corrected.

Belus gave her a small smile. "I shouldn't have worried you like that. I should have waited until I had more information." Belus leaned forward and pushed the plate of cookies closer to her.

She chuckled at his blatant bribery and took another cookie. "What about you?" she said over her mouthful.

Belus perked his brow in surprise. "What about me?"

"What did you think about Danato's choice?"

"You mean other than it sucked?"

"Yeah."

"I thought the same thing I thought when we were facing the decision of killing Olivia."

"What's that?"

"That we can kill people, but we can't kill ghosts."

Cori considered that statement and realized he wasn't just being philosophical. Even years after Olivia's death, she was haunting Danato through a radio—perhaps not literally her, but still. And now, with the sorceress' threat gone, her corpse was still threatening them with a magical breach. Whatever that turned out to be.

"I thought about what you said yesterday, about your concerns with my ability to make decisions that go against my heart."

"Oh?" Belus didn't change his expression. There was no eagerness for him to hear more, but she suspected he wanted to know what she had to say.

"I think you're making the same mistake that Renee made."

"Renee?"

"She thinks that I'm foolish for putting myself in harm's way to save the people I love."

"As one who has benefited from that foolishness, I can hardly criticize it."

"But you do think that my love makes me naïve." Belus didn't answer. "Efrat always says that I look at the world like it's a fairytale that has to have a happy ending."

"Do you?"

"I hope for a happy ending, and I fight for one, but I only do that because I know what the alternative is. But..." Cori reached down and twisted her wedding ring.

"If Ethan suddenly changed—if he turned into someone unrecognizable... someone that could threaten lives—threaten our son's life..." Cori glanced at the door as if she suspected that someone might hear the words she was about to speak. She looked at Belus. His eyes were wide and unblinking, waiting for his answer. "If I had no other options available—and I mean, the apocalypse is coming, and there isn't an inch of duct tape in the entire world type of scenario—then, yes... I would kill Ethan to protect everyone else." Cori felt a shiver come over her body as if someone were walking on her grave. "I just hope that I never have to make that decision. I'm not sure I could survive having to kill someone I love."

Belus reached over and gripped her hand. "Hopefully, there would be someone around who loves you enough to take the burden off you." Cori stared at Belus, once again trying to quantify the sacrifice he made by killing his best friend. It wasn't just the guilt of being an executioner he brought on himself, but also the years of bitterness he created by being the triggerman. He and Danato had only just recovered from those difficult years. There was no way to reconcile that sacrifice with the gratitude it should elicit.

Rather than attempt to address the complex set of emotions that Belus's veiled offer was unpacking, Cori just reached for another cookie and stuffed it in her mouth. "These are really good," she mumbled, trying to extinguish the emotional tension in the room.

"I don't think you're naïve, kid." Belus drew his hand away. "But I do know you're willing to take big risks without truly weighing the outcome of your actions."

"That's because there is never enough time."

Belus smirked and sipped his coffee. "I think we will eventually find a solution for Duke's predicament, but we will have to be patient. Ultimately, we have to find an answer that will satisfy Duke's morality, not ours."

"In the meantime, what happens to Riley?"

"That will be up to Danato."

Cori twisted another of her rings as she considered what the outcome of a new—or rather old—face would do to the prison.

"Do you miss them?" Belus nodded to her rings.

Cori shrugged.

"I've been thinking a lot about your rings since we spoke with Levi. He said that spells die with their creators."

"Yeah, so."

"So, Ethan technically created the spell, but he used Ogana's dark magic to activate it."

"Right, and Ogana is dead, so the batteries have gone dead."

"But the spell is still in place, only dormant."

Cori thought about that. "Like a record. The music is there; I just have to start up the turntable to hear it."

"Exactly."

"I suppose if one were to get a witch or a mage to shove some power back into them, that would start the music again—so to speak."

Belus nodded, eyeing her carefully. She knew he was evaluating her reaction and gauging her enthusiasm as natural or obsessive.

"Is that something that we would want to do?"

"I'm not sure, but I wouldn't advise bringing it up to Danato until we know exactly what is going on with Ethan. As I said before, we need to be patient."

"Thank you," she said, giving the words as much meaning as two singular words could have. He nodded, and she smirked uncontrollably. "Okay, I'm going to go before I can't resist hugging you." Cori stood up and dusted the crumbs off her pants.

"No hug? That was why I made the cookies."

Cori laughed at his joke, but he shifted off his chair and opened his arms to her. She had apparently underestimated his guilt. She leaned down to hug him, but the phone in his office rang, interrupting the rare moment of Belus-instigated affection. He headed in to answer it while she slipped her coat on.

"Yeah," Belus gave a gruff greeting to the person on the other end. She waved goodbye at him through the open door, but he held up a single finger, bidding her to wait. Though he was listening intently to the person on the phone, he turned his attention to her and stared her down. "How long? ... No, I mean, exactly how long ago?" There was a long pause as this determination was made. Belus checked his watch and relaxed. "Have you gotten hold of Danato? ... Alright, Cori and I will take care of it." Belus hung up the phone and came out to his small kitchenette.

"What will we be taking care of, and why did I get volunteered for it?"

"You got volunteered because I said so. I got volunteered because no one can find Danato." Belus pulled out a steak brander from his silverware drawer and turned the gas up on one of his stove burners. He placed the metal "dad gift" into the flame and turned his attention back to her. "Heaton just reported to the infirmary. About twenty minutes ago, he and Jordan lost track of their catch—a transmorph."

Cori rested her head back and groaned at the ceiling. She hated transmorphs. Not just because of her previous encounter with them, but because they were a determined and vengeful race. Tracking them down always proved to be difficult—and time-consuming. "It's loose in the prison," Cori asked, suddenly realizing she could no longer trust anyone. Anyone. She glanced at her watch, trying to determine how long she had been at Belus's house. He caught the glance but said nothing. She had been there long enough for cookie baking, so she was certain that Belus was not a transmorph.

"Jordan might be able to track her down, but we can't trust her now, either. We'll need to find Daniel first—they can't mimic his power. Efrat too. We'll clear Jordan and then coordinate a prison-wide search."

"Prison wide? That's going to take days. The minute someone leaves our sight, we'll have to check them all over again."

"I'm hoping we can get help with that. Lift your shirt."

"Excuse me." Cori blanched at the request until she saw Belus pick up the mini cow brander.

"Oh, come on, Belus, that's gonna scar," she pleaded, but knew it didn't matter. She lifted her shirt, and Belus didn't hesitate to place the hot metal against her skin. She was impressed at how well she took it—only minor cursing and no squirming other than to beat her fist against the counter. He placed the rod back into the fire and started rolling up his sleeve. Cori touched the big white "B" that was turning pink on her belly and chuckled. "Patty cake, Patty cake," she mumbled.

Belus took the hot iron out and marked his forearm with a B as well. She was also impressed at how well he took the pain—barely even a twitch in his lip. When he was done, he shut off the burner and pulled his sleeve down. "Don't show that to anyone. That's just for us to keep track of each other. Everyone else, as far as I'm concerned, is a suspect."

"Okay, Baker's Man." She gave him a mocking salute. "Let's go find our bad guy."

56

ORI STOOD IN THE elevator beside Belus and smacked her radio, trying to get the singing to stop. It was on more than one channel, so she was having trouble finding a clear signal to speak with anyone. When she first heard it, she thought it was Olivia and nearly threw the device into the wall, but it wasn't her voice.

"What is this?" She turned to Belus, who was equally baffled. "Is that French?" Cori pulled the radio close to her ear, trying to hear the low, quiet vocalization on the other end. "Who is this?" Cori spoke into the walkie. The singing continued, unencumbered by her interruption. Rather than listen to the creepy melodic voice, she clicked the device off.

The elevator doors opened, and she was happy to see that her call to arms had not gone unanswered as she thought. Several of the guards were waiting for her on the transmorph level, where they would start their search. Step one in the protocol was, of course, to secure the existing transmorphs. The only worse than an escapee was multiple escapees.

"Alright, let's get to work," she started speaking forcefully the moment she stepped from the elevator. "Belus and I will perform security checks on all of you before we—"

"Ma'am," Trevor spoke up from the middle of the pack. He stepped out in front of the others. "We have something else we need to deal with first."

"More important than a missing transmorph," Belus asked with his usual lack of appreciation for the guard's intelligence.

"Yeah." He nodded at Belus and turned his attention back to Cori. "We don't usually see this kinda stuff. Not here, anyway. Danato runs a pretty tight ship. We all do as we're told, ya know?"

Cori glanced around at the uncomfortable faces behind Trevor. Something had them upset, and it wasn't just twins in a crowd. "What is it, Trevor?"

"It looks like somebody wanted to send a message. And... uh... they did it in blood."

"Blood?" Cori frowned at his macabre statement.

Trevor nodded for her to follow, and she glanced at Belus before moving.

"Gentlemen," Belus interjected, as the other men started to move with Trevor. "With a transmorph on the loose, it would be best for all of you to keep your distance until we can verify your identities." The men seemed to understand Belus's paranoia and dispersed, allowing them to follow Trevor into the next section without an entourage.

Midway through that section, they found a guard bent over his knees, panting. "What's wrong with—" Before she could finish the question, the man vomited on the floor. She gave Belus another worrisome look, but he didn't know anything more than she did. "Trevor, what's going on?"

Trevor ignored the sickly man and headed to the next door. Before opening it, he turned back to face her. His expression was not of disgust or fear, but sympathy. "The boys tried to do CPR, but... he was already gone."

"Gone? Who? Who's in there?" Cori immediately thought of Ethan.

Trevor didn't answer; he just opened the door for her. Cori rushed inside, fearing the worst, but she still wasn't at all prepared for the scene she found.

"Oh, my God." She stopped in her tracks when she saw the blood. Bright red sullied the prison's beautiful white floor. Up and down the corridor, drips and puddles, splatters and streaks. There was far too much to believe one person had contained it.

Cori stared at the body in the middle of it all. Although his dark clothing showed no sign of red, heavy strokes of crimson smeared the floor around him along with dappled footprints.

The guards had obviously rushed to his aid, sliding through the blood to revive him. They were, after all, well-trained in first aid. The first few moments were critical, as she and Belus knew firsthand. Cori knew they had done their very best.

And yet, there he lay. A pale face with glassy black eyes staring up at the ceiling. He was gone.

He's dead. A voice whispered inches from her ear, but only in her mind. The familiar call of the sorrow demon felt like yesterday to her, but she didn't have time to drop to her knees and sob as she should have—as she wanted to. She had to be strong and ignore the wrenching ache in her chest that felt like the start of a heart attack. Her day was only beginning, and this wouldn't be the most difficult part of it. Not by a long shot.

Cori heard a soft, somber melody behind her. She turned to look and saw Trevor thump his walkie, much as she had, trying to figure out what was going wrong with it. He played with the volume, trying to make the singer more intelligible, but the voice remained a whisper on the other end.

"Cori," Belus whispered. She turned to him and found him facing the section break they had just come through. Her eyes tracked the red splatters that traveled up the wall, turning into legible smears–two words written in blood. She didn't know what they meant, but she was certain they weren't meant for her.

"Trevor," Cori snapped at him. "Shut that off and bring me Callin."

"Callin? But he's still recovering." Trevor looked at Belus for a saner request.

"Then put him in a wheelchair," Belus advised.

"Yes, sir," Trevor rushed off to do his bidding.

Cori stared up at the words, trying to understand the level of psychosis that was required for this type of violence. "What does it mean?" Cori asked Belus. "Doth Se-ola," Cori sounded out the words.

"Doth so-la," Belus corrected. He looked down at Daniel McGrath's body. "It means dead soul."

Cori shook her head. "What kind of sick joke is that?"

"It's not a joke." A familiar Irish accent sounded behind her. Naturally, the transmorph nearest them had taken Daniel's form—a mockery on top of what was already a travesty. For a moment—only a moment—she allowed herself to look at the creature as if it were really Daniel. She imagined it was all a horrible mistake and she could speak to him. Though there was no ill will between them anymore, she still had a burning desire for closure. As if telling him goodbye would somehow make this moment less jarring. "That's what they call me," the Daniel transmorph said.

"Is that so?" Cori hated bantering with transmorphs, but since they were technically witnesses to this crime, they were the only ones who knew what had happened to him. "Why do they do that?" Cori approached the facsimile.

"Cori," Belus cautioned.

"I know." She paused just on the red line. "What is a dead soul?"

"That's what I am." Daniel motioned to himself. "Legend has it that dead souls are men that are born with an empty space in place of their souls. They are constantly trying to fill it. So, they take the souls of others." Daniel motioned as if pulling a rope toward his heart. His eyes glittered with amusement, but there was also a coldness there too. "But that's not really true, of course."

"No, few legends are, though."

"The truth is, a dead soul isn't born empty. They are born with the soul of a dead man. It's how they get their power. It's also how they get their hunger. Hunger for death."

Cori shook her head, fighting away the tears that were going to come out sooner or later. "Is that why you killed him?"

"Me?" he shrugged and banged on the bars in front of him. "I didn't leave this cage."

"There is blood at your feet." Cori pointed down at the red drops, indicating that Daniel had, at some point, been standing in front of this cell. "And there." She pointed to another puddle of blood in front of the next cell. She wasn't sure, but she thought she saw more in front of the next cell. "This was an execution."

"And he was an executioner! If he had his way, my race would be extinct!"

"That is because your race is a parasitic bane! If I had my way, you would already be extinct."

Daniel cocked his head and looped his arms through the bars. "You don't want a war with us, girl."

"There is already a war."

"Oh, no, darlin'. The war has only just begun. That..." Daniel motioned to his own lifeless body. "...was just a warning shot to announce our presence."

Cori looked back at Daniel's body and took a breath. "That..." She looked back at the transmorph. "...was you writing your death sentence." Cori wiggled her finger toward the farther cells. "Four death sentences if the blood is speaking clearly."

Daniel shook his head. "It doesn't matter."

"Funny, it doesn't matter to me either." Cori moved to the clipboard between the cells and wrote a note on it. "Four hours," she said to the creature. "In four hours, you will be exsanguinated. Or do you prefer the incineration method?"

"You don't have that authority."

"I do." Belus joined her and took the clipboard.

"You don't want to put your name on that record, Belus. No sense in getting caught up in Danato's debts."

Belus signed his name across the entire page, nice and big. Cori took the clipboard back and hung it up, while Belus did the same with the remaining clipboards in the section. It would no doubt be the largest number of prisoner executions ever done in one day, but no one was going to feel guilty about it.

As she stared down at Daniel's body, she couldn't help but remember that no one was able to get a hold of Danato. Rather than trying to radio him on random channels, she just pulled the alarm on the wall.

57

D ANATO STOOD IN THE elevator, listening to the Irish folk ditty coming over his walkie. He had already scolded the singer for keeping the communal line busy, but it hadn't stopped him. He supposed one of the guards had made it into the alcohol reserves again. As he listened a little longer, he finally recognized the quiet voice on the other end.

"Daniel? Is that you?"

The singing stopped, and he heard a throaty chuckle coming from over the line. "Aye, it's me."

"Are you drunk?"

"Nah, but I wish I were."

"Why are you blocking my line? What are you doing?"

"Me? Oh, I'm not doing anything anymore." Daniel's voice sounded brittle. "Nothin'. No more."

"Daniel, what's wrong? Where are you?"

"I don't know where I am. The world's gone black, and I'm all alone with my thoughts. God help me." Daniel chuckled. "I'd like to say that I'm scared, but truly, there's nothing to be frightened of anymore."

"Daniel, you're not making any sense," Danato snapped at him. "What's wrong with you?"

There was a long pause. "I'm dead, Danato."

Danato stared at the radio in his hand as if it had suddenly come to life. The temptation to smash it into a thousand pieces was nearly overwhelming, but his curiosity got the better of him. "If you're dead, how are you speaking to me?"

"I don't know. I was all alone. Just me and my thoughts, here in the dark. Then I heard my name. Would you tell her something for me?"

"Who?"

"My wife. Would you tell her I'm sorry? I should've trusted her judgment. I should have always trusted her judgment."

Danato stared at the radio, wondering if these were really Daniel McGrath's final words or if it was a sick joke. He hoped that it was all just a sick joke. He wanted it to be a horrible, insensitive prank. Something he could yell about later.

"Do you want me to tell her anything for you?" Daniel asked.

"Who? Jordan?"

"No, your wife. Olivia."

Danato threw the radio into the wall of the elevator. The plastic shell shattered, spilling the guts of wires and batteries on the floor. Nothing more came from its speaker.

Danato stared at the doors of the elevator, incapable of digesting the conversation he had just had. Unable to reconcile the world he knew with the world that no mortal man could ever know. All he knew was that something terrible had just happened.

The elevator let out a *ponk* when it reached its destination, which was odd since he hadn't pressed a button yet. He hadn't even decided where he was going. Apparently, he was going to the part-time level.

As the doors opened, he saw Callin approaching the elevator with the help of one of his guards. They both looked up at him, surprised. Danato looked between their worried faces. "Gentlemen?" He stiffened up, looking over Callin. "What exactly do you think you're doing?"

"Warden," the young man said and even bowed his head slightly, as if he were meeting royalty. "We were just coming to find you."

"We?" Danato nodded to the recently shifted man next to him. "Why is Callin being moved?"

"Cori ordered me to bring him down to her."

"Why did she order that?"

Trevor's mouth gaped like a fish, but he didn't speak.

"Well, don't keep him waiting, Trevor. Give him your report," Callin said.

"I think she wants him to help to find the missing transmorph."

"Transmorph!" Danato's temper flared. He wanted to know why no one had informed him, but then he remembered that his radio had been off prior to his conversation with Daniel. Which he now suspected was more guile than tomfoolery. "Why hasn't the alarm gone off? We need to gather everyone and get everyone cleared."

"The guys decided not to sound the alarm. It just wasn't something to see if ya didn't have to."

"What are you talking about?"

Trevor looked at Callin.

"The alarm may not be necessary anymore," Callin contributed. "Trevor here discovered something on his way to get me. We think it's your missing transmorph. We hope it is, anyway."

Danato furrowed his brow. He had a slew of questions, but he resisted asking them. He wasn't sure what was going on, but Trevor seemed flustered by more than Danato's overbearing personality. And unless he was mistaken, Callin seemed a little disturbed as well. "Show me."

Callin nodded and turned to walk without Trevor's help. He only made it to his second step before collapsing to the ground like he had rubber legs. Trevor rushed to help him, but Danato shooed him away.

Danato dipped his arm under Callin's and assisted his rise with a tight grip around his back. "I can do it on my own," Callin grumbled.

"Bullshit," Danato grumbled right back. "This is the only time your kind ever does need help, so don't be a dick about it."

"I wasn't..." Callin sighed. "Thank you."

"Where are we headed?" Danato looked at Trevor. "Lead the way, young man."

"This way." Trevor jogged ahead.

Danato helped Callin into the next section behind Trevor. Once they were through the door, Danato saw a bloodied body lying on the floor in the middle of the section. His heart leaped into his throat as the memory of his recent conversation haunted him. But he could already tell that it wasn't McGrath. The petite form was decidedly female.

Nevertheless, new nightmares entered his thoughts. There were a few females in his employ, and even though Trevor had already indicated that Cori was upstairs, he couldn't put the concern out of his head until he saw a face.

Danato dropped his assistance to Callin and ran to the body in the center of the room. In his absence, the werewolf plopped to the floor like a marionette with cut strings. Trevor moved to help him, but he waved him away, content to stay where he had landed.

Danato bent down to examine the woman. He thankfully didn't recognize her face. However, that only brought more questions to mind. She was a long-haired redhead with beautiful features. Features that were clear and defined, even in death.

This wasn't a transmorph.

The body was bloody with rents and tears in the flesh. Transmorphs couldn't continue the pretense of human mockery after death. Their forms sagged against their cartilage frames. In death, they looked like melted human remains. Not to mention, stab wounds rarely affected transmorphs. This woman was a human being and had, no doubt, passed into death painfully.

Danato examined the jagged cuts in the flesh, which were certainly not done by a knife or sword. They were the wounds of a crude weapon or perhaps an animal mauling.

Danato looked at Callin. "Did you do this?" he asked, seeking the only logical connection he could to make sense of what he was seeing.

"Me?" Callin laughed, motioning to his incapacitated state.

Danato stood up straight. "Did you get out?" Danato turned his attention to Trevor. "Was he already out when you got here?"

Trevor frantically shook his head.

"Don't be ridiculous, Danato. If I had gotten to that girl in my wolf state, there wouldn't be a drop of blood to find, let alone a body."

"Then who did this? This had to have been done by an animal."

"I know," Callin said, disappointment in his tone.

"Who is she?" Danato asked Trevor.

"I think this is our missing transmorph, sir," Trevor answered.

Danato shook his head, frustrated by the man's ignorant conclusion. "This is not a transmorph!" Danato pointed to the body. "This is a human being!"

"I would beg to differ," Callin interjected before Trevor could bury his face deeper into his chest. "There is something very distinct in her scent."

"She is flesh and blood." Danato went so far as to push his foot against the woman's hip. "This is bone, not cartilage. This isn't a transmorph."

"I know what you know, Danato," Callin said more firmly, asserting he was not another vacant-headed lackey. "I don't understand it, either, but look closer." Callin nodded to the body, his eyes narrowing on the form like it was something to be wary of. "Something isn't right about it. The muscles, the organs." Callin's eyes shifted back to Danato. "Take it from someone intimately familiar with mammalian flesh. That is not a human being."

Danato shifted himself down into a crouched position and looked over the eviscerated body again. It wasn't part of his job description to perform autopsies or surgeries, but much like anyone, he had a basic understanding of human physiology. As he looked over the interior structures, he noticed something odd. The organs didn't seem to be positioned right.

He didn't want to surmise what that meant. He trusted Callin's nose, but to claim the woman was a transmorph was premature.

Danato drew himself up. He didn't want to dwell on answers he couldn't get without the help of a doctor. "Why is she here?"

"The hunters brought her in," Trevor answered.

"And now, instead of being put in a cage, she is lying on the floor of my prison, dead. How did that happen?"

"Tell him the rest," Callin told Trevor.

"Tell me what?"

"I don't really know for sure," Trevor dithered. "I could have been mistaken."

"Tell him," Callin insisted sternly.

"When I came through the first time—to get Callin... I saw a woman. She was... feedin' on her."

"Feeding on her?" Danato quickly inventoried his carnivorous female prisoners.

"She was eating from the body—like a zombie or something."

"Danato," Callin interjected. "I saw her run through my section shortly before Trevor arrived."

Judging by the grave look on Callin's face, he probably could have assumed the answer, but he asked it anyway. "Did you recognize her?"

Callin nodded and paused as if he wanted to give Danato the opportunity to cover his ears and refuse to hear the truth. Unfortunately, he didn't have the option to pick the truths he wanted to hear. "Who was it?"

"It was Nevia Jordan."

Danato turned away, hiding his emotions behind shock and irritation. He was surprised at how affected he was by the information. He had only worked with Nevia a short time, but he respected her a great deal. Her rational mind and calm facade didn't match the actions that Trevor was accusing her of, but Callin had no reason to lie. He wouldn't identify her if he weren't sure.

"There's something else you should know," Callin added. "She's going through werewolf puberty."

Danato looked back at him and shrugged. "I've never heard of cannibalism in half-breeds. Certainly not in quarter heritage."

"I'm not sure if this qualifies as that."

"If she's eaten from a corpse that has a face like hers, I qualify it as cannibalism."

"I just mean that killing by means of biting could look like eating."

Danato looked at the body again. The body was an ugly mess of torn tissue. The woman's neck looked as if a solid bite had been taken from it. It was beyond what he thought human teeth could be capable of, though.

"There is no way she could have done this. She's like 90 lbs."

"I can't speak for how, but Nevia was covered in blood. She had to be the one to kill her. In cases of extreme stress, all mammals are capable of great feats of strength. Even the petite ones."

"What could stress her enough to kill and eat another person?"

"Maybe she knew the guy who got murdered?" Trevor posed.

Danato and Callin looked at him, sharing in the shock of yet another morsel of necessary information being doled out much too late. "Who got murdered?" They both asked.

Trevor motioned two fingers over his eyes. "The guy with the laser eyes."

"Daniel is dead?" Danato felt a shiver run over his entire body. He didn't have answers for the haunting conversation he had just had with the man and probably never would, but that didn't stop his mind from conjuring thoughts about heaven and hell and other useless theological lessons.

"Yeah." Trevor nodded. "That's what I was saying before. We didn't set off the alarms 'cause we didn't want Ethan to run in and see him that way. When we couldn't find you, we called Belus. He and Cori are looking over the... crime scene—or whatever—on the transmorph floor." Danato started moving just as Callin found the strength to push himself off the floor. "Did she know him?" Trevor asked after Danato.

"That's her husband, you idiot," Callin snapped just as Danato pushed through the door to leave the section.

By the time Danato reached the elevator, he expected Callin to be in his dust, but he had kept up just fine.

The doors were open and waiting for them. The moment they stepped foot inside, the prison alarm sounded, announcing to anyone still out of the loop that danger was afoot on the transmorph level. Danato could only think about one thing as the door closed.

Ethan.

58

HEATON HAD FINALLY RELAXED with the help of his pain meds, but he wasn't quite asleep when Nevia came into the room. Covered in blood and panting, she fell to his bedside. "Heaton," she rasped.

"Jordan, what the hell happened? Are you hurt?" He struggled to reach for her, to check her wounds, but she clasped his hands and kissed them.

"I'm sorry. I'm so sorry."

"What's wrong? What are you talking about?"

"I wasn't fast enough."

"For what? Did she get away?"

Nevia looked up at him, eyes fearful and teary. She shook her head. "No, she's dead."

"That's good. How did you kill her?" Heaton asked, noticing the blood around her mouth.

"You need to know that she's different. Like she said, I think she was telling us the truth. She is a hybrid."

"Ohh, please no." Heaton let his head fall back. "Why do you think that?"

"Because of the smell..." Nevia rested her head against Heaton's hands and took in several labored breaths. When she looked up, she seemed calmer. Determination had returned to her eyes. "I have to go."

She moved away, but Heaton pulled her back. "Wait, no, tell me what happened. Why are you covered in blood?"

"I can't stay. It's too dangerous."

"Jordan! I'm your partner, for fuck's sake. Tell me what's going on!"

Nevia stared at him, her eyes as bright and as big as saucers. She moved to sit on the edge of his bed. He shifted back slightly, concerned that her movements might have implied desire, or worse. "You are my partner," she said firmly. "You're the only man I can trust. Do you understand? You are the only man I can tell."

Heaton swallowed hard. "Jordan, whatever you did... We'll deal with it. Okay?"

"Do you trust me, Heaton?"

Heaton's eyes flickered over hers. He could see something there. Something predatory. The truth was, he didn't trust her. He still hadn't come to terms with the danger that lurked inside of her. But he suspected she was speaking in terms of her instincts and her intellect. "Yeah, I trust you."

"Then heed my words. You can't trust anyone. Do you understand? Not anyone. Except me. Trust me."

Nevia leaned in close to his ear, and it took everything he had not to flinch away to protect himself. She placed her hand on his chest. He knew his heart was racing, but he could also feel a tremble in her hand. She was no doubt coming down from her adrenaline high.

Nevia's sweet susurrations could have lulled him back to sleep if she had been speaking lullabies or reading to him from the Hobgoblin lineage, but she wasn't. Her words were pure acid to his heart. A nightmare among nightmares. He wasn't sure how so few words could instill so much terror, but magical breaches and time bubble ruptures paled in comparison to the damage of those few words.

When she pulled away, she looked Heaton in the eyes. Worry on top of worry mounted in her expression. The same worry that was trickling through his body, forcing him to steel himself against a painful reality that had yet to solidify in his mind.

The alarm sounded, muffled by the interior walls of the infirmary. Nevia looked up through the window behind his bed. Her eyes tracked the movement outside. Her gaze returned to his, somber and guilt-stricken. "I have to go," she whispered. "I know you won't forgive me, but it doesn't matter. I'll never forgive myself."

"What do you—" Nevia kissed him. It was a hard, meaningful kiss that belonged on another man's lips, but he didn't pull away.

She released his lips, her gaze flickering over his body as she drew away from the bed. "I'll take care of it."

"Jordan," he said insistently, as she turned her back to him. "What are you going to do?"

She stopped in the door frame and looked back at him. "Don't follow me." Nevia disappeared as swiftly and quietly as she came.

"Jordan!" he yelled after her, but she didn't return. He wanted more answers than the few she had provided. The least of which was why her lips tasted like blood.

59

ALARMS BLEATED ACROSS THE prison, drawing everyone of importance to the transmorph level. Ethan had only just learned of Heaton's arrival in the infirmary when they started going off. The fact that a transmorph was loose somewhere in his prison was not only worrying him, but it was pissing him off. As if his week wasn't difficult enough. His only hope was that with Daniel on site, they wouldn't have to endure the same trials that they had done the last time a transmorph got loose.

As he jogged up to the fourth floor, several guards passed by on their way back down again. They each caught his eye on the way by and immediately looked away. He considered asking them where they were headed since the trouble was up, but then he noticed the blood on the palms of their hands. Someone was hurt.

Ethan's thoughts turned to Cori. Transmorphs had a long memory for revenge. They no doubt still resented her escape from their grasp. He quickened his pace, skipping steps until he reached the door. He ripped it open and ran onto the level.

He caught sight of two men in the section talking. They both paused and looked at him, giving him the same look of concern as the men in the stairwell. His heart began to race. It couldn't be her. It had to be someone else. He couldn't lose her.

He ran to the next section and found still more guards standing around, chatting. They each looked at him, their expressions sinking terror into his already nervous mind.

"Sir." One of the larger men, Blake, stepped forward, blocking his path before he could speed past them. "You should hang back. Your missus has this one under control."

"Cori?" Ethan started breathing again. "She's in there?"

"Yes, sir. I think this one is best left to her."

Ethan frowned and shook his head. "I'm sure she's doing fine, but I still need to report to the scene." Ethan shifted to move around him, but Blake stepped into his path again. Ethan couldn't keep himself from laughing. "What are you doing? You don't actually think you can stop me from going in there, do you?"

"No, sir. Not with my body, but I'm hoping that you'll listen to my words."

"What's..." Ethan looked around at the sullen faces that were also bidding silently for him not to go. "What's going on?"

"Sir, if you would just let me go announce your presence. I'm sure that Cori would be able to—"

"I need a report, Blake!"

Blake's jaw tensed, and he glanced at his fellow guards as if asking permission from them to speak. "There's been a... murder, sir."

Murder.

That was the only word Ethan could focus on. Not a death. Not an accident.

A murder.

Ethan didn't bother listening to more of Blake's pleas. He just pushed him out of the way and ran to the next section. Had he listened to the man, he might have saved himself some pain. At the very least, he wouldn't have the image of his best friend dead on the floor and two bloody words indelibly written across his mind.

60

D ANATO HEARD ETHAN'S LAMENTED scream long before he reached the scene. Callin's footsteps increased beside him, along with his hissing breaths. More than once, the werewolf grabbed his shoulder to support his tired and no doubt achy muscles, but he refused to slow down. It wasn't until then that he remembered Callin wasn't just there to offer Ethan camaraderie. Daniel had worked side by side with Callin on more than one occasion. They had no doubt become close. Close enough to be injured by the news of his death.

Danato stopped outside of the last door, where the guards gathered to gossip about what they had witnessed beyond that point. He turned to Callin. "Are you sure you want to see this?"

"Are you?" Callin asked. At any other moment, Danato might have taken it as a werewolf challenge of character, but he assumed Callin might have been attempting to offer the same consideration as he had to him.

Danato had never considered himself to be Daniel's friend. With such a complex history together, they had only just reached a level of respect that qualified them as colleagues. However, it was in that same sordid history that he felt an attachment. He and Belus had known Daniel longer than anyone in the prison's employ. And that time equated to a connection, no matter how he preferred to define it.

"I have no choice," Danato stated firmly, determined to do his job regardless of his feelings.

Callin glanced at the door. "I don't think I do, either."

"Very well." Danato turned to enter the section. He paused a moment for Callin to grab his shoulder for support before proceeding.

As they stepped into the section, a sickening smell—the smell of a butcher shop or a meat processor—greeted them. It was the smell of blood. Too much blood.

Callin's hand slipped away from his shoulder. He wasn't as immune to the streaks of red across the white canvas as a carnivore should have been. However, that was always the hypocrisy of the meat eater. The blood was never as alarming on your plate as it was coming directly from a warm body.

Danato could barely digest the scene except to note the sheer amount of blood he was seeing on the floor and painted across the walls. He also noticed that his successor was nowhere to be seen. Whatever emotions Ethan had been feeling, he had gone off to express them in private.

That was for the best, he supposed. He would be of no use to them in his burgeoning state of grief.

Danato moved into the center of the room and stood over the body of the man who had once caused him great ire and frustration. As he stared down at Daniel McGrath, he wondered two things. How had the most lethal man he had ever met gotten himself killed? And how had his wife killed his murderer with nothing more than her bare hands—and teeth?

Cori cleared her throat behind him. "Danato."

He turned back, expecting to see Cori weeping and prepared to throw herself in his arms, but neither was the case. It was true that her face held several pains—the least of which had to be the trauma of witnessing a murder scene of this magnitude.

"Sweetheart." He shifted to move to her, but she took a quick step back. He was insulted by the rejection. They had certainly had their share of arguments in the last few days, but he didn't feel he deserved such a staunch dismissal. Then he noticed the tremble in her hand as she raised it to signal for him to put the brakes on his gesture of comfort. She was holding it together, but just barely. He stood up tall, relinquishing his desire to hold her. "Report," he said firmly.

Cori pointed her shaky finger at the first cell, just behind her. "We believe that the first stabbings happened there. He must have killed one of the attackers because there was ash—"

"Attackers?" Danato frowned. "More than one?"

"One of the inmates from the first section is missing. They came at him together. I assume that while he was distracted with the first one, the other one came up behind him. There was an injury..." Cori demonstrated on herself with an imaginary knife. They stabbed the knife up through his chin... and into his..." Cori cleared her throat again. "...skull."

Danato watched Cori dutifully report the death of Ethan's best friend with as much detachment as she could muster. This being the first time Cori had to encounter a messy human death at the prison, he thought she was doing well. He knew, sooner or later, something like this would come up, but not like this. Not an outright murder. Not someone that everyone knew as a friend.

"As you can see from the ceiling tile, he did try to defend himself, but the trauma to his brain must have enabled his power because that was the only damage we found." Danato looked up at the exposed pipes and wiring. Something was sparking, threatening to start the place on fire, but he wasn't worried about that at the moment. "We believe he was walked down this line of cells allowing each of the transmorphs to stab him—Ides of March style."

"Jesus," Danato whispered as he realized why the blood was all over the room instead of just under the body.

"Somewhere..." Cori pointed to the row of cells on the other side. "...over there..." She pressed her fist into her mouth, willing her voice not to crack as she spoke. Her tears were forcing their way out, despite her efforts to remain reticent. Danato wanted to embrace her and alleviate her burden of stress, but he needed this report. And by the looks of Belus, standing at the far end of the section, staring vacantly at nothing, he would not be able to offer it any more intelligibly than Ethan could at this point.

"Around that cell is when he most likely officially died. The drag marks indicate that the transmorph had to drag him to his current position. The words were most likely written on the wall after that."

Danato looked at the wall, which did nothing to increase his grief. If anything, the big red words stirred his anger. This was not an impromptu murder. This was a targeted execution. This was revenge.

"They said that this is the start of a war," Cori whispered. "Daniel was just a warning shot."

Danato turned back to Cori. He could see the underlying worry in her eyes, not just for Daniel, but for him. He looked over at the transmorph nearest him. It had taken on Daniel's form, complete with stab wounds and glassy eyes, making him look like the living dead. "Who? Them?" Danato chuckled, downplaying her concerns. "They are always threatening to start a war."

Cori looked at Daniel's transmorph. She couldn't seem to take her eyes off the risen corpse behind the bars. It was even more frightening than the real one. Danato rested his hand on her shoulder. "You've done very well, Cori. If you want to take a break, I can handle the rest of this."

Cori looked at him and shook her head. "I have to do this. Ethan is in no condition to and..." She looked at Belus, who was still just standing across the room, staring at nothing. "I need to do this." Cori looked back at Callin. "We need to find the one who did this."

"We already did. It's dead."

Cori breathed a sigh of relief that sunk her shoulders and head. "How?"

"Never mind all that for now. We are safe." He rubbed her back. "I'll send for the doctor to collect the body."

"He's already been sent for." Cori stood up straight, as if she had been called back into play by the coach. "I've asked the nursing staff to assist with the cleanup. Belus is going to start work on the requisition orders to get his body transferred to Ireland so he can be buried on his mother's farm. We think he would have wanted that." Danato glanced at Belus, surprised he was entertaining yet another breach of protocol on body disposal. However, this was a different situation for everyone.

"And... we've approved termination for the entire floor." Cori was still trembling, but her eyes seemed to instantly dry as she looked at the transmorphs responsible for this bloodshed. "I believe consorting and murder is enough of a charge to warrant that."

Danato looked at the transmorph behind him. The blasted thing had changed from Daniel to Olivia. He wasn't sure any of them had been here long enough to know her, but apparently, at least one of them had. Cori frowned at the infrequent impersonation. She was familiar enough with the woman from her prison photo to recognize her. Not that it did her any justice. Nor did the transmorph, but he might have been remembering her a bit more angelic than she actually was. In his eyes, she had always been perfect.

"Can you do it, Danato?" his wife asked. "Can you kill me again?"

Danato noticed the clipboard next to the cell. Belus's signature was visible even from here. He smiled at his John Hancock bravado. He was about to offer a sarcastic retort to the transmorph when he heard and felt the crackle of electricity.

"I can," Efrat said.

Danato hadn't noticed him come in. Callin limped clear of the energy pouring off of him. Judging by the look on his face and the blue rivulets crawling up his arms—which were putting holes in his black shirt—he had no intention of joining the investigation.

"Efrat? What are you doing here?" he asked.

Efrat paused to look at Daniel's body. Danato wasn't sure he was close with the man, but he was certain that Ethan had earned enough loyalty from him to be angry on his behalf. He looked at the transmorph in front of Danato and started moving again.

"Efrat?" Cori moved to intercept him.

"Stay back!" he demanded, stilling her steps instantly. He stopped in front of Danato, who was not as easily scared off. He had seen this version of Efrat before. This was the man who had fought him time and time again—trying to free himself from his oppressor—namely Danato. "Get out of the way, Danato. I don't want to hurt you," Efrat warned him.

"What are you going to do?"

"Something you should have done years ago."

"We are handling this." Danato raised his hands, trying to appeal to his logic. "There is a protocol."

"Fuck protocol," he said through gritted teeth and moved around Danato. He tried to grab him, but the electrical current peeling off him was too much, and he recoiled from it. "Get clear now! I won't say it again." Efrat balled his fists, and a swirling ball circled his hands like an electron cloud around an atomic core.

"Danato!" Cori screamed as she backpedaled. "Run!"

Danato realized Efrat had no intention of offering a warning shot and did exactly as Cori suggested. He ran.

An explosion of blinding light and painful static electricity filled the room. The energy hit him like a blast wave, propelling him to the floor. The thunderous bang demanded he cover his ears or lose his hearing altogether.

Danato rolled over to chastise Efrat for his erratic and volatile behavior, but the elemental wasn't finished. He moved down to the next cell and did the same, charging his hands to impossible heights before releasing the energy like a cannonball at his target.

Danato closed his eyes as the next indoor lightning strike took place only yards away from him. Efrat moved down to the next transmorph to offer the same preemptive execution. Danato couldn't wait to see the damage he had done to the transmorph, so he slid across the floor to see into the first cell.

Another lightning strike made him clench his eyes shut, but between that and the next, he saw into the cell. Never mind the melted metal bars or the scorch marks on the walls. It was the blackened blob of goo on the floor that surprised him. Efrat had dissolved the creature. Transmorphs were not easy to kill: exsanguination or cremation were the only sure techniques, but apparently, high-voltage elemental electrocution was also effective.

He couldn't say he approved of this, but as he saw Efrat move around the far cells to finish his massacre, he didn't even attempt to stop him. He would enlighten him later on the reasons for protocol and why half-cocked plans rarely benefited the prison. However, as a student of Cori's antics, he wasn't sure that Efrat would listen to anything he had to say on the subject.

61

ETHAN HAD NEVER ATTEMPTED to fight a dragon outside of the gym before. Penelope's state of trance was the only thing that made him question his decision to attack her.

His fist landed hard against her belly, but the fat deposits barely warbled at the impact. Since she let out a deafening roar, he must have given her some pain.

"Did you know!" he yelled, not caring if anyone heard him openly conversing with the creatures behind the prison.

How dare you. Her mind spoke to him, chastising his physical confrontation or perhaps just the interruption of her prayer circle. The other dragons stopped their lyrical mooing and turned their attention to Ethan.

"My friend is dead!"

And what participation do you blame us for?

"I blame you for your reticence. I blame you for not using your power of sight to help us. I blame you for standing by while yet another body lies dead at my feet!" Ethan screamed at her.

The doth seola is not our concern. His magic is divined from sources beyond the earth. We only concern ourselves with maintaining the magic of this realm.

"You could have stopped this!"

Penelope twisted her head back and forth as if she were denying the accusation, but she continued to shake her head, spewing dragon spit all over him and the snow at his feet. *Does my body not afford the power to heal? Does my blood not provide the inducement of magic? Must you grind my bones to raise the dead as well?*

"You could have warned me of this event! Then I could have saved him!"

If you wish to save your friend, then you must understand the magic of his birthright.

Ethan stepped away from Penelope to get a better view of her face. It was difficult to discern emotions, but he could see her narrowed eyes and flaring nostrils. "Save him? He's already dead."

Human flesh dies. Souls ascend. Daniel McGrath may be a human vessel, but his core is of magic. And his is a magic that does not die.

"You mean dark magic?"

It is not of earthly or human origin. We dragons can see magic. Shades of greens and blues for earth. Blacks and grays for human energies. The doth seola possesses red magic.

"Red magic?" Ethan murmured. He couldn't help thinking about the devastating power that Daniel wielded. Did his power come from... hell?

Magic is not about religion. The dragon answered his thought. *These concepts have no place here. Magic is energy. Just as there are positives and negatives in nature, so must there be positives and negatives in magic. Some attract. Some repel. Some are balanced. Some are chaotic. All are dangerous. Including your own.*

For the first time in a long time, Ethan didn't feel like the world was collapsing around him. There was hope. Maybe someone didn't have to die for the sake of this prison.

"My magic?" Ethan looked at his hands as if they might somehow be the tools to implement this so-called mage power. "Can I save him with my magic?"

No.

"What is the point of this magic if I can't even use it?"

Your skill is still premature. Spontaneous and sporadic. There is still time to learn it, though.

"And what will I learn to do? What is a mage?"

My kind distinguishes your magic as purple. Your magic is not altogether separate from other magics, but it is substantially more unique.

"What does that mean?"

It means you are very rare.

"Why didn't you tell me this before?"

Because it will do nothing to change your path. It will do nothing to ease your pain. And it will not change the course of life and death for your friends.

Ethan looked to Addy's grave, which was plush with grass. He had tried to save her, but it only brought her to a colder grave. "What about the breach? Can I stop that? Can I change this course? Can I dig her up and burn her?"

No, the seed has been planted. We must let it grow.

"Why?"

To protect the earth.

"From what?"

This is not your concern yet. The breach is our responsibility. We will fight the battles. You must worry about the war.

"The war? What war do I have to fight?"

Penelope shifted her head and returned to mooing once more. The other dragons joined her, and just like that, the conversation was over. As usual, Ethan was left with half-truths and more questions than when he started.

62

C ORI FOLLOWED DANATO AS he carried Efrat into the infirmary. She was certain he was averse to offering the man assistance of any kind, but given that his power usage had put him into a state of physical shock, Cori demanded he be brought to the infirmary for care. Thankfully, Efrat's exertion had also reduced his tangible shock to nearly nothing. It wouldn't last, of course. It never did, but hopefully, it was long enough for the nurses to care for him.

Belus had excused himself to work on the paperwork, but she knew he couldn't take looking at Daniel's corpse one more minute. Not that he would have left the scene before Danato arrived, anyway. Cori had been so concerned about Ethan's reactions she hadn't even considered Belus. Daniel was like a son to him. Losing him was no different to him than if Danato had to lose Ethan.

The thought of how deeply Daniel's death would affect everyone around her made Cori wonder about outrageous solutions. Where was Gypsy now with her forked paths? Where was the genie to wish it all away? Where was the hero?

Cori already knew the answer. The hero was dead. Daniel McGrath was dead. He may not have considered himself a hero, but she knew him to be one. And she solemnly swore to herself she would do everything in her power to honor his memory.

Cori held the door for the doctor as he wheeled the stretcher in with the body bag. She had been thankful to be rid of the view of Daniel's pale skin and dead eyes, but somehow, the body bag was more frightening. Proof that the diagnosis was final.

Deceased.

Cori could already picture the big red letters stamped on his prison file.

Callin followed the doctor in, bracing himself on the door handle as he did. Cori knew he was still recovering from his evening of expansive changes and was hardly a threat, but she still moved away from him to avoid any unnecessary contact.

"Can someone tell me what the hell is going on?" Heaton hollered from behind the nurse's station. "Has anyone seen Jordan? She was talking like a crazy person earlier."

Danato dropped Efrat into a wheelchair brought by the nurses. He instructed them to let him know as soon as he was conscious.

"Who's the stiff?" Heaton asked, nodding back to the stretcher.

The entire room seemed to freeze, including the nurses. Everyone exchanged looks as they all realized that somewhere in the melee of the missing transmorph and murder, no one had informed Heaton of his partner's demise.

Cori's eyes locked onto Danato, fearful and already wetting with tears. Ethan's reaction was a torrid display of emotion. Belus's response was to be stony and quiet. What would Heaton do? The man who had worked side by side with Daniel daily for years.

Cori opened her mouth to speak, but she was terrified of answering. She was on the precipice of losing herself to her own emotions, as it was. She wasn't sure she had enough countenance left to offer Heaton. In truth, she just wasn't ready to watch another man's heart crushed.

"Is that Eve?" Heaton asked, his mood becoming somber.

"Who's Eve?" Danato asked before offering the answer.

"The transmorph that Jordan and I brought in. She slipped out of our grasp. I told him to tell you about it." Heaton pointed vaguely to the doctor.

The doctor nodded, confirming that his duty was to inform Danato. However, the day had not gone as anyone had planned.

Danato motioned for the nurses caring for Efrat to move along, and they continued to wheel him down the hall. "Our communication has been a little disjointed today." Danato shifted, blocking Heaton's view of the body. "Cori and I have been working on putting things back in order. Why don't you and I talk so we can finally get the beginning of this puzzle put in place?" Danato moved to Heaton and put an arm over his shoulder, urging him to move into another room.

Before they could make it around the corner to a more private location, the remaining nurse at the hub popped up and held out the phone. "Doctor, they have the transmorph on the west end. Which room do you want to do the autopsy in?" the woman asked much too loudly.

If Cori had been in reach, she would have throttled the woman. As it was, she gave her the most vicious glare she could muster.

"Transmorph?" Heaton pulled away from Danato, silently accusing him of a lie, though Danato had not technically spoken one.

"Never mind that Heaton. I need your report." Danato once again tried to take him by the shoulder, but Heaton rejected the contact like a poisonous snakebite. He was outright glaring at Danato now.

"What is this?" Heaton moved back and looked at everyone's uncomfortable gazes before settling his eyes on the body bag beside her.

"Heaton, what did I say about bed rest?" the doctor interjected. Cori glanced at him, impressed he actually had a compassionate bone in his body.

"Who's in the bag, Danato?" Heaton leveled a hard stare at him. His question was not so much a query as a demand for information.

"Let's go talk."

"Later."

"Now," Danato said firmly, trying his best to bully Heaton for his own good.

Heaton's eyes narrowed into fine slits. "You tell me who is in that bag right now." Heaton jutted his finger at the body. "Because I know who is and isn't in this room. I also know that Danato Calibria doesn't coddle his employees unless something pretty fucking awful has gone down."

Danato shifted, glancing at the floor before bolstering his shoulders for the news that no man or woman wanted to deliver. "Heaton, I'm sorry, but... Daniel has been killed."

Heaton said nothing. He didn't move an inch except to tense his jaw. Cori waited for the delayed reaction, but Heaton didn't speak. There was no lamentation or outcry.

Heaton's head finally bowed, and his eyebrows rose high on his face. "And?"

"And what?" Danato asked.

"Do you want to explain to me what happened to my partner, or should I wait for the paperwork?"

Danato nodded and took a breath. He had no doubt expected the same riotous reaction Cori had. The fact that

Heaton was remaining calm and lucid was throwing him off.

"We believe the transmorph that escaped from you, along with another she released, disguised themselves as someone he knew. They stabbed him to death."

Heaton shook his head. "How the fuck did they get away with that?"

"He managed to kill one of them, but he was stabbed through the head. We believe he was unable to use his power after that."

"Daniel's a hard man to kill." Heaton glanced at the gurney, presumably thinking his diagnosis was a mistake. Cori shook her head slightly, letting him know that there was no chance of a mistake. Heaton caught the movement and watched her for a moment, as if assessing her mood. So far, she was still holding it together, but that didn't stop the tears she was holding back from slipping free from time to time.

Callin surprised her by pressing into her back. She jumped and looked up at the werewolf. His eyes were pinned on Heaton, narrowed in a silent query. Cori wasn't sure if he was smelling something from Heaton or if he was responding to his physical cues. Regardless, Callin didn't like Heaton's *tone*.

Heaton released her from his appraisal and turned his attention back to Danato. "Jordan said that the transmorph was dead. The one that escaped. Eve, she called herself."

"Yes, that's correct."

"How was she killed?"

Danato shook his head. "Let's wait for the doctor—"

"Stop fucking mothering me!" Heaton went so far as to take a step toward him. Since there wasn't much of a difference in their height, Heaton didn't have to crane his neck to meet him eye to eye. "What did the body look like?"

Danato was still reluctant to answer, but since Heaton wouldn't budge, he summed up the report he had shocked Cori with earlier. "The body looked like it had been mauled. The stomach was eviscerated."

Heaton swallowed hard and took a step back. Cori thought he was taking that news even harder than Daniel's death, although the emotions were doubtlessly just piling up now. A missing sock might be the thing to eventually throw him over the edge.

"There seems to be some dispute about her species' designation. I need the doctor to look at her further."

"Who killed her?" Heaton asked.

Danato glanced at Callin. "Callin saw Jordan coming from the direction of the body and..."

"And?" Heaton insisted he continue.

"One of my guards claims he saw her eating the body."

As shocking as the news had been to Cori when she heard it, Heaton seemed calm. His demeanor shifted into something she would have suspected to be guilt.

She wasn't sure how Heaton could be responsible for his partner behaving like a cannibal.

"You said you saw Jordan," Danato spoke a little quieter. "What did she say to you?"

Heaton turned his attention to Danato—his eyes glazed over in a humorless stare. "Nothing. Just that the bitch was dead."

Heaton moved toward the gurney, and Danato shifted to stop him. Heaton slowly turned his head, silently objecting to being treated with kid gloves. The big man seemed to understand that Heaton was not interested in his assumptions about his emotional tolerances, so he lowered his barring arm.

Heaton reached the body bag and reached for the zipper. Cori touched his hand before he could unzip the bag. "Heaton," she whispered in a plea. He held his hand still under hers, though she wasn't actually restricting his movement. She was about to beg that he not inflict himself with so much pain, but Callin moved his hand to hers. He tugged her fingers away from Heaton and pulled her back a little to give the man space.

Callin held onto her hand for a moment, giving it a soft caress. She glanced down at the contact that made her far more uncomfortable than she wanted to admit. He may have been doing it to console her, but since his mind was still recovering from animal hormones, she couldn't trust that it was his only motivation. She pulled her hand back and crossed her arms.

Heaton ripped the zipper down on the bag and flapped it open unceremoniously. He looked down at Daniel's face. His cold, dead eyes were still staring at the ceiling. The puncture in his chin had bled down his neck and chest.

Despite everything that Heaton saw, he reached down and checked his neck for a pulse. He held it there for a long while, searching for a heartbeat—no doubt begging for one. But much as the doctor had confirmed, there was no sign of life. Daniel may have had accelerated clotting and reduced healing time, but he had lost too much blood to recover.

Heaton moved his hand up and caressed Daniel's cheek fondly. He shook his head and chuckled. "I always knew this was how our friendship would end. I just thought I would be the one in the body bag." Heaton leaned down and kissed Daniel's forehead. "Goodbye, my friend. My brother. My pain in the arse." Heaton took in a long breath and looked up at the ceiling, containing his budding emotions. "I need to find Jordan."

"She's gone," Belus announced, sneaking in the door behind the doctor. "The guards on the roof reported seeing a woman riding out on horseback about a half hour ago."

Cori looked around at the disappointed faces. No one could blame the woman for wanting to leave, but leaving before she explained herself seemed suspicious. As if cannibalism wasn't already putting her in the question mark category.

"I hate to ask this," Cori said. "Are we sure that was Jordan and not the transmorph? Is there any chance that the other body could have been misidentified?"

"No," Callin answered resolutely.

Belus looked at Danato for further confirmation. He shook his head. "The face was mostly unharmed. Height and weight were all wrong. Whoever that woman was, she was unknown to this prison."

"Why would she run?" Cori looked at Heaton for the answer. "She had to know we would have questions." He stared back at her, not willing or not wanting to speak for her.

"If she's gone feral, I need her back here," Danato announced to no one in particular.

"No." Heaton zipped Daniel's bag back up. "She isn't feral." Cori wasn't entirely sure what the definition of feral was for werewolves, but she doubted it was a far cry from what other animals experienced.

"Heaton, I know you want to protect her," Danato said soothingly. "No one is going to mourn her victim, but she—."

"She saw what that bitch did to her husband!" Heaton snapped. "If ripping her heart out made her feel better for even a minute, then it's justifiable."

"I'm not concerned about the woman she killed. I'm concerned about her. She was eating from the body."

Danato tried to implore the gravity of her actions, but once again, Heaton seemed to want to hide from that accusation.

"Jordan has her issues," Heaton mumbled. "But we were dealing with them."

Danato's sympathy seemed to evaporate as he shifted his chin a little higher. "What do you mean you were dealing with them? Did you know about this?"

"She's not feral. She's hormonal."

"That's a very fine line when dealing with werewolves."

"I swear to you on my life, Danato. She is in control. She is just angry and torn up. That's all. Don't send the collectors for her," Heaton pleaded. "Wherever she is going, whatever she is doing..." Heaton paused as if he were figuring something out. "She isn't going to hurt anyone. She just needs space to heal. And to figure out what the hell is wrong with her."

"Werewolf matters are very delicate. Even if I choose not to send out the collectors, I will have to report her actions to the Council of the Moon."

Heaton grimaced. Cori wasn't sure what that would mean for Nevia. The little she knew about the council was that mixed breeds were only recently allowed the privilege of inclusion into the werewolf population. If Nevia turned out to be a smudge on their clean record, they might be inclined to take decisive action against her as a warning to others.

Heaton looked at Callin, but he had nothing redeeming to contribute. He was, after all, loyal to Leona, the council's new leader.

"I don't think she was eating the body," Heaton said.

"Trevor saw her." Danato argued.

"Not for sustenance, anyway. Not for hunger." Heaton turned his gaze to Callin. "I think she ate from that thing for a purpose."

Callin narrowed his eyes at Heaton and shook his head. "That prospect isn't going to appease Danato any more than her being feral."

"What?" Danato asked, finally approaching the group.

As if being blocked in on all sides reminded the doctor he had a job to do, he excused himself and pushed the gurney forward to take the body for processing. Assuming Belus could get approval for his paperwork, Daniel would be headed for Ireland soon.

Danato cleared the way for the doctor and returned to the now free-standing circle. As everyone shifted to a comfortable distance, Cori made it a point to step closer to Danato and away from Callin.

"What are you two speculating?" Danato asked.

"Blood-scenting," Callin answered when Heaton didn't.

Danato's brows knit tightly together. Cori noted that Belus had the same look of disbelief on his face. "I thought that was a myth." Danato crossed his arms.

"What's blood-scenting?" Cori asked anyone.

"It's a tracking method," Belus explained.

"But she can already—And why would she—I mean, the woman is already dead?" Cori fumbled around, every question in her head at once. "What's to track?"

Callin took his turn to explain to her as well as the others who may have had some of the same questions. "Blood tracking isn't about an individual's scent. It's specific to the species. Human, werewolf, transmorph, we all have a different olfactory profile."

"But she can already smell the difference between us. She could easily tell us apart."

"Yes, but she has difficulty tracking because her senses are so broad. She smells too much, so to speak."

"So how is blood tracking different from regular tracking?"

"It's not," Callin said. "At least not from Jordan's perspective. She will use all of her skills to track the scent in the same way, but the blood-scenting allows her to distinguish the scent more easily." Cori must have looked just as baffled as she felt, because a small smile perched on Callin's lips. He turned to speak more directly to her. "If a wolf tastes particular meat. For example, my wolf is very partial to rabbits. After tasting rabbit, I became partial to its flavor. My senses have become attuned to its scent above all others because I want it more than other animals." Callin's eyes danced over hers, and for a moment, she felt like the rabbit he wanted so desperately.

"It's no different from you craving a cookie after you smell some baking in the oven," Heaton explained more simply. "The first time you ever smelled a cookie baking, you knew it smelled good, but once you tasted it... You forever know that cookies smell like that, and you don't even have to open the oven door to know what's baking."

"However, in Jordan's case," Callin continued. "Her sense of smell is already accelerated well beyond a normal wolf's perception. She can smell the cookies before they hit the oven."

"And from three blocks away," Heaton added.

Callin nodded and looked at Danato. "If she is blood-scenting, it means she is trying to attune herself to one specific smell. To block out all other distractions. And the only reason she would do that is if she plans on hunting whatever she has blood-scented."

"So much for her not hurting anyone," Danato said rather acridly.

Heaton tipped his head. "No one worth saving."

Danato narrowed his eyes at Heaton. He had no love loss for transmorphs and whatever Nevia had killed would likely fall into the same category, but Danato didn't prefer to play the part of the executioner.

"What is Jordan going to do?" Cori asked. "Go hunt down every transmorph on the continent by herself and... eat them?"

Heaton contemplated this, licking his lower lip. "No. She's not doing it by herself." Heaton turned to leave, but Danato grabbed his shoulder, stalling his exit.

"What do you think you are doing?

"My job."

"Your job is to hunt down creatures for imprisonment, not for death penalties."

"My job is to protect my partners." Heaton turned back to face Danato. "I've already lost one. I'm not losing another."

"And where will you go to help her?"

Heaton paused as if logic had just caught up to him. "I'll find her."

"If you find her, then you will bring her back to me."

Heaton stared at Danato.

"Is that going to be a problem for you, Heaton?"

"Yeah, it's going to be a big problem."

Danato lowered his grip on Heaton's shoulder and bolstered his chest with a deep breath. Heaton didn't flinch at the ire shedding off Danato's tensed body. "You're going through a lot right now, Heaton. The least of which is a nearly broken back. I want you to do as the doctor says and get plenty of bed rest. When you've calmed down and had more than a minute to deal with the loss of your friend, then we will discuss when you can return to duty."

"You bloody..." Heaton stifled his verbal anger, but it was still dripping from his cold expression and tensed jaw.

Danato glanced down, noting that Heaton was balling his hands into tight fists. He took a slight step away from him. "Go ahead," Danato said calmly. "If that will make you feel better." He moved his hands behind his back, inviting the man to lash out.

Belus took a few steps back from the men. Callin moved away as well, pushing her along with his barring arm.

Heaton and Danato faced off for several more seconds as Heaton debated the invitation. Even as the tension rose, Cori hadn't expected Heaton to swing, but he did.

She gasped as the hunter's fist clipped Danato's chin. Despite Callin's protective arm, she tried to lunge forward as if there was anything she could do to stop it.

To her shock, Heaton took another shot, snapping Danato's face back the other way. It was the third slapping impact on Danato's cheek that caused her to scream in agony.

"Stop!" Cori dropped to the floor, no longer able to contain the tears or trembling that had been detaching her from reality for the last hour. "No more! Please!"

She hadn't thought her display would do anything to dismantle the rage in the room, but when she looked up, she saw the men looking down at her pitiably. There was some slight guilt in Heaton's eyes, but his tears were still not freely falling.

He rubbed his face and stalked away. Danato turned and watched him go, no doubt making sure he returned to his bed. "I want a guard posted on his door." He looked at Belus. "He doesn't leave this prison until he has calmed down. I have a feeling he knows where Jordan is, or at least where she is headed."

"Are you going to send out the collectors?" Belus asked.

Danato frowned and shook his head. "I'll confer with the council. This is as much a werewolf issue as it is a prison issue." Belus nodded and headed out to fulfill Danato's requests.

Cori suddenly felt ridiculous, kneeling on the floor, and stood up again. She should have been retrieving the guards, not Belus. Despite the momentary breakdown, she was happy to have disrupted the scene. Bruises were already forming on Danato's chin, but they were superficial wounds. There was little that Heaton could do to truly harm Danato—at least not with his fists.

Danato looked at her and reached his hand out to caress her tear-filled cheeks. "Why don't you take a break? I'm going to track down Ethan and fill him in. If he's ready to hear it." Danato left the infirmary, leaving her and Callin alone—save the nurse at the hub, who was catching up on the latest Hollywood gossip.

Callin smiled at her and motioned to the door. "I think perhaps Danato neglected to mention that I should be placed back in my confinement."

Cori knew that was the appropriate protocol, but she would have preferred to leave him there.

"I promise, I am as weak as a mouse. I won't be any trouble to you."

Cori disagreed, given that she had not been able to break free from him a moment ago, but she hadn't truly been fighting for her life. And as it was, he looked drained now that the danger had passed. She nodded and motioned for him to go out first.

He took a small wobbling step forward, then looked back at her. "Would you mind terribly being my crutch?" He lifted his arm for her to provide assistance. Once again, the protocol would have demanded a wheelchair, but she suspected Efrat had run off with the last one. "I swear on my honor as a wolf. My thoughts may not be entirely pure at the moment, but I am in control of my actions."

Cori sighed, wondering why she had ever bothered to read her manuals. It was so rarely she was put in a circumstance that allowed the rules to be followed. She ducked under Callin's arm, and together, they made their way back to his confinement.

63

“**Y**OUR EMOTIONS ARE ERRATIC,” Callin pointed out in the confines of the elevator. She had left him to lean against the wall while she leaned on the opposite side, staring at the dull sheen of the interior metal. It was not nearly enough to see her reflection, but she could make out the movement behind her should she need to duck from an attack.

“Can you blame me?” she said sourly.

“Were you close with Daniel?”

Cori considered that. “Not especially, but we had our moments. He helped me give birth to my son, so that was a pretty intense bonding moment for us.” As she remembered that memory, Cori felt a little ashamed she hadn't considered Daniel to be a close friend. They certainly had some kind of relationship. Something that fell more into the category of respect than love. It was an odd twist, considering that they had started out disliking each other. “What about you? Were you close?”

“Daniel was an easy man to like. He had many qualities I respect. I will miss him.” Cori glanced back, noting the dismal expression on Callin's face as he considered a future that did not include his friend. "I'm sorry that I was unable to help you more today."

"The transmorph didn't get away. That's all that matters."

"I'm also sorry about yesterday morning." Cori looked away, refusing to offer any forgiveness for the incident. "I know I've lost your trust. That was not my intention."

"You're a werewolf. It's just your nature. I can hardly blame you for it."

"Yes, I am a slave to those pesky hormones. Still am." Cori glanced at Callin, but he was making no attempts to attack her. "It's alright, I'm still in control. Just perhaps a little bolder than usual. You know, I wasn't just talking about the rabbit earlier."

"What?"

"Blood lust is a powerful thing to a werewolf."

"What are you talking about?" Cori shifted, putting her back to the wall. She touched the hilt of her gun. "Do I need to use this?"

Callin's eyes tracked her movement, and he shook his head. "Please, don't. I really am in a great deal of pain just standing here."

"Then why are you talking about blood lust."

Callin chuckled. "I'm trying to explain my behavior. As I told you before, during the change, my wires get crossed. Lust becomes hunger. However, now that I am coming back into my own mind, my hunger is becoming lust again."

Cori stared at him, her fingers still grazing the metal of her weapon.

"Your flavor is still on the tip of my tongue. It's making me a slave to your scent. I want more of you. So very much more."

"Do you really think now is the time to be propositioning me?"

"My body knows no time beyond now. I know what I am asking is out of line, and I will most certainly regret my words in a few short hours, but for now, I beg you to relieve my hunger."

"See, it's the word hunger that is making my fingers twitch." Cori danced her fingers over the hilt of her gun, reminding him it was still an option.

"Trust me, it's not your blood I want to taste anymore." Callin's eyes danced over her body, glittering with unadulterated lust. "Think about it, Cori. I am but a slave to my desires. You could be my master. I will do anything you command of me. Anything that my body is capable of, anyway." Callin smirked at her.

Cori considered the power she held over him. It wouldn't be the first time she had seduced a werewolf on the cusp of his recovery to gain an advantage that suited her.

But could she?

Could she truly weigh the life of one man against another?

Callin was nearly thirty—the age of disrepute among werewolves. Surely, he wouldn't last as long as Vince had. At best, he had three years before the change destroyed him.

Duke easily had fifty years of life left to live. Wasn't a handful of years a more logical exchange? The more she rationalized it, the more trivial Callin's sacrifice of life seemed to her.

For a moment, just a moment, Cori was ready to do it. She was resigned to make decisions that held the balance of two lives in her hands. Perhaps it was the trauma of seeing Daniel dead, but something inside of her was more determined than before to find a solution to the problems around her. She was ready to repair the broken pieces of her family, even if that meant losing a piece of herself.

The doors to the elevator opened, revealing the top floor instead of the part-time level button she had pressed. With the new open floor plan, she could see the Medusa statue without leaving the lift.

The idea had seemed fanciful at first, but now it seemed to have potential. She could convince Duke that Callin made the choice voluntarily. She would tell him that the werewolf sensed his body was depleting and that his death was not long in the future. That would satisfy him. That would keep him from surrendering to his guilt again.

Callin stepped forward and looked out at the wrong floor. He turned to her, his lurid stare now suspicious.

He may not have entirely understood her plots, but he no doubt smelled the treachery on her.

As she continued to stare at him, his suspicion fell away and something akin to disappointment and possibly even fear took its place. There was a small part of her that was proud of that. She was tired of being the one afraid all the time. Besides that, he needed to know he was not invincible, and she was not without options.

"Wrong floor, Cori," Callin said firmly.

Cori relinquished her devious thoughts and pushed the button for the part-time level again. It took a moment for the elevator to agree with her surrender, but eventually, the doors closed, and they descended.

Callin's efforts to seduce her ceased, and he turned away from her to sulk on his side of the elevator for the remainder of the ride.

Though she had the presence of mind to forego such an emotionally motivated plan now, she wondered if that would change in the future. Perhaps at his next lunar phase, Cori would have the stomach to choose between the lives of two men. Maybe when two years were outweighed by forty-nine, she could find the strength to be a villain.

64

HEATON HAD NO TROUBLE getting past the guard Belus had posted at his door. However, the guard would likely claim otherwise when he woke up.

He slipped down the hall to the nurse's hub, where a young woman named "Judy" was reading a beauty magazine and humming to herself. He wasted no time covering her mouth and lifting her from her chair. She squealed through his hand. He only needed to get her to the storage closet, which he planned to open with the keys hanging off her belt.

As he struggled with the lock, the woman bit his hand. He grunted and leaned in close to her ear. "If you stop biting me, I will put you in this closet unharmed. If you don't stop biting me, I will punch you in the face like the guard down the hall."

The woman released the grip of her teeth and turned her head in the direction of the downed guard. Heaton hadn't actually punched him. He had used a sedative on him, but he didn't mind giving her the impression he could knock a man out with one punch.

The woman patted her fingers on the door as if choosing door number one. She even went so far as to assist him with the keys. She got the door open in no time, and he shoved her in. When she turned around, he gave her a stern look. "Do I need to gag you?"

The woman shook her head frantically and sat down on the floor, preparing for her extended stay. Heaton closed and locked the door, which only opened from the outside. That was how most of the extraneous rooms in the infirmary worked—extra holding cells—just in case.

He checked for onlookers and jogged to the hub. Under the counter was a small fridge, which provided a quick stash of sedatives, painkillers, and several boxes of dragon shakes. Heaton pulled out one box and tucked it under his arm. The natural fast acting steroid was just what he needed to get his back healed up.

He took a few painkillers and another sedative and headed down to the truck dock. There was a truck scheduled to go out that night, and he planned to be on it.

Heaton arrived just as the final boxes were being loaded. The night shift loaders looked at him as he approached. One of them stopped in his tracks and shook his head. "You aren't supposed to leave," he said and moved to close the door to the truck.

Heaton intercepted him and injected him with the sedative he had stolen. Unfortunately, the second man was not within reach. The man dropped what he was doing and ran toward the back wall, where a big red alarm lever begged to be pulled.

Heaton cursed, knowing he was in no shape to leap off the dock and tackle him.

The man made it to the wall, but before he could make it to the switch, a right hook from out of nowhere, at least from his perspective, dropped him to the floor.

Heaton stared at Callin, who was standing and walking on his own—a far cry from earlier in the day. He turned to Heaton and crossed his arms. "I'm coming with you."

"Excuse me?"

"You heard me." Callin took some easy but measured strides to the stairs before carefully ascending to the platform. "I'm coming with you."

"You mean you're heading back home?"

"No." Callin shook his head. "I'm going with you to get Jordan."

"I'm afraid that's not going to work for me."

"Whatever is happening to her is beyond your textbook education. You are going to need me. Especially if she has gone feral."

"She hasn't gone feral."

"As Danato said, there is a fine line between hormone imbalance and feral. You don't want to stand in the path of a feral fem-wolf. I don't care how small she is."

Heaton remembered the taste of blood on Nevia's lips. The glitter in her eyes was like a wildcat. There was something off about her. If it was just grief, he could deal with that. If it was something more, then he might not be able to help her.

On the other hand, he wasn't completely sure Callin could be trusted. After all, Nevia specified that he should only trust her.

"I know you're hiding something, Heaton. I know Jordan is in trouble. I know that you are worried about her. I also know that whatever this trouble is, you've stopped trusting your friends to help you deal with it. What exactly are you two going up against that you can't ask for help with?"

"I appreciate your heroics, Callin, but what's happening here has nothing to do with you. You would be wise to stay the hell out of it." Heaton ducked into the truck and started to lower the door.

Callin stepped into the path of it and blocked the descent. It took some effort for him to do so, which meant he was still not at full strength and was likely still in significant pain. "I think you'll find that my involvement in this world is becoming more and more inevitable, but politics aside... I want to help."

"Why? Is this about Jordan? Are you going to turn her into the council?"

"I can't promise that the council won't need an explanation from us, but no, I have no intention of turning her in like a criminal." For a moment, they both just stared at each other, arms up, face-to-face, waiting for the other to either give in or give up.

"Look," Callin broke the silence. "I smelled what she smelled on that transmorph. I smelled blood. I smelled bowels. I smelled the tar rubber of parasitic skin. It wasn't quite human, but it definitely wasn't a transmorph—not like the ones we know. If this is something new... If these things have evolved yet again..." Callin released his hold on the truck door and stepped back. "You and I both know that transmorphs are a far greater risk to humans than rabid werewolves. Some would say they are the greatest risk to humanity. If you don't want my help with that, then good luck to you both."

Heaton rolled his eyes. "Alright, you can come with me, but I call the shots. We go where I say? We do what I say?"

Callin smiled, but nodded respectfully. Heaton allowed him passage and closed the truck door. He gave the door a heavy thump with his fist, and soon, the rumble of the truck engine announced their departure.

Heaton situated himself across from Callin on a crate. There wasn't much light to see, but as his eyes adjusted, he found Callin staring at him. "Where are we going?" he asked.

"To a swamp," Heaton said somewhat begrudgingly since he knew it meant asking for a favor that would put him in debt to a very childish man. Callin perked a brow but didn't ask the specifics. "You mind handing me that tarp?" Heaton pointed at the heavy cloth beside Callin. "It's cold as shit in here."

Callin reached over to grab the cloth, and Heaton took his chance. It would be his last, since the werewolf was getting stronger by the minute. He pulled his blade from his ankle and shoved it into Callin's side between his ribs.

Callin yelled—partially a growl. "What do you think you are doing?" Even in the dark, his eyes shined brightly with threat.

"I can't trust anyone, so you are going to have to prove yourself to me."

"What do you want?"

"Stand up—and don't fucking try anything because I swear to god I will kill you if I have to."

The fury in Callin's eyes turned to confusion, as if he was doubting Heaton's state of mind. "Easy, Heaton. I'm not your enemy. I'll do what you want." Callin eased himself up carefully off the crate.

"Now... take down your zipper and pull your better half out."

"What?" Callin grimaced.

Heaton nodded his head, pressing the knife ever so gently into his rib. "I call the shots, remember?"

Callin took a moment longer to question the resolve in Heaton's eyes before complying. "Okay, okay." The werewolf undid his pants slowly and revealed his member.

Heaton glanced down, twisting his jaw. "That's a fine-looking cock, my friend."

Callin looked perturbed, but he didn't flinch at the compliment. "And what exactly will I be doing with this fine cock of mine?"

Heaton gave him a small smirk. There were about a dozen things he could think of that he preferred Callin do with it. Unfortunately, they weren't on his list of priorities at the moment.

"Take a piss."

65

C ORI FELT USELESS IN more ways than one. It didn't matter that her rings were no longer functioning. The events of the day were proof that not every problem could be solved with magic. Not only was there nothing she could do to stop Daniel's death or Duke's containment, but there was also nothing she could do to fix it.

She had done her best to console Ethan, but his grief was turning bitter. Rather than listen to him bicker with Danato about trivial things, she decided to spend some time alone with her grief. However, when she reached the top floor, the new home of the prop room, she found she wasn't alone.

Riley stood before Duke's statue, staring at the man carved in perpetual stone. She would have preferred to turn around and slip back into the elevator, but the *ponk* had already sounded her arrival.

Riley turned and looked at her. "Cori, right?"

She nodded.

He looked back at Duke. "It feels strange."

"What does?" she asked, hardly able to politely avoid the conversation.

"Looking at it from this side. I know years have passed. I know I don't really exist anymore, but it feels like there should be a way to go back. To redo the timeline."

"How would you change it?"

"You mean besides not going into the statue?"

"Yes."

"I'd probably punch that lousy Texan in the face instead of taking his guff."

"That lousy Texan has saved my life on multiple occasions."

"That's good," Riley snapped and nodded. "That's good that you and Ethan got the good guy version of Duke. I didn't, though. I got the cocky, selfish prick... and I paid the price for knowing him." Riley turned to face her. "I get it, Cori. I'm the usurper now. I'm the wrench in your world. But right now, for me, the world is one big ass wrench."

"I don't know what to do about that."

He looked puzzled for a moment. "You don't have to do anything. I'm not asking for your sympathy. I just need you to know that the one man in this whole scenario that deserves a punch in the goddamn face is Duke, but he's in there. So, you see, from my perspective, he is still behaving like a coward."

"Well, as soon as we figure out a way to yank him back out, you two can have a proper showdown."

Riley chuckled under his breath and shook his head. "Duke isn't coming out of that statue."

"No?"

"No. Danato's going to have the statue decommissioned."

"What do you mean?"

"He's been burned by it twice now. He will pack it up in a nice tight box and then pour concrete over the top of it. That way, no one can get hurt by it ever again."

"Danato's not the same man you remember. He'll give us time to save Duke."

Riley snorted. "He's already written up the paperwork for it—just needs his stamp of approval." Cori frowned, appalled by any plans to permanently—more permanently—entrap Duke. "I guarantee by the end of the week; Duke will be just a big crate."

"Why are you telling me this? Do you want to rub it in my face? Do you have any idea what I have been through today?"

Riley shifted uncomfortably and nodded. "Yeah, I heard about all that. I'm sorry you lost another friend." Riley stared at her a moment as if he were trying to figure her out. "Maybe you're right. Maybe Danato has changed, and I'm sure Duke has, but I'm just bitter about how my turnaround went."

"I'm sorry about that too, but I don't have room in my life for another bitter man. So, if you're sticking around, you are going to have to find a different schtick because that one is all used up."

Riley cracked a smile and nodded. "Alright. What do you have room for in your life?"

Cori sighed and shrugged. "I have a vacancy for a lousy but sweet Texan and a rarely sober Irishman." Cori's eyes watered. "Have you got any of them?"

Riley bit his lip and shook his head. "No, I'm sorry. I could work on an accent, but I doubt I would ever be able to replace either of them."

Cori shook her head, agreeing he was no match for the positions.

"Is... there anything I can do?" Riley asked tentatively, as if he knew the answer was no, but felt compelled to ask out of pure politeness.

Cori took a breath and tipped her head apologetically. "Can you give me the floor?"

Riley glanced back at the big empty area that was littered with glass displays, artifacts, and specialty enclosures, but no people. "Yeah, sure." He nodded and tucked his hands in his pockets. He headed toward the elevator. He looked back after pushing the button. "Ah... Cori, Danato told me that Ethan might need a few days to grieve. Since Duke is... out, he asked me to take over some of my former duties. To help out."

"Okay."

"He said that I should report to you for my assignments until Ethan is back on his feet?"

Cori nodded. "Just take care of the guards. They were never under my domain, anyway. That was always Ethan's territory."

"And what exactly is your domain?" Cori narrowed her eyes at him, unsure if he was being sarcastic or not. "Just so I don't step on any toes."

Cori shrugged, not sure how to describe her mismatched duties as of late. "Everything else, I guess."

Satisfied with that, Riley stepped into the arriving elevator and left her to wander the floor alone.

Cori trekked through the endless maze of junk that, surprisingly, all seemed to have a home now. Each large piece had a platform, and each small piece had a dedicated cubby. The dangerous pieces were enclosed in glass, and the *really* dangerous pieces were locked down in small closets marked "Danger" or "Caution." The truth was, of course, they were all dangerous. From forks to dead rats, they all had a purpose that someone had created them for. Good or bad, they disrupted the natural order of the world with purposeful magic.

As helpful as her rings had been for her, it wasn't as if they couldn't be used as a weapon in the wrong hands. That was why Clark had tried to kidnap her. Had he succeeded, she might have found herself in the same situation as Efrat—locked up in a high-security prison until she agreed to do as he commanded.

Cori looked down at the Spirit of Pamola. The original glass globe had been broken by her and Efrat when she helped him and the other elementals escape their captivity. Somehow, Danato and Belus figured out a way to get the dreaded winter storm back in the containment of a new globe. Otherwise, there wouldn't be a top floor anymore, just a big freezer. Not to mention, the cost of heating the building would be astronomical.

As she moved through the displays, she felt the fabric of her shirt catch on something. She looked back just in time to see the pedestal holding the oil lamp wobble. The lamp responsible for her wish relocation toppled toward her. She instinctively reached out and caught it. As the metal touched her skin, she dropped it to the floor as if it had burned her. It rattled against the tile.

"No, no, no!" She wiped her hands on her pants and looked around as if searching for a witness to yet another of her stupid mistakes. She had just gotten out from under the genie's debt, and three minor inconveniences were the punishment for rejecting his granted wishes. She didn't want a new one. "No more wishes. No more wishes. Please."

She waited for the genie to emerge and grant her "wishes," but he didn't show up. Maybe she had used up her wishes. Was the lamp expired for her?

She waited for nearly five minutes, watching the lamp for signs of a smokey wisp, but nothing came out of it. When all was clear, she carefully picked the lamp up by its handle only and placed it on the pedestal.

Cori decided that this was not the best place to get alone time and headed back to the elevators. Before she could reach for the button to call on it, a voice called out to her, "It is time."

"Shit," Cori whispered and turned back to see the face of the mysterious voice. Somewhere beyond the globe, but before, the Teddy Bear from hell was a man she could only describe as a god.

"Genie?" she questioned, although there was no way she couldn't recognize the seven-foot-tall man with hardened muscles and inky black tattoos all over his body.

"Hello, Corinthia." He smiled.

Cori raised her hand to block out the blinding light that seemed to outline the genie's body. She didn't dare look away, though. The wavy tendrils of a perfect star grew and blocked out everything around her except him. In the midst of pure white, she could see his tall and robust physique. His bald head and bare chest had smooth amber skin, every inch covered in tattoos. The black ink looked like obsidian against the white backdrop. Each sinuous symbol represented a partition of a spell—a spell that had been cast centuries upon centuries ago to draw down the power of the universe so that man could wield it.

He was magnificent, and it took everything inside of Cori not to touch him. To do so would be to defy all logic and bind herself to his power. It was suicide, she assumed, but what a beautiful death it would be. Despite her knowledge of this, she still gravitated toward his aura, trying to feel the warmth of his skin.

"Genie?" Her mouth gaped as his radiance dimmed enough for her to see his face. She stared at him, ever in awe of his near godlike allure. A small smile tipped the edge of his lips. He was no doubt amused by her stunned gawking. "What are you doing here?"

"Your third and final inconvenience has recently been rendered. Your debt to be released from your wishes has been paid."

"I know. Thank you."

The genie bowed his head slightly.

"I never thought I would see you again."

The genie's eyes twinkled as he flickered his gaze over her face. "Did you miss me?"

Cori nodded. "Yeah, I think I did."

"That pleases me."

Cori gasped and pointed to the statue behind her. "You can help us. You can release my friend."

"No, I'm afraid the affairs of man hold no interest for me."

"I'll gladly take another punishment for my impertinence. How many minor inconveniences to free my friend? Better yet, how many to turn back time so I can stop all of this?"

"Time is not a weapon to be played with by humans. You know that better than anyone. And I am not a tool to be used as frivolously as you desire."

"People are dead, Genie. I need your help."

"I am not here to help you, Corinthia. I have already helped you. I am here to collect my debt."

"Your debt?"

"Yes, it's time to receive my payment."

"Payment? For what? I've given my three sacrifices. My debt is paid. You just said so."

"That was in exchange for the wishes being ungranted."

"I don't understand."

"You don't remember." The genie stepped to one side and motioned back toward the radiance he had arrived from. Within the beautiful glow, she saw herself bleeding and dying on the prison's floor. Ethan crouched over her, begging the genie for her life. She was writing in blood the words she couldn't speak for herself. "You could not speak. You would not have been returned to your world without the verbal agreement. I bent the rules for you. To allow you to return."

Cori looked at the genie with wide eyes as she shook her head. "Yes, you did. And I am eternally grateful for that."

"You would have died had I not allowed the deviation from my rules. You exist because of my graciousness."

"I don't deny that your gift was generous."

"It was not a gift. It is very difficult for a genie to defy his restraints. You have no idea what a sacrifice it was for me."

"I'm sorry. I didn't understand that. I was only thinking of myself." Cori reached to touch his cheek—to somehow express her regret for any pain he endured because of her. He drew his face back, and she froze. He glanced at her hand and clicked his tongue.

"Careful. Sticky. Remember?"

She did remember, but it was hard to resist the temptation. "What happens if I touch you?" she asked, not dropping her hand just yet.

He smiled. "A thousand and one empires rise and fall in the span of a heartbeat."

"Would it kill me?"

The genie perked his brow, surprised she was still considering it. "I think it best we don't find out."

Cori lowered her hand, finally giving up on the idea of touching a god. "What do you want from me?" She looked back at the image in the light.

"I have given you your life. That debt must be repaid. I have come to collect as much in return."

Cori shook her head, looking over the room behind her for an escape, but there was nowhere to run from a genie. She also knew there was no arguing with him. And his power was far too great to trouble herself with a battle.

Her thoughts turned to Ethan and her son, Danato and Belus, all the people who would be lost without her. They had already lost too much.

"I'm not ready to die." She turned her pleading eyes to the genie. "Give me another bargain? Just a few more years. I'll do anything." She knew she shouldn't offer an open-ended commitment to such a being, but at that moment, she didn't care. A plague on the world was better than leaving her family at that moment. It was, once again, selfish, but her heart demanded no less.

"I cannot wait any longer. My time grows short."

"Your time grows short. You're dying?" she asked, suddenly more concerned about him than herself.

"I cannot die, but the spells are starting to fray." He rolled his arm, showing the underside where the tattoos were fading.

"Then what?"

"Then nothing." He shrugged. "I am released back into the universe. As if I never was."

Cori wasn't sure what the exact definition of death was, but she was pretty sure that still applied. "I'm sorry. I guess I should have saved my last wish to free you."

The genie shook his head. "I only exist because I am not free. My cage may not be gilded, but there is something to be said for the gift of self-awareness." He took a step forward. "I appreciate the thought of the offer, though. It means I chose the right vessel."

"Vessel?"

"Yes. A body. A real body. Flesh and blood. So that I might taste the sweetness of your fruits, smell the earthly air, and feel the touch of another on my skin."

"You want to be human? But you're beyond human already. You're better than us."

"I am more powerful, to be sure, but I am not real. I am an idea manifested by a spell and perpetuated by the magic that resides in every living being on this planet."

"What happens if you become human? What are you then? Are you still a genie?"

"Then I will be a living god."

Cori frowned. If Danato didn't like the idea of a sorceress running around on the earth. He really wouldn't like a flesh and blood god. "You can't do this."

"I can."

"There has to be another way."

"The pact has already been made," he said.

"What pact? I didn't make a pact."

"I assure you it was made."

"But I didn't know what I was agreeing to. You never told me."

"That does not matter."

"Of course it does!" Cori took a step back. "Everything about our last interaction was detailed out like a damn divorce proceeding. There is a book in Danato's office with more litigious bullshit than a cell phone contract. Don't tell me I entered into a pact without knowledge, consent, or my bloody signature written in triplicate!"

"You did not."

"There! See! It doesn't count!"

"I mean, you did not enter the pact."

"I...!" Cori tipped her head. "What?"

The genie closed his eyes and took a soothing breath before opening them again. "I am not here to collect you, Cori. I am here to collect your son. He is the one I made the pact with."

FELICIA JEDLICKA

Curses & Sacrifices

Book 12

The Warden

Curses & Sacrifices

Sneak Peek

GYPSY BREATHED A SIGH of relief as the skid hit the rooftop. She put the brake into place and shut down the helicopter's engine. It had been a long trip and even with her uploaded flying lessons; she wasn't comfortable with the variable weather conditions this far north. As if gale force winds weren't enough to tighten her grip on the cyclic, there was always the occasional glass-shattering blast wave to worry about... or dragons.

Gypsy unstrapped herself and peered out the windshield at her arriving escort. Despite the early hour, the prison's security was on point. The lookouts had no doubt called in their impromptu guests the minute they caught sight of the helicopter over the dark horizon.

Gypsy climbed out of the cabin and approached her favorite spark plug. She was legitimately pleased to engage with Efrat again, but she was a little disappointed not to see her favorite Texan by his side. His particular charm was growing on her. She was certain that he didn't reciprocate that sentiment, but time was usually a better predictor of her friendships than first impressions.

Efrat slowly moved his arms forward and away from his sides—the equivalent of cocking a gun in his case. She bit her lip, trying not to mock him with an unrestrained grin. Nevertheless, she raised her hands a little to reveal her empty palms, surrendering to his authority. She knew he was dangerous—more dangerous than he was given credit for, but much like Daniel McGrath, she could see a reluctance in his armament. He had no desire to hurt her. Not yet anyway.

"Since when did the roof become our official landing pad?" Efrat called to her over the slowing whir of the chopper's blade.

Gypsy shrugged and glanced back at her newly acquired bird. It cost a pretty penny, but it hadn't come out of her account, so she didn't have to worry about it. "I'm afraid my employer doesn't understand the meaning of the phrase no-fly zone. And he hates traveling by land. Too slow."

"Your employer sounds like a douchebag."

Gypsy tipped her head and perked her brow. He wasn't wrong. Her employment had been more than satisfactory on the money front, and there were certainly perks to having such a powerful man in her corner, but his personality required a degree of tolerance... and coddling. "Where's your other half? I was looking forward to being greeted by some down-home southern charm."

Efrat frowned and averted his eyes to the ground. "He's inside of the Medusa statue."

"Oh." Gypsy wasn't quite sure what that meant, but by the look on Efrat's face, it wasn't good. "Can't get him out, I take it?" Efrat shook his head despondently, jaw tight as if he were fighting back more emotions than he preferred to reveal to her. "Rough week then?"

Efrat glared at her, but she held back any inclination of amusement so he knew she wasn't mocking his distress. She wasn't unfamiliar with the loss of a colleague and she considered it one of the more underrated griefs that people had to endure. Recognizing her sincerity in the statement, he scoffed and nodded. "You have no idea."

"I'm sorry. I know you and Tex were friends."

"Duke," Efrat corrected a little defensively. Never mind that the man's given name was Duane. His nickname was as much a part of his identity as his southern accent. Or at least it had been.

Gypsy could feel the moment getting heavy. If they continued on this path, there was bound to be hugging or tears—and there was no need to embarrass the man like that. "How about I kick these two douchebags out of my chopper and we can fly off to Tijuana together?"

Efrat looked back and the chopper. His frown softened, and he let his lip tip up a little. "I'd love to, but knowing my luck I would short out the engine and we would crash and burn before we made it to the equator." Efrat showed off his dazzling blue hands.

Gypsy shrugged. "Well, it would be a hot ride either way."

Efrat's brow dipped at her semi-flirtatious morbidness. "You really are a strange cat, you know that, right?"

"Strange as they come." Gypsy shifted to see who had come through the roof exit. She met eyes with Cori. She was dressed in a black coat two sizes too big and her hair was blowing in her face, but they recognized each other instantly. "Ah, crap," Gypsy mumbled. She had anticipated having an altercation with the woman. Cutting her hand off was bound to have some lasting consequences for their already turbulent relationship. However, she had hoped to at least get off the roof before the fisticuffs began. It was too damn cold up here and the lighting was shit. "I don't suppose an apology will get me out of this fight."

Efrat glanced back at Cori's approach and stiffened his back upright into a proper little soldier. Whatever levity Gypsy had developed in the conversation had instantly evaporated. "I don't think so," Efrat said quietly. "She's having a worse week."

Gypsy wondered what was worse than losing one of their own, but she didn't have time to inquire.

Cori moved toward her, eyes bright with venom that increased with each step. There wouldn't be any chance of making peace with the woman now. At best, she could have a proper row with her and exhaust the anger out of her once and for all.

Cori stopped beside Efrat and looked her over. Gypsy recognized the attempt to search her for weapons, but the woman was not skilled enough to identify anything beyond the bulge of a gun holster. Not that it mattered since, like the last time she visited, Gypsy was under strict orders not to harm "the good guys," unless absolutely necessary. The fact that cutting off Cori's hand became necessary last time was not her fault. Strictly speaking, it was Cori's fault. The woman's doggedness had been extremely inconvenient to her rescue efforts.

"What the hell are you doing here?" Cori asked, not bothering to hide even a sliver of her contempt.

Gypsy was relieved she hadn't outright attacked her, but that didn't mean Cori wasn't poised for any excuse to start a fight. Gypsy needed to be very careful about what she said, so she didn't set the woman off.

"I've come for the other hand," Gypsy announced with a wicked smile.

"You bitch!" Cori only hesitated a second before pulling her gun.

Thank you so much for reading. I hope you
enjoyed the ride and if you aren't getting
off here, I encourage you to sign up for my
newsletter so I can return your generosity
with new release updates and special offers.

Sign-Up

You can also find me on Facebook or visit my
website. Keep reading!

Website

Facebook

AUTHOR

As a Nebraska native, and a small-town girl at that, I have very little to occupy my time beyond imagining a world outside of my own reality. By the grace of God and the seat of my pants, I have kept my waning attention span on the task of becoming an author.

So here I am, an indie author, peddling my words in cyberspace and enduring my comeuppances with an unwavering determination. I may not be a professional, and I certainly am not perfect, but if you've made it this far, you have to admit, this smartass yokel does spin quite a yarn.

From the self-inflicted sweatshop conditions of my unairconditioned childhood home, to the arthritis reaping positions of a sedentary lifestyle, I bring to you: my sarcasm, my oddity, and my heart. Take it with a grain of salt or a teaspoon of sugar, but take it for what it is: a story born of the mind, translated to paper, and gifted to you.

I thank you for your readership and even more for your support. Please recommend this book to your friends and family via any social media that you use. Word of mouth is still the best advertising and is greatly appreciated.

Most importantly, keep reading. I'll keep writing.